A Complete Report of the Trial of Dr. E. W. Pritchard for the Alleged Poisoning of His Wife and Mother-In-Law

AP
AP\
LHc

E. W. Pritchard

A COMPLETE REPORT

OF THE TRIAL OF

DR E. W. PRITCHARD,

FOR

THE ALLEGED POISONING OF HIS WIFE AND MOTHER-IN-LAW.

REPRINTED, BY SPECIAL PERMISSION, FROM THE "SCOTSMAN."

CAREFULLY REVISED BY AN EMINENT LAWYER.

With an Accurate Portrait.

EDINBURGH:
WILLIAM KAY, 5 BANK STREET.
1865.

PREFACE.

Dr Edward William Pritchard is a native of England, where he became a member of the Royal College of Surgeons in 1846. He voyaged in the Pacific and Northern Polar Seas, and went to Egypt and other countries bordering on the Mediterranean. He was afterwards located at Filey, in Yorkshire, and married a Miss Mary Jane Taylor, daughter of Mr Michael Taylor, a retired silk and lace merchant, residing at the Grange, near Edinburgh, by whom he has five children,—the eldest about thirteen years old. He latterly settled in Glasgow, about the year 1859, where, in consequence of many contributions to medical science on the subjects of cancer and gout, the influence of vegetable medicines on diseases, and others, he soon became known as a man of superior attainments. His popularity was also greatly enhanced by his activity in connexion with public institutions,—among others, the Glasgow Athenæum, of which he became director.

While thus in the enjoyment of a popularity and success apparently due to merit and activity, the attention of the public was attracted to him by a horrible circumstance which occurred in his house on the 5th of May 1863. He was then living in No. 11 Berkeley Terrace, Berkeley Street. The occurrence, as set forth in the columns of the *Glasgow Herald* of 6th May, was as follows:—

"*Lamentable Occurrence—Young Woman Burned to Death.*—Yesterday morning, a melancholy accident occurred in the residence of Dr E. W. Pritchard, situated No. 11 Berkeley Terrace, Berkeley Street. The house, which is at the north side of the street, consists of two flats and attics, the servant's sleeping apartment being in the top flat fronting the street. About three o'clock, one of the constables stationed in the vicinity of the dwelling observed the glare of fire through the attic window, and immediately proceeded to the front door and rung the bell. The door was opened by Dr Pritchard, who slept in a bed-room on the second floor, and who had been wakened a few minutes before the bell rung by his two sons, who slept in an adjoining apartment, calling out "Papa, papa." The doctor rose, and, on opening the room door, he was alarmed to find smoke in the lobby; and on proceeding to the room in which his sons slept, he learned that they had been awakened by smoke and the cracking of glass. It was quite apparent then that the house was on fire; and after leaving his boys in the lobby leading from the street door, he rushed up to the attic flat, pushed open the door of the servant's sleeping-room, and called out Elizabeth, but received no answer. The apartment was so completely filled with smoke that he could not enter; and on proceeding down stairs for the purpose of raising an alarm, the bell rang, and he admitted the constable. Dr Pritchard told him that the servant slept on the attic flat, and on proceeding thither, and reaching the door of the apartment, they were unable to proceed farther in consequence of the smoke and flames. The alarm was immediately conveyed to the Anderston Police-office, and then to the central engine station, by telegraph, and the brigade was speedily in attendance, and extinguished the flames. On entering the sleeping apartment on the top flat, a sad spectacle presented itself. The poor woman, whose name was Elizabeth M'Girn, was found in bed dead, her body being a charred mass. The bed was placed at the north-west corner of the room, and the body lay at the front of the bed, the head towards the west. The body was lying on its back, the left arm being close by the side, and the right arm appeared to have been in a bent position; but the fire at this part had been so strong that the arm, from the hand to the elbow, was entirely consumed: the head was a charred mass, and the flesh was burned off the breast, the ribs being visible. The limbs of the deceased were comparatively uninjured, in consequence of being protected by stockings and blankets, but the toes, which had not been protected by the blankets, were charred. The fire had evidently broken out at the head of the bed, because, at this part of the apartment, the floor was burned through, and the joists forming the roof of the drawing-room were considerably charred. The roof of the house, with the exception of a portion at the back, was entirely destroyed. Dr Pritchard, on returning home, about eleven o'clock on Monday evening, observed that the servant's apartment was lighted. He entered the house, and, contrary to his usual custom, he did not call her to ascertain whether or not he had been wanted. After visiting the apartment in which his boys slept, for the purpose of ascertaining if they were comfortable in bed, he retired to rest about twelve o'clock. It is said that the poor girl, who has met such an untimely death, was in the habit of reading in bed; and the supposition is that, after she had fallen asleep, the gas jet, which was close to the head of the bed, had ignited the bed-hangings, and that the deceased had been suffocated by smoke. This is the more apparent from the position in which the body lay, because if the deceased had not been suffocated while asleep, she would have made some attempt to escape, and been found in a different position. The neighbour servant of deceased happened to be out of town with her mistress, and possibly, in her absence, the girl M'Girn had read longer than usual, and fallen asleep without extinguishing the gas. The damage to the dwelling is, we understand, covered by insurance."

Such is the story as told by the newspapers of the day, and which, as regards all that took place inside of the house prior to the visit of the policeman, behoved to have been taken from the lips of Dr Pritchard himself. There were additions made to it afterwards which imparted to it a more mysterious aspect. It was said that the insurance office demurred to the payment of the sum required to cover the loss, but upon what ground they placed their objection—subsequently withdrawn—was not ascertained. It was also reported that the girl was pregnant, but we have no official authority for the statement, nor are we aware that any judicial examination was made of the body. It was asserted that the door of the servants' bedroom was found locked outside. This does not agree with the statement in so far as that may be supposed to come from the policeman.

But, apart from these statements, which, if they had been true, might have led to further investigation on the part of the authorities, it is impossible for any one to read the story which we have given without feeling that it does not support the theory assumed for the manner of the girl's death. We may pass over certain coincidences as being merely curious—that, for instance, of Dr Pritchard coming to the door (dressed, it is to be presumed, for there is nothing to the contrary in the statement) only after the policeman rang, though he admits having been up a considerable time before that; the absence of Mrs Pritchard and the other maid; the exception on this particular night of his usual act of seeing and questioning the servant as to whether he had been wanted; we say nothing of the difficulty of burning a volume of a book so as to take away all trace of it; and the insurance is too common a thing to deserve much attention. But it requires a large amount of very easy credulity to believe that the girl, under the circumstances stated, would either not have escaped by the door, (only a few feet from the bed), or made an attempt in that direction, or at the very worst would not in "the lie" of the body, and in the contraction or contortion of the muscles, have exhibited some of the ordinary indications of pain. We can easily conceive a case where, by the sudden influx from another quarter of a great body of smoke, a person in a deep sleep may be so suddenly caught by asphyxia as to be choked as she lay, yet even in that case there will always be some contraction or contortion; but in the case we are examining the smoke had its *beginning* in the room; it was therefore under the law of progress, it was close by the sleeper, and it is scarcely possible to conceive that a young active woman would not have been quickened by the first touch of asphyxia either to an attempt at escape, or a voluntary or involuntary action of the muscles. Such absolute quiescence as set forth would seem to amount to a physical impossibility. The only presumption which can make the story quadrate with natural laws, is that the girl was dead, or under the influence of a soporific, before the fire was kindled. As to the means of the death, or the hand that applied the flame, these must be left to the judgment or imagination of the reader.

The report of the trial, which we are enabled to give from the unquestionable authority of the reporters of the *Scotsman*, will speak for itself. After the summing up of such a judge as the Lord Justice-Clerk, it would be presumption in us to offer any remarks either on the evidence or the verdict.

TRIAL OF DR PRITCHARD.

FIRST DAY—MONDAY, JULY 3, 1865.

THIS morning, at ten o'clock, the trial of Dr Pritchard, on the charge of murdering his wife and mother-in-law, commenced before the High Court of Justiciary. The judges on the bench were—the Lord Justice-Clerk, Lord Ardmillan, and Lord Jerviswoode.

The facts of this remarkable case have been so prominently brought before the notice of the public, that we need not do more than briefly indicate the more important points connected with it. On the 21st March last, the accused was apprehended by the police authorities of Glasgow, and placed in custody, pending the investigation of certain suspicious circumstances connected with the sudden death of his wife. The respectable position held by Dr Pritchard in the society of Glasgow, and the practice as a physician which he had been enabled to attain in the course of a six years' residence in that city, had awakened an unusual degree of interest in the public mind on the fact of his apprehension becoming known. Deep and painful excitement was occasioned, which was rather strengthened than diminished by the mystery invariably attached to the prosecution of all criminal inquiries in Scotland. When first apprehended, it was the received opinion that the charge to be preferred against the prisoner merely related to the death of his wife, but it soon became evident that the matter at issue was much more serious. For some time previous to her decease, Mrs Pritchard had been in a delicate state of health, and her mother, Mrs Taylor, wife of Mr Taylor, silk mercer, Edinburgh, had gone through to Glasgow to nurse her during her sickness. Mrs Taylor took up her abode in the house of Dr Pritchard, and ministered to her daughter's comfort; but while so engaged, she was seized with illness, and died suddenly, about three weeks previous to the day on which the prisoner was apprehended. Apoplexy was assigned as the cause, and as Mrs Taylor was about seventy years of age, no public attention was awakened, and the body was accordingly conveyed to Edinburgh, and buried in the Grange Cemetery. Circumstances closely following on this, however, awakened grave suspicions. Mrs Pritchard died shortly after her mother, and a report was circulated that she had been cut off by gastric fever. The family ground at the Grange was fixed on as the place of interment, and arrangements were made for the funeral without delay. The body was taken through to Edinburgh by rail, and Dr Pritchard accompanied it to the house of his father-in-law, where it was to await burial. The deaths of the two ladies occurring within so short an interval of each other, coupled with certain hints which they had received, set the police on the alert, and while Dr Pritchard was absent in Edinburgh they instituted inquiries which led to a warrant being issued for his apprehension. Previous to the last rites being paid to his wife, Dr Pritchard returned to Glasgow by the late evening train; but on stepping from the carriage at the railway station in Queen Street, he was taken into custody and conveyed to the Police-office. Meanwhile, the authorities had transmitted to Edinburgh information of what had been done, and at the same time had issued a warrant for a *post-mortem* examination of the body of Mrs Pritchard previous to its interment. The discharge of this duty was entrusted to Professor Douglas Maclagan (assisted by Dr Arthur Gamgee) and Dr Littlejohn, and resulted in the first place in the ascertainment of the fact that death had not resulted from natural causes. Subsequent examination of the intestines disclosed the presence of minute particles of antimony in the liver of the deceased. The official determination of this point having fully confirmed the suspicions entertained against the prisoner, it was resolved to prosecute wider investigations into a case that had now assumed a grave and mysterious aspect. The next step taken was to order the exhumation of the body of Mrs Taylor from the Grange Cemetery. This was done upon the 31st March, and the vital parts were preserved for chemical analysis. The analysis was conducted by Professor Maclagan, Dr Littlejohn, and Professor Penny, of Glasgow; and, after a protracted examination, a report was given in, which attributed the death of Mrs Taylor, like that of her daughter, to the presence of antimony. On these important facts being elicited, Dr Pritchard was fully committed on the charge of murder.

Since the memorable case of Madeline Smith, no criminal trial which has taken place in Edinburgh has been looked forward to with such deep and general interest by the public. The smallest scrap of information likely to throw any light upon the matter has, since the incarceration of the prisoner, been eagerly sought after, and not a few speculations have been hazarded regarding the final result. Nor has the interest been confined to Glasgow, where Dr Pritchard was so well known, and where his high position as a citizen brought him prominently before the notice of the community. The merits of the case in all their bearings have been keenly canvassed in every part of Scotland, and have also awakened a large share of attention in England. The mystery that ever attaches to cases of poisoning, the double crime of which the prisoner is accused, his near relationship to the deceased ladies, and the respectable profession to which he belonged, have all contributed to this result. The fact, also, that there is an apparent absence of any motive for the commission of a crime of so aggravated a character, has added to the interest felt in the case, and has naturally increased the curiosity felt by the public in regard to the evidence which may be in possession of the authorities to prove the crimes which they have charged against the prisoner. Representatives of the press from Liverpool, Manchester, Leeds, Newcastle, Shields, Dundee, Glasgow, Dumfries, and a number of other places, have come to Edinburgh to attend the trial, and for these extra accommodation has been provided in Court. Several improvements and alterations have during the week been carried out in the Court and the adjoining rooms, to promote the comfort of the large number of witnesses and others attending the trial.

Shortly after eight o'clock this morning, Dr Pritchard was conveyed from the Calton Jail to the lock-up room below the High Court of Justiciary. He was driven up in the ordinary police van, the presence of which in the streets gave intimation to the public that the prisoner was being removed for trial. Large crowds of people were accordingly attracted, and numbers followed the van as it drove up the High Street in the hope of gaining a glimpse of its occupant. Beyond the curiosity thus excited, however, the removal was effected with great quietness.

Half-past nine o'clock was fixed for opening the doors of the Court to the public, but for a considerable time before that hour numbers of people began to assemble in Parliament Square. As was to be expected, the applications for seats were greatly more numerous than the Court-room could accommodate; and with the view, therefore, to prevent confusion, and to afford the greatest possible convenience to those who were to take part officially in the proceedings, a series of regulations were issued making arrangements for ingress and egress. These regulations state that no one, except the judges, will be allowed on the bench without an application to the Court; that no one will be allowed within the bar except those engaged in the case; that no one, except reporters, will be admitted at the door of the reporters' seat, which is situated immediately behind the dock; that the side seat opposite the jury-box is to be kept exclusively for the Glasgow reporters; that two seats behind the Faculty seat will be kept for reporters of the provincial press; and that one of the side galleries will be kept for advocates. Admission to the public side-gallery was obtained by special order. Those having special tickets of admission were admitted previous to the doors being opened, so that by half-past nine a good number of people had assembled in the Court. As soon as the doors were opened a rush for seats took place. In a very short time the whole available space devoted to the accommodation of the public was taken possession of by those privileged to be present. The galleries, both upper and lower, were packed, and every inch of standing-room was gradually occupied. As the hour for the commencement of the trial approached, the greatest excitement prevailed among those in Court, and anxiety to catch the first glimpse of the prisoner as he should enter the dock was generally manifested.

At three minutes past ten the prisoner came up the steps, and took his place in the dock. He was dressed in deep mourning, and, on taking his seat between the two policemen, he removed his hat, and gazed quietly around him. He is a tall, stout, well-built man, rather prepossessing in appearance, and with striking sharply-defined features. He wears his hair long, is slightly bald, and has a large bushy beard. The expression of his countenance was sad; but he appeared quite calm, and his manner was composed and collected. When the judges took their seats, he rose and bowed to the bench, but immediately afterwards resumed his seat. Considerable attention was attracted by the brother of the panel entering the dock, and taking his seat beside the prisoner. Previous to doing so, he shook Dr Pritchard warmly by the hand.

There appeared on behalf of the Crown, the Solicitor-General, Mr Gifford, and Mr Crichton; Mr Andrew Murray, jun., W.S., Crown-agent. For the prisoner—Mr A. R. Clark, Mr Watson, and Mr Brand; Mr Buchan, S.S.C., agent in Edinburgh; Mr James Galbraith of Galbraith and Maclay, in Glasgow.

The Clerk then read the indictment against the prisoner, which was as follows:—

"Edward William Pritchard, now or lately a doctor of medicine, and now or lately prisoner in the prison of Glasgow, you are indicted and accused at the instance of James Moncreiff, Esq., Her Majesty's Advocate for Her Majesty's interest: That, albeit, by the laws of this and of every other well governed realm, murder is a crime of an heinous nature, and severely punishable: yet true it is, and of verity, that you, the said Edward William Pritchard, are guilty of the said crime, actor, or art and part: In so far as,

"(1.) On one or more occasions between the 10th and 25th days of February 1865, both inclusive, the particular occasions or occasion being to the prosecutor unknown, within or near the dwelling-house, in or near Clarence Place, Sauchiehall Street, Glasgow, then occupied by you, the said Edward William Pritchard, you did wickedly and feloniously administer to, or cause to be taken by, Jane Cowan or Taylor, now deceased, wife of Michael Taylor, now or lately silk and lace merchant, then residing in or near Lauder Road, in or near Grange, Edinburgh, and now or lately residing with Ann Taylor or Cowan, in or near High Street, Musselburgh, in the shire of Edinburgh, in tapioca and in porter or beer, and in a medicine called Batley's Sedative Solution, or one or more of them, or in some medicine to the prosecutor unknown, or in some articles or article of food or drink to the prosecutor unknown, or in some other manner to the prosecutor unknown, tartarised antimony, and aconite, and opium, or one or more of them, or some other poison or poisons to the prosecutor unknown; and the said Jane Cowan or Taylor having taken the said tartarised antimony, and aconite, and opium, or one or more of them, or other poison or poisons, so by you administered or caused to be taken, did in consequence thereof die on or about the 25th day of February 1865, and was thus murdered by you, the said Edward William Pritchard. Likeas,

"(2.) On repeated occasions, or on one or more occasions between the 22d day of December 1864, and the 18th day of March 1865 inclusive, and in particular on the 8th, 9th, and 21st days of February 1865, and on the 13th, 14th, 15th, 16th, 17th, and 18th days of March 1865, the particular occasions or occasion being otherwise to the prosecutor unknown, within or near the said dwelling-house in or near Clarence Place, Sauchiehall Street, Glasgow, then occupied by you, the said Edward William Pritchard, you did wickedly and feloniously administer to, or cause to be taken by, Mary Jane Taylor or Pritchard, now deceased, your wife, and then residing with you, in egg-flip and in cheese, and in porter or beer, and in wine, or one or more of them, or in some medicine to the prosecutor unknown, or in some articles or article of food or drink to the prosecutor unknown, or in some other manner to the prosecutor unknown, tartarised antimony and aconite, or one or other of them, or some other poison or poisons to the prosecutor unknown; and the said Mary Jane Taylor or Pritchard, having taken the said tartarised antimony and aconite, or one or other of them, or other poison or poisons so by you administered or caused to be taken, did in consequence thereof die, on or about the 18th day of March 1865, and was thus murdered by you, the said Edward William Pritchard."

After the indictment had been read, several objections were made to it by Mr Watson, for the defence. The Solicitor-General, for the prosecution, replied to them at great length. Finally, however, after a consultation on the bench, they were held to be inadmissible, and decision was given accordingly that the trial be proceeded with.

The Lord Justice-Clerk said—Edward William Pritchard, you are charged under this indictment with the crime of murder. How say you: Are you guilty or not guilty?

Prisoner (firmly)—Not guilty, my Lord.

The empannelling of the jury was then proceeded with. In the course of the balloting, when the name of Mr John Adair, temperance hotel-keeper, High Street, was called,

Mr A. R. Clark rose and said—A letter has been addressed from Mr Adair to the following effect:—

"319 High Street, Edinburgh, June 24, 1865."

The Lord Justice-Clerk—Who is it addressed to?

Mr Clark—It is addressed to Mr John Strachan, in Glasgow, I suppose to be communicated to the agent for the panel, and it was communicated to the panel's agent with a letter from Mr Strachan. Mr Clark then read the letter, which was to the effect that the writer (Mr Adair) had received a summons to attend the trial of Dr Pritchard as a juror, and was likely to be drawn, and stating that his business urgently required his attendance during the week, and that, moreover, he had formed a strong conviction in regard to the case; and concluding by requesting Mr Strachan, if he came in contact with the counsel, "to get an old acquaintance out of the dilemma."

Mr Clark, after reading the letter, stated that he would leave the matter to his Lordship.

The Lord Justice-Clerk—It is a mere device to get escaping as a juryman. Let Mr Adair go to the box.

Mr Clark rose and said—Then, my Lord, I challenge him peremptorily.

Mr Adair was accordingly allowed to leave.

The following gentlemen were then empannelled as the jury:—

Robert Graham, dairyman, Broad Wynd, Leith.
George Sim, writer, 7 Cambridge Street, Edinburgh.
Thomas Legat, farmer, Pinkiemains.
Andrew Turnbull, grocer, High Street, Portobello.
John Blair, merchant, North Berwick.
James Charles, ironmonger, 18 Broughton Street, Edinburgh.
Thomas Inglis, grocer, 11 Lothian Street, Edinburgh.
David Norrie, shipowner, Baltic Street, Leith.
Thomas Stark, tobacconist, 81 West Port, Edinburgh.
John Brown, flesher, Penicuik.
Robert Frater, farmer, Law, Linlithgowshire.
Thomas Thomson, grocer, Elmfield Place, Dalkeith.
John Mathison, cabinetmaker, 7 Vennel, Edinburgh.
William M'Cartney, sea-gravel merchant, New Street, Fisherrow.
William Young, blacksmith, Raw Smithy, Kirknewton.

The evidence for the prosecution commenced at half-past eleven.

Sir Archibald Alison—By Mr Gifford—I am Sheriff of the county of Lanark. [Shown declarations dated 22d March and 21st April 1865.] These declarations were emitted by the prisoner at the bar in my presence freely and voluntarily, in his sound and sober senses, after receiving the usual warning.

Peter Morton—By Mr Gifford—I am a clerk in the Sheriff-Clerk's office, Glasgow. [Shown declaration dated 22d March 1865.] That was emitted by the prisoner at the bar in my presence, freely and voluntarily, in his sound and sober senses, and after being duly warned.

Robert Wilson—By Mr Gifford—I am a clerk in the Sheriff-Clerk's office, Glasgow. [Shown declaration dated 21st April 1865.] This was emitted by the prisoner in my presence in his sound and sober senses, freely and voluntarily, and after receiving the usual warning.

The Solicitor-General moved that the medical witnesses for the Crown should be allowed to be present in Court during the evidence to be given of the facts.

Mr Clark said he had no objection to that, and made a similar motion as to the prisoner's medical witnesses. He, however, objected to their being present at the giving of scientific or medical opinions.

The Court granted both motions, with the qualifications proposed by Mr Clark.

Catherine Lattimer—By the Solicitor-General—I am a widow. I was at one time in the service of Dr Pritchard, the prisoner. I was with him for ten years. I left his service on the 16th of February last. I was cook. A brother of mine became unwell and died in Carlisle in October last. I left Dr Pritchard's house in October to visit my brother. He was dead when I arrived. I was away about a fortnight. Mrs Pritchard was living in the house when I left. She was quite well when I left. She had not been complaining then that I knew of. They were living at that time in Clarence Place, one of the divisions of Sauchiehall Street. I cannot give the date when I returned, but it was in October. When I returned to Glasgow, Mrs Pritchard was not very well; she was complaining. What was the matter with her? She said it was cold. The house consisted of four floors, one of them a sunk floor. On the sunk floor there were two bedrooms, kitchen, larder, and cellar. Before I left in October, and after my return, Mary M'Leod was the other servant in the house; she was the only other servant. She and I slept together on the sunk flat. On the dining-room floor there were consulting-room, dining-room, and pantry; the dining-room was to the front, and the consulting-room and pantry to the back. The drawing-room floor consisted of drawing-room, ante-drawing-room, and two bed-rooms. One of these bed-rooms was called the spare bed-room. One of the children slept in the other bed-room sometimes, and latterly it was occupied by Mr King, who boarded with Dr Pritchard. He came in October, and after he came he had that room. The floor above consisted of two good bed-rooms and a nursery, and another small bed-room. Dr Pritchard and his wife slept in one of the bed-rooms, one of the children slept in another, and two of the children in the nursery. Thomas Connell, another boarder, slept in the small bed-room. The youngest child slept in the room with Dr Pritchard and his wife, in a separate bed. The youngest child is five years old on the 27th of this month, the next was seven last May. The others were named Charles and Horatio, but I forget their ages. Dr Pritchard had five children altogether; the eldest was eleven years old, I think. Only four of them lived in the house. The eldest, Jane Frances, lived with her grand-mamma, Lauder Road, Edinburgh. When I left to go to Carlisle, and when I returned, the household consisted of Dr Pritchard, his wife, four children, two boarders, Mary M'Leod, and myself. When you returned, Mrs Pritchard was ailing, and said she had caught a cold? Yes. Was she confined to bed? No; not when I came home. She was laid up two days after. Was that long after you came home that she took to her bed? Not very long. Can you tell us how long? It could not be more than a few days. How long was she confined to bed? Four or five days. Was she sick? Yes, at times. How did the sickness show itself? I did not see it, sir. Did anybody tell you? Yes. Did she tell you herself? Yes. Did Mrs Pritchard herself tell you that she was sick? Yes. What did she say to you? She said she was very often sick; she made no further remark. Did she tell you that she had attacks of vomiting? Yes. That was what you meant by the sickness, I suppose? Yes.

Mr Rutherford Clark—Was that what Mrs Pritchard told you, or Mary M'Leod? They both told me.

The Solicitor-General—Did any medical man attend her at this time? Dr Gairdner was the first. But before going to Edinburgh, when she was unwell and complaining of sickness, as you mentioned, did any medical man attend her at that time? No; not that I know of. After within four or five days being confined to bed, did you see that she got better? A little better; not much. Do you remember her leaving to go to Edinburgh to visit her mother? Yes. When was that? I cannot remember the date. But do you remember the month? Was it in November? How long was it after you came home? I think it would be about the end of November. Did she appear to be quite well then? No, not quite well. Did she tell you of her sickness or vomiting down to the time you went away, or till near it? It was near it. Did she take any of the children with her? I do not remember. Do you recollect when she returned from Edinburgh? Yes. When was it? It was a few days before Christmas. Did anybody come with her? Her mother and daughter. That was Mrs Taylor and Miss Pritchard, the eldest daughter? Yes. How did she appear to be in health when she returned from Edinburgh? A good deal better. Do you know whether she had any sickness or vomiting immediately after her return from Edinburgh? I think it would be a while after that—a week or more. Was her husband, the prisoner, living in the house with her at home, before she went to Edinburgh? Yes. And also after she returned? Yes. He remained at home? Yes.

The Lord Justice-Clerk—The time she was away also? Yes.

The Solicitor-General—After she returned from Edinburgh, did you see the sickness upon her yourself, or are you speaking merely of what she told you? I heard her; but I did not stand by her. Retching or vomiting? Yes. When was this? This began about a week after her return, as near as I can remember. Was it a frequent thing with her this vomiting? I very seldom heard her. Did you hear it from herself? Not always from herself. Did you hear it frequently from herself? No, just sometimes. What did she say to you about it? She complained of being sick so often, and could not tell the reason why.

The Lord Justice-Clerk—Was it after her return? Yes.

The Solicitor-General.—Did she ever tell you how often she was sick in a day? No; I don't remember that. Did she tell you when it was she was sick, what time of day it was, whether before eating or after it? It was sometimes after and at times before eating. Where was it that you heard her sick and retching? It was once in the pantry after she had come out of the dining-room. Was that very shortly after she came from Edinburgh? No, it was about three weeks. Did you see her daily? Yes, I generally saw her every day. Did you see whether she was falling off in health or not? Yes, I thought she was looking worse.

The Lord Justice-Clerk—When did you first notice that she was looking a great deal worse? I first noticed it when she was vomiting in the pantry. From the time you heard her retching in the pantry, did you notice the decline in her appearance? Yes.

The Solicitor-General—What kind of falling off was it? How did she look? She looked pale and losing her strength. Did she often speak to you about it, about her being frequently sick and unable to account for it? No, not often. Was she so ill as to be confined to bed after her return from Edinburgh and before you left? She was confined to bed before I left. When did she take to her bed, after her return from Edinburgh I mean? It would be about three weeks or a little more.

The Lord Justice-Clerk—That was just about the time you heard her retching in the pantry? Yes.

The Solicitor-General—Do you think you can recollect the day? I cannot. On what day were you to have left her service? I was to have left on the 2d February, Candlemas-day, but Mrs Pritchard was very ill that night, which necessitated me to stay a little longer till they got another servant. That is the reason you remained on till the 16th? Yes, on account of her illness and the other servant not having come. Then you remember that she had been very ill upon the night before you was to have left? Yes, I should have left next day, and would have left had it not been for that. That was on the 1st February? Yes. Tell us what was the first thing you saw wrong with her on the 1st February? It was sickness and cramp. When did it come on? at what time of the day? In the evening after dinner; about six o'clock. When had she dinner? Between three and four o'clock. Did the prisoner dine with her? Yes, I think so. Was that the day you heard her sick in the pantry? Yes. Was that the only day you heard her sick in the pantry? The only day. Then we have got the date of the occurrence now; the day before you were to have left, viz., the 1st of February? Yes. Where did she come from to go to the pantry? From the dining-room. Was the doctor in the house at the time? I cannot say. Did you go to assist her? Yes, sir, I did. Did she call for you? She rung the bell for me, and I went upstairs. What bell? Her bed-room bell. She had gone upstairs herself, had she? Yes.

The Lord Justice-Clerk—That was her own bell she rung, after she had gone upstairs? Yes, sir, the bell in her own bed-room.

The Solicitor-General—How long after you heard the sickness in the pantry was it that she rung the bell? About half an hour or twenty minutes. Did you go up? Yes. And how did you find her? Very ill. Was she in bed? Yes. With her clothes on? Yes, with her clothes on. Did she speak to you? Yes, sir; she said she had quite lost her senses. Just try to remember the words she used. She said, "Catherine, I have lost my senses; I never was so bad as this before." Did she complain of anything in particular? No, sir; she took cramp directly after. After you went up? Yes. You mean the cramp seized her after you went up? Yes, sir. Where did the cramp affect her? In her hands, and down her side. Her tongue was affected, she said.

By the Lord Justice-Clerk—It appeared to affect her speech a little.

The Solicitor-General—Did you observe the state of her hands? The fingers of her hand were straight out, and the thumb twisted underneath. Did she seem to have no power to put them straight? No, sir. How did she look, what was her face like? Rather flushed. Did she say any more than you have told us? No, sir. Did she not tell you to get anybody, did she not ask for the doctor? No, she did not ask for the doctor then. The doctor was not in the room? No, he was in the consulting-room, I think. Did you not go to the consulting-room, and call him up? I went down stairs for him and called him up, and he came. He came from the consulting-room? I think he did. Did he go up with you to the bed-room? Yes. Did he give her anything? Yes, I think it was a little spirits and water. The first that he saw of this attack of illness was when he went into the bed-room with you? Yes, sir, as far as I know. What did he say, or did he say anything at all? Not that I remember. What did he do? He rubbed her hands with me. Did you say anything about the cramp? I said it was very strange. Did he make any remark? No, sir; not that I remember. Did his wife say anything to him? No, sir; I did not hear her say anything particular. She seemed in great pain. Where was the pain? It was cramp in the stomach.

The Lord Justice-Clerk—What did you say about her stomach? There was pain there, sir.

The Solicitor-General—The cramp was painful, and she felt pain in her stomach? Yes. Did she tell her husband that she had been insensible? I cannot remember that. I cannot say whether she did or not; but she said so to me. How long did you remain with her? Till she was quite free from the cramp. How long was that? About half-an-hour. About what o'clock would it be when you left her? Perhaps about seven. Did you leave her husband with her? I think he was with her. When did you next see her? I saw her that night again about nine or ten o'clock. How was she then? She was easier then. She was much better. Was she in bed? Yes; she was taken down to the spare room. The doctor ordered a fire to be lighted there for her. That is a bedroom off the drawing-room? Yes. Was she able to walk down? No; the doctor carried her down. Did you see her that night again? Yes, later the same night. It was about eleven o'clock when I saw her last. How was she? Better. But not well? Not well, sir. When did you see her next after that? I would see her next day. At what time? About eleven o'clock in the forenoon. Was she in bed? Yes. How was she? A good deal better. What did she complain of, or did she complain of anything? She did not complain of anything. Did she not complain of weakness? No. Did she complain of sickness? No. Nothing about that? Nothing. How long did she remain in bed? She remained in bed from that time. How long? Perhaps nearly a week—till

Mrs Taylor came. Did she remain in bed from that time till her mother—that is, Mrs Taylor—came? Yes. Did you see her every day? Yes. Did you see much of her? Just going to see how she was. Sometimes I took her something to eat. Was she to your knowledge sick during that time, after she took to bed, before her mother came? Yes, I heard that she was. Did you hear that from herself? Yes, I think I did. She told me herself that she had been very sick Was this every day, or not so often? No; sometimes she would miss a day. Did the other servant, Mary M'Leod, wait upon her as a rule? Yes. And who was it who took her food into her before Mrs Taylor came? Mary M'Leod in general. And who cooked it? I did. Was it told you, as the cook in the house, that what she got did not lie on her stomach? No, sir. Did you speak to Mrs Pritchard herself about her sickness? Yes, sir, sometimes. About the cause of it? Yes. I made the remark that it was strange that nothing would do her good; that nothing would take it away, and stop the sickness. What did she say? She said nothing seemed to stop it. It was generally slops she was sick after—often tea. She told you so? Yes. Did anybody else cook her food at the time before her mother came except you? No, sir. Who made her tea? It was generally given in the dining-room in a cup, and sometimes it was put into the teapot in the dining-room. Who took it up to her room? Mary M'Leod. Did anybody else take it, or do you not know what became of it after it got into the dining-room? No, sir, I do not know anything about it after it got into the dining-room. During the ten years you were in the service, before the time you have mentioned—after your return from Carlisle—was she ever sick? No, sir, not that I know of. And her sickness began after you returned in October? Yes. Was she able to go into the drawing-room occasionally before her mother came? Yes. She was generally confined to bed, but went into the drawing-room sometimes? Yes; she did not lie all day. You mean she lay the most of the day? Yes. I think Dr Cowan came to see her before her mother came? Yes. Do you remember when he came? How long before her mother? About two or three days. He came one day and went away the next? Yes. He remained all night? What time of the day did he go away, do you remember? By the train sometime in the evening. Where was Mrs Pritchard when he went away? I think she was in the drawing-room. The prisoner was at home? Yes. He was never from home during the time you have been speaking to? No; not that I know of. Did anything remarkable occur on the night of the day that Dr Cowan left? It was either that night or the next that Mrs Pritchard had the first cramp. Was she not cramped on the 1st February, the night before you were to have gone away? Yes; and Dr Cowan was there before that. Dr Cowan only came a day or two before her mother came? Yes.

The Lord Justice-Clerk—How long before you went away did Mrs Taylor come? About a week. You went on the 16th? Yes. Then Mrs Taylor came about the 9th. How long before that would it be that Dr Cowan came? I cannot tell; but Dr Cowan was gone when she had the first severe cramp. Was it the day he left? It was either that night or the night after. I think it was the night after.

The Solicitor-General—Do you mean that it was that night or the night after that she told you she had been insensible? It was the night after he left. That she said she had been insensible? Yes, that was the first cramp she had had. I thought it was on the 1st February? Yes it was, I think. It was on account of that illness that you did not go away on the 2d February as you intended? Yes. That was the occasion of the first cramp? Yes. You say that on the afternoon of the day before you had intended to go away you heard her sick in the pantry? Yes. That was about six o'clock? Yes. And in about twenty minutes or so she rang the bell, and you went up to her, and she told you she had been insensible, which she had never been before? And the cramp came upon her when you were there, and twisted her fingers? Yes. That was about seven or eight o'clock? Yes. She had had cramp then? Yes. On the night that Dr Cowan left, or the night after, when did you first hear any alarm about her being ill? That was the first. About what o'clock was it? About six o'clock, when she was in the pantry. Do you remember an alarm about midnight one night that she was taken ill with cramp? Yes. And that was the second time she had taken cramp? Yes. Was it after you had gone to bed? No, I was not in bed. Did you hear her calling out pain? Yes. How was she calling out? As if she was in trouble—in pain. Where did the calls come from? From the bed-room. Which bed-room? the spare bed-room? The top bed-room. She had been taken back there? Yes.

The Lord Justice-Clerk—She was back again in her own bed-room at the time this second attack took place? Yes.

The Solicitor-General—How long had she been out of her own bed-room—how long had she been in the spare bed-room? She might be out of that room about a fortnight or more.

The Lord Justice-Clerk—You mean she had been in the spare bed-room about a fortnight? Yes.

The Solicitor-General—If she went to the spare bed-room on the 1st February and remained there for a fortnight, it would be the 14th when she went back to her own bed-room?

The Lord Justice-Clerk—The second attack would be very soon before you left? Yes.

The Solicitor-General—When you heard her cry out about midnight, was it before her mother came, or after? It was before. Just think a little. Was that not the night Dr Cowan left? Yes, I think that would be the night that Dr Cowan left. I thought she had had no cramp before Dr Cowan came, but I think she had had the first attack before he came.

The Lord Justice-Clerk—You were confusing those two attacks together? Yes.

The Solicitor-General—You now remember it was the 1st of February, the day before you should have left, that she was taken ill about six o'clock in the afternoon, and rung for you, after she had gone up into her bed-room; and it was after she had returned to her own bed-room upstairs, and you think on the night Dr Cowan left, that she cried out with pain about midnight? Yes. When you heard the calls of pain from the bed-room, what did you do? I went upstairs to see what was the matter. What did you see? Mrs Pritchard was in bed, seemingly in great pain. Anybody with her? The doctor was with her.

The Lord Justice-Clerk—You mean the prisoner? Yes.

The Solicitor-General—And his wife, Mrs Pritchard, was in bed? What state did she seem to be in? She seemed to be under the influence of chloroform. She said she had taken chloroform.

The Lord Justice-Clerk—Then she was not insensible? She told you she had taken it? Yes.

The Solicitor-General—She knew you, and spoke to you? Yes. And said she had taken chloroform? Yes. Was she much excited? Very much. In what state was the prisoner himself? Quite calm. He did not say anything. He stood by Mrs Pritchard, and tried to soothe her. What more did she say to you? She called for a doctor. She said she would like to see another doctor. Tell us the words she used. She said, "I want to see Dr Gairdner: fetch Dr Gairdner." That was in the presence of her husband? Yes. Was it to you she said that? Mary M'Leod entered the room just after that, and she sent Mary off for the doctor. Did you notice her hands? Yes. What state were they in? They were all drawn together with the cramp. Was she calling for another doctor before Mary M'Leod came into the room? I did not hear what she said before. Mary M'Leod came straight in after me. Did you do anything to her hands? I rubbed her hands till the cramp left them. Did Mary M'Leod bring Dr Gairdner? Yes. Did he come immediately? Yes. Did you hear Mrs Pritchard tell the doctor what was the matter? Yes, she told him she had taken some chloroform, and she did not blame the doctor—that she never liked chloroform. Did she say who had given it to her? No; she said, "I do not blame the doctor." She meant Dr Pritchard. She did not tell you that he had given her the chloroform? No. Did she complain of having been sick that night? No, she did not complain at that time. At any time that night did you see the mark of vomiting? No, not that night. Had she any champagne that day that you know of? No. Or any wine? No. Was she in the habit of taking wine or spirits of any kind? No; she was very temperate. Did you, during the whole time of your service, ever see her the least under the influence of drink? Never. Had she any vice of that sort? No. When did she take her last meal the night when you heard her cry about midnight? I cannot tell anything she had except a cup of tea that night. That was the last thing she had, as far as I know. Did you remain with her all night? Yes. Did the prisoner remain also? No; he went into another room. He went into the spare bed-room? Yes. In what state was Mrs Pritchard during the night? Very quiet and calm. Was she any trouble to you? No. Did she sleep? Only a little. Did she complain of thirst? Yes. Do you mean that her thirst was remarkable? Not very remarkable. Did you give her anything? Just water. Did her thirst continue next day? I think it did. But not very remarkable? No. Did you attend her next day? I was in the room two or three times. Was you there sufficiently long to see that she required drink? Yes. Was anything got for her? I just gave her water and a little ice in it. Did she seem to be very weak during the night and next day? Yes, very. I believe Dr Gairdner called the following day? Yes. Were you present when he saw her? No. Then it was after Dr Gairdner's last visit that Mrs Taylor came? Yes. Now, I want you to think back upon the occurrences of that night. When you went up to the bed-room and heard her cry out with pain about midnight, tell us whether you did not hear her say anything besides what you have already said here. Did you hear her saying anything to her husband? She said they were all hypocrites together. She meant the doctors. She was under the influence of chloroform and very excited.

By the Lord Justice-Clerk—Was that when she was calling for Dr Gairdner? It was when Dr Gairdner was there. Tell us as exactly as you can the very words. She bid the doctor not cry, and said, "If you cry, you are a hypocrite." That was her husband? Yes. Was he shedding tears? I did not notice it till she said that, and I did not see it then. She said, "Don't cry, or you are a hypocrite?" Yes; and she said, "You are all hypocrites." Did she add that? Yes, when Dr Gairdner and Dr Pritchard were standing by the fire. Did she say who had done it? No. Was Dr Pritchard shedding tears? I did not see him. You did not see him weeping? No. Or pretending to weep? No; he stood over Mrs Pritchard at the bedside, but I can't say I saw him weeping. Did you think he was? Well, I thought so by what Mrs Pritchard said. You mean, that by what she said you thought he was weeping when he was standing over her at the bed-side? Yes. Then, was it when he was standing over her at the bed-side that she said, "Don't cry?" Yes. To the best of your recollection did she say, "Don't cry, you hypocrite," or, "Don't cry, for if you do you are a hypocrite?" Yes, these were the words; she said, "If you cry you are a hypocrite."

At this stage of the examination Dr Gairdner, who had been sitting with the other medical witnesses in the Court, was requested to leave the Court.

The Lord Justice-Clerk—Then I understand the words were, "Don't cry; if you do, you are a hypocrite?" Yes. Was it at the same time that she said, "You are all hypocrites?" Yes, when Dr Gairdner and Dr Pritchard went to the fireside. But was it at the same time? Not at the same moment, but it was the same night. A short time afterwards? Two or three minutes afterwards. What were the words she used? "You are all hypocrites together." Did she use the word "Doctors?" No; just "You are all hypocrites together." That might have included you as well as the doctors? I do not know.

By the Solicitor-General—When she said to her husband, "Don't cry," did she say it was he that did it? No. You heard nothing like that? Nothing like that. Were you constantly in the room? All that night. Before Dr Gairdner came, when she said she wanted another doctor, and named him, did she say anything about hypocrites? No. It was when Dr Gairdner was there that she said that? Yes. A day or two after this, Mrs Taylor came? Yes. And was Mrs Pritchard in bed when Mrs Taylor came? Yes, I think she was. From the time you heard her cry at midnight till her mother came, was she confined to bed? Yes. And after her mother came till you left she was generally confined to bed? Yes. Always? Generally. She got up till her bed was made, and then she went to bed again. Was there any other serious attack of illness after her mother came? Yes, she had cramp after her mother came. How long after? It would be perhaps two or three days after. When did it begin? It was in the afternoon or evening, but I saw her at the time. When had she dinner? She would have something about one o'clock. Did she seem to be in the same state on this occasion as she was on the occasion when you went up at midnight? Not so bad. Was the cramp the same? Yes, it was in her hands, but not so bad. Was she complaining of pain in the same way? Yes. And seemed to be suffering? Yes. Had you heard of this attack being upon her before you went up and saw her? Yes. Long before? No, not long; I think it was that that took me up. Was she recovering when you saw her? Yes, she was recovering, and said to her mother: "I am not nearly so bad this time as I was last." Where was the prisoner when she was attacked this time? I don't remember whether he was there or not. Do you remember what day of the week this was on? No, I cannot. But it was a few days after her mother came? Yes. Had she any other attack after this before you left? No. You left on the 16th—after your successor came—leaving Mrs Pritchard in bed? Yes. Did you come back to the house after that? Yes, several times. When did you call first? It would be a week after I left.

The Lord Justice-Clerk—Did you go to a situation in Glasgow? No, I stayed with a friend. On the 23d you called back? Yes, I think it would be a week from the time I left.

The Solicitor General—Do you remember the day that Mrs Taylor was taken ill immediately before her death? I saw Mrs Taylor on Friday morning, and I think she died that night or towards Saturday morning. But I did not know of her death till the Monday. I had not been in the house. On the Friday—the last day of Mrs Taylor's life—you called at Dr Pritchard's house and saw her? Yes. What time of day was it when you saw her? It would be about eleven o'clock in the forenoon. Did you see Mrs Taylor first? I saw Mrs Taylor during the time I was in the house. I went to take Mrs Pritchard's youngest child out a walk. What passed between you and Mrs Taylor? I asked how Mrs Pritchard was, and she said, "Well, Catherine, I don't understand her illness; she is one day better and two worse." That was all. That was the last word I had with Mrs Taylor. Did she say what was wrong with her? No she did not. Anything about her sickness? No, she did not mention the sickness. Did you see Mrs Pritchard herself? Yes; after Mrs Taylor's death I saw her. But upon that Friday? Yes, I saw her. I was in Mrs Pritchard's bed-room when I asked Mrs Taylor that question, and when Mrs Taylor told me that she was better and worse. How did Mrs Taylor herself seem at that time? She looked wearied, and not so well, I thought; but she did not complain of anything. She was up and dressed? Yes, and going about. Before you left, Mrs Taylor slept with her daughter on the high floor, I believe? Yes, always while she was there.

The Lord Justice-Clerk—In the same room? Yes.

The Solicitor-General—And acted as her nurse and attendant as a mother might be expected to do? Yes.

The Lord Justice-Clerk—The prisoner did not sleep with his wife at that time? No. He slept down stairs? Yes.

The Solicitor-General—After Mrs Taylor came, did you continue to make all her food, or did Mrs Taylor make some of it herself? Mrs Taylor made some of it herself. It was not your duty to attend upon her at her meals, and to take up her dinner or tea, and you cannot speak about that? No, I took her up very little. Sometimes I took her up a potato; she liked a potato, and said it stayed best with her—and sometimes a poached egg. But anything prepared in the kitchen was cooked either by you or by Mrs Taylor after she came? Yes. When did you call again after this Friday? On Monday morning. You were there the Monday after Mrs Taylor died? Yes. And that was when you first heard of it? Yes. Who did you see that day? Dr Pritchard was in the lobby when I went in. Did he say anything to you or you to him? He said they had a sad house to-day. The two servants were standing in the pantry, and I went past him to them. I asked what was the matter, and they said Mrs Taylor was dead and taken to Edinburgh. Did you see Mrs Pritchard? Not that day. When did you next see her? I think it was the next day—Tuesday. Was she in bed? She was just coming out of her bed-room into the drawing-room. Did you go into the drawing-room with her? Yes. How was she? She was very poorly, and in grief about her mother. Was she very emaciated—very thin? Yes, very thin. And weak? And weak. Did she tell you anything about her health at this time? No, she did not. Do you remember preparing some tapioca for Mrs Taylor and Mrs Pritchard? Yes, well. Do you recollect what day it was? It would be a few days after Mrs Taylor came to the house. Do you remember the day of the week? I scarcely can. Didn't you forget to get it on the Saturday? Mary M'Leod went to order it for anything that I know. I did not see who brought it. Is there anything that brings to your recollection that it was a Monday? I cannot bring that to my recollection. But it was shortly after Mrs Taylor came? Yes. Who ordered you to prepare it? Mary M'Leod told me that Mrs Pritchard would like a little tapioca. She brought the message to you to prepare it? Yes. Where did you get the tapioca? It was brought from Burton and Henderson, the grocers. Who gave it to you? I cannot positively say. It was brought down into the kitchen. I think very likely Mary M'Leod would bring it to me. What was it in? In a paper bag. Had the bag been opened apparently when it was brought to you? I did not notice whether it had been or not. You made some tapioca? Yes. Did you take it to the ladies or send it up? There was about half a breakfast cup full made, and Mary M'Leod took it up to the dining-room to Mrs Taylor. She said she was not to take it to Mrs Pritchard herself, but that Mrs Taylor would take it to her. Do you know how long it stood after it was made before it was taken up? It stood about half-an-hour or twenty minutes in the dining-room.

Mr Clark—How do you know? Mary M'Leod told me that it was there.

The Solicitor-General—Did you see it there yourself? No, I cannot say I did. Then you know nothing about it except what Mary M'Leod told you? Nothing. Did you speak to the ladies about the tapioca afterwards? No. Did you say anything to them about its not being very nice? I asked Mrs Pritchard how she liked the tapioca, and she said, "It was not very good, Catherine, it was rather tasteless;" and I think Mrs Taylor made an observation of the same kind. Did you yourself not say that it would not be very nice? I said it was rather thin made, being the first that I had made, and that if I had known it would stand so long, I would have made some fresh. I thought the standing had made it worse. That was in consequence of what you had heard about its standing so long? Yes. Did you yourself put anything into the tapioca? No. What was in it besides water? Nothing but the tapioca and the water. Any salt? I don't think there was salt or sugar in it. Mrs Pritchard liked to put sugar in anything she got herself. But you put no substance into it that could hurt anybody? No. Nothing at all? Nothing. Did you put anything into any of the food which you cooked? No. What was done with the packet of tapioca after you had made some for the ladies on that occasion? Just left it in the closet in the kitchen. Did you find it in the closet after the prisoner was apprehended, along with the police? When Mr Gemmell asked for it I told him what I had heard. You went to the press, and got the bag of tapioca? I cannot remember whether it was Mary Paterson or myself, but I told Mr Gemmell there would be some of it very likely in the house, for anything I knew. Did you see it there? Yes, it was in that closet. Who was the officer who was present? I think it was Morton or Murray. [Shown a paper bag.] Is that it? It may be it, for anything I know. I cannot swear to the bag. Is that what was found in the press by Murray, in your presence? Yes. The bag that was found in the press was taken possession of by the officer? Yes.

The Lord Justice-Clerk—When was it found in the press? It was the week when I was taken back to Glasgow. I was staying in Sauchiehall Street at the time. When you were taken back there did you find the remainder of the tapioca in the kitchen press? Yes. I went to see if it was there.

The Solicitor-General—It was immediately after the prisoner was apprehended? No, not immediately, but he had been apprehended. It was after I was brought back from Edinburgh to Glasgow. And that bag which has been shown to you is the same sort of bag? Yes. About the same size? Yes.

The Lord Justice-Clerk—Did you find the remainder of the tapioca in the kitchen press? Yes. What was done with it? It was given to Mr Gemmell, the Procurator-Fiscal, and the officer Murray, who was with him.

Cross-examined by Mr A. R. Clark—Did the prisoner and his wife live happily together? Yes. Was he attentive to her in her illness? Yes. Do you remember seeing Mrs Pritchard after Mrs Taylor's death, and speaking about a nurse? Yes. When was that? It was after I left her service. I asked Mrs Pritchard if she would not like to have a nurse. This was after Mrs Taylor's death? Yes. What did she say? She said, "No, Catherine; I do not like strangers." Did she say anything more? Nothing. Just think a little—"It was my own fault," she said, "that I have not got a nurse, for the doctor wished me to get one."

The Lord Justice-Clerk—Meaning her husband? Yes.

By Mr Clark—Are you satisfied that she had an attack of cramp before Dr Cowan came? I think so. The first attack was before Dr Cowan came, and the second after he left. When you heard Mrs Pritchard call out at midnight upon the occasion you have spoken to, were you and Mary M'Leod both down stairs? Yes. Who went up first? Me. Were you in the room before Mary came? Yes; she came immediately after. Then whenever Mary came in did she tell you to go for the doctor? Yes. That was the first thing that she said? Yes. And the first thing you heard? Yes. Dr Pritchard was in the room when you went up? Yes. She had said nothing that you heard until she told Mary M'Leod to go for Dr Gairdner? She did not say anything particular; but she seemed to be in great pain under the influence of chloroform. She said nothing that you heard about this time of hypocrites? Not at that time. Was Dr Gairdner in the room at the time the word was used? Yes. And it was not used before he came? No. Who else was in the room besides Dr Gairdner? Dr Pritchard, Mary M'Leod, and myself. Were you in the room all the time Dr Gairdner was there? Yes. Was Mary M'Leod in the room all the time Dr Gairdner was there? Yes. I think she was. And you heard all that was said during that time? Yes. And saw all that was done? Yes. Mrs Pritchard was very much excited you said during that time? Yes. When you got the tapioca, was it not Mary M'Leod that brought it to you? I think so. Have you any doubt about that? It was brought down stairs into the kitchen. And by Mary M'Leod? Yes. Did it appear to be unopened when you got it? I thought so. I did not notice it ever having been touched. After you made the tapioca you put the bag away in the closet? Yes. You did that yourself? Yes. When it was found in the closet was it in the same condition as you had left it? I cannot say that. Did it appear to be in the same condition as when you put it there? Yes. You did not make any more tapioca in the bag? No.

By the Lord Justice-Clerk—There was just one making of tapioca? Just one that I know of.

By Mr Clark—Dr Pritchard kept medicine, I believe in his house? Yes; but I did not see much of it. I thought there was chloroform in the house. But did he not keep it in the consulting-room? No, I did not notice any. Was he not in the habit of dispensing medicine? No; I think he generally gave prescriptions for his medicines. Were there no bottles or other things of that sort in the consulting-room? Yes. There were a good many bottles, but I did not know what they contained. You know that things of that kind were kept in the consulting-room? Yes. Was the place in which they were kept open or locked? Sometimes open and sometimes locked; it was not always locked. Was Dr Pritchard in the house at the time the tapioca was brought? Yes, so far as I know.

MARY M'LEOD—The Solicitor-General—How old are you, Mary? Seventeen in October.

You were in the service of Dr Pritchard in Glasgow, I believe? Yes. When did you go there? In Whitsunday 1863. Were you housemaid and nurse? Yes. You would be under fifteen when you went, were you? Yes. You remember Catherine, the cook, going to Carlisle to see her brother? Yes. Was Mrs Pritchard quite well when Catherine was away, or did she turn ill when she was away? She had a little cold. She was well otherwise? Yes. And did her cold continue to distress her for some time? Yes. You knew that she went to Edinburgh about the end of November to her father's? Yes. Now, between the time that she first took ill, when Catherine was away and her going to her father's, was her health generally good or bad? She did not complain of anything in particular. Was she sometimes sick before she went to Edinburgh? Yes. Did you see her sick yourself? Yes. Was she vomiting? Yes. Was the sickness frequent or seldom? She was often sick. Before she went to Edinburgh, was she often sick? Not so often as she was after she returned, but still often. You had charge of attending her bed-room? Yes. When was she generally sick—at what time of day? Sometimes in the afternoon. After dinner? Sometimes after dinner, and sometimes before dinner. Before she went to Edinburgh, was she confined to bed for some time. I do not mean immediately before, but some time before Catherine returned from Carlisle? Yes. How long, according to your recollection? Not very long. Did she ever pass a day without being sick and vomiting? Yes. Was that immediately before she went to Edinburgh, or further back? I mean, did she get better for some time before she went to Edinburgh? Before that, and when she was confined to bed, was she generally sick every day? Sometimes she was not sick every day. Then all you can say is that she was very often sick, but that she sometimes got better before she went to Edinburgh? Yes. Was there any doctor attending her besides her husband before she went to Edinburgh? No. Did she get any medicine, so far as you know? Yes. What medicine? I could not say what. What like was it—powder or liquid? Liquid. And what colour? White. Did you procure it for her? Yes. It was some white liquid in a doctor's bottle? Yes. Was it clear like water or white like milk? White like milk. What it was you don't know? No. Did she get anything else? Yes; red powders. Where were these got, do you know? Did you buy any of them? No, I ordered them. Who told you to get them? The doctor gave me a line to go for them. The prisoner there? Yes.

The Lord Justice-Clerk—Did he give you a prescription to get them? Yes.

The Solicitor-General—And some of these powders were in the house after the prisoner was apprehended? Yes. And I think you told where they were to be found? Yes. [Several powders were produced.] When did she return from Edinburgh? Some time before Christmas. Was it a long time before Christmas or a short time before Christmas? It was part of a week. And her mother came with her and remained a short time? Yes. And her eldest daughter? Yes. How long did they remain? Was it two or three days or longer? Longer than that. After she returned from Edinburgh had she any sickness? Yes. Immediately after or sometime after? Sometime after. How was she when she came back? Did she appear to be better? She seemed to have a little cold. But no sickness? No. And no vomiting? She was sick soon after she came back. How long after? A few days. What was the sickness you saw a few days after she returned from Edinburgh? She was vomiting. Where? In the pantry. That adjoins the dining-room? Yes. At what time of day was it? It was at night.

By the Lord Justice-Clerk—At what hour of the night? About twelve o'clock at night.

By the Solicitor-General—Did she leave the dining-room to go into the pantry? Yes. Did she leave any one in the dining-room when she left it? No. Had she been there alone? Yes. How long had she been alone from the time the rest of the family had gone away? Not long. Her mother was with her then? Yes. Had they gone to bed? They had gone to their bed-rooms, but whether they had gone to bed or not I can't say. You mean the mother and daughter? Yes. And Dr Pritchard, the prisoner, where was he? Upstairs. In his bed-room, too? Yes. Then was it just after the others had retired to rest that you heard her go into the pantry and become sick? Yes. Where were you at the time? I was downstairs. And you heard her retching? Yes. Did you go to her? Yes. In the pantry? Yes. And how did you find her? She was vomiting. Was she very sick? Yes. Did she say anything to you? No. She did not speak? No. Did you not speak to her? No; I gave her hot water. Did she ask for it? No. She said nothing to you or you to her? No. Did you see any more that night? Did you go up to her bed-room with her? No. Well, when did you see her next? I saw her next morning. In her bed-room? Yes. And how was she? She was a little better. Did she remain in her bed a part of the next day? Yes. Till when? Till between twelve and one o'clock. She got up then? Yes. Before that she had been getting up to breakfast at the usual time? Yes. What was the usual time? About nine.

Did she seem unwell when you saw her next day—that day she remained in bed till twelve or one o'clock—did she look ill? Yes. Now, after this, did sickness come upon her frequently—was she sick every day after this? No. Not every day? No. Was she sick often? Yes. Almost every day? Yes. And when was she generally sick—what time of the day? Between four and five o'clock.

By the Lord Justice-Clerk—Was that after dinner? Yes. What was the dinner hour? Half-past three o'clock.

By the Solicitor-General—Then she was commonly sick about an hour after dinner? Yes. Was she sick at any other time of the day commonly, or was she only sick once a-day? Sometimes she was sick at other times.

By the Lord Justice-Clerk—At what other times was she sick? Sometimes in the forenoon.

By the Solicitor-General—How long after breakfast? About one o'clock. And when did she commonly breakfast? About nine o'clock. Now, I am speaking of the time before she took to her bed, and was confined to her bed. Was she sometimes sick during the night? Yes. How do you know that? Sometimes she would tell me herself. And you had to remove her slops from the bedroom? Yes. Did you see from these that she had been sick during the night? Sometimes they would be emptied by the doctor. How do you know that? Mrs Pritchard would tell me.

By the Lord Justice-Clerk—Mrs Pritchard would tell you that she had been sick during the night? Yes. And you did not observe anything that looked as if she had been sick? No. Did you hear how that came to be? No. How did she come to tell you that the doctor emptied the slops? There was no one in the room to do it but him. Then it was your own opinion that he did it? Yes. Then she did not tell you that? No.

By the Solicitor-General—Did Mrs Pritchard ever tell you that the doctor had taken away what she had vomited? No.

By the Lord Justice-Clerk—Now, you must try and speak out; it was from your not speaking out that that mistake was very nearly arising, and it might be a very serious one.

By the Solicitor-General—Did she frequently complain to you of having been sick during the night? Whenever she was sick during the night she remained in her bed for a time next day. And upon these occasions she told you she had been sick during the night? Yes. What did she say about her sickness? She said, "I wonder when this sickness is going to stop." Was that a thing that she said once, or that she said to you often? Often. Was she able to account for it by what she had eaten, or in any way? No. Now, when did she take to her bed permanently after returning from Edinburgh? I mean, when did her last illness begin? Do you remember Dr Gairdner coming? Yes. How long before that was it that she first took to her bed for a long time? I do not remember.

By the Lord Justice-Clerk—Had she been confined to bed for some time before Dr Gairdner came? Yes.

By the Solicitor-General—How long had she been confined to bed? Was it a few days, or more? A few days. Do you remember where she was when she was seized with sickness before taking to bed before Dr Gairdner came? Do you remember her being taken ill when she was writing in the consulting-room? Yes. Tell us all that you know about that. How do you know that she was writing in the consulting-room, and how do you know she was taken ill? Tell us the story. I was in the consulting-room, and saw her writing there. How long was that before Dr Gairdner came—was it a few days—was it about the beginning of February? I do not remember. But it was some time before Dr Gairdner came? Yes. Now, then, after you were in the consulting-room, and saw her there writing, what next did you see of her? She came out to the pantry, and was vomiting there. Were you in the consulting-room when she went into the pantry? No. You saw her come out, and go into the pantry? Yes. And heard that she was sick? Yes. What time would that be? About three o'clock in the afternoon. Was it after dinner? No. It was before dinner? Yes. How long was it before this that you had seen her writing? Not very long. She was very sick in the pantry? Yes. You heard that from the sound, or did you go in and see her? I went in and saw her. And she vomited? Yes. Where did she go after leaving the pantry? Upstairs to her bed-room. Did you go with her? Yes. Was that on the top flat? Yes. Was she weak? Yes. Did she need help upstairs? Yes. Did you take anything up to her? Yes. What? Hot water for her feet. Where was the prisoner at the time? I think he was out when she was vomiting in the pantry. Did you see him after she had gone upstairs to her bed-room? Yes. How long after? When I came down stairs. Was Catherine there? Catherine was down stairs. She had not gone up? No. About what time of day was it that you saw the doctor when you came down?

The Lord Justice-Clerk—How long after she had taken ill? Almost directly. I suppose he came in just in time for dinner? Yes.

The Solicitor-General—The dinner was at half-past three? Yes. Did you go up with him to his wife's room? No. Did he go up himself? After he had his dinner, I think he went up.

By the Lord Justice-Clerk—Did you tell him she had been taken ill? Yes.

By the Solicitor-General—Before dinner? Yes; if he went up before dinner, I don't recollect. You mean that he may have gone without your recollecting? Yes. But you do recollect his going up after dinner? Yes. Was Mrs Pritchard put to bed? Yes. Were her clothes taken off? No. What seemed to be the matter with her when she had got into bed, anything but the weakness after such sickness as she had in the pantry? No; she did not complain of anything to me except cold. She said her feet were cold. Anything about her hands? They were cold, too. Was anything else the matter with her feet or hands except that they were cold? No. Did she say anything about that attack to you? Did she give you any account of it? No. How it happened that she was so sick? No. Did she say anything at all? No; not that I remember. Did you see anything of her during the night? Yes. What did you see of her? The bell was rung by her about seven o'clock at night, and Catherine went up. Did you not go up? She went up for me. I was out at the time. Then, you only heard that from her? As I was coming in, Catherine was coming down stairs. Did you go up then to your mistress's room? Catherine came down and wanted the doctor to come up; and both the doctor and Catherine went up. Did you go up with the doctor? No; I went down stairs to make some tea. When did you go up? They wanted me to light the fire in the spare room, and to bring Mrs Pritchard down there. You did light it? Yes. Who told you to do that? Either the doctor or Catherine. Did you see her brought down? Yes. How was she brought down? She was brought down in the doctor's arms. He carried her? Yes. Was she confined to bed after this for some time? Yes. How long? A few days. Did you see her during these few days? Yes. Was she attacked with sickness? Yes. When she was in the spare room after she had been carried down by her husband, in attending to the room as housemaid, did you see what she had vomited? Yes. And did you speak to her about her sickness, or did she speak to you? Sometimes I would be in the room when she was vomiting. Was the vomiting severe when you saw it? Sometimes it was worse than others. From what you saw of her, can you tell us when that usually happened, was it after she had had something commonly, or before? Sometimes she would be sick after she had something. Who took her food to her when she was in the bedroom? Sometimes it was taken by me and at other times by Catherine. Was it ever taken up by anybody else? Sometimes the doctor took up her breakfast to her and sometimes he did not. Did he sometimes take her tea up to her? Yes.

By the Lord Justice-Clerk—You have seen the doctor take up her breakfast? Yes. And her tea also? Yes.

By the Solicitor-General—Was it he commonly who took up her tea, or was it you or Catherine? It was taken by the three of us. It was sometimes the one and sometimes the other.

By the Lord Justice-Clerk—Either you or he or Catherine took up all that was got in the way of food? Yes.

By the Solicitor-General—Did Catherine take food to her often, or very seldom? When Catherine was there she took it up very often. As often as you? I don't recollect. You remember that occasion before Dr Gairdner was called in about the attack of illness which she had? Yes. When did you first hear of it? My first intimation of it was by Catherine going upstairs. Did you hear Mrs Pritchard cry out with pain? Yes. About what time of night? About twelve o'clock or past twelve.

The Lord Justice-Clerk—You and Catherine went up? Yes.

The Solicitor-General—Which of you were in the room first? Catherine. Was she long in before you, or were you close together? Yes. How did you find Mrs Pritchard? She was undressed and in bed.

By the Lord Justice-Clerk—What did you see remarkable about her? She had been seized with cramp.

By the Solicitor-General—Did she seem to be in pain? Yes. Was she excited? Yes. Did she complain of pain in any particular place? Not to me. Or in your hearing? No. Just of pain generally? Yes. Was her husband there? Yes. What was he doing? He was attending to her. But what was he doing to show his attention—was he rubbing her hands or doing anything else to relieve her? Catherine and he were putting hot and cold water on her hands. Was he excited, or quite cool and calm? He was excited—he was sorry that Mrs Pritchard was ill. How did he show his sorrow—was he crying? Yes. Did she say anything to him? I did not hear her say anything to him; I was sent away for Dr Gairdner. Before you went away for the doctor, did you hear her say anything to him when he was crying? I heard her saying something to him after I returned. Not before you went away? Not that I recollect. Before you went away for the doctor, what did she say about a doctor? Whenever I went into the room, she said, "Go away for another doctor directly, Mary." Did she say anything else? She said, "Be sure to go; I want another doctor." Was Dr Pritchard crying at this time? It was after I returned that he was crying. Are you sure he was not crying before you went away? I am not sure.

The Lord Justice-Clerk—You are not sure that it was before or after? I am not sure. I saw him crying after I returned; but I am not sure if he did so before.

The Solicitor-General—Are you really not sure that he was not crying before you went away for the doctor? I am not sure whether he was crying before or not; but I am certain that he was crying after I returned. Now, what was it she said to him after you returned; you told us that she said something, what was it? She asked him not to cry. Did she say why? She said, "Don't cry, you hypocrite; if you cry, it was you that did it." As far as I can remember, these were the words. Was Dr Gairdner present when she said this, or was it before he came? I think he was in the room, but I don't remember very well. Now, I do not want to press you about anything, but I wish you to remember as exactly as you can. Was what you have told us now not said before you went for the doctor, when Mrs Pritchard was crying out that she wanted another doctor, and telling you to go? I think it was after. Did she only say that once? I do not think I heard her more than once. Now, after this did Mrs Pritchard become very unwell till her mother came? Her mother came in a day or two afterwards. Did her sickness continue till that time? Yes. And anything else excepting sickness—cramp? I do not think she was attacked with cramp between that night and the time that Mrs Taylor came. After Mrs Taylor came, how was Mrs Pritchard—was she confined to bed chiefly? Yes. And were you frequently with her when Mrs Taylor was there? Mrs Taylor slept with her and attended upon her. But did not you continue as housemaid to wait upon the room, and you saw Mrs Pritchard I suppose every day? Yes, several times. Did you speak to her about the way in which she was every day? I always asked her if she was better. How did she say she was? Sometimes she said she was much the same; sometimes that she was a little better, and at other times she was worse. Was she sick every day during the time her mother was with her? She was not sick every day that Mrs Taylor was with her. Was she sick most days? (After some hesitation.) She was sick almost every day. But these days when she was sick, was she sick only once a-day, or generally more than once? I cannot tell. Did she complain of thirst? Yes. Great thirst? Yes. Anything else? Of great heat in her head. Anything else—pain in her stomach? Yes. Was Dr Pritchard in the house all the while that Mrs Taylor was there? He was not in the house all day. Not all day; but was he living at home? Yes. And took his meals at home? Yes. When had he dinner generally at that time? At half-past three. When had Mrs Pritchard her dinner usually when her mother was with her? Between one and two generally. Was Dr Pritchard sometimes with her when she took her dinner? He was sometimes in the room with her when she dined. Often? He would not be every day. He would not be there every day—that is not an answer to the question. Was he commonly there when she had her dinner? Not so often as not. Who made her tea? Sometimes I did, and sometimes the cook. Who poured it out for her? It was poured out for her in the dining-room. By whom? By the doctor, or by whoever was at the table. Did you see it done? Yes. Who else was at the table except the doctor? Her mother. It was sometimes poured out by the doctor, and sometimes by Mrs Taylor? Yes. Who prepared her bread and put the butter upon it? Mrs Taylor, when she was there. And who else when she was not there? It was done by herself. What I mean is, did Dr Pritchard ever put the butter upon her bread? Yes.

By Mr Clark—Have you seen this? Yes.

By the Solicitor-General—After Mrs Taylor's death—on the morning of the 25th February—who was in the habit of taking Mrs Pritchard's meals to her? Her tea was generally taken up to her by the doctor or one of the children. That is, he either took it up himself from the dining-room, or sent one of the children with it? Yes, or me. Her breakfast and her tea were sent up from the dining-room? By whom was her dinner taken up after Mrs Taylor's death? Generally by me.

By the Lord Justice-Clerk—With regard to the dinner, did you take it straight from the kitchen? Yes.

By the Solicitor-General—What did her dinner consist of? Chicken or fish. Anything else? That was what she generally liked. Before Mrs Taylor's death, did she send you to a druggist's to buy a bottle of Batley's Solution? Mrs Taylor sent me. How long before her death? The Monday before. Where did you buy it? At Murdoch Brothers. Did she give you a bottle to get filled, or did you buy it there? She gave me a bottle to get filled. Is that the sort of bottle [bottle No. 85 produced]? Yes. Is that the same bottle you took? I could not say; but it is something like it. How much did you pay for it? 8s. 4d. Did you give it to Mrs Taylor with the mixture or solution in it? Yes. Did you see the bottle, or one like it, after Mrs Taylor's death? Yes. Where? In the bed-room. Did you find it in her pocket? No. Was Mrs Taylor in good health herself from the time she came till the day before she died; or did you see anything the matter with her? She was complaining. When did she begin to complain? She had a cold when she came. When did she begin to complain about anything else? She never complained of anything else till the day before she died. What did she complain of to you the day before she died? She wanted to be sick. What time of day? About five o'clock she said to me she was not well. That is Friday the 24th? Yes.

The Lord Justice-Clerk—In the morning? No, the afternoon. She was unwell, and wanted to be sick? She said she wanted to be sick, and could not vomit.

By the Solicitor-General—After five; was that long after five o'clock? It was between six and seven. Did she say what she thought was the matter with her? She said she thought it was from being confined too much in the same room. Did she say she thought she had got the same complaint as her daughter, Mrs Pritchard? Yes. This was between six and seven? Yes. Well, what did she do then? She came down stairs from her daughter's bed-room. Was it not her daughter's bed-room where she said she wanted to be sick, and that she thought she had the same complaint as her daughter? Yes. Where did she go after she came down stairs? I think she went into the dining-room or drawing-room. Did she not go to the consulting-room and write letters? Not at that time. When was that? After tea. Where had she tea? In the dining-room. Anybody with her at tea? Yes. Who? All the family.

By the Lord Justice-Clerk—Was the prisoner there? Yes. And the children? Yes; I did not see her taking tea, but she was in the dining-room when the tea was on the table.

By the Solicitor-General—What time was that? About seven or past seven. When did she leave the dining-room? I came down stairs and left her there. You said she was in the consulting-room later at night; did you see her there? I went down stairs, and she came to the stairhead and called upon me, and sent me out for sausages for her supper. And you went and got them? Yes. And when you came back you found her writing in the consulting-room? I knew that she was there.

The Lord Justice-Clerk—How did you know it? Because she was not in the dining-room.

The Solicitor-General—Did you not see her there? No. Did you not see her again that night? Yes. What was the first you saw of her that night after you came back with the sausages? She met me going upstairs to the drawing-room. And she must have come out of the consulting-room, for she was not in the dining-room? Yes. You had come up from the kitchen yourself, I suppose? Yes. What did she say to you? Nothing. What o'clock would it be? About nine o'clock. Where did she go at this time when you met her in the stair? I think she went up to her daughter's bed-room, where she slept. When did you next see or hear of her? Up in the bed-room. Were you sent for when the bell was rung, or soon after she went up? Yes. How long after? Not very long. But was it two or three minutes, or an hour or so? It was more than two or three minutes.

By the Lord Justice-Clerk—Was it about half-an-hour or a quarter of an hour? About half-an-hour—I don't think quite as much.

By the Solicitor-General—You answered the bell? Yes. What was she doing—was she in bed when you went up? She was sitting on a chair. And she wanted hot water? Yes. Did she say why she wanted it? She said it was to make her vomit. Did you go for the water? Yes. Where was Mrs Pritchard at the time? In her bed. Did Mrs Taylor take the hot water when you took it up to her? Yes. Did Mrs Pritchard give you any message when you went up for the water? She desired me to go for the doctor. Did you go for the doctor? Yes. Where did you find him? He was engaged in the consulting-room. Do you mean there was a patient with him? Yes. Did he come to Mrs Pritchard's bed-room, where his mother-in-law was? Yes; but not then. How long after? Very soon after. Do you mean within a few minutes? Yes. After the person who was with him went away? Yes. Did you go with him yourself, or did you go up before him? The bell was rung again before the doctor went. And did you go up? Yes. And what did you find? Mrs Taylor in the bed-room. What was she doing—was she as well as she had been, or worse? She appeared to me much the same; she was not any better at any rate. But was she not worse? She was worse when I went up the third time. What was wanted the second time the bell rung? More hot water. And you took it up? Yes. Did she take it? Yes. Did she try to vomit both times that she took the water? Yes. Did she succeed? She did not vomit, but threw up a little water. Did the bell ring the third time? Yes. Was that before the doctor had gone up? The doctor was up then. How did you find Mrs Taylor then? She was sitting on a chair. What state was she in; did she seem sensible or insensible? Insensible. How was her head? Hanging down.

By the Lord Justice-Clerk—Was she still in the chair? Yes.

By the Solicitor-General—Was her head hanging down on her breast? Yes. How were her eyes? I think they were shut. Was Mrs Pritchard still in bed, or had she got up beside her mother? She had got up beside her mother. The prisoner was in the room? Yes. What was done? She was put to bed. Without taking her clothes off? Yes. Who lifted her? The doctor and me. Was Mrs Pritchard herself sick that evening? Yes. Did you see her? Yes. Was that when her mother was in the bed-room, or before she had gone up? Before she had gone up. Was it after she had had her tea? I don't know if she had any tea that night or not. Did you not see her vomiting the tea? If she had tea that night I don't know of it.

The Lord Justice-Clerk—Did what she vomit appear to you to be tea? I forget what it was like. Was it after tea-time when Mrs Pritchard became sick? Yes.

The Solicitor-General—After Mrs Taylor was lifted into bed how long did she live? Till about twelve or half-past twelve; I think a little past twelve. Was anybody sent for? Yes, Dr Paterson. Did you go for him? No. Did he come? Yes. How long before she died? I think it would be between ten and eleven when he was there. Did Mrs Taylor ever speak again that you heard after she was put to bed? I don't think she did. And she died just when the doctor and you laid her down in bed? Yes. With her clothes on? Yes. When was Mrs Taylor's body removed? On Monday. Mrs Pritchard, you said, had been sick the evening before her mother died. How was she afterwards? She was a little better on the Saturday and Sunday, but she was sick on Sunday afternoon. Was she not vomiting on Saturday or Sunday? She was vomiting on Sunday. On Saturday did she not vomit? No, not that I remember. Was Dr Pritchard at home on Saturday? Yes. Was he at home on the Sunday? Yes. When did he go to Edinburgh? On Monday. After her mother's death, was Mrs Pritchard brought down to the spare bed-room? Yes, she was brought down when Mrs Taylor died. Was she able to walk down? I did not see. What time on the Sunday was it that she was sick? In the afternoon—after dinner. Where did she dine that day? She dined in the drawing-room, past four o'clock. Was anybody with her? Two Miss Lairds were in the room with her, but they did not dine with her. Was Dr Pritchard there? No. Where was he? In the dining-room. Was the dinner sent from the dining-room to her? Yes. Who took it up? I did. What was it? Roast-beef and potatoes. Anything else? No. Who gave it to you to take up? The doctor. When did she become sick? Sometime in the afternoon. How long after dinner? It was shortly before tea. On the Monday Dr Pritchard went to Edinburgh? Yes; I think so. I don't recollect if he went to Edinburgh, but I know he left the house along with Dr Taylor. When? He left to go to Edinburgh by the eleven o'clock train. Had Mrs Pritchard her breakfast before he went? I don't remember. I think she had. Was she ill after breakfast? No; she got up almost directly. She got up before Mrs Taylor's body was taken away.

By the Lord Justice-Clerk—Then she was not sick on the Monday morning? No, I don't think she was.

By the Solicitor-General—Did she go into the drawing-room after breakfast that Monday morning? Yes. Did she vomit in the drawing-room shortly after going in? No; not that I remember. She lived for about three weeks after this? Yes. Did she get better, or did she continue ill the whole time? Much the same. Was she chiefly confined to bed? She generally got up about one o'clock. And remained up till when? She would go to bed at ten, and sometimes later. Do you mean she remained up till bed-time at night? Yes. In the drawing-room? Yes. Did you see a good deal of her every day? Yes. Was she commonly sick every day after her mother's death? She was much the same. Was she then sick two or three times a day? No. Generally only once? Sometimes twice. Can you tell me the times of day at which she was commonly sick? Sometimes before, and sometimes after breakfast. Was it most commonly before breakfast, or after it? After breakfast. And what was the other time? In the afternoon. At what time—after dinner? Yes. How long after dinner? Fully an hour. I don't think you mentioned how long after breakfast it was that she usually became sick? Two hours. Did you sometimes see her vomiting? Yes. And see what she did vomit? Yes. What was it commonly that she vomited when she vomited after breakfast? She vomited her breakfast. Did you think you saw tea in the stuff she vomited? I never took any notice of it. Do you remember getting anything from the doctor to give to her before supper one night—did you get a bit of cheese to take to her? Yes. When was that; was it the week that Mrs Pritchard died, or the week before? I think it was the week before; but I am not certain. What like was the bit of cheese he gave you? It was a piece of cheese. What size was it? Not very large. Was it new cheese or old? It was new; we had it in the house.

By the Lord Justice-Clerk.—But was it soft or hard? It was soft.

By the Solicitor-General—Did you take it to Mrs Pritchard? Yes. Did you see her taste it? Yes. What did she say? She asked me to taste it. Did she ever ask you to taste anything before? I don't think she did. And did you taste it? Yes.

By the Lord Justice-Clerk.—How did it taste? It tasted hot. You mean like pepper? Yes.

By the Solicitor-General—Was there anything peculiar about it except the hot taste? No. Did it make you very thirsty? No. Think again; did it make you thirsty? I don't remember if it did. You don't remember. Did it make you thirsty after eating it? It is not a thing you could have forgotten. No. Did you never say so?

Mr A. R. Clark took exception to this question.

After discussion, the question was withdrawn; and the witness being recalled, the examination was resumed.

The Solicitor-General—Did the cheese produce any peculiar sensation in your throat? Yes. What was it? A burning sensation. How much of the cheese did you take? A very small bit. Had you ever felt the same sensation in your throat before? No. Did Mrs Pritchard take the rest of the cheese? No, it was left uneaten. Soon after taking the cheese did you become thirsty. Rather thirsty. Do you remember getting some camomile tea from anybody to take to Mrs Pritchard? Yes. Who did you get it from? It was left in the bed-room by Dr Pritchard, to give to her. Did you see him leave it there? I saw him taking it up, and then I saw it in the bed-room after. Were you in the bed-room when he brought it in? Yes. What was it in? A jug. Did the doctor pour out any of it to his wife? Yes, into a wine glass. Did he tell you what to do with it? He said it was for Mrs Pritchard. Did you give it to Mrs Pritchard? Yes. Was there any reason why he did not give it himself? (No answer.)

By the Lord Justice-Clerk—Was it to be given to her at the time or afterwards? When she wanted a drink.

The Solicitor-General—You gave her some of it? Yes. Did she appear to be anything the worse of it? She vomited it.

The Lord Justice-Clerk—Immediately after taking it? Yes.

The Solicitor-General—When was this? That was the week before she died. The week before she died did you get some egg-flip to give her? Yes. From whom? From Mary Patterson. That's the girl who came to succeed Catherine as cook? Yes. About what time of day did she give it to you? At night. Where? In the kitchen. Did you get the egg-flip in the pantry in a tumbler? Yes. That was before the hot water was poured upon it? Yes. Who gave you the tumbler with the egg-flip in it? Mary Patterson told me to get it in the pantry. I took it down stairs, and Mary put some water upon it there. Did you see her taste it after she put the water on it? Yes. Did she say anything when she tasted it? She said, "What a taste it has." What time of the night was it—I think you said it was at night? Between eleven and twelve. Did you take the flip up to Mrs Pritchard? Yes. Was the doctor in the room when you took it up? Yes. Did Mrs Pritchard get some of it? Yes, she did.

The Lord Justice-Clerk—Did you taste it? No.

The Solicitor-General—How much did Mrs Pritchard take? About a wine-glassful. How long did you remain in the bed-room with Mrs Pritchard the night that she had the egg-flip? Till between three and four in the morning. Did the prisoner remain in the bed-room too? Yes. Was Mrs Pritchard sick that night? Yes. How long after she had taken the egg-flip was she sick? Very soon after.

By the Lord Justice-Clerk—Was it half-an-hour or an hour? Less than half-an-hour. And at four in the morning when you left her you went down to Mary Patterson? Yes. How did you find her? She was asleep. In the morning after the egg-flip had been given to Mrs Pritchard, did Mary Patterson tell you whether it had had any effect upon her?

Mr Clark objected to the question, and the witness was removed.

The Lord Justice-Clerk asked on what ground Mr Clark objected to the question.

Mr Clark—On the ground that it is hearsay evidence.

The Solicitor-General said he would not press the question if the objection was pressed.

The Lord Justice-Clerk said there could be no doubt about the competency of the question; referring as it did to what was going on in the house about the time of the occurrence.

Mr Clark—I should have thought the proper witness to have spoken to that would have been Mary Patterson herself.

The Lord Justice-Clerk—Oh, of course, she must be called.

Witness recalled, and examination resumed by the Solicitor-General—In the morning after the egg-flip had been given to Mrs Pritchard, did Mary Patterson tell you if it had had any effect upon her? No. Did she tell you whether she had been sick or not? Yes,

I think she told me that she had been sick. When did she say she became sick? During the night. Did she say how long after taking the egg-flip it was that she became sick? She never mentioned the egg-flip at all. Did she not? No. Think again; did she not tell you how long it was after taking the egg-flip that she became sick—did she tell you, or have you forgotten? If she told me, I don't remember it. Did she say that anything else had been wrong with her except that she had been sick—anything about her throat? I don't think so. Did she say that she had felt a burning sensation in her throat? No. And that she had vomited? She said she was vomiting during the night. And how did she account for it? (No answer.) Now just remember, you must tell us the truth—you take an oath to do that. Did Mary Patterson speak about the egg-flip next morning? No. And when she told you she had been sick she never referred to the egg-flip? No. And did she not say she had a burning sensation in her throat? Not that I remember. Did she account for her sickness in any way? No. It was the morning after she had tasted the egg-flip that she told you she had been sick during the night? Yes. Did you, in the course of the week that Mrs Pritchard died, on the Tuesday or the Wednesday, give her any port wine? Yes. From whom did you get it? It was left in the bedroom in a bottle by the doctor. How much did you give her? A wine glassful at a time. Did you give her more than one wine glassful? Not at a time.

By the Lord Justice-Clerk—Was it just one glass you gave her, or a glass at one time, and a glass at another? I gave it her more than once.

By the Solicitor-General—Do you mean more than once that same day, or on other days? On other days. Now, was she sick after getting it, or was she not? She was not. Do you mean that she was never sick after getting it? I do not remember. On Friday the 17th, the day before she died, did you see her in the morning? Yes. How was she then? I asked her if she was better, and she said she could not tell. Was she in bed? Yes. Was she in bed all that day? Yes. Did her bell ring for you in the afternoon? Yes, about five o'clock. Did you go up? Yes. Did you meet her before you got to her bed-room? Yes; she was on the stair-head, at the drawing-room landing. Was she sleeping in the spare bed-room at that time? Yes. Was she dressed or undressed? She had on her night-gown. What did she say to you? She pointed to the floor, and said, "There is my poor mother dead again." What more did she say? To take her into the bed-room. I went down stairs, and called Mary Patterson up, and we put her to bed. Did she seem to be raving? Yes. When you got her into bed, was she quiet? No. What did she say or do? Mary Patterson and I began to rub her hands, and she asked us to rub her mother and never mind her. Did her hands appear to be cramped? Yes; and they were very cold. Was her speech clear, or thick and broken? Quite clear. Did she become quiet or sensible while you remained there? She became quiet. Where was the prisoner at this time? He was out. Before her bell rung she had been in the bed-room alone? Yes. Had she had anything to eat or drink shortly before she rang the bell that you knew of? No. When had she tea? In the morning. Had she not got tea that afternoon? No. When had she dinner? Between one and two. When did the prisoner come home? Very soon after I had gone up to her. Was he in the room with her while you were there? He went into the room as I was coming out. How long had you been with her? Not very long. Was any other doctor sent for? Not at that time. Afterwards that same day? Yes. Who? Dr Paterson. Were you present when Dr Paterson was with her? I was in the room when he came, but when he came I left the room. Did you remain in the room during the rest of the night till the time she died? Yes. When did she die? I could not tell the hour, but I think it would be about one o'clock. Was the doctor present at the time? Yes. Was he in bed with her when she died? Yes. Where were you? I was lying on the sofa for some time, and then I was told to get mustard for her. Was the doctor undressed, or had he lain down in his clothes? I think he had on his drawers, but I could not say. When you were still lying on the sofa, did you hear her speak to him? Yes. What did she say? "Edward, don't sleep; I feel very faint." Was it after that the doctor sent you to get mustard? It was when I was told to get it. Was it by the prisoner you were told to go and get mustard? He asked me to go down and get it, and she said to be quick. And you went down to get the poultice made? Yes. Did you bring it up? Yes. And it was applied to Mrs Pritchard's stomach? Yes. Did she seem to be any better, or much the same when you came back, and the poultice was applied? She was not any better. Were you sent upon any other message? I was sent for another one.

The Lord Justice-Clerk—Another mustard poultice? Yes.

The Solicitor-General—Did you go for it? Yes. And brought it up? Yes. What did you find when you came back to the room? Mrs Pritchard was in her bed. After I brought up the second mustard poultice I went down and called for Mary Patterson, and when we came up we found that Mrs Pritchard was dead. And Dr Pritchard, how did he behave when he found that she was dead? Was he beside her? Yes. What did he do or say? He said she was not dead. Was he weeping? Yes. Did he say anything to her after seeing she was dead, addressing her as if she was alive? He said, "Come back to your dear Edward." Anything else? Yes, he said a good deal. You mean a good deal in the way of addressing her? Yes. Was Mary Patterson present? Yes. Did he say anything about bringing a rifle? Yes. What was it? He asked somebody to bring a rifle and shoot him. After her death, and after this excitement by him, did he leave the house? Yes. Immediately after? No. How long after? I cannot say. Was it a few minutes, or a few hours? He wrote a letter or two, and went out to the post. Did you see him come in? I heard him come in. About what time of the morning would it be when he came in? I could not say. When he came in, did you hear him say anything? When he came in, I heard him say to Mary Patterson, "Mary Jane walked down the street with me, and told me to take care of the girls, but said nothing about the boys," and that she kissed him and went away. Had Mrs Pritchard in her lifetime ever seen the doctor using any familiarities with you?

Mr Clark objected to the question, and the line of examination.

Mr Watson said he objected to this question, in the first place, that it was not sufficiently precise, and, in the second, as disclosing the intention of the prosecutor to follow up a line of examination for which he thought they had laid no foundation in the libel. The question now put was not limited in point of time.

The Solicitor-General—It referred to last summer.

Mr Watson said, taking it as his learned friend had now put it, it was limited to the summer of the year 1864, several months before the earliest period which was mentioned in the libel. It had no connexion whatever with anything contained in the libel. The question which their Lordships had to determine was whether this matter, of which no notice had been given upon record, and of which it would have been exceedingly easy to give notice upon the record had it been intended to found upon it to any extent whatever, could be competently gone into now. He did not know the ground on which the Crown put their claim to go into this line of examination. Obviously it did not bear upon the crime which was set forth in the libel, or, if it bore at all, it could only be brought to bear as suggesting, or suggestive of, some kind of motive. Assuming that that was the correct view of the matter—and it was the only view which suggested itself to him—he had to submit that, in that view, this line of examination could not be gone into without any intimation having been given on the record. Mr Watson then cited several cases in which the Court had overruled attempts to lead evidence to suggest a motive where no notice had been given of the intention of the Crown to do so, and where such notice could easily have been given. In the case of Black, which would be found in "Irvine's Reports," page 281—a case of fire-raising—an attempt was made to show that the prisoner had insured certain property shortly before, so as to suggest motive. The Court declined to allow that line of examination on the grounds he had stated. In the Culsalmond Rioting Case, where a clergyman and others were accused of mobbing and rioting, an attempt was made to show a common purpose or motive on the part of the rioters which had not been set forth on the record, and that attempt was not allowed by the Court, because notice had not been given to the prisoners. It was usual for the public prosecutor to give notice that such and such was the motive on which he would try to prove that a panel had acted, and he could guard himself quite securely by saying "for that purpose or some other purpose unknown." It put the Crown to no disadvantage to give notice, but it put the panel to great disadvantage to go without it. In the present case, it would put the prisoner to great hardship, because the matter attempted to be proved did not lie within the four corners of the libel.

The Solicitor-General—My friend must have been aware from the investigation which has taken place what the line of examination is. I am afraid I would very gladly abstain from it, if I could convey to your Lordships the information necessary to enable you to determine the point without doing it; but I cannot see the possibility of that, and I must therefore of necessity indicate what the line of inquiry is.

Their Lordships then consulted for a few minutes, after which

The Lord Justice-Clerk said—The Court have thought it proper to consider this matter, and the result to which we have come is this, that we do not think this is a case at all within the rule of the cases cited by Mr Watson, one of them being a case where the prosecutor charged mobbing and rioting without allegation of a common purpose, which must necessarily be libelled in the case of mobbing and rioting. But here the difficulty which might have arisen is this—Whether these circumstances, occurring last summer, were not now to be brought forward for the purpose of proving the existence of malice at the time. There was some examination going to show that there was some secret misunderstanding, which I need not particularly refer to, between the prisoner and his wife. Now, in that state of the evidence, we cannot see that it is incompetent to prove what this question implies the Crown are intending to prove—namely, that the prisoner had familiarities with this woman which caused jealousies with his wife—because that would very materially bear on the question before the Court.

The Solicitor-General—I understand your Lordships' ruling is this, that I am to tender evidence bearing on the footing on which the prisoner and this girl lived before the time referred to in this libel, and down to the very period of his wife's death.

The Lord Justice-Clerk—Yes.

The witness recalled, and examination resumed by the Solicitor-General—Did Mrs Pritchard ever see her husband use any familiarities towards you? Yes; she did. What were they? (Witness hesitated to answer.)

The Lord Justice-Clerk—This is very unpleasant, Mary; but there is no avoiding it, and you must tell us the whole story. What was it? She saw him kissing me.

By the Solicitor-General—Where was the place? It was in one of the bed-rooms, was it not? Yes. And Mrs Pritchard came in just at the time? Yes. Did she speak to you about it afterwards? I spoke to her. When did this happen? Last summer. What did you say to her? I wanted to go away. And what did she say? She would not let me.

The Lord Justice-Clerk—What did she give as her reason for not letting you go away? She said she would speak to the doctor. What did she say about him? She said he was a nasty dirty man. When did the doctor first use any familiarities with you? Was it shortly before this? Yes. In the course of last summer? Yes. Did he get the better of you? (No answer.) He had connexion with you, had he not? Yes. Did you become with child to him? Yes. Did you tell him that yourself? Yes. What did he say? He said he would put it all right. When did this happen? Last year. Was it before Mrs Pritchard had seen him kissing you, or afterwards? Afterwards. Did he give you any medicine?

Mr Clark—Are we to go into questions leading to this that he gave her medicine for the purpose of procuring abortion?

The Lord Justice-Clerk—I would like first to know if a child was born. (To witness.) —Were you delivered of a child, Mary? (No answer.) Had you a child? (No answer.) Was there a child born? (Still no answer.) Had you a miscarriage? Yes. When did that take place? Was it in the winter? No. Was it in the autumn? Yes.

The Solicitor-General intimated that the next question he meant to put was if the prisoner gave her anything to produce the miscarriage.

Mr Clark—That is a matter which, if it was to be inquired into, we should have had notice of. What that has to do with the question of whether these murders were committed or not I cannot see. That was a matter which the prosecutor could have raised in a separate indictment, or in this indictment by a separate charge.

The Solicitor-General—I think it is material to the ends of justice here that it should be shown not only the footing on which he was living with this girl at the time, but also that, being a doctor, he in the course of that illicit intercourse used his professional skill and knowledge of his art for such a purpose. I think that is material with reference to the charge that is made against him here—using his professional skill and art for another purpose upon his wife and her mother. The bearing of that on the other evidence, not only for the prosecution, but for the defence, it would be improper, and might be prejudicial to the ends of justice, to dwell upon. But I think it is impossible not to feel that it is for the consideration of the jury with reference to the whole circumstances that may be brought out in evidence—on the prisoner's side it may be evidence of good character—evidence of living together with his wife on such terms as to exclude all notion of such a crime as that which is imputed to him here—that it should be known how he was living in his own house, and to what uses he was about the time in question applying the skill and practice of his art.

Mr Clark—That just seems to me to be this: that they want to use the alleged commission of another crime as proof of this crime. They don't suggest that as motive. The Solicitor-General says—"I want to use this evidence for the purpose of showing that, because he used his skill in this improper manner, it is probable he may have used it in the more atrocious manner charged against him in the present indictment." That is simply, I submit, putting the prisoner on trial for a crime which is not charged in this indictment. That was a perfectly competent charge, if the public prosecutor thought it his duty to make the charge, and to put it in the indictment. He has not dared to do so. He has not made any charge, I presume, because he knew he could not prove it, and he brings this girl as his witness for the purpose of putting the prisoner on his trial for an offence, on the allegation that it may be useful for the public prosecutor, to show that he used his skill improperly in one case, so that the inference may be drawn that he used his skill improperly on the occasions libelled. If the public prosecutor thinks that the ends of justice are to be gained by any such act, I challenge him to show any reason for it. It has nothing to do with justice. If he wanted to charge this crime, the justice was to have charged it in the libel, and not to have used the alleged commission of one crime spoken to by this witness, and by this witness only, as giving colour to the other offences which are charged here.

The Lord Justice-Clerk, after consultation with the other judges on the bench, said that the Court was of opinion that the last question was not competent.

By the Solicitor-General—Did this improper connexion between the doctor and you continue long after you had the miscarriage? No. Was it continued when Mrs Pritchard was in Edinburgh visiting her father? No. Hadn't he connexion with you when Mrs Pritchard was in Edinburgh visiting her father? (Witness here hesitated a long time, and seemed indisposed to answer the question.)

The Lord Justice-Clerk—It is necessary that you should answer the question, Mary. I sympathise with your very painful position, but it is necessary that you should answer it. Had he connexion with you at the time? Yes.

By the Solicitor-General—Had he also connexion with you after his wife's return to Glasgow and before her death? No. Did he ever speak of marrying you? [Witness became affected at this question, and began to sob. After a pause, she answered in the affirmative.] When did he first speak about marriage? Was it more than once? Was it before his wife turned ill? Yes. What did he say about marriage? Did he say he would marry you? Yes. Did he say when he would marry you? No. When he said he would marry you, did he speak of his wife? (A long pause by the witness.) What did he say about his wife when he said that he would marry you? (Another pause, the witness showing disinclination to answer the question.) Did he say that he would marry you if his wife died? Yes. Now, after I have suggested the matter to you, you will be kind enough to repeat what he did say to you? What was it he said? (A long pause.)

The Lord Justice-Clerk—Give us the exact words. Witness hesitated, and became apparently deeply excited. After a pause of more than a minute,

The Solicitor-General said—You cannot possibly like standing there, but you must if you do not answer the question. What were the words he said to you? (Witness still hesitated, and held down her head.) There is no reason why you should not say it. It is to avoid mistakes regarding you that might be made that I wish you to answer.

The Lord Justice-Clerk—Tell us what he said, because it must be known.

Witness was repeatedly urged by the Lord Justice-Clerk and the Solicitor-General to repeat the words, but only became more deeply excited. The scene lasted for several minutes, and produced a very painful impression in Court. At one time the witness murmured some words, but too faintly to be heard, and afterwards, though repeatedly urged from the bench, and by the Solicitor-General, she refused to repeat what she had said.

The Solicitor-General—Did he say he would marry you if his wife died? Yes. Was that several times? No, only once. What did he say then upon that one occasion? (Witness again hesitated.) This was before his wife took ill that he said that? Yes. Did he give you any presents? Yes. What was the first present he gave you? A ring. Was that last summer? No. Was it this year? No. When was it he gave you the ring? The year before last. What else did he give you? A brooch and a locket. [Shown a brooch in the shape of an anchor.] Is that one of the brooches? Yes. When did you get the anchor brooch? This year. Was it not very shortly before his wife's death? Yes. In the same month that she died? Yes. Did he give you his likeness? Yes. Did he give you more than one photograph of himself? Yes. Was his photograph in one of these brooches which he gave you? In the locket. Was there a photograph in it when he gave it you? Yes. There is not a photograph in it now; what has become of it? (Witness hesitated.) The Solicitor-General repeated the question. What became of it? (Witness faintly.) I tore it. I forgot to ask you when you were speaking about Mrs Pritchard's illnesses throughout from her return after Christmas until her death, was she afflicted with a violent purging as well as with sickness and vomiting? Yes. You had to attend in the chamber and empty it several times a-day? Yes. Did this purging accompany the sicknesses down to the end of her life? When she was sick, did she also purge in this way? Sometimes. Was it commonly? Yes. Do you know whether Mrs Taylor, on the last day of her life, was also affected in that way with frequent purging? Yes. When did you first observe it? On the Friday. What time of day? In the afternoon. Now, there was some tapioca got from Burton & Henderson during Mrs Taylor's lifetime, do you remember who bought it? Yes. Who was it? Master Kenneth, one of the children. Did the boy give it to you when he brought it in? Yes. How much was there of it? There was either half-a-pound or a pound in a paper bag. What did you do with it? I laid it on the lobby table. How long did it lie there before it was taken down to Catherine? It did not lie very long. Was it an hour or two, or a shorter time? A shorter time. Did you take it down to Catherine? Mrs Taylor took it down. Did you tell the prisoner that Mrs Taylor used Batley's medicine? I did not. Did you ever speak to him upon that subject at all? No.

Cross-examined by Mr Clark—Did you see Dr Pritchard cut the cheese that you took up to Mrs Pritchard? No. Had you taken the cheese into the supper-room? Yes. Who were at supper? They were all in the room. But who was all? All the children—Charley, Kenneth, and Horace, and Dr Pritchard, Mr King, and Mr Connell. They were there when you took in the tray, I suppose? Yes. With the cheese on it? Yes. And they were there when you got it to take away to Mrs Pritchard? Yes. Were they sitting at the table when you got it away with you? Yes, I think they were. And the cheese was on the table? Yes. Where was the doctor when he gave it to you? He was in the dining-room. Was he just sitting at the table? Yes. And it appeared to have been just as if he had cut it off at the table and gave it to you to take up? Yes. How much of that cheese did you eat? A very small bit. But just give me a notion of it? Was it more than a bean? No. How much did you take of it? A very little. Could you show me on the point of your finger how much it was? (Witness pointed at the tip of her finger, showing that it had been very small.) Before you had taken up the egg-flip to Mrs Pritchard, had you been with her that night? Yes. And continued to be with her till you went down for the egg-flip? Yes. Had she been ill before you went down for the egg-flip? Yes. Vomiting? No. Had she not vomited before you went down for the egg-flip? No. What had been the matter with her? She was worse that night. Was that before she took the egg-flip? Yes. Had she not been vomiting? Not that I remember. In what way was she worse? She told me she was not well. You stopped with her till about four o'clock in the morning; did she vomit more than once? No. Just once? Yes. Was she worse or better after the time that she got the egg-flip than she had been before, except for the vomiting? She was better after she vomited. Do you mean better than she had been before she took the egg-flip? Yes. Did you clean out the consulting-room during the time you were there? Yes. Did Dr Pritchard keep any medicine there? He used to keep medicine on the table for people that came in. Were there medicines in other places in that room except on the table? I could not tell. Was there a press in the room? Yes. More than one? Yes. How many? Two. Were these kept locked or open? One of them was always kept locked, the other was kept locked with the key in the door. Do you know if spirits were kept in the locked one? Yes. Have you seen the doctor taking spirits out of it? Yes. Do you know there were bottles in the one in which the key was left? Yes. What kind of bottles? All kinds of bottles. Medicine bottles? Yes. When you were in Dr Pritchard's service, who did you sleep with? With Catherine. All the time she was there with you? Yes. When the doctor spoke to you about marriage, did you think he was speaking in joke? Yes.

The Solicitor-General—What did you do with the rest of the cheese—I mean with the bit which Mrs Pritchard would not eat? I took it downstairs, and left it in the pantry.

The Lord Justice-Clerk—You say that the prisoner appeared to be in joke when he spoke to you about marriage. Now, you must tell us what he said. Come, now, there must be no more delay about it, the thing must be done. (The witness here hesitated some time, disinclined to answer the question.)

By the Lord Justice-Clerk—This is the last question you have got to answer, but if you do not answer it, I shall be obliged to send you to prison. Now, you may choose between these two things. The question you have got to answer is, what the prisoner said to you about marriage? He said that when Mrs Pritchard died, if she died before him, and I was alive, he would marry me.

The Lord Justice-Clerk—This is what I have taken down; see that it is right:—"What the prisoner said about marriage was that if ever Mrs Pritchard died before me, he would marry me." Is that right? Witness: before him.

The Lord Justice-Clerk—Did you say anything more than what I have taken down? No.

The Lord Justice-Clerk—Then you may go.

The next witness called was Mary Patterson, formerly in the service of Dr Pritchard.

Mr Clark suggested that, it being now past six o'clock, the Court might adjourn, as it would not be for the advantage of the prisoner that the sittings should be too protracted.

The Lord Justice-Clerk said that when the time was so limited as it was in this case, the Court were bound to sit longer to prevent the miscarriage of justice, and referred Mr Clark to the arrangement made in the trial of the cotton-spinners.

Mr Clark said he would be willing to enter into any arrangement which might be thought necessary.

The Lord Justice-Clerk then, addressing the jury, said—I hope that we shall be able to adjourn now till to-morrow. This is a case, I need not tell you, which will occupy several days, and it is not desirable that we should sit for long hours daily, which might be by no means conducive to the ends of justice. Accommodation will be provided for you in a hotel in this city, where I hope that you will be perfectly comfortable, and to which you will be conveyed upon the rising of the Court. If the proposed arrangement is carried out, we will adjourn at present to meet at ten to-morrow morning. We will require to wait a few minutes to see if the arrangement is agreed upon, and to draw up a minute.

The following minute was then put in and agreed to by the respective parties :—

"At this stage of the proceedings, it was moved by the counsel for the panel, and by the panel himself, that for their accommodation the Court should now adjourn the diet, it being expressly understood that the period of adjournment shall not be reckoned in the running of the letters of indictment."

The Court adjourned at half-past six o'clock to meet next morning at ten o'clock.

SECOND DAY—Tuesday, July 4.

The Court met again this morning at ten o'clock, and resumed the trial—the Lord Justice-Clerk, Lord Ardmillan, and Lord Jerviswoode presiding.

About a quarter-past ten the prisoner entered the dock, and took his seat. The brother of Dr Pritchard also entered the dock, and, having shaken hands with the agent for the defence, took his seat beside his brother.

During the whole of to-day's proceedings the prisoner maintained a calm and attentive demeanour. He seemed somewhat fatigued, but he appeared to take a deep interest in the examination of the witnesses, and more than once watched them attentively as they were questioned by the counsel.

The Court arrangements were admirably carried out. No crowding was permitted in the galleries or passages, and everything was done to promote the comfort of those engaged in the trial.

The crowd outside the doors was not so large as on the previous day; but this may be accounted for by the difficulty of procuring admittance.

The first witness called was Mary Patterson, servant to kotel-keeper, Glasgow.—Mr Gifford—You were engaged to be cook in the service of Dr Pritchard? Yes. When did you enter his service? On the 16th February last. You came to Glasgow from Forres, and knew nothing of Dr Pritchard's family before? No. Did you see the old servant whose place you were to take, Catherine Lattimer? Yes. When did she leave? The same night. Who were the inmates of the house when you came to it? Dr Pritchard and his wife, and Mrs Taylor, and four of a family; Mr King and Mr Connell, boarders; and Mary M'Leod; Mrs Nabb was there that night. Mrs Nabb is a person who assists in washing occasionally? Yes. Did you see Mrs Pritchard when you came? No. Where was she? She was confined to bed, I understand. And you were not up in her bed-room? No. Who took charge of the house? Mrs Taylor. She gave you directions? Yes. Did Mrs Taylor speak to you about Mrs Pritchard? Yes, she did so occasionally. Did she say anything to you about her when you first came? She said she could not understand her trouble; that she was sick and vomiting frequently, and got no sleep. Did you ask for Mrs Pritchard every day at Mrs Taylor? In general, every day. Did she tell you how she was? Yes; she said she rested very little during the night. Did she tell you more than once that she had been sick and vomiting? Yes, several times. You never saw any of the matter that Mrs Pritchard had vomited? No, except on her clothing. And you saw it on the bed-clothes? Yes. When did you first see Mrs Pritchard? The night of her mother's death. She died on the morning of the 25th February? Yes. When did you see Mrs Pritchard on the night of Friday the 24th? I saw her first well on for twelve o'clock that night. That was the first time you saw her? Yes. Tell us how you came to see her then? Mrs Taylor had been ill about nine o'clock, I understood, and Dr Pritchard had been called in, and Mary M'Leod went out a second time for Dr Pritchard, and she asked me to answer the door when she would ring; when she went out, I went up stairs to see if I could see anybody there, or if I could be of any service. You went to the top flat? Yes; and I stood near the top of the stair. Did you hear anything going on in Mrs Pritchard's room? I heard Mrs Pritchard saying, "Mother, dear mother, can you not speak to me?" Did the bed-room door open soon after that? Yes; and Dr Pritchard came out and told me that Mrs Taylor was gone. Did you go in? I went in then. Did you find Mrs Taylor dead? Yes; I put my hand on her forehead, and found it getting cold. That was the first occasion you had seen Mrs Pritchard? Yes. How long before that on that day had you seen Mrs Taylor? I saw her some time about seven o'clock in the evening. She was down in the kitchen speaking to me. Did she appear to you to be well? Well, she appeared to me somewhat peevish, as I thought from fatigue, in consequence of the night-watching with Mrs Pritchard. Did you see nothing of her again that night? No; not till I saw her dead in the bed-room. You were not very frequently up stairs? Very little. Your work was below? Yes. Had you been told not to come up stairs? Not at that time. When? I was told several times after Mrs Taylor's death. By whom? By Dr Pritchard. What were you told? I was told by him several times, before he went out to his calls in the morning, not to disturb Mrs Pritchard, as she was composed to go to sleep. When you found Mrs Taylor dead that night, did the doctor come back to the bed-room? He came in, after he came out and told me that Mrs Taylor was gone. What was done after that? Mrs Pritchard was in bed in a kneeling position, beside her mother, rubbing her mother's right hand between hers. Was Mrs Pritchard removed from the room? The doctor asked her to come down stairs, as he thought it was not agreeable for her to be there. She insisted she should be left a little longer with her mother, as she thought her mother was not quite dead. Mrs Pritchard said that? Yes. Were you sent down stairs to make the spare bed-room ready? Yes. To light a fire in it? Yes. By the prisoner? Yes. Did Mrs Pritchard and the prisoner come down to the spare bed-room? Yes; after I went up and told them that the bed-room was ready. How did Mrs Pritchard come down? She walked down, and the doctor accompanied her.

Lord Justice-Clerk—With his help? I don't think he helped her. He said he would carry her down. She said she would rather walk.

Mr Gifford—Had Mrs Nabb been sent for? Yes, Mary M'Leod was sent for her after she came from Dr Paterson. Did Mrs Nabb come? Yes. Did she and you go to the bed-room to dress Mrs Taylor's body? Yes. And you did so? We did. Were her clothes on when she died? Yes. As you were taking off Mrs Taylor's dress did you feel or hear anything in the pocket? Yes. I took off her clothes and laid them on the floor, and in doing so I heard the sound of a bottle along with a key in her pocket. Did you lift the dress? A little afterwards I did, and took out the bottle. What did you find in the pocket? I found the key of the storeroom, and a purse and a letter. [Shown No. 85 B.] Is that the bottle? Yes. Was there anything in the bottle? Yes; it was about half full. Of a liquid? Yes. What was the colour? It was a brown liquid, something like laudanum. Did you notice how full the bottle was? It was about half-way up the label. You read the label at the time? Mrs Nabb read it aloud. This part of it—"Two drops equal to three of laudanum?" Yes, she read that. You afterwards pointed out how far it was filled to Dr Penny? Yes. And he made a mark at the time? Yes. That is the mark [showing it]? Yes. Did you uncork the bottle? Yes. And smelt it? Yes. What did it smell like? It smelt to me like laudanum. What did you do with the bottle? I put it underneath a chest of drawers in the room. When you were dressing Mrs Taylor's body did you observe any mark upon it? Yes; it was all coloured on the left side.

Lord Justice-Clerk—What colour? A pinkish sort of colour. What shape of a mark? It was all coloured down the side—a purplish sort of colour.

Mr Gifford—When you had entered the bedroom at first, was Dr Paterson there? No. Dr Pritchard was? Yes. Did he make any remark to his wife? When Dr Paterson did not come, Mrs Pritchard said, "Edward, can you do nothing yourself?" He said, "No; what can I do for a dead woman? Can I recall life?"

Lord Justice-Clerk—That was, I suppose, immediately after you went into the room? Yes.

Mr Gifford—Was that after Mary M'Leod had come back and said that Dr Paterson was not coming? Yes. Did the prisoner say anything to his wife more about Mrs Taylor? He said that Dr Paterson said she was paralysed on the left side when he was there first. That was the same side that you had observed the mark upon? Yes. After you had dressed the body, did the prisoner come back to the room before you had left it? Yes. What did he say? He came and asked for the bottle that we found in Mrs Taylor's pocket.

Lord Justice-Clerk—Was Mrs Nabb there, too? Yes.

Mr Gifford—Did you take the bottle from below the drawers, where you had placed it? I did. Did you give it to the prisoner? I did. What did he say? He raised his eyes and hands and said, "Good heavens, has she taken this much since Tuesday?" What more did he say? He charged me to say nothing about it.

Lord Justice-Clerk—Give us the words he used? He said it would not do for a man in his position to be spoken of.

Mr Gifford—Did he say anything more? He said he would take the bottle down and show it to Mrs Pritchard. Did he take it with him? Yes. After Mrs Taylor's death did you wait on Mrs Pritchard, or was it Mary M'Leod? I waited very seldom—once or twice, or perhaps three times, with her food. Can you remember the first occasion? I saw her frequently—once a day, perhaps, until about the last week, when I did not see her so often. Was she in the drawing-room? Yes; most of the times that I saw her. Did you get orders from her in the drawing-room about what was to be brought in for dinner, or what was necessary for the house? Yes; sometimes. Had you ever been sent by the doctor to get anything for Mrs Pritchard before Mrs Taylor's death? Not that I am aware of. Do you remember the doctor asking you to get something for Mrs Pritchard one night? One night he brought in some woodcock and wanted me to cook them. Was that before Mrs Taylor's death or after it? It was before. Did you cook the woodcock for supper? I did. Who took it up? I do not know. The doctor brought it down. Do you remember before Mrs Pritchard died that a bell was rung? Yes; I remember that it rung the day before her death, in the forenoon, between twelve and one o'clock. Whose duty was it to answer the bells? Mary M'Leod's. Did you answer the bell on that occasion? I did; I answered it when it rang a third time. What did you do? I went to the consulting-room first, the door being a little open, and asked the doctor, who was there, if he had rung his bell, because I was not sure of the sound of the different bells. I got no answer. The door was a little open, but it refused to open to me with freedom, and I did not press it. The doctor was in the room. I know that, because when I was up the third or fourth step of the stair going towards Mrs Pritchard's bed-room, he asked me, "How is Mrs Pritchard now?" When you heard the bell ring a third time, you say you went to the consulting-room to see if it was the doctor's bell? Yes. The door of the consulting-room was partly open. What prevented the door from opening? I don't know. It appeared to me to be something behind the door. You went upstairs and the doctor came from the door of the consulting-room after you? Yes. And asked you how Mrs Pritchard was? Yes. I said I did not know, as he had told me not to go upstairs before he went out, as she wanted to go to sleep. Was it then he told you that? It was before he went out to make his first calls in the morning. Did you go upstairs after he came out of the consulting-room? I did. Did you keep looking down stairs to see if the doctor was following you? Yes. Did he follow you? He did. Anybody else? Yes; Mary M'Leod followed the doctor. Had she been with the doctor? I do not know where she came from. Had she been in the kitchen flat with you? No; she wasn't. Did you ask her about the bells? Yes; when I returned to the kitchen afterwards. Did you go to Mrs Pritchard's room? Yes. What did you find? Mrs Pritchard asked me to empty a certain vessel in the bed-room.

Lord Justice-Clerk—Where was she—in bed or sitting up? She was lying.

Mr Gifford—You took away the vessel? I did. Had the doctor followed you? I met the doctor near the foot of the bed, as I was going out. You went down stairs? Yes.

The Lord Justice-Clerk—Taking the vessel with you? No. Mary M'Leod took it out of my hand.

Mr Gifford—Had Mrs Pritchard been vomiting? Not that I am aware of, at that time. Was Mary M'Leod in the kitchen when you went down? She came down after me for hot water for Mrs Pritchard's feet. What did she say to you? Question objected to, and withdrawn. Do you remember the 8th of March—you took up Mrs Pritchard's dinner that day? Yes. What was the dinner? Curry. Who had ordered it? Mrs Pritchard herself. Did you see her after dinner? I did. Did she make any observation? She said she enjoyed her dinner very much, and wanted me to keep the remainder of it for her supper. Did she say on that occasion whether it had remained on her stomach? Yes; she had not been sick at that time, when I saw her.

Lord Justice-Clerk—Did she say she had not been sick? She had not been sick at the time I saw her. And how long after dinner was it that you saw her? Immediately after—taking away the dinner things.

Mr Gifford—Did she make any observation regarding her illness? Yes; she said she felt much better, and I said she looked much better than I had seen her before. She also said she could not make out what was the matter with her. She said she felt almost well, excepting when she was sick and vomiting. That was on the 8th of March? Yes. Then you did not see her for some days after that? Not in particular, that I remember. I might, and I might not. You remember the next Tuesday—the Tuesday in the week in which Mrs Pritchard died—of finding a plate with cheese somewhere? Yes, I found a small plate with a bit of cheese in the pantry in the morning. How big was the piece of cheese? A little bit cut off a cheese. What time of day was it when you found it? About seven in the morning.

Lord Justice-Clerk—What size was the cheese? There might be three or four inches.

Mr Gifford—Was it a piece of cheese that had come to the house before that? Yes. Did you hear that Mrs Pritchard had cheese for supper the night before? Yes. I learned from Mary M'Leod the night before that Mrs Pritchard had decided on taking cheese for her supper. When you found this piece of cheese did you do anything with it? I took up a little bit and ate it. How much did you eat? About the size of a good large pea. How did it taste? It had a bitter taste. Did you feel any peculiar sensation after eating it? I felt a burning sensation in my throat immediately after taking it, and inclined to sickness and vomiting. Did you get sick? Yes. Did you vomit? I vomited frequently. Immediately afterwards? About twenty minutes afterwards. Had you taken anything else that morning? I drank a cup of tea when breakfast-time came. Had you taken anything to eat or drink before eating the cheese? Nothing. How long did the sickness continue? Till after breakfast; some time before ten. You vomited more than once? Yes. Did you feel any pain? Yes; I felt a pain in my stomach and bowels.

Mr Gifford—Did you mention that to any one? I mentioned it to Mary M'Leod between eight and nine o'clock, and asked her to get me half a glass of spirits. Did she get spirits for you? Yes; about ten o'clock she brought me down a glass of spirits. Which you took? Which I took after I went to bed.

Lord Justice-Clerk—When did you go to bed? Between nine and ten o'clock in the morning.

Mr Gifford—Were you sick after that? No. How long did you keep your bed? I was up again some time before twelve o'clock. That was on Tuesday the 14th March? Yes. Now, next day, Wednesday, do you remember the prisoner speaking to you in the forenoon? Yes; he spoke to me several times that day. At what o'clock? Somewhere about dinner time. Did he not speak to you before that in the forenoon? (This question was repeated twice, and the witness said she did not remember just now whether he did so or not.) Well, about what did he speak to you at dinner time? I don't recollect just now. Then, in the evening of Wednesday did he speak to you? He spoke several times, I think, that day. Do you remember any particular conversation you had with him in the evening about something? He asked me at night to make some egg-flip for Mrs Pritchard. At what time would that be? Somewhere between ten and eleven o'clock at night. Did he call you up stairs? He called me up to the top of the kitchen stairs. You met him at the top of the stairs? Yes. Did you get an egg from him? Yes. Was it broken or whole? It was whole. What did he say? He told me to beat it up in a porter glass. Did you do that? I did. Where? In the pantry up stairs. Did he give you any more directions about it? He told me to beat it up very smooth, or Mrs Pritchard would not take it. Where did he go when you were beating it up in the pantry? He was once or twice in the pantry during the time; and one of the times he said he thought it was now pretty smooth, and he would bring me a bit of sugar, and I would put on some boiling water.

Lord Justice-Clerk—Did he go for the sugar? Yes. Where to? He went from the pantry into the dining-room, from the dining-room into the consulting-room, and then from the consulting-room into the pantry, and dropped the sugar into the tumbler.

Mr Gifford—What kind of sugar was it? Lump sugar. Was it in one or two pieces? There were two pieces, as far as I could see. Where was the sugar kept? I don't know. I think it was in the dining-room cupboard, as I took it to be, but I never saw into the dining-room cupboard.

Lord Justice-Clerk—Did you remain in the pantry all the time he was away? Yes.

By Mr Gifford—There is no direct communication between the consulting-room and the dining-room? You have to go into the lobby first? Yes. Did you notice the sugar that was dropt by the doctor into the glass? I took no particular notice of that further than that it was loaf sugar. And two pieces of it? Yes; there were two pieces. Did the doctor say anything? Nothing at that time. Did he tell you anything then about hot water? He told me before about the hot water. Did he say anything about whisky? Yes; he said he would add the whisky when it came up stairs. Did you take it upstairs? No; I left it in the pantry. And went down stairs for the hot water? No; Mary M'Leod passed when the doctor and I were in the pantry, and said that Mrs Pritchard was not ready for it yet, and that she would come down for it when Mrs Pritchard was ready to take it. When you heard that, what did you do? I left it on the pantry table. You laid down the glass with the beat-up egg and sugar in it on the pantry table? Yes. Did you go downstairs? I went downstairs. Did Mary M'Leod come down soon after? Yes. How long might that be? It might be ten or fifteen minutes? I could not say how long. Did she ask for the egg-flip? Yes. What did you say? I told her it was in the pantry, and she went up and brought it down. What did you do then? I put in the hot water into it. When you were mixing the water, did you say anything? I said I wished it might be warm enough, as the kettle had been some time off the boil. Mary M'Leod asked me to taste it, and I did so. Had it any peculiar taste? It had a bitter taste. How much did you take? I took about a teaspoonful of it. Did you make any remark about it to Mary M'Leod? Yes, I said it had a horrible taste, or a bitter taste. Did she take the egg-flip away? Yes. Did you feel anything after that? Yes; I grew sick immediately after tasting it. Had you any other feeling? Yes; I had the same feeling as I had with the cheese.

Lord Justice-Clerk—You mean a burning in your throat? Yes; a burning, bitter sort of taste in my throat. Had you a similar feeling in your stomach? Yes; I felt in the same way as I felt with the cheese the day before. Did you vomit? I vomited frequently through the night.

Mr Gifford—Did you continue sick any time? I did; I continued sick till about four o'clock in the morning. Did you vomit more than once? Yes. Was Mary M'Leod up stairs that night? Yes. Was she up till about four o'clock? Yes. Did she come down about that time? She came down to go to her bed about four o'clock. Did you tell her how sick you had been? I did. What did you say? I said, I thought I would have died without seeing the face of any one alive, alone in the room. Did you say to Mary M'Leod that your sickness was owing to anything? No. Did you say anything about the egg-flip to Mary? No; I said nothing at that time. Did you ask for Mrs Pritchard when Mary M'Leod came down? I asked where she had been, and she said in the room with Mrs Pritchard. I asked if Mrs Pritchard was so ill that she required both the doctor and her, and she said Mrs Pritchard would not allow her to leave the room, and that the doctor was in bed in the same room. You continued unwell that morning even after four o'clock? Yes; I was unwell the whole day after, but I did not vomit after four o'clock. When did you see Mrs Pritchard next? I did not see her till the Friday—the day before she died. And when did you see her first on the Friday? Sometime about twelve o'clock. Did the bell ring? The bell rang three times.

Lord Justice-Clerk—Three times constantly? Yes; the one after the other.

Mr Gifford—That was about twelve o'clock? Yes, in the forenoon, or between twelve and one. When the bell rang the third time did you go up? I did. When you went upstairs did you meet anybody? No. You went to Mrs Pritchard's bed-room? No; that was the day I went to the consulting-room door. Did you not go up that day? On Wednesday I went up; the bell rang three times. I am asking about the Friday—the day before she died—you saw her that day? Yes; the bell rang three times, and going up, I went to the consulting-room door. That was upon the Friday. Did you speak to her that day, on another occasion, about some chemises? Yes. When was that? That was the second time I was up; after I came down first I went back again. That was the Friday before she died? Yes; I went up to speak to her about chemises for the youngest daughter.

Lord Justice-Clerk—When was that? It was between twelve and one o'clock on the Friday. It was immediately after I was first in the room. It might have been twenty minutes after.

Mr Gifford—Who was in the room when you went up? The doctor. What was he doing? He was standing at the side of the bed. What was Mrs Pritchard doing? She was finishing drinking something out of a porter glass. Did she empty the glass? Yes. Who took it from her? The doctor took it from her and set it down on the side table. Did you speak to her about the chemises, and get directions what to do? Yes. She was quite intelligent then? Yes, she said she had a bit of cotton about the bed, and she sat up and looked for it, but she could not find it. I spoke to her about a piece of linen for a chemise. When did you see her next? Some time about five o'clock in the afternoon. Did the bell ring then? The bell rang with violence, and Mary M'Leod went to answer it. What did you hear next? Mary M'Leod came and called to me very sharp, "Come up stairs."

Lord Justice-Clerk—How long was this after you had been in the bed-room? Some hours.

Mr Gifford—She called you over the stair? Yes. Did you go up stairs? I did. What did you find? I found Mrs Pritchard going in at the bedroom door, or towards the bed, with Mary M'Leod. Did you and Mary assist her into bed? She was in bed before I got the length of assisting her. I saw her getting into bed. What state was Mrs Pritchard in then? She was in a state of excitement. What did she say? The first thing I heard her say was something about her mother. I could not repeat it, but I heard the word "mother." Did you go forward to the bed? I did. Did you assist Mary to do anything to Mrs Pritchard? I assisted to put the bed-clothes upon her. Did she say anything then? She said—"Never mind me; attend to my mother; rub her, and give her breath." Was Mrs Pritchard raving then? It appeared to me to be so. Did you continue rubbing her? Mrs Pritchard asked for one of the pillows, and I thought she thought it was her mother. She began to rub it with one of her hands. Did you rub Mrs Pritchard's hands yourself? Yes; some time after that. How did they feel? They felt cold. Were they cramped? I don't know whether they were cramped or not, but Mrs Pritchard said to me to rub her hands as she was afraid of cramp. I began to rub one hand, and she told me to take them both and rub them both. I did so. Did she get composed then? Yes. Did she get composed while you were rubbing her hands? Yes: she mentioned my name and said, "I did not know anything about this until the boys came in dressed." Had any of the boys come in? No. Did you know what she meant by that? No. How was she speaking, earnestly or incoherently? Earnestly, as I thought. Can you tell us the exact words she said when she became composed? The youngest daughter came into the room, and she asked who that was; I said it was Ailie. She said, "Is not Ailie to bed yet?" I said no; it was not time. She said she thought it was eleven o'clock. I said she must have been sleeping. Then she told Ailie to leave the room and go down stairs and see if Mary was getting ready the tea. She then said to me, "Oh! Patterson, rub my hands harder, because I am afraid of cramp all over." Did the doctor come in while you were still rubbing? Yes; and I left the room. Can you remember the exact expression she used about not knowing about this till the boys came in dressed? She said, "I did not know anything about this till the boys came in dressed." There were none of the boys there then. Was that at the same time she was speaking about her mother? It was after she left off speaking about her mother. When the doctor came you left the room? I did. Did he do anything before you left the room? No. Were you asked to prepare anything for supper that night? A little chicken which had remained over from her dinner. Did you prepare it for supper? I did. Did you take it up? I took it the length of the pantry. What happened then? I met the doctor there. He came out of the consulting-room and said, "Has Mrs Pritchard got her supper?" I said No, but there it was, and I was going up with it. It was in your hands? Yes; and I was going to take it up. What did he say? He said he would take it up for me. Did you give it to him? Yes. Did he go up stairs with it? I think so; but I returned immediately to the kitchen, and left him. What o'clock would that be about? Somewhat between ten and eleven o'clock, as far as I recollect. What was the next you heard after that? I do not think I heard any more till Mary M'Leod called me up about half-past one in the morning. What did she want you to do? She told me to get up and make a mustard-poultice for Mrs Pritchard. And you got up and did it? I did. Did you ask if you would go up with it? I gave it to Mary, and asked her if I would come up. What did she say? She said she would let me know if I was wanted. She went up with it. Yes. What happened next? Immediately the bell rang, and I went up. Did you go into Mrs Pritchard's room? I did. Who were there? Mary M'Leod and the doctor were there. Were the doctor and Mrs Pritchard in bed? Yes.

Lord Justice-Clerk—Did it seem as if they had been sleeping together? Yes.

Mr Gifford—Did you notice what condition Mrs Pritchard was in? I went up to the bed and looked at her, and handled her, and found that she was a good part cold. She was dead? Yes. How long was this after you had sent up the mustard-poultice? I don't think it would exceed five minutes. Did you notice that the mustard-poultice had been used? No; it had not been used. You saw it lying? Yes; the doctor pulled up her night-dress, and asked me to put it on, which I refused to do. I said there was no use to put mustard upon a dead body. When you said that, what did the prisoner say? He said—Is she dead, Patterson? I said—Doctor, you should know better than I. Did he say anything more? He said she could not be dead; that she had only fainted. Did he say anything more before he left the room? He asked Mary M'Leod to rush down for some hot water to put about Mrs Pritchard. But I said that it was no use to put hot water to a dead body. Did he leave the room then? No; it was sometime after. Did he say anything more? He said, "Come back, come back, my darling Mary Jane. Do not leave your dear Edward." Did he say anything more? Yes; he said, "What a brute; what a heathen; to be so gentle—so mild." What more? He asked me to kill him; and to take Mr King's rifle and shoot him.

Lord Justice-Clerk—Had Mr King a rifle in the house? Yes.

Mr Gifford—What more? I then said, "Doctor, don't provoke the Almighty with such expressions. If God were to shut your mouth and mine, I don't know how we would be prepared to stand before a righteous God." What did he say to that? He said, "True, Patterson, you are the wisest and kindest woman ever I saw." Did he leave the room then? I asked him to leave the room that I might dress the body, and he did so. That same night he had been in the kitchen for coals? Yes; he came down between eight and nine o'clock, I think. Did he say anything about his wife? He said he had his friend Dr Paterson in seeing Mrs Pritchard, and that he said she had taken too much wine. Did he say anything more about his wife? No; I said that it would be a pity if she would do the like of that. Did you dress Mrs Pritchard's body? I did; with the assistance of Mary M'Leod. After you had dressed the body did you see the doctor again? Yes; I went into the dining-room and told him I had made up a bed for him on the top flat. He was in the dining-room at the time. What did he say? He said, "Very good." Did he say he was going anywhere? He said he was going to the post-office. Did he appear to have been writing in the dining-room? I did not see, but he told me he had written some letters, one to his mother, and one to an intimate friend of Mrs Pritchard's. Did he go out? Yes. Did you see him when he returned? Yes; he called me upstairs, and I saw him at the top of the kitchen stair. What did he say? He said that she walked down the street with him, and said to him to take care of Ailie and Fanny, but that she never spoke about the boys, and that she kissed him on the cheek, and went away.

Lord Justice-Clerk—You understood him to be speaking of his wife? I understood so.

Mr Gifford—He went upstairs then? Yes; he went into the consulting-room, as far as I think. When were you next sent for by him? I sent him up a cup of tea when I returned at the time to the kitchen. He then came and called me up another time. When was this? A few minutes after. After he came in from posting the letters? Yes. What did he want? He wanted Mrs Pritchard's ring from me. Did you give him the ring? Yes; I gave him the ring and earrings. Now, did you take off the sheets and the bolsters and the pillow-cases off the bed in which Mrs Pritchard died? Yes.

Lord Justice-Clerk—You took them off that morning? Yes.

Mr Gifford—Where did you put them? I put them into the dirty-clothes press. Were you afterwards asked by Superintendent M'Call for them? Yes, after the prisoner was apprehended. Do you remember what day it was? It was the 20th March. When asked for these sheets, &c., by Superintendent M'Call, did you go and get them? I did; they were in the dirty-clothes press, just where I had put them. You gave them to Mr M'Call? Yes. [Shown a parcel containing two sheets, two pillow-cases, two towels, and a toilet-cover.] These are what I gave to Mr M'Call. Were they in the same state when you gave him them as they were in when you took them off Mrs Pritchard's bed? Yes. Did you also take off Mrs Pritchard's body clothes? I did.

Lord Justice-Clerk—Her night-dress, I suppose? Yes.

Mr Gifford—Where did you put them? I put them in the same place. In the dirty-clothes press also? Yes. Were you asked afterwards to give them up? Yes. And you gave them up to Mr M'Call also? I did. Look at these things and say if these are the things which you gave to Mr M'Call—a night-dress, a cap, a chemise, a knitted woollen semmet, a woollen polka or jacket, a pair of stockings, and three handkerchiefs. [These articles were produced and shown the witness.] When you gave these to Mr M'Call, were they in the same state as they had been when you took them from Mrs Pritchard's person? Yes. The sheets had a yellow stain when taken off the bed, had they not? Yes.

Lord Justice-Clerk—Were they all stained in that way, do you mean? There were stains on them all. Does that apply to the body clothes as well as to the bed clothes? There were some stains on the sheets.

Mr Gifford—On Saturday, 1st April, did you find anything in the kitchen pantry? (No answer.) Did you find a paper bag with something in it? Oh, yes, I found a bag of tapioca. Who was with you? Catherine Lattimer was with me at the time. [Shown bag.] Who did you give it to? I gave it to Mr Gemmell and the sheriff-officer, Mr Murray. The bag was about three-quarters full? Yes. All the time that you were in Dr Pritchard's house you did not use any tapioca? No, there was none used while I was in the house. Did you notice the bag standing in the kitchen press? Yes. It had never been meddled with all the time you were there? No. Were you frequently in the consulting-room? No; I was very seldom in it. Dr Pritchard did not keep his consulting-room locked? Not the door. Were there presses in the room? Yes; there were two. Was the door of the consulting-room itself kept locked while the doctor was out? No. It was always unlocked? Yes. Then, were the presses in the consulting-room kept locked? There was one that I never saw open at all. It was kept locked all your time? Yes; I have seen the other open sometimes. Was the one you never saw open kept locked? I do not know, for I never tried whether it was locked or not; but it appeared to be. The other you have seen open sometimes, what was in it? I could not say what was in it, but I have got eggs out of it from the doctor for the breakfast.

Lord Justice-Clerk—Is that the locked or unlocked one? The unlocked one.

Mr Gifford—Any time you noticed it was the key in the door? Yes. During the whole time you were in the house till Mrs Pritchard's death, was she ever down to the dining-room floor? Never to my knowledge. Never further down than the drawing-room? No. When you showed the doctor the bottle which you found in Mrs Taylor's dress the morning after she died, and when he said, "Good heavens! has she taken all that since Tuesday," did he say anything more? Nothing that I recollect except charging us to say nothing about it. Did he not say something about if she had told him? Oh, he did. What was that? He said, "If she had told me, I would have known what she was taking; besides, to send a girl like that for it!" Was that part of the same statement? Yes.

Lord Justice-Clerk—Was that after what you have already told us? No; it was before. Tell us all he said. He raised his hand and eyes towards heaven, and said, "Good heavens! has she taken this since Tuesday. If she had told me, I would have known what she was taking, and not sent a girl like that for it." That meant Mary, I suppose? Yes.

Mr Gifford—Did he say anything more besides charging you not to say anything about it? Not that I remember. Did he say anything about his not knowing? No; I took it for granted. He said that Mary had told him that we had found a bottle in Mrs Taylor's pocket.

Lord Justice-Clerk—Was that when he came to ask you for the bottle? Yes; and therefore I understood that he knew nothing about it.

Mr Clark—You said you did not know that Mrs Taylor was in the habit of taking the stuff you found in the bottle—Batley's Sedative? No. And the doctor told you to say nothing about it? Yes. Did you understand him at the time to mean that you were not to say that Mrs Taylor was taking that stuff? I understood him to mean that we were to say nothing about finding it in Mrs Taylor's pocket. Not to let on that Mrs Taylor had been taking it? Yes. That was all you understood? Yes. When you tasted the cheese in the morning, did you tell the doctor that you had been ill? No; I did not. You never did at any time? I did the morning after I tasted the egg-flip. I asked how Mrs Pritchard was, and he said she had had a very bad night. I said I had been very sick and vomiting during the night. He was in the pantry at the time, and as far as I remember he was gargling his throat after coming down from the bed-room. All you said was that you had been sick and vomiting? Yes. Who were in the house that night you made the egg-flip? Mr King and Mr Connell, and Mary M'Leod. All the people that usually slept there? Yes. After you left it in the pantry you did not see it till Mary M'Leod brought it down to the kitchen? No. How long would that be? It might be ten minutes, or perhaps longer or shorter, I could not exactly say. When Mrs Pritchard was raving, was she speaking loud? Not louder than her usual way of speaking. When she said she knew nothing about this till the boys came in dressed, you said she was speaking earnestly. Do you mean she spoke like a person not in her senses? I don't know. She spoke not wild-like, but in a quiet sort of mood. Was she speaking differently from the time when she spoke about her mother? No; but between the times she mentioned my name, and then I thought she knew me. The tone of voice from the beginning to the end was about the same? Yes; it was not in a wild, rough manner, but in a smooth way of speaking. Why did you think her raving? Because she spoke as if her mother was present when her mother was not present. How long would it be from the time she spoke about her mother and about the boys? It was only a few minutes. What time of the night did you leave her? I was not many minutes in the room—perhaps ten or fifteen minutes. Was she better when you left her? She appeared quite sensible when I left her. And out of pain? I did not think she was in pain, but she said to me she was afraid of cramp, and to rub her hands harder than I was doing. Was she better? You did not leave her until you had done all you could do for her, I suppose? The doctor came in, and I left the room. As to the presses in the consulting-room, you say one was locked, and one not. Which one did you never see open? The one beside the fire. There is one press in the same wall that the fire is in? Yes. And another in the wall opposite the fire? Yes. It was the one next the fire that you never saw opened? Yes.

Mr Gifford—When you told the doctor the night after you tasted the egg-flip that you had been sick and vomiting, what did he say? He said it would be a bad job if I would be laid up also. Did he give you anything? No; he did not. I returned to the kitchen. No more passed. When the egg-flip went upstairs to the bed-room, you never saw it again? No. Did you afterwards see the glass in which it had been? No; but I could not have distinguished it from other glasses. Did you usually wash the glasses? Sometimes I did and sometimes not. You never saw the egg-flip or the glass in which it was afterwards? No, not that I could distinguish it. There are two presses in the bed-room; one that you have seen open, and one that you have never seen open? Yes. Is the one press on the same wall with the fireplace? Yes; and that is the one I never saw open. There is just one window in the bed-room? Yes.

Lord Justice-Clerk—When you are looking out of the window, which of the presses is behind you? None. Which is to your right hand? The one which was sometimes open; and the one which was never open is to the left hand. When you told the prisoner that you had been sick and vomiting that night, did you tell him what was the cause of it, or what you supposed to be the cause? No; I did not say anything. The bottle that you found in Mrs Taylor's pocket was taken out of the room by the prisoner that same night? Yes. When did you next see it? The next time I saw it as far as I can recollect, I think was upon the Monday morning on which the body of Mrs Taylor was carried to Edinburgh, but I am not certain of the day. Where did you see it that day? On the corner of the chest of drawers under which I had put it in the room where Mrs Taylor's body was lying. Did you look at it particularly then? No; I did not take it into my hands. Did you observe whether the liquid was still in it? The liquid was still in it. You just let it stand then—you never meddled with it? I never touched it.

When did you see it next? The next time I saw it was in Superintendent M'Call's hands. Was that after the prisoner's apprehension? Yes. You were shown a bottle here, marked No. 85; was that a bottle of the same size and general appearance? Yes. I suppose you cannot say more precisely that it is the same bottle? No.

[As this witness was leaving the Court, one of the jurymen became faint, and was compelled to leave the Court. He was attended by Dr Littlejohn; and after being out for about ten minutes, returned, and took his seat in the box, when the proceedings were resumed.]

Mary M'Leod recalled and re-sworn—Solicitor-General—You were in Dr Pritchard's house after his wife's body was taken to Edinburgh? Yes. On the Tuesday the police were in the house, and you saw Superintendent M'Call there? Yes. Did you give him a bottle? Yes. [Shown bottle.] Is that the bottle you gave him? It is very like it. It is the same looking bottle and the same looking label? Yes. And there was a dark-coloured liquid in it? Yes. You said that was like the bottle that you saw after Mrs Taylor's body was dressed? Yes. Where did you find it? It was in a drawer. In what room? The chest of drawers was in the bed-room when Mrs Taylor died, but they were taken to the lobby; and it was in one of these drawers that the bottle was found. The chest of drawers had been in the room when Mrs Taylor died, and also when Mrs Pritchard died; but they had been shifted into the lobby by the time Superintendent M'Call came to the house to search, and in one of the drawers of that chest of drawers you found the bottle and gave it to him? Yes. Was there any other bottle like it in the house that you knew of? No.

Lord Justice-Clerk—How did you come to look for the bottle in the drawers? Did any body ask you to do so? Yes. Who was it? Captain M'Call.

Solicitor-General—What bottle did he ask for? For the bottle that was found in Mrs Taylor's pocket after her death.

Jessie Bryden or Nabb—Mr Crichton—You go out as a washerwoman, and have been employed sometimes by Dr Pritchard's family? Yes. Do you remember being sent for the night that Mrs Pritchard died? Yes; it was between twelve and one in the morning. Was that to assist in dressing the body? Yes. Mary Patterson and I dressed the body. Did you see anything found in Mrs Taylor's pocket? Yes; a bottle. [Shown a bottle.] Is that the bottle? Yes. Did you read the label? Yes. [Shown label.] Is that it? Yes. What kind of liquor was there in it? It was brownish in colour, and rather thick. How full was the bottle? About three parts full. The liquid did not come under the label.

Lord Justice-Clerk—That is to say, it stood above the lower edge of the label? Yes.

Mr Crichton—Did you see what was done with it? Dr Pritchard took it down stairs. But, before that, did Mary Patterson do anything with it? Yes, she put it upon the drawers. Upon the drawers or under the drawers? I think it was under the drawers, because we were both on the floor at the time, raking the clothes up. Did you see the doctor after that? Yes, he came into the room, and said that Mary M'Leod had told him that we had found a bottle in Mrs Taylor's pocket. He asked Mary Patterson to give it him, and she knelt down and gave it him. He looked at it, and said, "Good heavens, has she taken all that since Monday?" Did he say anything more? He said she ought not to have got a girl like that to buy it for her, but she ought to have asked him to buy it for her, and he would have got it; then he said she had been in the habit of taking it for years. Did he say anything about Mrs Taylor's illness? No; he said she had been indulging in liquor for a few days, and had taken an overdose of the opium.

Lord Justice-Clerk—By which you understood him to mean Batley's mixture? Yes. Did he say anything more about it? He said to us to say nothing about it, because it might lead to a little trouble. When did he say that? At night in the bed-room. Did he speak to you again about this bottle? Yes; next morning in the consulting-room, between eight and nine o'clock, I think. Who was there? No one but myself. I had gone in to make up the fire. What did he say then? He said to take no notice to any one about the bottle. I asked if it was dangerous, and he said yes; it was poisonous when one took too much of it. Anything more? He did not say anything more then. Do you remember seeing Mrs Pritchard one day in January when you were there? Yes. When was that, do you remember? I cannot remember the dates, but I know it was in the month of January. Had you been carrying up coals to the bed-room? Yes. Did you hear anything before you went into the room? Yes. I heard Mrs Pritchard retching very much indeed. Did you go in, or did you wait a little? I waited a little. What happened next? She rang the bell very violently, and then I went in. Where did you find Mrs Pritchard? Leaning over the basin-stand. What time of day was this? About seven o'clock in the evening. Did she ask you to give her anything? Yes, she asked me to give her a drink of cold water. Had she been down stairs before that? Yes; she came out of the dining-room, and went up to her bed-room. Had she been down at tea? Yes.

Lord Justice-Clerk—Very shortly before? Yes.

Mr Crichton—Did she ask for anything else? She asked me to put her to bed, and give her a bottle of hot water for her feet, as she was very cold. Did you assist her into bed? Yes. Did she complain of the sickness after she was in bed? She only said she did not know when that sickness would cease. Did she say anything more about it? No. Lattimer came in, and I left the room.

Lord Justice-Clerk—Did you get the bottle of hot water for her? No; Lattimer attended to her.

Mr Crichton—Did you see Mrs Taylor the week before she died? Yes; on the Wednesday night during the week in which she died. Did she say anything to you about Mrs Pritchard's illness then? Yes. Tell us what she said? She said she could not understand Mrs Pritchard's illness, for she was one day well and another day very ill, and that she had been very ill the night before. Did she say how she had been ill? She said she had been very ill—sick and vomiting all the night through. Did she say anything about cramp? No. Were you washing in Dr Pritchard's house after Mrs Taylor's death, upon the 9th of March? Yes. Were you in Mrs Pritchard's bed-room that night? Yes. Were some soiled bed-clothes taken off the bed by you? Yes. Did they appear to have been soiled with vomited matter? Yes. Did she say to you she had been sick? Yes; she told me she had been sick, but that she was not aware of it till she awoke in the morning.

Lord Justice-Clerk—She had vomited in her sleep? Yes.

Mr Crichton—Had Mrs Pritchard spoken to you frequently about her sickness? Very seldom; I saw her very seldom. Did she ever tell you how she was when she was in Edinburgh? She said she felt much better when she was in Edinburgh. You pointed out to Professor Penny the quantity of liquid which was in the bottle when you saw it last? Yes.

Cross-examined by Mr Clark—You told us the conversation that passed betwixt you and Dr Pritchard, when he came in when you and Mary Patterson were dressing Mrs Taylor's body. Have you told us all that passed? Yes. Was Mary Patterson present during the whole time of the conversation? Yes. Was anybody else present besides Mary Patterson and you? No. Was Mary M'Leod not there? No.

Lord Justice-Clerk—When you showed Dr Penny the quantity of liquid that had been in the bottle, was there anything in the bottle? No; it was then empty. Did you see the bottle more than once? I only saw it the night I was in Mrs Taylor's room; and I saw it again empty.

THOMAS ALEX. CONNELL.—By Solicitor-General—I am a student of medicine. I boarded with Dr Pritchard at one time. I went to him in November 1863. I remained till after his wife's death. I was in his house when his wife went to Edinburgh in November last. I remember her going to Edinburgh. I spent the Christmas and New Year holidays with my father at Helensburgh; and I was away when Mrs Pritchard returned. I found her at home when I came back. I came back shortly after the New Year. She appeared to me in pretty good health when I returned. I knew she had been ailing before she went to Edinburgh. After my return in January, I observed that she became unwell again. She told me she had a cold. She did not complain of anything else particular. One night, I remember her complaining in the doctor's presence of being unwell. This would be, I think, the third week of January. It was in the dining-room. The doctor and myself were there. It was after tea. She said she felt unwell, and would go to bed. I don't remember her mentioning how she felt unwell. It appeared to me as if it had come suddenly upon her. She left the room. I don't remember her ever coming down to breakfast after that. I don't remember of her ever coming down to her other meals after that. I did not see her again till after her mother's death. Before her mother's death, and when you were in the way of seeing her, did she ever complain to you of sickness? No, I don't remember. She never said much to me about how she felt. That was the only occasion that I remember when she complained of illness in my presence. I next saw her the week after her mother's death. During that time I generally asked the doctor every morning at breakfast time how she was. Sometimes he said she was greatly better, and sometimes he said she was falling off. He did not at that time say what was the matter with her. Shortly before her death, and after Mrs Taylor's death, he told me that he thought it was gastric typhoid that was the matter with Mrs Pritchard. He had not before that given any name to her illness. He mentioned sickness as one of the symptoms of her illness. He said the sickness came on whenever she had eaten anything. He mentioned this several times. He mentioned cramp as a symptom of her illness. Did he tell you that the cramp came on at night generally? I heard that from Mrs Taylor. Did you hear about the cramp from the doctor at all? No; I heard that from Mrs Taylor. The only symptom of illness which the doctor told me of was the sickness. Mrs Taylor said Mrs Pritchard was sick every time she tasted food, and was sometimes attacked with cramp in her arms and hands. She said the cramp came on after tea, and at night. Mrs Taylor once spoke to me about being sick herself. She said she was sick after taking some tapioca that had been prepared for Mrs Pritchard. She said it had been prepared for Mrs Pritchard, and taken up to her room, and she refused to take it, and Mrs Taylor took it, and about an hour and a-half after, she was seized with sickness and with vomiting. She told me that the sickness and vomiting continued about an hour. I understood her to say it was severe sickness and vomiting. She also said she was very glad that Mrs Pritchard had not taken it, as it might have proved fatal in her delicate state. She said she would send the tapioca back to the shop, for it was bad. Did she say that her sickness and vomiting were like those with which Mrs Pritchard was afflicted? She said something of the kind, but I cannot remember the words. But although you don't remember the words, the idea she conveyed to you was that her attack was like Mrs Pritchard's own? Yes.

By the Lord Justice-Clerk—I cannot tell the day that this occurred. It was shortly after Mrs Taylor came.

By the Solicitor-General—I was told Mrs Taylor died at an early hour on Saturday morning. I had seen her upon the Friday. It did not appear to me that there was anything the matter with her when I saw her. I noticed no change upon her. I always thought her a strong healthy old lady. I saw no difference on her on the Friday. She took tea that night with the doctor and myself, and the rest, in the dining-room, just as usual. That was about seven o'clock. She left the dining-room shortly after, as she was in the habit of doing. She generally went to Mrs Pritchard's room after tea. I next heard of her about half-past nine o'clock. The doctor came and told me that she was taken suddenly ill, and desired me to go for Dr Paterson. That was his purpose in coming to me. Just tell us what passed between Dr Pritchard and you upon that occasion. He merely came into the room and said Mrs Taylor was taken suddenly ill, and asked me to go for a doctor. I asked what was the matter with her, and he said he thought it was apoplexy. I went for Dr Paterson, and he came in about ten minutes after. I was not present when Dr Paterson was in the room. I saw Dr Pritchard for a few minutes, shortly after Dr Paterson left. I asked him whether Mrs Taylor was any better. He replied that she was not. I asked if it was apoplexy, and he said it was. The next I heard of Mrs Taylor was next morning. The doctor came to my room early in the morning and said something which at first I could not catch; but when I awoke and understood him, it was that Mrs Taylor had died about half-past twelve o'clock. He said she had died very calmly and peacefully. Afterwards he told me she was not conscious for some time before she died, but that she had recovered consciousness for a few minutes immediately before she died. I left the house next day. I returned about a week afterwards—on Monday, 6th March. I saw Mrs Pritchard that day in the drawing-room. I asked her how she felt, and she said she was pretty well. The doctor was in the room at the time. I thought, from her appearance, that she was getting better. She looked convalescent; but her face looked rather haggard. I saw Mrs Pritchard again about a week before her death—again in the drawing-room. She seemed much about the same in health as when I had seen her before. She did not tell me anything about herself. The doctor was not present, and she asked me to go for him. She did not say why she wanted him. I got him for her. I never saw Mrs Pritchard again while she was alive. I asked the doctor about her generally every morning. He said she was getting better, and that he thought she was coming round.

Lord Justice-Clerk—How long did he continue to say that? Until the day she died.

Examination resumed—He complained of being worn out by being kept up so often at night watching her. Anything about her having worn him out in the same way before? I asked him if he was not worn out sitting up at night. He said he was, but she had often done the same thing for him when he was ill. I understood him to mean that he did not grudge sitting up, for she had done as much for him. On the night before Mrs Pritchard's death, the prisoner gave me a doctor's prescription to get for him, and told me to go to the Glasgow Medical Hall. I went and got two phials containing a liquid preparation. I gave them to the prisoner. I did not read the prescription. That was about nine o'clock in the evening. The apothecary's shop was in Elmbank Street. [Shown a prescription.] That is in the doctor's handwriting; but I cannot be sure if it is the one he gave me. I brought the prescription back from the apothecary's, and gave it to Dr Pritchard, along with the phials. [Shown phial.] This is about the size of the phial, and that is like the colour of the stuff that was in it. The prisoner, when he gave me the prescription, said it was for his wife. I was told of Mrs Pritchard's death on the following morning by Mary M'Leod. I used to be frequently in the doctor's consulting-room, but not for six months before Mrs Pritchard's death. I went in when I wanted to get a book from the library. There were a few tinctures kept in a cupboard in the consulting-room. There were two cupboards, but the tinctures were kept in the one which was in the same wall as the window. When you are looking out of the window, this cupboard is on your right hand. There were no tinctures or any other medicines kept elsewhere that I know of. The doctor was not in the habit of making up medicines for his patients, to my knowledge. It was not his practice to send medicines to his patients since he came to Glasgow. I never saw him making experiments with chemicals or compounding drugs in the consulting-room or elsewhere. [Shown two copies of "Lett's Medical Diary," and a copy of "Blackwood's Scribbling Diary."] These are all in Dr Pritchard's handwriting.

Cross-examined by Mr A. R. Clark—I remember Mrs Pritchard going to Edinburgh last year. I remained in Dr Pritchard's house in Glasgow while she was in Edinburgh. I was ill in November during the time that she was away. I had sickness and cramp. I took ill first about dinner-time and vomited, and could scarcely sit up. I was ill for a fortnight after that. I was only away from the dinner-table, however, for three or four days during that time. I was ill again in February. Every morning after breakfast I was sick, and that continued about two hours every day. It was about half-an-hour before breakfast when my sickness came on. My illness did not continue every day. It lasted a week in the beginning of February, and then it came on again towards the latter end of February. I cannot tell where the breakfast was made; nor can I say where the tea was made; but it was always poured out at table. It was brought up made. Sometimes Catherine and sometimes Mary M'Leod brought it up.

By Solicitor-General—The prisoner was in the habit of pouring out some of the tea at the table and sending it up to his wife by the servant. I have seen the doctor once or twice go away as if to take up the tea himself. Shortly after Mrs Taylor came to the house, I was sick once or twice. That was a third attack. I never felt sick after any other meal except breakfast—and that not every day. I vomited; the sickness always produced vomiting. In November I was troubled with cramp. It was the same sort of sickness in February that I had in November. It was after meals in November too. I was first taken ill at dinner time, but after that I could not take any food without being sick. The cramp returned now and again in February, but not very often. It was generally in my hands. I was not able to account for the sickness. I mentioned it to the prisoner. He said he was afraid it was gastric typhoid. After my sickness in November, whenever I was well enough to go home, I went to my father's. I never had any sickness at my father's.

By Mr Clark—The prisoner was ill like myself in November in the same kind of way.

By Solicitor-General—And he was ill sometimes in February also. I cannot tell if he was as ill as I was, but he was ill in the same way.

By Lord Justice-Clerk—Besides the sickness, vomiting, and cramp in November, I also suffered from constipation greatly. I don't remember suffering from anything else.

By Solicitor-General—In February I had constipation now and again, but not regularly.

Richard John Christian King—By Mr Gifford—I am a medical student. I went to board with Dr Pritchard in the end of October last. Mrs Pritchard seemed to be in good health then. I remember her going to Edinburgh. She was a little delicate before she left. I remember her coming back. She was pretty well when she returned; she got worse after her return. I am not sure that the prisoner ever spoke to me about her. He said that gastric fever was the matter with her. After her return from Edinburgh, she was sometimes confined to bed. I remember Mrs Taylor coming. Mrs Pritchard was confined to bed then. I saw Mrs Pritchard only once while Mrs Taylor was there; that was in the drawing-room. I remember the morning after Mrs Taylor died. I saw her the night before from seven till half-past eight. I saw her in the consulting-room; she was writing letters. She appeared to be quite well: I next heard of her at ten o'clock. The prisoner told me that she was dangerously ill. I asked what was the matter. He said apoplexy. I went to bed between eleven and twelve, and was awoke after twelve by one of the servants, who told me the doctor wanted me. I got up. I saw the doctor; he asked me to go to the telegraph-office, and to telegraph to Mr Michael Taylor, of Edinburgh, that Mrs Taylor, his wife, was dangerously ill. The doctor told me at that time that she was dangerously ill; he did not say at that time that she was dead. I went and telegraphed that she was dangerously ill. When I returned, the doctor asked me to go back to the office, and telegraph that she was dead. He then told me that she was dead before, but that he did not want to alarm the old gentleman. After Mrs Taylor's death, I never saw Mrs Pritchard; she was always upstairs. I remember the night before her death. I came in about eleven and went to bed. I was awoke between a quarter and half-past twelve by Mary Patterson. I rose and went into the doctor's room. He was in bed beside Mrs Pritchard. Did you look at Mrs Pritchard? Yes; I did. What state was she in? She was dead. The doctor said she was not dead, and asked me to go for Dr Paterson. I went and saw Dr Paterson, and told him to come, and he said he would. When I came back to the house, one of the servants met me, and told me that the doctor was not coming. No reason was assigned to me for his not coming. I then went down to the Victoria Hotel for Mr Michael Taylor, of Edinburgh, who was living there. I can't remember which of the servants it was who told me to go to the Victoria Hotel, but it was one of them. I brought Mr Taylor up to the house. I slept in the room next to Mrs Pritchard's. I have heard her vomiting during the night—not frequently, but more than once—five or six times. I did not hear her vomiting in the mornings.

JANET HAMILTON, dressmaker, Glasgow.—Solicitor-General—I am a dressmaker in Glasgow. I was acquainted with Mrs Pritchard, the prisoner's wife. I was in the habit of making dresses for her, and I occasionally went to see her. I remember being sent for to go and see her shortly before her death, in the same month that she died. It was on Wednesday, 8th march. I went about nine o'clock in the morning, but I did not see Mrs Pritchard till in the forenoon, when I saw her in the drawing-room. How was she looking that day? She was looking very well it appeared to me; but when I saw her before it was after her mother's death, and she looked very grieved like. What did she tell you about her illness? She said she did not understand this retching, and that if it left her alone she thought she would be all right. I asked what she was taking in the way of medicines, and she said very little. She said the retching came upon her always after food, and that she was often sick at night. Did she account for her weakness in any way? No; she said she did not understand it. I had asked her what her trouble was, and she said that was what she would like to know, but that she did not understand it. She said afterwards that it was very strange that she was always well in Edinburgh and ill at home. The answer I gave her was that perhaps it was because Edinburgh was her native air. She said she did not know about that. Was there anything about her manner or expression which struck you when she said that? Well; I did not think about it particularly at the time, except that she looked very serious. She said she didn't know what was wrong with her. She said she was very anxious to know about her illness, and that she thought she would very soon get better if the retching would leave her. I understood from her that that was the only thing the matter with her.

WILLIAM TENNENT GAIRDNER.—Mr Gifford—You are Professor of Medicine in the University of Glasgow? I am. Do you know the prisoner? I do. Do you remember receiving a message requesting you to call upon the prisoner? I do. When? On the night between the 8th and 9th of February. It was during the night and between the 8th and 9th of February? Yes. At what o'clock? I think between twelve and half-past one. I cannot come nearer the time. Had you retired? I had not. I was making preparations for a lecture next morning. What was the message? It was to come and see Mrs Pritchard. Did you go immediately? Immediately. Had you ever seen her before? Never; so far as I know.

Lord Justice-Clerk—Never as a patient? No.

Mr Gifford—You met Dr Pritchard at the house? Yes. Did he take you to his wife's bed-room? Yes. Did he tell you before he introduced you what was the matter with her? In general terms. What did he say? He said she had been very sick, and that her stomach was not able to bear food. I think he said she had been some weeks so. Did he say anything more? Not just at that time, I think. I mean before he introduced you? I think not. When he had introduced you, did he still continue to speak to you about her symptoms? At intervals; but I cannot remember exactly. When he introduced you, how did you find Mrs Pritchard—was she in bed? I found her in bed, lying on her back, with a considerably flushed face, and in a state of pretty considerable excitement. She then, I think, told me herself she had been sick. You said that the prisoner went on to speak of her symptoms? Yes. Did he say anything about spasms? He did; but I cannot remember whether I got the first information of the spasms from him or from her. Was any opinion expressed by the doctor as to what was the matter with her? The only thing I recollect was after the spasms became known to me, and he then said that it was catalepsy. Did he mention that any other medical man had seen her? He mentioned that Dr Cowan, of Edinburgh, had seen her. Did he say if Dr Cowan had ordered anything, or what? I think afterwards he said that Dr Cowan had ordered stimulants, and he said that his wife had had chloroform, but whether by Dr Cowan's orders or not I do not know. Did he say his wife had had the stimulants? I think so. He said she had had champagne. You spoke to Mrs Pritchard, I suppose? Oh, yes. Did she say anything about having sent for you? Yes. What did she say? She began by apologising for not having sent for me sooner. She said that Dr Cowan was an old friend of the family, that though she had wished to send for me, she had sent for him on that account, and made a kind of apology to me for not sending for me before. I told her there was no necessity for apology, because all that she had done was perfectly natural and perfectly right. Did she say anything about her own brother? Yes, she said she was aware that I was a class-fellow of her brother. Who was her brother? Dr Michael Taylor of Penrith. Did she seem to know that her brother was a college friend of yours? Yes. You had some other conversation with her about her symptoms, and how she felt? Yes; we had a good deal of general conversation about her symptoms. What state did you find her in? She had been sick. I found her to a certain extent exhausted, but not by any means extremely so. She had a pretty good pulse. There was nothing in her symptoms indicating immediate danger; and the most remarkable thing about her symptoms was the violent state of mental excitement she was in, and the spasms of the hands.

Lord Justice-Clerk—There was no immediate danger from exhaustion? I thought not, from the state of the pulse, and the general aspect of the patient. But the most striking symptom was the excitement and the spasms in her hands, of which she told you? Yes.

Mr Gifford—Did you yourself observe the spasms in the hands? I did. She held her hands outside the bed-clothes above her head, and I saw that the wrists were turned in, and the thumbs somewhat inverted towards the wrists—a very peculiar state of the hand. I think it was owing to her mentioning this that Dr Pritchard used the word catalepsy. Did you form any opinion as to the cause of her excitement? I thought that she was intoxicated. You attributed it to the stimulants? I did. I attributed it to the combination of champagne and chloroform. Did you make any further examination? Yes. What did you do next? I then withdrew to the fire in order to warm my hands, with the view of making an examination of her person, and I had no sooner moved towards the fire than she began to scream out at the top of her voice, "Oh, you cruel, cruel man," or something like that, "you unfeeling man; don't leave me;" and I then returned to the bed and said I was not going to leave her. I then returned to the fire, and was warming my hands; and in the midst of this she was in a state of most violent hysterical excitement, screaming out various exclamations, which after a little while I ceased to take any notice of, because I thought she was not responsible for them at all, because I thought they were the exclamations of an intoxicated woman for the time-being, and paid no attention to them; but the general purport of them was a remark about my being extremely unfeeling in leaving her alone and going to the fireside. Then I returned to her, and I examined her person: I took up the bed-clothes and examined the belly, and I asked particularly both at her and Dr Pritchard if there was any chance of her being pregnant—pregnancy being a frequent cause of vomiting. I found there was none; and then, after various other inquiries, and feeling her pulse, looking at the state of her skin, and so on, I came very soon to the conclusion that she was not in a state to give any evidence at all about her own previous history that night, and I just gave the orders I thought necessary, and left her. Did you order that the stimulants should be discontinued? Yes.

Lord Justice-Clerk—To whom did you state that? To Dr Pritchard and to her; but I repeated it more emphatically to Dr Pritchard than to her, because I told him very decidedly that I thought this was very bad practice, and that she was to get no stimulants whatever until I saw her again.

Mr Gifford—From what you observed, did you see any symptoms of catalepsy in her? No. You formed a distinct opinion that there was no catalepsy? I may explain that I hardly know what catalepsy is. It is not a disease of ordinary medical experience at all. Most of what we know of it is from books; and what is written about it is to a great extent apocryphal; therefore, I don't presume to be an authority upon catalepsy. Do you remember of her using any expression while you were there, to you or to any one, about hypocrites. I cannot say. She used a great deal of language in that hysterical state of which I did not take any notice, and in fact deliberately and intentionally ignored.

Lord Justice-Clerk—You intentionally paid no attention to it? Yes. I thought it was as well to show her that I did not wish to give attention to every little expression. Were any of the servants present? I have great difficulty in remembering that. My attention was concentrated upon Mrs Pritchard. I have some recollection of Lattimer, but none at all of the other servant, and Lattimer I think I saw chiefly at the following visit. You left that night? Yes. Did you say anything to Dr Pritchard before you left? I spoke to him in strong terms about the impropriety of this stimulating practice, and said it was very bad practice. He said it had been ordered by Dr Cowan. He rather seemed to indicate that he concurred with me in disapproving of the champagne, but asked me if she was to get no more chloroform. I said, "No, no stimulants and no medicine till I see her again." Did you arrange when you were to see her again? Yes; I was to see her the same day of which this was the morning. Did you call? I called between twelve and one o'clock. That was the 9th February? Yes. Did you see Dr Pritchard? I did. He said Mrs Pritchard was better, and quite quiet. Did you go to Mrs Pritchard's bed-room? We went to her bed-room, and I found her quiet. Free from fever? Yes. Had you any conversation with her? Yes. In general terms I assured myself that she felt better, and that she had not vomited since I saw her; but she still had the remains of the spasms in her hands.

Lord Justice-Clerk—That was about twelve hours after your former visit? Yes.

Mr Gifford—Dr Pritchard was there the whole time? He was. How long might you be there? About ten minutes. What did you direct? I directed that she was still to get no stimulants and no medicine, and that when she required food she was to get a boiled egg plain, and milk and bread, but nothing else; and I told her that my object was to make her diet as simple as it could possibly be, in order that there might be no possibility of her taking anything that would disagree with her. That is, nothing that would produce sickness or sit heavy on her stomach? Yes. I think I told her that if her stomach had fair-play it would digest milk and the simple food I indicated. Did you say anything more to Dr Pritchard? I simply repeated generally what I had said to her.

Lord Justice-Clerk—You said if her stomach had fair-play it would digest milk? I do not wish it to be understood that I used these words. I do not remember the exact words; but I endeavoured to impress her with the idea that her stomach would digest a simple thing when it would not digest complicated things; and that she must not load it with medicine and with a variety of food, but that she must go back to perfectly simple food.

Mr Gifford—Did you form any opinion as to what was the matter with her? I was very much puzzled. You are confining yourself to the one visit, doctor? Yes. What did you think of her? I was very much puzzled. I thought she was intoxicated the evening before—drunk, in fact; but beyond that I formed no very decided opinion. Did you say, on leaving on the second visit, that you would return again? I do not think I fixed any time. Did you think her case required serious and constant attention? Yes. Just tell us what was your impression of it? My impression was, that if I had been a general practitioner, in attendance upon her, I should probably have seen her every day, or twice a-day; but there was a doctor in the house, and my habit is to act as a consulting physician, not as a general practitioner.

Lord Justice-Clerk—You considered that you had been called by the prisoner as a consulting physician? Yes.

Mr Gifford—This was upon the 9th. Did you return next day? No; I never saw her again.

Lord Justice-Clerk—Were you ever sent for again? No.

Mr Gifford—Had you to leave town? I had to leave town for a distant engagement on the Friday, and before leaving town I wrote a note or sent a message to ascertain how Mrs Pritchard was, and received for answer that she was better. I then left for my engagement, and returned on the Saturday afternoon. On my return, there was a patient waiting for me; and while I was engaged with the patient, I believe Dr Pritchard called and left word that his wife was better, and that I need not call. Did you write to your friend Dr Taylor, in Penrith, about the case? Yes. I think it was on the 9th February, the day after my second visit. What was your reason for writing him? My reason was that I was puzzled, and that I thought the practice bad in so far as stimulants were concerned at least, and that I wished to be backed up and aided by his suggestion. Were there any symptoms of gastric fever upon Mrs Pritchard that you observed? I did not think there was any fever at all.

Cross-examined by Mr A. R. Clark—You said you did not understand what was the meaning of the word catalepsy which the prisoner used? It was not I that applied the word to the case. I do not say it was, but I thought you said you did not understand the meaning of the word as applied? No; it seemed to me to have no application to the case. Had you known the prisoner before? Yes. Long? More or less, I think, for about a year; but I don't remember how long? About how long? I think for one or two years. My connexion with him has been chiefly seeing a few cases with him in consultation.

Lord Justice-Clerk—You knew him as a medical man for a year or two previous? Yes.

Mr Clark—Was his nomenclature correct? Witness—In this case? Mr Clark—No; generally. Had he any peculiarity in the way in which he spoke of disease? Well, I can't answer that question. Did you not observe anything peculiar in his nomenclature of disease? Perhaps it was occasionally a little at random. What was it you observed in him? I have no very distinct impression. You say it was perhaps a little at random.

What do you mean by that? I mean by that that I do not think he was a model of accuracy and wisdom and caution in applying names to things. Well, without being a model of wisdom and accuracy and caution, what was the way in which he spoke of disease? Describe the way in which he spoke of disease. I have said before that there was nothing that caught my attention. At the same time, was there not something which did catch your attention? I think he was rather a careless man in his ideas; slip-slop a little. Was that through ignorance, do you suppose? I cannot tell. Was he a skilful man in his profession? I had not enough to do with him to tell you that. Tell me what symptoms you observed in Mrs Pritchard when you saw her on the second day? I think the chief symptom was the remains of the spasm. What was the state of her pulse? It was pretty quiet. What was the state of her tongue? I have no distinct impression about the state of her tongue. Her colour? Her colour was good, but rather high. Was she very prostrate? I think not. You said you wrote to her brother after you saw her the first night? Yes. Did you indicate to him that there had been anything more than improper treatment?—did you indicate to him that there had been any foul play? Witness—You mean poison? Mr Clark—Yes. Witness—Certainly not.

Dr James Paterson—Solicitor-General—Are you a doctor of medicine in Glasgow? Yes. How long have you been in practice there? Upwards of thirty years. I believe you were at one time Professor of Midwifery in the Andersonian University? Yes. It is not, properly speaking, a University. You may call it the Andersonian Medical School. For how long were you Professor there? For twenty-two years. Did you resign? I did, about two years ago. Where is your house? No. 6 Windsor Place, Sauchiehall Street. That is another division of the street in which Dr Pritchard lived? It is. Do you remember being called to Dr Pritchard's house in February last? I do. Do you remember the day of the month? It was on Friday evening the 24th February. Was that the first time that you had been called there? The first time that I ever crossed his threshold. What time of night were you called? Between half-past ten and a quarter to eleven. Did you see Dr Pritchard? I met him in the lobby or hall of his own house. Tell us, if you please, what he said to you? He conducted me into his consulting-room on the first floor, and then he told me that his mother-in-law, while in the act of writing a letter, had suddenly been taken ill, had fallen off her chair upon the floor, and had been conveyed up stairs to the bed-room. Did he say how long before your visit this happened of the old lady tumbling off the chair? I think he said about half an hour or an hour before I came. I asked if he could assign any reason or cause for the suddenness of the attack. He said his mother-in-law and Mrs Pritchard had been partaking of some bitter beer, as I understood, for supper, soon after which they both became sick and vomited, and both complained that the beer was much more bitter to the taste than usual. You are telling us now what he said to you on your first arrival in the consulting-room, where he and you were alone together? I am. He said that they could not have taken more than a third part of a pint each, because there was still some remaining in the bottle. I said I could not think it possible that either Allsopp's or Bass's beer could produce such an effect, and that the attack must depend upon some other cause. Allow me to ask you, why did you mention Allsopp's and Bass's beer? These were the only two that struck my mind at the moment. Did he point to the beer bottle on the table? Afterwards, but not at this time. I then asked him in regard to the previous state of his mother-in-law's health, and I asked particularly with reference to her social habits, when, by a particular insinuation, he led me distinctly to understand that she was in the habit of taking a drop occasionally.

Lord Justice-Clerk—Drinking spirits, you mean? Yes.

Solicitor-General—What else did he say? He stated also that Mrs Pritchard had been very poorly for a long time past with gastric fever; and that some days previously he had telegraphed for his mother-in-law to come through to keep her or attend to her in her illness. We then went up stairs to the bed-room. On entering, I observed Mrs Taylor lying on the edge of the bed nearest me. She was lying on her right side with all her clothes on, and on her head a half-dress cap with a small artificial flower. She had all the appearance of there having been a sudden seizure? Yes; and Mrs Pritchard, in her night dress, with nothing on her head, and her hair very much dishevelled, was in the same bed, but underneath the bed-clothes, and sitting up immediately beyond her mother. Tell us the appearance of the old lady. On examining Mrs Taylor, my impression was that she had previously been in very good health.

Lord Justice-Clerk—But was she dead or living? She was living at this time. She gave you the indication of a person who had been in good health? So far as I could judge from appearance.

Solicitor-General—Not touched by illness or emaciated? No. A healthy-looking old lady? I should say so. She seemed to me to be rather above the ordinary size, good looking, well-formed, altogether I should say a very superior-looking person for her time of life, and certainly not having the slightest appearance of being addicted to the use of spirituous or intoxicating liquors. On examining her face it was rather pale, but the expression was calm or placid. The eyelids were partially closed, the lips were rather livid, the breathing slow and laborious. Her skin was cool, and covered with a clammy perspiration. The pulse was almost imperceptible, and she seemed to me to be perfectly unconscious. On my opening up the eyelids I found both pupils very much contracted. From those symptoms, and judging from her general appearance, my conviction was that she was under the influence of opium, or some other powerful narcotic, and I at once pronounced my opinion that she was dying. That was your opinion? Yes; decidedly. To Dr Pritchard, who was beside you all the while? Yes; on my doing so, Pritchard said something in an undertone of voice, apparently unwilling that my opinion should be heard by the ladies, which was quite natural and quite common. We retired a little from the bed-side, went near to the fire-place, and I then stated distinctly that she was dying. Pritchard said she had frequently had attacks of a similar kind before, but never one so severe. I said that nothing we could do would have the slightest effect, but that, as a last resource, we might try mustard poultices to the soles of the feet, the calves of the legs, and the inside of the thighs, and as quickly as possible administer a strong turpentine enema. That is an injection? Yes. Pritchard at once proceeded to prepare the enema, and he said he had a little before given her one in which he had administered a glass of brandy. The old lady lay apparently comatose, or unconscious; but on being roused a little, and the head and shoulders slightly elevated, there was a degree of consciousness came on, and the pulse became perceptible at the wrist. Was that rousing the first thing you had done to test whether she was really conscious or not? It was. And what you meant by saying that she was seemingly unconscious before was, that she was not manifesting consciousness before? Yes.

The Lord Justice-Clerk—All the symptoms manifested unconsciousness, did they not? Yes. The pulse was first perceptible at the wrist? Yes; I directed Pritchard's attention to the pulse, and he then clapped the old lady on the shoulder and said, "You are getting better, darling." I looked at him, and shook my head ominously, as much as to say, "Never in this world."

The Solicitor-General—She gave no promise to you of being better? None. A slight fit of retching now came on, and she put up a small quantity of a frothy kind of mucous, immediately after which the coma or insensibility returned—the breathing became more oppressed, more laboured, and the alvine evacuations were passed involuntarily. I then concluded that the case was utterly hopeless, but Pritchard administered the enema. What then? I left the room and went downstairs accompanied by Pritchard, and we went into the consulting-room. I repeated my opinion that she was in a state of narcotism.

The Lord Justice-Clerk—That is to say, under the influence of opium or some narcotic? Yes.

The Solicitor-General—Narcotism was the expression you used? Yes. Pritchard then said the old lady was in the habit of regularly using Batley's Sedative Solution, and that she had a few days before purchased not less than a half-pound bottle of the medicine, and that he had no doubt, or it was very likely, that she might have taken a good swig of it. That was his expression? Yes. There was little more said at that time in regard to the state of Mrs Pritchard. You know Batley's Solution? I know it, but I very seldom used it. Had Mrs Taylor anything of the appearance of an old lady who had been in the practice of using such a medicine? My impression was that she was not what is called an opium-eater, or one who used opium to any great extent. She presented no appearance of that? That was my opinion. Would you recall to your recollection the bed-room again, and tell us what you observed of Mrs Pritchard? While attending to Mrs Taylor, I was very much struck at the same time with the appearance of Mrs Pritchard. She seemed exceedingly weak and exhausted. Her features were sharp or thin, with a high hectic flush on her cheeks, and her voice was very weak and peculiar—in fact, very much resembling the voice of a person verging into the collapsed stage of cholera. The expression of her countenance conveyed to me the idea of a kind of silly or semi-imbecile person at the time. At first I was inclined to attribute her appearance to the recent severe attack of gastric fever, which I was told by the prisoner she had had, and her symptoms aggravated of course by the great consternation and grief not unnaturally caused by the sudden and alarming condition of her mother. At the same time I must say I could not banish from my mind the idea, or rather the conviction, that her symptoms betokened that she was under the depressing influence of antimony. You mean that that impression or conviction came upon you at the time while in her presence, and that you could not get quit of it? Certainly. I did not put a single question to Mrs Pritchard.

The Lord Justice-Clerk—The impression was created entirely by her appearance? Yes, and the general symptoms of the case. I then left, and went home about half-past eleven.

Solicitor-General—Were you sent for again in the course of that morning about one o'clock, and did you afterwards get another message not to come because she was dead? A little before one o'clock my door-bell was rung. I was in bed, but Mrs Paterson happened to be sitting up. She opened the door, and a girl asked me to come directly and see Mrs Taylor. I refused to go, because I was certain that I could be of no service; and as I was very much fatigued with the previous day's work, I was very unwilling to rise; but I sent my compliments to Dr Pritchard, saying that if he really thought I could be of use he was to send back word, and I would then rise and visit her. Your house was only a short distance from his in the same street? 195 yards. Did any message come back? No message came back, and I did not go; but about ten o'clock on Saturday morning, the 25th, an elderly gentleman called upon me. Was that Mr Taylor, the husband of the old lady? I afterwards learned that it was. Did he inform you that she was dead? He came for the death certificate. You refused to give a certificate? I said I was surprised that Dr Pritchard had sent for a certificate, and that as a medical practitioner he should have known that it was not given to the friends, but to the district registrar. Were you afterwards applied to by the registrar? On Friday, 3d March, I received through the Post-Office a schedule from the registrar, in which I was requested to fill in the cause of Mrs Taylor's death, and duration of her disease. You refused to do that? I did so, and sent it back with a note accompanying it, directing his attention to the circumstance. When did you see the prisoner after that? On Wednesday forenoon, 1st March. I met him accidentally in Sauchiehall Street, near my own house. On coming up to me, he said I had been very correct in my opinion with regard to his poor mother-in-law, and he added that he would feel obliged if I would visit Mrs Pritchard next day at eleven o'clock, as he required to be in Edinburgh at the funeral of his mother-in-law. I at once agreed to visit at his request. And did you go? Yes; on Thursday, 2d March, about eleven o'clock in the forenoon. Did you see Mrs Pritchard? Yes. She was in bed. How did you find her? She was still very weak and prostrate, and in a weak voice she expressed her satisfaction and her gratitude at my calling. Then, in a very earnest manner she asked me if I really thought that her mother was dying when I saw her. I said most decidedly I did; and I had told Pritchard so. She then clasped her hands, looked up, and feebly exclaimed, "Good God, is it possible?" and burst into a flood of tears. I put some questions then as to the previous state of her mother's health, and especially if she was habitually addicted to the use of Batley's Sedative Solution. She told me that her mother's health generally speaking was good, but she suffered occasionally from what she called neuralgic headaches, and for relief of these attacks she did take a little of Batley's Sedative Solution; but she added, that it could not be said that she was in the habitual use of that medicine. I then questioned her with regard to herself. She told me that for a considerable time past she had suffered very much from sickness, retching, and vomiting, with severe pains in the stomach and throughout the bowels, accompanied with purgings, great heat and uneasiness about the mouth and throat, and a constant urgent thirst. I examined her tongue. It was very foul, and of a lightish brown colour. Her features were still very sharp and deeply flushed. Her pulse was weak, contracted, and very rapid. Her skin was moist, but defective in animal heat, and altogether she presented an appearance of great general prostration. Her eyes were watery, but clear and intelligent. I prescribed for her small quantities, at short intervals, of champagne and brandy to recruit her strength; small pieces of ice occasionally to relieve the thirst and irritability of the stomach. If she tired of these, I said she should have recourse to granulated citrate of magnesia as a cooling effervescing drink, and have a sinapism or mustard-poultice applied over the pit of the stomach. So far they were verbal directions which you gave her? I also recommended small quantities, at short intervals, of easily digested nutritious food, such as beef tea, calf-foot jelly, chicken soup, arrowroot, and so on. I then wrote a prescription for twelve grains of camomile, twenty-four of blue or gray powder, twelve of powdered ipecacuanha, and six grains of aromatic powder, the whole to be carefully mixed up, and divided into six equal parts—one powder to be taken every day. That prescription was with the view of relieving the biliary disturbance, and soothing the mucous lining of the alimentary canal. Did you give the prescription to herself? I did, and told her to show it to Pritchard when he came home in the evening, and to tell him what I had ordered. I never saw Mrs Pritchard again until within four or perhaps five hours of her death. Between the visit of which you have given us an account, and the last time you saw her before her death, did you see her husband, the prisoner? I did. When? On Sabbath evening, the 5th March. About nine o'clock he called at my house. What did he say? He told me his wife had been very much relieved by the medicines and treatment I had ordered; that she relished very much the small quantities of champagne and brandy, and felt refreshed by the cooling effervescing draught and the ice. What did he say further? He said that she was still very weakly, and the stomach still irritable. I recommended the continuance of the stimulants and nourishment, and to pay most particular attention to the state of the alimentary canal—the stomach and bowels. Nothing more passed at that interview? No. Then I suppose the next occasion you have to speak of is that visit a few hours before her death? On the 17th of March—the Friday evening—Pritchard called upon me personally, I think about a quarter to eight o'clock in the evening, and requested me to go with him to see Mrs Pritchard. Did you go? I did. And went up to the bed-room and saw the lady? Yes. Mrs Pritchard was in bed, in a sitting position, supported by pillows. What appearance did she present? I was very much struck with her terribly altered appearance. She seemed quite conscious. I went up to her bedside, and she caught my hand, and I could see a half smile of recognition upon her countenance. She very soon began to mutter about her having been vomiting. Pritchard was standing behind me, and he volunteered to say that she had not been vomiting—that she was only raving. She complained of great thirst, and Pritchard poured some water out of a caraffe into a tumbler, and gave it to her to drink. At the same time he said, "Here is some nice cold water, darling." Did she drink it? She drank it. I observed her countenance very much changed from what it had been when I last saw her. There was a peculiarly wild expression; the eyes were of a fiery red, and sunk-looking. Her cheeks were hollow, sharp, pinched-looking, and still very much flushed. Her pulse was very weak, and exceedingly rapid. Her tongue, how was it? It was of a darkish-brown colour, very foul; and she immediately began to grasp with her hand, as if to catch at some imaginary object on the bed-clothes. She muttered something about the clock; and Pritchard said he thought she referred to the clock or timepiece on the drawing-room mantelpiece. There was no clock in the room where she was. I expressed my surprise at the great change and alarming appearances, and I asked Pritchard how long she had been entirely confined to bed since I saw her. He said only since morning; that yesterday or yesterday afternoon, she was in the drawing-room amusing herself with the children. I again expressed surprise at her alarming condition. Her condition was alarming? Yes, certainly. Anything said about her sleep? He said she had not slept for four or five days or nights. I then said we must endeavour to do something to relieve her, and, if possible, procure some refreshing sleep. We left the bed-room and went downstairs, and I then prescribed thirty drops of solution of morphia, thirty drops of ipecacuanha wine, five or ten drops of chlorodyne, and an ounce of cinnamon water. This was to be repeated in four hours, if the first draught did not give relief. That is, did not procure sleep? Quite so. Did you write the prescription? I did not. Pritchard wrote the prescription at my dictation. Did you ask him to write it? No; I said it was unnecessary to write it, it was so simple that he might make it up himself. I was anxious to save time, and give relief as soon as possible. What did he say to that? He said he kept no medicines in the house excepting chloroform and Batley's Sedative Solution. Did you say anything to that? I asked if he did not keep a small stock in order to meet any emergency, and particularly for night work, and he said he did not. Did that strike you as anything strange? It certainly did.

Lord Justice-Clerk—You mean that it is not a usual thing for a medical practitioner? Yes. Medical men in extensive practice must keep medicines in stock, especially for night work, if they have much night work to go through.

Solicitor-General—And he wrote it to your dictation? So far as I know. You did not look at it? No. You assumed he would write it correctly? Certainly. [Shown No. 13.] Is that in his handwriting? I think it is. I am sure it is. Does that conform to what you told him to write? Yes. What next occurred? I then left the house, and I heard no more of it till about one o'clock on the following morning, which was Saturday. And what did you hear then? At that time my door bell was suddenly loudly rung, and on going to the door I found a young man, who requested me to go to Mrs Pritchard immediately, as she had become much worse, and was thought to be dying, if not dead. I proceeded to dress myself at once. In less than three minutes after that my door bell was again rung, this time by a servant girl; and as I opened the door she said, "You need not come; Mrs Pritchard is dead." And you did not go to the house again? No. And you have mentioned to us the only visit you ever paid to the house, and all you saw of those two ladies? Certainly; I never crossed the threshold of the house except on these occasions. Did you ever say to the prisoner that you thought his wife, Mrs Pritchard, had taken too much wine? I never did. And you have mentioned to us quite accurately everything you ever ordered for her? Yes. You are quite sure you never recommended Dublin stout for her? No; I never did.

Cross-examined by Mr Clark—You mentioned that Mrs Taylor had not the appearance of having been in the habit of using opium? That is my candid opinion. Have you had experience in cases of that kind? I have. And Mrs Taylor did not resemble any such patient? I think not. Why did you judge that she was not addicted to the use of opium? If a person is in the habit of taking opium to a great extent, you generally find that they are not very good in colour. They are generally thin in features, and hollow about the eyes—in fact, not of a healthy appearance generally. And Mrs Taylor, being stout and healthy-looking, as far as you could judge, you concluded that she was not addicted to the use of opium? That was my impression—at least not to any great extent. I do not say that she never took opium at all, but merely that she was not an habitual consumer of opium. What do you mean by not being an habitual consumer of opium? do you mean that she did not take it constantly, though she might take it by way of medicine? That is what I meant. And when Dr Pritchard said to you that she was in use to take opium, you thought what he was saying was not true? That was my impression after I saw the individual; I took it for granted before I saw the individual. After you saw the individual, you thought the statement was not consistent with fact. I thought so. Now, when you were with Mrs Taylor that evening, did you examine attentively the condition of Mrs Pritchard? I only glanced at her—I did not put a question to her. I formed a diagnosis from the symptoms that were present. By merely looking at her? Yes; just as I am in the habit of forming an opinion of any patient I see for the first time. But you did not examine her at that time as a patient, did you? Certainly not. But you formed the conviction that she was under the influence of antimony? Yes. Had you ever seen before a case of poisoning by antimony? Yes. How many? Perhaps two or three. What were they? Young children. Did you ever see a case of poisoning by antimony in the case of an adult? No. Now, I understand, when you translate the words "depressing influence of antimony," you mean that she was being poisoned by antimony? I was under the idea that she had been getting antimony for some time past. I had nothing to judge from but her appearance. Do you mean she was getting antimony medicinally, or for some other purpose? Of course, I could form no opinion as to how or by what means she was getting antimony. Was the condition you have described one to which a patient could be brought by the medicinal use of antimony? Not exactly the medicinal use, but a long-continued use: a judicious practitioner would not carry it to such an extent as to produce such debility and prostration. Did you mean to convey to us that she had been taking antimony medicinally, or that she was being poisoned by antimony? My impression was that she was being poisoned by antimony. And you formed that conviction by looking at her? Yes. Simply from looking at her? Yes; judging from symptomatology—the science of signs of disease. Now, as you thought Mrs Pritchard was suffering in that way from antimony, did you ever go back to see her again? I did not, and I believe that I never would have been called back again if I had not met Pritchard accidentally on the street. Why did you not go back? Because she was not my patient. I had nothing to do with her. Then, though you saw a person suffering from what you believed to be poisoning by antimony, you did not think it worth your while to go near her again? It was not my duty. I had no right to interfere in any family without being invited. Dr Paterson, is it not your duty to look after a fellow-creature who you believe is being poisoned by antimony? There was another doctor in the house. I did the best I could by apprising the registrar. Did you tell Dr Pritchard? No. You did not mention it to him? I did not. Had I been called in consultation with another medical man, I should certainly have considered it my duty to have stated distinctly my medical opinion. But you stood upon your dignity, and did not go back to see what you believed to be a case of poisoning? I had no right. No right? I had no power to do it. No right? I was under no obligation. You were under no obligation to go back to see a person whom you believed was being poisoned with antimony? I took what steps I could to prevent any further administration of antimony. By never going back to see her? No; I beg your pardon. What did you do? By refusing to certify the death. Had there been a *post-mortem* examination of Mrs Taylor's body, I believe that in all probability the drugging with antimony would have gone no further, at least at that time. But still it comes to this, that, although you had the impression, you never went near her again until you were called in by Dr Pritchard? Yes. Well, did you find her labouring under the same symptoms or similar symptoms to those you observed when you were with her on the 2d March? Yes. You still believed her to be suffering under poisoning by antimony? I did; and I prescribed accordingly. Did you see her alone on that occasion? I did. Did you give her any indication of what you thought was her ailment? I did not mention antimony to her in the slightest. Did you mention poison to her? I did not. Did you give her any idea that she was labouring under anything other than natural disease? I did not consider that she was labouring under natural disease. Question repeated. I did not. Why? Because the treatment I prescribed for her, provided she got nothing else, was quite sufficient, in my opinion, to have very soon brought her round, taking it for granted that my prescriptions were carefully walked up to, or rather my advice—not prescriptions. It was Dr Pritchard that asked you to visit his wife upon that occasion? Yes. Did you mention to him your opinion as to his wife being poisoned by antimony? I did not. It would not have been a very safe matter to do that. Why did you not visit her the next day and see that your advice had been acted on? I did not consider at all, sir, that she was my patient, and I had no right or title to go back and visit her. I would have considered myself intruding upon the family had I done so. You had been asked to visit her by the prisoner himself on the 1st March? I believe that if I had not met him accidentally, I would not have been asked. You have no right to say that, doctor. Well, I understood that visit more in the light of a friendly call of condolence under painful, trying circumstances, than as a medical visit. Had you ever been intimate with Mrs Pritchard before? No. Why did you call to pay a visit of condolence to a person you never saw before? It was at Dr Pritchard's request. To condole with her? I could conceive of nothing else. What was the use of calling on a person whom you did not know to condole with her? I had seen her at her mother's deathbed. Were you not called as a medical man? I don't think so. I understood Dr Pritchard was attending her himself; that I was only to call during the day, and when he came back in the evening I had nothing to do with it. But when you saw something so specially the case, why did you not call back? Simply because it was none of my business; I did not consider it my duty. She had her own husband there—a medical man. Having been in a house where you thought there was poisoning going on, you did not consider it your duty to go back? I had discharged my duty, as far as I thought was incumbent upon me. By prescribing certain things, and not knowing whether the prescription was followed? In any case where a consultation is held, the consulting physician has no right to go back to see the patient. Then it was the dignity of your profession that prevented you from going back? It is the etiquette of our profession. That was one reason why I did not go back. I did not say it was the only one. In any case where I had been called in for consultation, were I to go back, it would be a breach of the etiquette of my profession. You said you wrote to the registrar. Did you write first, or did you get a letter from the registrar before you wrote to him? I got the schedule sent to me in the first place. That was about Mrs Taylor? Yes. I got no notice with regard to Mrs Pritchard.

Solicitor-General—It was to visit Mrs Taylor, who was thought to be very ill upon the 24th February, that you was called in? Yes. That was only what you was called in for? Only. You were not consulted about Mrs Pritchard at all? No. Was your meeting with Dr Pritchard accidental? Purely accidental. What time of day was it? About eleven o'clock in the forenoon; and he told me that he was going from home, and would be obliged if I would call and see his wife next day. You had no reason to suppose, and do not suppose, that he was coming for you? Certainly not. And it was, therefore, from your accidentally meeting him at eleven o'clock that one day, and his asking you to call at eleven o'clock the next, that you thought it was an accidental invitation? Purely. You said that it might not have been safe for you to communicate your suspicions to Dr Pritchard himself? It would not have been very natural, certainly. You mean that your suspicions concerned himself? I would rather not answer that question.

Mr Clark—You did not communicate that to any of the family—that is, Dr Pritchard's family? No. Nor the Taylor family? I never saw any of the Taylor family, unless Mr Taylor himself, when he came for the certificate.

Solicitor-General—You told us that you wrote to the registrar, Mr Struthers? I did. That letter has been destroyed? I know the letter verbatim. I wrote it very guardedly.

Mr Clark—Is there a copy in existence?

Solicitor-General—I have a copy taken from the witness's dictation.

Lord Justice-Clerk—You must have the destruction of it proved.

Solicitor-General—I shall do so now.

James Struthers—By Solicitor-General—I am registrar of deaths for the Blythswood district in Glasgow. The prisoner's (Dr Pritchard's) house was in the district. I received intimation in the usual way of the death of Mrs Taylor in his house on the 25th February, between twelve and half-past twelve in the forenoon. It was given by Mr Taylor, her husband. I asked him who was the medical attendant. He mentioned Dr Pritchard and Dr Paterson. He mentioned that Dr Paterson had been called in some little time before her death, and I asked him if I might send to Dr Paterson, as I did not consider him (Dr Pritchard) as the medical attendant. He said he should prefer I should send to Dr Paterson for the certificate. I accordingly sent Dr Paterson the usual printed form of the Registrar-General with blanks to be filled up. This was on the Thursday the 2d March. I got a certificate returned blank, with a note. I am sorry to say that the note was not kept. It recommended me to apply to Dr Pritchard, which I did, and I afterwards got a certificate from Dr Pritchard, which certified that the primary cause of death had been paralysis, the duration of which had been twelve hours, and the secondary cause had been apoplexy, the duration of which had been one hour. Dr Pritchard got a similar schedule when he came to register the death of Mrs Pritchard upon Monday the 20th March, at ten o'clock forenoon. At the time he called he signed the entry in the register, and gave me the certificate, which stated that the primary disease and cause of death had been gastric fever, the duration of which had been two months.

Dr JAMES PATERSON—This witness was then re-called.

Solicitor-General—State to us the terms of the letter, as well as your memory serves you, which you sent to the registrar.

Witness—The letter was dated No. 6 Windsor Place, 4th March 1865, and addressed :— Dear Sir,—I am surprised that I am called on to certify the cause of death in this case. I only saw the person for a few minutes a very short period before her death. She seemed to be under some narcotic; but Dr Pritchard, who was present from the first moment of the illness until death occurred, and which happened in his own house, may certify the cause. The death was certainly sudden, unexpected, and to me mysterious." Then followed "I am, dear Sir," &c., and I signed my name. I rendered emphatic the words "the cause of death," by having them underlined.

Mr Clark—That was the whole letter? I believe so, *literatum et verbatim*. And there was no postscript? There was no postscript. Was that letter sent off the date it bore? I sent it off that day through the post office, directed to James Struthers, registrar. When I was asking you whether you had taken any means for the protection of Mrs Pritchard, this was the communication you referred to? Yes. And the only communication you referred to? The only communication, and I had three motives for making it. Never mind the motives, but you say this was the only communication? The only communication. And Mrs Pritchard was not mentioned in it? No. You did not make any communication whatever to any one of Mrs Pritchard's family? No. Nor to any one? Nor to any one. I spoke of the matter in my own family; that was all.

Lord Justice-Clerk—In answer to a question from the prisoner's counsel, I think you stated that your impression when you first saw Mrs Pritchard, and afterwards when you saw her on the 2d March, was that she was being poisoned by antimony. That was what you said? Yes. Now I want to know exactly what you mean by that. Do you mean that you believed that some person was engaged in administering antimony to her for the purpose of procuring her death? But to me unknown. But was that your meaning? Yes, that was my meaning.

Dr JAMES MOFFAT COWAN—Mr Gifford—You are a Doctor of Medicine in Edinburgh? I am. Are you in practice? Not now, and I have not been for several years. I am a Doctor of the University of Edinburgh. Were you a relative of the late Mrs Pritchard? I was. What relation were you? Well it was rather distant; perhaps you will be able to trace it. Her grandfather and my grandfather were brothers; that is the relation. (A laugh.) You were second cousins, then? Yes. Do you remember getting a letter from the prisoner some time in February last? I do. Do you remember when it was? I think I saw Mrs Pritchard on the 11th, and I would get the letter on the 10th. You have not the letter now, I think? I have not got it; I unfortunately destroyed it. What did the letter say—what was its import? The import of it was, that Mrs Pritchard had been ailing for some time, and that he (Dr Pritchard) was becoming very anxious about her case. He wished to call in another medical man in Glasgow. Did he wish you to come through and see her? He did. Well, did you go? Yes, I went. On the 11th? Yes, on the 11th. Did you go to Dr Pritchard's house? Yes. When did you reach there? About four o'clock, or between four and five o'clock—at dinner time. Where did you find Mrs Pritchard? She came down stairs from the bed-room to the drawing-room to see me there. She met you in the drawing-room? Yes. Was Mrs Taylor there at that time? No. You know that she went afterwards? At my desire she went afterwards. Have you any reason for saying that it was the 11th of February? Well, I have no particular reason except that to the best of my recollection that was the date. It was a few days before Mrs Taylor went through? It was two days before that.

Lord Justice-Clerk—I was only there once in February, and that visit was two days before Mrs Taylor went to Glasgow.

Mr Gifford—Did you see the prisoner before you saw Mrs Pritchard? He met me in the lobby, and I inquired after Mrs Pritchard, and he said she was very much better that day, and that she would be down to see me in the course of a few minutes. And you went to the drawing-room? Yes. When you saw Mrs Pritchard in the drawing-room, how did you find her? I found her very much better than I expected to have found her. Did you put questions to her as to what her symptoms were? Yes; she said she had been troubled with considerable irritability of the stomach, that she could not retain food on her stomach, and had been vomiting for some time back. Did you put what questions you required in order to enable you to judge as a medical man? Well,

I did not go exactly as a medical man; I went more as an old friend, but I did ask one or two questions. Then what did you say or do? In the first place, I saw she had erred in coming down stairs, and I ordered the application of a mustard-poultice to her stomach and to take ice, and if there was much prostration I advised small quantities of champagne, with ice. The prisoner was present during the whole interview? Yes. Did you remain over night? I did. You dined there, I suppose? I did. Did anything occur in the evening about Mrs Pritchard? While I was sitting in the dining-room with the children, Dr Pritchard came down from the bed-room and told me that Mrs Pritchard had been vomiting again, and requested me to accompany him to the bed-room to see her, which I did. To her own bed-room? Yes. You saw her? Yes, and she told me she had been again vomiting. What did you do? Nothing. She at that time complained, I remember, much of feeling a desire for food, and yet she could not retain it, and I proposed to administer beef-tea injections to see if that would do any good. Was she in bed when you left her? She was in bed at that time. Did you see her next morning? I did. Was she down at breakfast? No. In her own bed-room? Yes. Was this before or after breakfast? It would be the first thing in the morning. How did you find her? Much the same as on the previous night. Did anything particular occur? No. Did you return to Edinburgh that evening? Yes; I stayed in Glasgow during the day. Did you see her that day again? Yes; I saw her when I left, but nothing particular occurred that made any impression upon me.

Lord Justice-Clerk—You went back to Edinburgh on the day after you went to Glasgow? I did.

Mr Gifford—Was it you that took the message to Mrs Taylor to go to Glasgow? I did. Who gave you the message? Well, it was Mrs Pritchard's desire that her mother should come through and wait upon her. It was my proposal partly, and she acceded to it. You suggested it? Yes. There was a large family, and I thought she required undivided attention. And you saw Mrs Taylor? Yes; and she went next day.

Cross-examined by Mr Clark—You knew Dr and Mrs Pritchard well? Very intimately. During the whole time they were married? Yes. Did they live happily together? Exceedingly so. Down to the time Mrs Pritchard died? To the last moment—at least to the last moment I saw her. When was the last time you saw her? I saw Mrs Pritchard at Mrs Taylor's death. You never heard of any disagreement whatever between them? The very reverse. And they appeared to you to be very affectionate as husband and wife? Exceedingly so. I never heard him speak a disrespectful or unkind word of her or to her, and I never heard her speak a disrespectful or unkind word to him or of him. On the contrary, they both spoke in the absence of each other very kindly? Exceedingly so. How did he and Mrs Taylor stand? Well, he was Mrs Taylor's idol. Do you remember of Mrs Pritchard's body being brought to Edinburgh. I do. It was taken to her father's house in Lauder Road? Yes; I accompanied it to the house. Did the prisoner accompany it? He did. It was in a coffin, of course? It was. When it was taken to the house, was the coffin opened? It was, at Dr Pritchard's desire. For what purpose? To gratify the servants. They were very much attached to her, and it was done that they might have a last look at the body. What day was that? It was on Monday the 20th. Now, just tell us what passed on this occasion? The coffin was opened, and was in the bed-room at the time it was opened, and the servants were in the room, and Mr Taylor was in the room; Dr Pritchard exhibited a great deal of good feeling on the occasion, and kissed her; and after some time we retired.

Mr Gifford—Were you well acquainted with Mrs Taylor? Yes. You had known her for a great many years? All my life. You were intimate with her? Yes. You visited her frequently? Oh, very. She was a person of temperate habits? Very temperate habits.

Lord Justice-Clerk—Have you seen much of Dr and Mrs Pritchard during the last two years? A good deal. And visited them frequently at Glasgow? Well, I was *not in* the habit of visiting them very frequently, but occasionally, and Mrs Pritchard and Dr Pritchard were frequently through to Edinburgh. You saw more of them at that time? Yes.

MARGARET DICKSON—Solicitor-General—I was in the employment of Mr Michael Taylor, the husband of the late Mrs Taylor, who died in Glasgow. I was in his service four and a half years till April last. His wife lived in the house with him till she went to Glasgow in February last. I was the only servant in the house. They lived in Lauder Road. I remember Mrs Pritchard coming from Glasgow on a visit in November last; and she remained till a few days from Christmas. She had been complaining when she came; but she got better with us. She was pretty well when at Lauder Road. I heard no complaint. She was not confined to bed any day or part of a day, and took her meals with the family. During that visit she was never sick to my knowledge. On Thursday, 30th March, I was present at Grange Cemetery when Mrs Taylor's body was taken from the grave. I saw the coffin opened, and saw the body. I recognised it as that of Mrs Taylor in presence of Dr Maclagan and Dr Littlejohn. Before Mrs Taylor went to Glasgow in February, she was in good health. She was so all the time I was in the house. She had no particular illness—no complaint. So far as I know, she was of temperate habits. I never saw anything to the contrary. I have seen her take a little whisky and water during dinner, but never at any other time. I never saw her affected by it. I was also present with the same doctors when Mrs Pritchard's body was handed over to them on the 21st March. I identified Mrs Pritchard's body.

MICHAEL TAYLOR—Solicitor-General—The late Mrs Taylor, who died in Glasgow in February last, was your wife? Yes. Before she went to visit your daughter, Mrs Pritchard, in February last, was she in good health? Only middling: she had been complaining a good deal. What had she been complaining of? She had been delicate for years, and subject to very violent perspirations. Did she also complain of neuralgic headaches? Occasionally. Did she take anything for her headache? Batley's Solution. Had she taken that for years? For five or six years. Am I right in saying that it was for the headache she took it? No; for the perspirations. Excuse me for asking the question, but was she of temperate habits? Perfectly so. In every respect? Yes. She did not make herself the worse of any kind of liquor or of opium? I sometimes observed a great inclination in her to sleep, which I supposed was caused by the medicine. After she had taken the medicine? Yes. She took it in your presence? Never. You knew she was taking it? For some years after she had begun taking it, I did not know what it was. I knew that she was taking medicine, but I did not know the name of it till last year. But you knew she was taking the thing the name of which you now know to be Batley's Solution? Yes. Your daughter was with you upon a visit from the end of November until a few days before Christmas last year? She was. She had been ailing before she came. How was she when she was in your house? Very delicate. Anything more the matter with her than being very delicate? She had very little appetite. She took her meals with you, and did not eat very much? She ate very little. Was she confined to bed while in your house at all? She might get up about ten or eleven o'clock in the forenoon.

By the Lord Justice-Clerk—After she had been with us for some little time, she got up to breakfast. This was when she got better.

By the Solicitor-General—She did not always breakfast with the family even after that.

Lord Justice-Clerk—She got somewhat better while she was staying with you, and was more in the way of getting up to breakfast? Yes.

The Solicitor-General—Did she complain of anything? She complained of sickness. Was that once or oftener? Frequently. At what time of her visit did she complain? In the latter end of November or early part of December. Was it when she first came? She frequently complained of sickness. All the time she was with you? Yes, more or less. What did she say about it? Well, I do not know particularly. She complained that she was weak, and occasionally sick. She said nothing about it? Nothing particular. Did you ever see her sick? I have heard of her being sick; she has been obliged to leave the table from being sick. Was that two or three times, or only once? I think I heard of it two or three times; but I am not very certain. Was she very much better when she went away from you than before she came? She was a little better. You were telegraphed to from Glasgow that your wife was dangerously ill, and then that she was dead? Yes. You received the two telegrams together? Yes. You went through to Glasgow? Yes, by the first train. You went to Dr Paterson's house in the morning? Yes, on the Saturday morning. Who had told you to go there? Dr Pritchard asked me if I would go down and register the death. And you went to Dr Paterson's first? Yes, to ask him to give me a certificate as to what was the cause of Mrs Taylor's death. It was Dr Pritchard who sent you to Dr Paterson? Yes. Did Dr Pritchard tell you what your wife died of? I think he said it was apoplexy or paralysis. Had your wife ever any fits? Not to my knowledge. I mean of any kind? No. I believe you were present when your wife's body was disinterred in presence of the doctors? Yes. And Mrs Pritchard's also? Yes. (Shown letter.) Is that a letter you received from Dr Pritchard? Yes. It is dated 9.3.'65. The passage I want to read to you is this:—"I am very much fatigued with being up at night with dear Mary Jane, who was very much worse yesterday, and passed a wretched night. Wednesday has been a periodic day with her during this illness, and she always dreads it. Her prostration is extreme, and her appetite quite failed. Dr Paterson has recommended Dublin stout, and some very simple medicine." I see that passage here.

Cross-examined by Mr Clark—Were you frequently iu Glasgow? I may say a week in every month. Were they living happily together? I never saw anything to the contrary. Did they appear to be living happily? Yes. And affectionately? Yes. Did she appear to be very kind to him? Yes. And he to her? Yes. When you went to Glasgow, you always went to their house? I generally stopped three days at a hotel, and after finishing business I generally stopped Saturday, Sunday, and Monday at their house. That was in each month? Nearly in each month. Perhaps it might not be quite a month. Upon the average, I would say one week a month. You spent two or three days in their house in each month? Yes. Do you remember when you were in Glasgow of stating something to Mrs Pritchard about a nurse, or did she speak to you about a nurse? The doctor wrote that he was either going to get a nurse, or had got one. But did Mrs Pritchard? Never. Do you remember Mrs Pritchard saying to you that she did not want a nurse? She may have said so, but I remember the doctor wrote saying he was going to get a nurse, or had got one, and it is quite possible Mrs Pritchard may have said that, but I cannot remember. You said you knew that Mrs Taylor took Batley's Sedative, though you did not know the name of it? I knew she was taking medicine. Do you know where she got it? She got it at Duncan & Flockhart's, and at Fairgrieve's, in Clerk Street. These were the two places she got it at? Yes. You did not know the quantity she took? No. Only that she did get it and took it? Yes.

At this point, the Court adjourned till ten next morning, having sat till six o'clock.

THIRD DAY—Wednesday, July 5.

The Court met again this morning, and resumed the trial — the Lord Justice-Clerk, Lord Ardmillan, and Lord Jerviswoode presiding.

The Solicitor-General, Mr Gifford, and Mr Crichton conducted the prosecution; and Mr A. R. Clark, Mr Watson, and Mr Brand appeared for the prisoner.

At five minutes past ten the prisoner took his seat in the dock, and immediately after his brother entered and took his seat by his side. The prisoner during the day preserved the calm and attentive demeanour which has characterised him since the commencement of the trial.

The first witness called was Alexander M'Call, Superintendent of Central District of Glasgow Police—Mr Crichton—I am Superintendent of the Central District of Glasgow Police. I apprehended the prisoner on Monday, 20th March. He was searched then. [Shown Nos. 9 and 10.] These letters were found on him. I visited his house, Clarence Place, on Tuesday, 21st. I searched his repositories. [Shown Nos. 19 and 20.] I found these in the consulting-room. I got a bottle from Mary M'Leod. [Shown 85 B.] That is the bottle. She took it out of a chest of drawers which was standing on the stairhead in the passage on the top flat. There was a brownish-coloured liquid in the bottle. It was about half-full—up to about the middle of the upper label. I went back next day, the 22d. [Shown No. 86 C.] I took possession of these seven paper packets. I found them in the consulting-room. [Shown No. 87 D.] I got this quart bottle in the same room in a locked press; I think it was ginger-wine that was in it. The key of that press I found in the prisoner's pocket when apprehended. It was the press next the fire. [Shown 88 E.] I found this small phial also in the consulting-room; there are the remains of a label bearing "Timon." I found that in another press in the consulting-room—in an unlocked press. [Shown 89, 90, and 91.] These are three vials, two corks, and a glass-stopper. I got these in the unlocked press in the consulting-room. [Shown 92 G.] This phial I got on the mantel-piece in the ante-drawing-room. The cork now in it I believe was in it then. On the 23d I was back in the house, and got some things from Mary Patterson. [Shown 96 L.] I got these from Mary Patterson. [Shown 97 M.] This bed-linen I also got from her. I was there also on 30th March. [Shown two bank pass-books, Nos. 100 and 101.] I got both these in the locked press in the consulting-room. Nos. 96 and 97 I handed to John Murray on the 29th, in the same state in which I got them. On 13th April I handed to Dr Penny all the bottles which have now been shown to me. [Shown Nos. 12, 13, and 14.] I found these in a desk in the consulting-room. They are two prescriptions and an envelope. [Shown 32 to 37 inclusive. I found these letters in a bookcase in the consulting-room. [Shown Nos. 22 to 28 inclusive.] I found these letters in the same bookcase. [Shown Nos. 15 and 16.] I found this prescription and envelope on 30th March on a table in the same room. [Shown Nos. 17 and 18.] I found this prescription and envelope on the same day, and on the same table. These were all the medical prescriptions I found.

Cross-examined by Mr Clark—I did not take all the bottles in the consulting-room. I left thirty-five phials or bottles in the unlocked press. In the locked press there was a bottle of brandy, a bottle with whisky, and some bottles labelled chloroform. The medicines were in the open press. These thirty-five bottles were examined by Drs M'Leod and M'Hattie in the place, and found to contain drugs which were not poison. I took all the bottles except the thirty-five. I gave the key of the locked press to the prisoner's brother, Charles, on 31st March, and what became of the bottles left in it I don't know. I handed over to the prisoner's agent the medicine bottles which Dr Penny did not retain; I handed them over in the same condition in which I found them. [Shown Nos. 32 to 37.] These were found in the bookcase in the consulting-room.

John Murray—Mr Crichton—I am a sheriff-officer in Glasgow. [Shown No. 96 and No. 97 M.] I got those from Mr M'Call, and handed them over to Dr Maclagan in the same state in which I got them from Mr M'Call. [Shown No. 84 A.] I got that parcel of tapioca from Mary Patterson on Saturday, 1st April. I took it to the County Buildings, Glasgow, sealed it up, and handed it to Dr Penny, Glasgow, in the same state in which I had got it, except that I had sealed it up. [Shown No. 95 K.] I purchased this packet of tapioca from Messrs Burton & Henderson, tea and coffee merchants, Glasgow, on the 14th April. I attached a label to it, and gave it to Dr Penny in the same state in which I got it from Burton & Henderson, except that I attached a label to it.

John Campbell—By Mr Gifford—I am manager of the Western Branch of the Glasgow Apothecaries' Company, 251 Sauchiehall Street. I have known the prisoner by sight for four years. He has not been in the habit of making purchases at our establishment till within the last eight or nine months. I have my books here, and the purchases he made are entered therein. He had a running account with us. [Shown No. 58.] That is an excerpt from our books of Dr Pritchard's account. That account contained the following entries:—1864, Sept. 19,—10 grs. strychnine; Nov. 4,—½ oz. tincture conii (*i.e.* hemlock); Nov. 16,—1 oz. laudanum, 1 oz. tartar emetic; Nov. 24,—1 oz. tincture aconite; Dec. 8,—1 oz. Fleming's tincture aconite; Dec. 9,—1 oz. tincture conii; 1865, Feb. 4,—1 oz. tincture conii; Feb. 7,—1 oz. tartarised antimony, 1 oz. tincture aconite; Feb. 9,—1 oz. tincture aconite; Feb. 11,—2 oz. tincture digitalis; Feb. 18,—2 oz. tincture conii. I have my books here from which this was excerpted. I made the excerpt and compared it carefully with my books. Dr Pritchard invariably got the articles mentioned here himself. He came to the shop and ordered them himself. Some he took away with him, and some were sent home. Some orders were taken by myself, and some by an assistant. The orders taken by the assistant were:—On November 24, 1 oz. tincture aconite; on December 9, 1 oz. tincture conii; on February 4, 1 oz. tincture of conii. I did not get the orders for these personally, but all the other orders were given to me personally by the prisoner. I am satisfied that the whole of these articles, not only those ordered from myself, but from the assistant, were furnished from our establishment. All the articles that I have read are poisons. Look at entry under date November 16—1 oz. tartar emetic. Is that a large quantity? Yes. What is the ordinary dose when used as an emetic? Two grains. How many grains are there in an oz? 435¼ avoirdupois. An oz. is not a usual quantity for me to sell. I never sold an oz. to a medical man in Glasgow before. On February 7th, I sold another oz. of tartarised antimony. The quantity of antimony which I sold the prisoner struck me. How much tartarised antimony may you have sold during a year to the medical profession in Glasgow and the whole public? I think two oz. would serve us for twelve months. For the whole of your trade? Yes; for the whole of our trade. Have you a very large trade? A very large dispensing business. Under date November 24 I observe an entry—"One ounce tincture of aconite." That is a large quantity—an unusual quantity to sell to one individual. There are other two entries of an ounce each also. The quantity I sold to the prisoner struck me as very unusual. It was Fleming's tincture of aconite I sold to him on 8th December. The difference between that and the other kind is, according to the new British Pharmacopœia, that Fleming's is six times stronger than the ordinary tincture of aconite. I believe an ounce or two ounces of Fleming's would cover the whole of my business during a twelvemonth. Fleming's is the kind principally prescribed in liniments. We do a large dispensing business. There is an entry of an ounce of tincture of digitalis on February 11. Was that an unusual quantity? Well, it is not unusual. What are the other articles in the account which I have not asked you to read—what is the principal article? Chloroform. The quantity of chloroform sold to the prisoner from July 13 to December 9, 1864, was very large, being 132 oz. That is a very unusual quantity. How much chloroform do you sell to the general public or to other medical men? I could give you no idea, but it has no relation at all to what the prisoner got—nothing like it in quantity. Do you mean that the prisoner got more than all your other customers put together? Yes. We supply medicines to a great many medical practitioners in Glasgow. I have been a dispensing apothecary for twenty-three years. In all my experience I never furnished so much poison to any medical man. [Shown label I, No. 94, being six phials.] These are the kind of phials we use for tincture of aconite and for all purposes. I can recognise on one of the phials part of the label "Aco." I recognise these labels as portions of labels such as we use. When we furnished these phials we always labelled them. The hand-writing that is on the part of the label remaining on the phials I recognise as the handwriting of one of my assistants. His name is Mr Rose.

JOHN CURRIE—Mr Gifford—I am a chemist in Glasgow, and my shop is in Sauchiehall Street. I have known the prisoner since he came to Glasgow, fully three years ago. He came to my shop frequently and made purchases. I have my ledger here showing his account; but I have also made an excerpt from that account, showing the articles with which the prisoner was furnished from my shop. That excerpt is a correct one. The excerpt was then read by Mr Gifford, and was as follows:—1865, February 18.—Two ounces solution morphia; one ounce Fleming's tincture of aconite. March 8.—Solution of atropine, one drachm, with two gr. to drachm. March 9.—Solution of atropine, one drachm, with two grs. to drachm. March 13.—Half-ounce of Fleming's tincture of aconite. March 14.—Solution of atropine, one drachm, with two grs. to drachm. March 16.—Solution of atropine, one drachm, with five grs. to drachm. The witness proceeded to say—All these articles were furnished to the prisoner. I could not say decidedly which of them were furnished to him by myself personally; but some of them I prepared, while others were prepared by my assistant. They were just sent to order. Dr Pritchard generally came himself and ordered them. To the best of my knowledge all these articles were furnished to Dr Pritchard at the dates specified. You know that? They were furnished from my shop at the dates, so far as I could possibly say. You have no doubt of these articles being provided? No; I have none.

Mr Clark—You say that because you saw these entries in your book? Yes. And that is all you know about it? No; I furnished some of the articles myself. They were ordered either by the prisoner or by his direction, and sent to him.

Mr Gifford—To the best of my knowledge I put up the tincture of aconite which was sent on the 18th of February, although I would not swear to it. Unless I saw the label I could not swear to it. Then on the 7th of February I put up several phials for drops for the ear. I think I prepared the first solution of atropine on 8th March, and one or two of the other articles, but I could scarcely be positive. I am not sure whether it was I or my assistant who made up the half-ounce of aconite supplied on 13th March. I was in constant attendance at the shop. I rather think my assistant gave the most of the solutions of atropine, although one or two I gave myself. The prisoner generally gave his orders himself verbally. He did not often send written orders.

Cross-examined by Mr Clark—You have no recollection of these articles being supplied to Dr Pritchard further than that the entries are in your book? I have. What recollection have you? I prepared some of the articles, and I know they were sent to Dr Pritchard. How do you know they were sent to him? My assistant told me so. Your assistant told you; but you do not know of your own knowledge? Yes I do, for I provided some of them myself. Did you send them away yourself? I sent away the three dozen of phials, and I supplied the first ounce of aconite; I am pretty certain of that. But you would not swear to it? No. Then, as to anything else, all the information you have is what your assistant told you? I know the articles were sent. They were all entered by myself, and my assistant told me distinctly they were sent. That is just what your assistant told you. It is that, then, you are speaking from? But I provided some of them myself. I know you spoke to the aconite and the phials? Yes; and some of the atropine. But, as to the rest, it is only from what your assistant told you that you know? I have no reason to doubt him. That is another question. What is his name? Girvan Brown; he is not a witness in this case.

DR DOUGLAS MACLAGAN—Solicitor-General—Dr Maclagan, you are Professor Medical Jurisprudence in the University of Edinburgh? I am. And have been long engaged as a medical practitioner in Edinburgh? Yes. For many years? Yes. And I believe you have also devoted considerable attention to chemistry? Yes; in its toxicological relations. In connexion with poisons? Yes. On the 21st March last, I believe, you made a *post-mortem* examinacion of a body that was submitted to your examination, represented to be the body of Mary Jane Taylor or Pritchard? Yes. And you prepared a report of that *post-mortem* examination? Yes.

Dr Maclagan read the following report:—

Medical Report by Drs Maclagan and Littlejohn of post-mortem *examination of body of Mrs Pritchard.*

EDINBURGH, *March* 21, 1865.

We, the undersigned, in virtue of a warrant of the Sheriff of Lanarkshire of yesterday's date, concurred in, of this date, by the Sheriff-Substitute of Edinburgh, at No. 1 Lauder Road, Grange, examined a body identified in our presence as that of Mary Jane Taylor or Pritchard, by the following witnesses :—Mary Raynor or Taylor, sister-in-law of the deceased; Michael Taylor, father of the deceased; Catherine Lattimer, servant; and Margaret Dickson, servant.

The body appeared to be that of a healthy woman, of about the age stated on the coffin-plate—thirty-nine years. It was free from putrescency. There was moderate *post-mortem* lividity and *rigor mortis*. Nothing was observed externally, except a yellow stain on the right side of the abdomen, looking like the remains of a sinapism. The expression was placid. The pupils of the eyes natural.

Head.—The vessels of the scalp were not loaded with blood. The veins on the surface of the brain were moderately full, especially at the posterior part. There was considerable effusion of serum under the arachnoid membrane on the top of the brain, but not at the base. The brain itself was healthy, both as regards vascularity and consistence. The ventricles contained only a small quantity of serum.

Organs of Respiration and Circulation.—The windpipe was healthy. The right lung was quite healthy. The left lung was slightly adherent to the walls of the chest, at its apex, where there was a firm mass of old tubercular deposit, of the size of a hazel nut, of cheesy consistence, and unaccompanied by any traces of recent morbid action. There was a small amount of serum in the pericardium. The heart contained a little fluid blood in both cavities; rather more in the right than in the left ventricle. In the right ventricle there was a small fibrous clot. The heart and its valves were healthy.

Organs of Digestion.—The gums and mucous membrane of the mouth were exsanguine, the lips dry, the pharynx and gullet perfectly healthy. The walls of the abdomen were loaded with fat, and so were the omentum and mesentery. The viscera presented no morbid appearance externally. The liver was natural: the gall-bladder full of bile. The spleen was healthy. The kidneys slightly congested. The stomach contained about three drachms of pinkish-gray ropy fluid, with some small masses of tenacious mucus mixed with it. The mucous membrane was generally healthy, but on the posterior wall, near to the cardia, there was a patch of punctiform redness over a space of two inches square. The small intestines were lined with light gray mucus. The colon and rectum contained some yellow feculent matter, which nowhere was of solid consistence. The ileum, for about three inches of its length, at a part beginning about three inches above its termination in the colon, was closely contracted on itself. The mucous membrane of the rectum, throughout a good part of its extent, presented a superficial dark discoloration, as if some black pigment were embedded in its substance. There was slight ramiform injection of the greater part of the mucous membrane of the rectum. There were several small patches of the same appearance at various points throughout the colon, and a few spots of similar vascular injection in the small intestines.

Urinary and Genital Apparatus.—The urinary bladder contained about eight ounces of brownish yellow urine; the womb and its appendages presented no morbid appearance beyond a slight ulceration of the cervix uteri.

We have to report that this body presented no appearances of recent morbid action, beyond a certain amount of irritation of the alimentary canal, and nothing at all capable of accounting for death. We have therefore secured the alimentary canal and its contents, the heart and some of the blood, the liver, the spleen, the left kidney, and the urine, in order that these may be submitted to chemical analysis.

(Signed) DOUGLAS MACLAGAN.
HENRY D. LITTLEJOHN.

Solicitor-General—That is a true report? That is a true report.

Read your chemical report, Dr Maclagan, now. Dr Maclagan read a part of his report, dated 11th April 1865, but he was interrupted in the reading in order that Drs Gamgee and Littlejohn might speak to the parts of the report referring to what they had done during Dr Maclagan's absence in London.

[Dr Arthur Gamgee, assistant to Dr Maclagan, and Dr Littlejohn, were here called, and gave evidence that the statement in Dr Maclagan's report of what they had done in his absence in London was a correct statement.]

Dr Maclagan was again called, and read the remaining portions of the report. The following is a complete copy of the report :—

Chemical Report by Dr Maclagan. Death of Mrs Pritchard.

EDINBURGH, 11*th April* 1865.

I have subjected to chemical examination the various organs, and contents of organs, removed by Dr Littlejohn and myself from the body of Mrs Mary Jane Taylor or Pritchard, at the *post-mortem* examination on 21st March, and I have to report the following as the results which I have obtained :—

It having been stated to me that antimony was suspected in this case, immediately on returning from the *post-mortem* examination, I made a trial experiment in presence of Dr Littlejohn, and my assistant, Dr Arthur Gamgee, with three drachms of the urine, and obtained from this unmistakable evidence of the presence of antimony. Being obliged, in consequence of the death of a relative, to go to London, and having, by the above experiment, ascertained that my researches must be directed towards the discovery of antimony, I requested Dr Gamgee, in conjunction with Dr Littlejohn, to carry on the following preliminary process in my absence. The whole contents of the intestines were evaporated to dryness on a water bath, so as to obtain a solid residue; one-half of this residue was digested with water acidulated with tartaric acid, and filtered, by which a solution measuring two ounces and five drachms was obtained, in which any antimony present in the intestines would be found. One ounce of this fluid was subjected to a stream of sulphuretted hydrogen gas, and the orange-yellow precipitate which formed was collected on a filter and washed. This precipitate, and the remainder of the tartaric acid solution, were reserved for my examination on my return to Edinburgh on the 24th March. I then subjected these materials to the following examination. The orange-yellow precipitate was boiled in a tube with pure hydrochloric acid, and the solution thus obtained was mixed with water, when a white precipitate formed. The fluid containing this precipitate was again subjected to a stream of sulphuretted hydrogen gas, and again gave a deposit of an orange-yellow colour. One fluid drachm of the tartaric acid solution was treated by Reinsch's method, and another fluid drachm was treated by Marsh's process. By each of these well-known methods, and thus operating upon a quantity of fluid corresponding to a forty-second part of the contents of the intestines, I obtained unequivocal evidence of the presence of antimony. By digesting a small quantity of the dried residue of the intestinal contents with distilled water, filtering and subjecting the filtrate to Reinsch's process, I readily ascertained that the antimony was here present in the form of a compound soluble in water. There are only two preparations of antimony occurring in commerce which are soluble in water; the one of these, the chloride, is a strongly acid, dark brown, corrosive fluid, totally unsuited for internal administration; the other is what is known scientifically as tartarised antimony, and popularly as tartar emetic, a colourless substance, possessed of comparatively little taste, and in daily use as a medicinal agent. I have no doubt, and shall assume in the following statements, that the antimony found in Mrs Pritchard's body was taken in this form. The remainder of the acid solution, amounting to one ounce and three drachms, was subjected to a process intended to determine the quantity of antimony present in the contents of the intestines; but though the presence of this metal was determined with the greatest facility, I found that the amount yielded by the materials which I used was too small to enable me to weigh it with sufficient accuracy. I also made an experiment with the contents of the intestines, directed towards the discovery of vegetable poisons. It is sufficient on this subject to say, that the result was entirely negative. I then subjected to analysis the following fluids and solids removed from the body of Mrs Pritchard.

1. *Contents of Stomach.*—These amounted to little more than half-an-ounce, and were free from all odour of any poisonous drug. They were subjected, in the first place, to what is known as "Stas's process," for the separation of vegetable poisons, but not a trace of any of these was detected. The whole residues of this operation were preserved and subjected to examination for antimony, but none was found.

2. *The Urine.*—The presence of antimony having been already ascertained in this secretion, the remainder, amounting to seven ounces, was employed to determine its quantity. The process followed here was a well-known one, by which the antimony is obtained in the form of sulphuret, after destroying the organic matter by means of hydrochloric acid and chlorate of potash. The quantity of sulphuret was readily weighed, and found to be rather more than one-tenth of a grain (0·1078 grain.) This corresponds to nearly one-fourth of a grain (·218 grain) of tartar-emetic.

3. *The Bile.*—A little more than half-an-ounce of this fluid was obtained from the gall-bladder. By Reinsch's process fifty minims readily gave an antimonial deposit. The remainder of the bile, amounting to four drachms, was used to determine the amount of antimony in it, and it yielded sulphuret of antimony, corresponding to more than one-tenth of a grain (0·121 grain) of tartar-emetic.

4. *The Blood.*—The total quantity was six and a-half ounces. One ounce was subjected to Reinsch's process, and readily gave evidence of the presence of antimony.

5. *The Liver.*—The weight of this organ was found to be thirty-six ounces, a portion weighing less than four ounces (1460 grains) was subjected to Reinsch's process, and a sufficient amount of antimony was found to coat rather more than four square inches of copper foil. Although the existence in the liver of an abundance of antimony was to my mind satisfactorily established by the appearance of the coated copper foil, I deemed it right to employ a portion of the product thus obtained for confirming, by another test,

he presence of antimony in the body of Mrs Pritchard. For this purpose a piece of the copper foil, one inch long and half-an-inch broad, was boiled in a dilute solution of pure caustic potash, the copper foil being from time to time freely exposed to the air. The coating disappeared from the copper, and a solution was obtained, which, when acidulated with hydrochloric acid, and subjected to a stream of sulphuretted hydrogen gas, gave an orange precipitate, which again was dissolved in strong hydrochloric acid; this acid solution gave, on being mixed with water, a white turbidity, which again was turned orange by sulphuretted hydrogen. Another portion of the coated foil, measuring half-an-inch square, was heated in a fine glass tube, with a view to ascertaining the presence or absence of arsenic, which occasionally exists as an impurity in compounds of antimony. No arsenic, however, was found, nor had any been observed in the previous trial of the contents of the intestines by Marsh's process. Finding antimony thus abundantly in the liver, I made an experiment to determine its actual quantity in that organ. For this purpose I operated upon one thousand grains, by the process described above for determining the presence of antimony, and obtained an amount of antimony in the state of sulphuret (0·1234 grain) corresponding to a quarter of a grain (0·25 grain) of tartar-emetic; the amount contained in the whole liver being almost exactly four grains (3·93 grains.)

I next examined the remainder of the solid organs removed from the body of Mrs Pritchard, and have to state, that I have found more or less of antimony in the whole of them. I operated in no instance upon more than 350 grains, in every case following Reinsch's process. I thus obtained the evidence of the presence of antimony in the spleen, kidney, muscular substance of the heart, coats of the stomach, coats of the rectum, brain, and uterus. On the 29th of March I received from the hands of John Murray, sheriff-officer, Glasgow, two parcels of clothes, with sealed labels attached to them, with a view to my examining some stains upon them. One of these labels bore, "Police Office, Glasgow, Central District, 23d March 1865. Found in the house of Dr Pritchard, 131 Sauchiehall Street, and referred to in the case of himself. (Signed) A. M'Call, Audley Thomson." The label was signed by John Murray in my presence, and initialed by me. On the back of the label was the following list of the articles attached to it:—"One night-dress, 1 chemise, 1 night-cap, 3 handkerchiefs, 1 knitted woollen semet, a pair of worsted stockings, 1 woollen polka." The other label was similarly dated and signed, the list on the back being—"2 sheets, 2 pillow cases, 2 towels, 1 toilet cover." I examined such of the stains on these articles as appeared of importance, confining my experiments to a search for antimony, and I have to state, that whilst with many of the stains the result was entirely negative, I found antimony on the following:—1st, On the chemise, from a stain obviously of discharge from the bowels, and which had been marked by me A. 2d, On one of the sheets, distinguished by me as No. 1, in a stain marked by me B. 3d, On the other sheet, distinguished by me as No. 2, in a stain obviously of urine, marked by me A. 4th, On a toilet cover, in a stain of a reddish colour, looking like a wine stain. It is hardly necessary to state that the materials employed in all these chemical operations had been ascertained to be entirely free from all metallic impurity. From the experiments, the details of which are given above, I have been led to the following conclusions:—1st, That Mrs Pritchard had taken a large quantity of antimony in the form of tartar emetic. 2d, That having regard to the absence in her case of any morbid appearances sufficient to account for death, and to the presence in it of a large quantity of a substance known to be capable of destroying life, her death must be ascribed to the action of antimony. 3d, That it is most unlikely that this poison was taken in a single large dose. Had this been the case, I should have expected to have found some more decided evidence of irritant action in the mouth, throat, or alimentary canal. 4th, That from the extent to which the whole organs and fluids of the body were impregnated with it, it must have been taken in repeated doses, the aggregate of which must have amounted to a large quantity. 5th, That from the large amount found in the liver, from its ready detection in the blood, and from its being found passing so copiously out of the body by the bile and urine, it is probable that some of the poison had been taken at no greater interval than a period of a few days previous to death. 6th, That I am inclined to believe that it had not been administered, at all events in any great quantity, within a few hours of her death. Had this been the case, I would have expected to have found at least some traces of it in the contents of the stomach, and more in the contents of the intestines; whereas none was found in the former, and the amount found in the latter seems to be amply accounted for by the bile impregnated with the poison discharged into them from the liver. 7th, That the period over which the administration had extended cannot be determined by mere chemical investigation, but must be deduced from the history of the case, with which I am unacquainted. Douglas Maclagan.

The Solicitor-General—That is a true report? Yes.

Dr Maclagan then read the following report, giving the results of a *post-mortem* examination of the body of Mrs Taylor made by himself and Dr Littlejohn:—

Medical Report by Drs Maclagan and Littlejohn of Post-mortem Examination of body of Mrs Taylor.

Edinburgh, 30th March 1865.

In virtue of a warrant of the Sheriff of Lanarkshire, dated 28th March 1865, and concurred in on 29th March by the Sheriff-substitute of Mid-Lothian, we this day, at the Grange Cemetery, examined the body of Mrs Jane Taylor, who was buried there at the beginning of the present month. The coffin was exhumed in our presence, and was found to bear on the plate "Jane Taylor, died 25th February 1865, aged 71 years." A portion of the earth from above the coffin was secured for chemical examination. The coffin, and subsequently the features of the deceased, were identified in our presence by the following witnesses:—Mr Michael Taylor; Dr M. W. Taylor; Margaret Dickson; James Thomson; John Moffat; David Glen; and Robert Grant. The coffin was entire. The following were the appearances observed by us in the body of Mrs Taylor:—

Externally, it presented the appearance of great freshness. There was some red *post-mortem* coloration of the shoulders and back. The abdomen was slightly green over a space of not more than four inches by three. There was a little mouldiness on the face, but there was no putrefactive disfigurement of the countenance. The expression was placid, and a little florid colour was visible on the cheeks.

Head.—The scalp was not congested. The dura mater was firmly adherent to the skull at several points, especially at the frontal bone, and in the right temporal fossa, at which places the inner table of the skull exhibited rough elevations and depressions, to which the dura mater was attached. These were of old standing. A small quantity of fluid blood, which had exuded from a vein torn in removing the skull-cap, was found on the upper part of a posterior lobe of the left hemisphere. It was entirely a *post-mortem* occurrence. The blood was at once washed away by a little water poured gently upon it, and the brain and membrane beneath it were found quite in a natural state. There was a small amount of sub-arachnoid effusion, obviously also a *post-mortem* phenomenon, as it was found only at the back part of the brain, and was unaccompanied by any appearance of inflammatory action. The blood-vessels of the brain were not congested. The ventricles contained less than a teaspoonful of clear serum. The brain throughout was remarkably fresh. Every part of it was most carefully scrutinised, but at all points it was found perfectly healthy, both externally and internally, equally as regards consistence, colour, and structure. There was a trifling amount of atheromatous deposit on the coats of the vessels at the base of the brain, but much less than might have been expected in a person seventy-one years of age.

Organs of Respiration and Circulation.—The mucous membrane of the trachea was little, if at all, altered by putrefaction, being only slightly reddened, and lined by a little colourless mucus. The lungs were remarkably healthy, there being no trace of anything noteworthy about them, except some old adhesions of the left pleura. The pericardium was healthy, and contained no serum. The heart was large, and weighed sixteen ounces. It had a considerable layer of fat over its surface, was slightly dilated, particularly on the right side, but all its valves were quite healthy. There was about one ounce and a half of fluid blood, along with a fibrinous coagulum in the right ventricle. The left ventricle was almost empty. The venæ cavæ contained half coagulated blood. The aorta was quite free from atheromatous deposit.

Organs of Digestion.—The gums and mucous membrane of the mouth, the pharynx, and gullet, were perfectly healthy. The walls of the abdomen were loaded with fat, and so were the omentum and mesentery. The stomach contained five ounces of turbid yellow fluid, and some small masses of undigested food. The mucous membrane was free from disease, and presented only some *post-mortem* blackening at several points, and a yellow coloration from contact with the contents. The intestines presented diffuse *post-mortem* redness externally at several points, but nowhere exhibited any distinct morbid appearances. A portion of the ileum, about four inches in length, and about three feet above the cæcum, was closely contracted upon itself. The small intestines contained only a lining of pinkish-gray mucus. There was a small amount of yellow fluid fæces in the cæcum and rectum. The large intestines elsewhere contained only a lining of pinkish-gray mucus. The mucous membrane of the intestines everywhere was perfectly healthy. The rectum at one or two points, especially close to the anus, presented slightly the appearance of a black pigment matter imbedded in its mucous membrane. The other organs of the abdomen were healthy.

Urinary and Genital Apparatus.—The bladder was contracted, and contained only a little mucus. The uterus and its appendages were healthy.

We have to report that we have not been able to discover in the body of Mrs Taylor any morbid appearance capable of accounting for her death, and are of opinion that the cause of her death cannot be determined without chemical analysis. We have therefore secured for this purpose, the alimentary canal and its contents, the heart and some of the blood, the liver, the spleen, the kidneys, the bladder and uterus, and a portion of the brain, which have been left in the custody of Dr Maclagan.

DOUGLAS MACLAGAN.
HENRY D. LITTLEJOHN.

Lord Justice-Clerk—That report is signed by yourself and Dr Littlejohn? It is.

Solicitor-General—And it is a true report? Yes.

Dr Maclagan next read the following report of the chemical analysis of the various things mentioned at the end of last report:—

Chemical Report by Dr Maclagan. Death of Mrs Taylor.

EDINBURGH, 13*th April* 1865.

I have subjected to chemical examination the various organs and fluids removed by Dr Littlejohn and myself from the body of Mrs Jane Taylor at our *post-mortem* examination on 30th March, and have to report on them as follows:—

Contents of the Stomach.—These, which amounted to five ounces, were, in the first place, subjected to the process known as that of Stas, for the detection of the active principles of vegetable poisons. The result, however, was that no trace of any of these was detected. A special test was also applied, with the view of discovering in the stomach meconic acid, one of the characteristic constituents of opium, but in this also I was unsuccessful. The residues of the above process were reserved to be tested for metallic poisons, and a preliminary trial, by Reinsch's method, having revealed in the contents of the stomach the presence of antimony, I subjected the whole to a process by which I was enabled to determine the amount of this metal. This process was as follows:—The materials were boiled with pure hydrochloric acid and copper foil, so long as the latter continued to receive on its polished surface a deposit of antimony. The foil thus coated was boiled with a weak solution of pure potash, the foil being from time to time exposed to the air, and the antimony was thus dissolved. The fluid, after being acidulated with hydrochloric acid, was subjected to a current of sulphuretted hydrogen gas, and yielded an orange-coloured deposit of sulphuret of antimony. This was further purified by dissolving it in a weak solution of sulphide of sodium, from which it was again precipitated by hydrochloric acid and weighed. Assuming, for reasons to be afterwards given, that the antimony existed in the form of tartar emetic, the amount of this represented by the sulphuret which I obtained from the stomach was a little more than a quarter of a grain (0·279).

Contents of Intestines.—The whole contents were evaporated at a gentle heat on the water bath, and a dry residue obtained, which weighed four hundred and thirty grains. Ten grains of this residue, on being subjected to Reinsch's process, yielded a characteristic deposit of antimony. To determine in what form this antimony existed, other ten grains were treated with distilled water, the solution filtered, and the fluid subjected to Reinsch's process. A characteristic antimonial deposit was obtained, thus proving that this metal was present in a soluble form. There are only two soluble forms of antimony met with in commerce. One of these, the chloride, is a dark-coloured, acid, corrosive fluid, totally unsuited for internal administration. The other is what is known scientifically as tartarised antimony, and popularly as tartar emetic, a colourless substance possessed of comparatively little taste, and in daily use as a medicinal agent. I have no doubt that it was in this last form that the antimony had been taken which I found in the alimentary canal of Mrs Taylor. I endeavoured to determine, by the process formerly mentioned, the amount of antimony in the contents of the intestines, and for this purpose one hundred grains of the dried residue were boiled with hydrochloric acid and copper foil. The amount of foil coated was one and a-half square inches, but the deposit was too small to enable me with confidence to make it the subject of a quantitative determination.

A piece of the coated copper, half-an-inch square, was heated in a tube to ascertain the presence or absence of arsenic, which occasionally occurs as an impurity in tartar emetic, but none was found.

The Blood.—Of this, six and a-half ounces were obtained at the *post-mortem* examination. One ounce was subjected to Reinsch's process, and a characteristic antimonial deposit was obtained.

The Liver.—This organ weighed two pounds six and a-half ounces. Two hundred and twenty grains were subjected to Reinsch's process, and two pieces of copper foil were coated with a characteristic deposit of antimony. One of these was made use of to confirm, though this was not necessary, the fact, that the deposit on it was antimony. For this purpose it was, by the process already described, converted into sulphuret, which again was dissolved in strong hydrochloric acid. The solution thus obtained became milky on the addition of water, and on being a second time exposed to sulphuretted hydrogen gas again yielded the orange-coloured sulphuret. These reactions are conclusive as to the deposit on the foil being antimony. I determined the amount of antimony in the liver. For this purpose I operated upon a thousand grains by the method already described, and obtained a quantity of sulphuret, indicating that the liver contained rather more than one grain and a tenth (1·151 grains) of tartar emetic. I also examined the other solid organs and tissues removed from Mrs Taylor's body, in each case following Reinsch's method, and in each case obtaining on the copper a characteristic antimonial deposit. I thus found that there was more or less of antimony present in the muscular substance of the heart, the spleen, the kidney, the coats of the stomach, the coats of the rectum, the uterus, and the brain.

Lastly, As Mrs Taylor's body had been exhumed, I thought it my duty to examine some of the earth in which it had been interred, although this was superfluous, from the facts that the soil of the cemetery was dry and the coffin entire. For this purpose I boiled eight ounces of the earth in water, filtered and concentrated the decoction, and subjected it to Reinsch's process, but it was found not to contain a trace of soluble antimony, and was therefore incapable of impregnating with this metal any body buried in it.

Cross-examined by Mr A. R. Clark—I understand that the first experiment you made was the experiment made upon the urine? Yes. When you obtained unmistakable evidence of the presence of antimony, by what process did you arrive at the conclusion? By performing Reinsch's process, and getting the characteristic violet deposit upon the copper. You did not carry it further? No. That is the way you obtained unmistakable evidence of the presence of antimony? Yes. In your opinion as a chemist is that conclusive proof of the presence of antimony? I should not consider a case thoroughly worked out on that alone, but as a trial experiment, to my mind it was quite unmistakable. Is it unmistakable? I think so. Being unmistakable, is there any necessity of going further? It is better, I think, in every case to carry assurance to the minds of other people by adding a further corroborative test. I understand that in your opinion the characteristic deposit upon the copper is conclusive of the presence of antimony? Yes; quite satisfactory to my mind. I understand that Reinsch's process consists in producing upon the copper foil a certain coloured deposit? Yes. That is the beginning and the end of the process? Yes; properly speaking. That deposit which you procured upon the copper may be subsequently tested in other ways, but that is not an essential part of Reinsch's process? No. But I understand you proceeded so far as to get this deposit on the copper by Reinsch's test, which you held to afford unmistakable evidence of antimony? Yes, in the urine. After you had done so you had to leave for London, and the preparatory work was done by Drs Gamgee and Littlejohn. Were the rest of the experiments conducted by yourself? Yes. The whole of them? Yes. From the beginning to the end? Yes. You performed the experiments upon the contents of the intestines with a view to enable you to determine the quantity of antimony? Yes. The result was that you found a quantity so small that you could not determine it by weight? Yes; by that particular process. The exact quantity in the intestines was so small that you could not make it out? I could not make it out as a quantity. I could not weigh it satisfactorily. In these intestines what did you operate upon? Upon the remains of the fluid that had been prepared in my absence by Dr Gamgee and Dr Littlejohn. Upon nothing else? Nothing else. Only upon the solution which Dr Gamgee gave you? Yes. Upon a portion of it? Yes. Now, I should like you to tell me whether you handed any portion of the solution to Dr Penny? None of the solution. Did you hand any part of the intestines to Dr Penny? Yes; some of the dried residue. You yourself did not know how the solution was prepared, or in what way the previous preparatory process had been carried through of preparing it? I was merely informed that they had followed the instructions which I had given when I went away. Would you tell me, referring to your report, what was the amount of antimony that you found in the liver? (After referring to report.) A quarter of a grain to the thousand grains, corresponding to tartar of emetic. But of sulphuret of antimony? ·1234 of a thousand grains. In making these experiments you did not find any traces of mercury? I did not; not at the time.

Solicitor-General—You gave to Dr Penny a variety of articles that were taken from the body of Mrs Pritchard, and also from the body of Mrs Taylor? Yes. Just be kind enough to tell us what you handed to him from Mrs Pritchard's body. Yes; a note made at the time by myself contains a short record of the proceedings. I delivered to Dr Penny at the University, from the body of Mrs Pritchard—(1) a portion of the rectum, (2) the piloric half of the stomach, (3) about half a kidney, (4) a portion (half) of the spleen, (5) a portion of the heart, (6) a portion of the brain, (7) 255 grains of dried contents of intestines. 225 or 255? Well, I am not very distinct about that. You gave him upwards of 200 grains? Yes. Then a portion of liver, and a portion of blood. In glass bottles? Yes; all the things were either in jars or bottles. You handed them over to Dr Penny in your laboratory at the University? Yes. Of Mrs Taylor's body you delivered to Dr Penny what articles? First, a portion of liver; second, a portion of heart; then, one kidney; then, 100 grains of dried contents of intestines; about one-half of the stomach; a portion of the rectum; and a portion of the blood. I believe you found no mercury in your examination of the contents of the intestines? No. You were requested subsequently to make an examination of a part of the residue of the contents of the intestines of Mrs Pritchard? Yes. When was that? Last week. What I operated upon were the remains after the process that had been conducted by Dr Gamgee and Dr Littlejohn in my absence, and which had remained locked up.

Lord Justice-Clerk—Tell me what you made an examination of? It was the solid residue that had remained after the tartaric acid fluid had been filtered through.

Solicitor-General—And with what result? I determined the presence of mercury, and found a considerable quantity of antimony remaining in it. Just give us as accurately as you can the result, and state how much antimony was found? I got a clear fluid by operating upon that residue with chlorate of potash and hydrochloric acid; and then passing sulphuretted hydrogen, I got a precipitate of a dirty orange colour, which was collected, washed, and boiled in strong hydrochloric acid. The yellow colour disappeared, and the precipitate became black. The hydrocloric solution was then mixed with water and tartaric acid, and it gave an orange precipitate which, when collected and weighed, amounted to 0·082, equal on the whole to 1·265 of sulphuret of antimony. Is that one grain and 265 decimal parts of a grain you mean? Yes. That is about a grain and a quarter is it not? Yes; rather more.

Lord Justice-Clerk—In what quantity of solid residue? In the whole that remained.

Solicitor-General—What would be the weight of it? It would be impossible to estimate the weight, because it had been in water, and had then been kept in a jar. It was not a thing to be weighed. In short, it was more antimony than you found in the contents of the intestines after the precipitate obtained by Dr Littlejohn and Dr Gamgee? Quite so. Dr Littlejohn and Dr Gamgee treated the solid residue of one-half of the contents of the intestines, in my absence. They filtered the clear tartaric acid, and the result is given in my first report. The solid matter of that not dissolved by the tartaric acid was kept on the filter. It was that that was operated upon, and therefore it was the solid residue of the one-half of the intestines, minus, of course, what had been dissolved by the tartaric acid. Then it was so much antimony which their process had not extracted? Yes.

Lord Justice-Clerk—It was about a grain and a quarter? Yes; a grain and a quarter of sulphuret. And what is that in tartar emetic? It is equal to 2·56 of tartar emetic.

Solicitor General—That is rather more than two and a-half of tartar emetic? Yes, rather more than two and a-half. Now, you have spoken of the precipitate you obtained becoming black? Yes. What did that indicate? It indicated the presence of sulphuret of mercury. Did you make a quantitative analysis to determine the amount? Yes. How much mercury did you find? It was 0.0509 grains—500 parts of a grain—the twentieth of a grain.

Lord Justice-Clerk—That was mercury—in what form? I cannot tell in what form.

Solicitor-General—Did you estimate the total quantity of tartar emetic contained in the whole of the intestines from what you recovered? I made a corroborative experiment along with that which I have just narrated on a little fresh portion of the dried contents. I took fifty grains of matter that had never been operated upon by any person before—what had been got by simply evaporating to dryness. I worked by the process of chlorate of potash as before, and I got 0·138 of sulphuret of antimony, corresponding to 0·280 of tartar emetic. And what was the weight of the whole dried contents of the intestines? 1020 grains generally.

Lord Justice-Clerk—So that the whole tartar emetic was? In the whole of the contents of the intestines it would be 5·712.

Solicitor-General—What do you mean by the contents of the intestines? That which had originally been got out of the intestinal canal from the stomach down to the rectum, and which had been evaporated to dryness as the first stage of the proceedings.

Cross-examined by Mr Clark—Did you find any mercury in making that last experiment? I did. What was the amount? The amount in the experiment with the fifty grains of sulphuret of mercury was 0·0308 grains—300 parts of a grain. In conducting your original experiments, did you carry any of them further than the mere obtaining the deposit on the foil? Yes; I boiled the copper foil in potash, so as to get the sulphuret of antimony. In all cases? No. Speaking of Mrs Pritchard's body, in what cases? It was partly on the tartaric acid solution. What do you mean by partly? That process was followed out of testing the antimony by means of the solution in potash, both with the contents of the intestines and with the liver. In the other cases you rested satisfied with obtaining the deposit on the copper? I think in all the other cases. In making these experiments which you have referred to upon the bed-clothes, and so on, did you carry your test further than the coloured deposit? No. In the case of the examination of Mrs Taylor, did you proceed to the close of the experiments, or did you rest satisfied with the coloured deposit? I carried out the experiments in regard to the contents of the intestines and the liver? In the other cases you did not? No.

Dr Frederick Penny—Solicitor-General—You are Professor of Chemistry in the Andersonian University of Glasgow? Yes. You have, I believe, given much attention to chemistry for many years? I have. Including great attention to the subject of poisons? Yes. You received from Professor Maclagan of Edinburgh the things which you heard mentioned in the witness-box a little ago? I did; on the 10th April last. You made a chemical analysis of these? I did. Dr Penny then read the following report:—

Report of Analysis in the Case of the Death of Mrs Pritchard.

"Andersonian University, Glasgow, *9th May* 1865.

"On Monday, the 10th of April last, I received from Dr Douglas Maclagan, at his laboratory in Edinburgh, the following articles, all of which were certified to have been taken from the body of Mrs Pritchard:—

"No. 1. Pyloric half of stomach.
 " 2. Nearly half of kidney.
 " 3. Portion of rectum.
 " 4. Portion of spleen.
 (These four articles were contained in a stoneware jar.)
 " 5. Portion of liver in a glass jar.
 " 6. Portion of brain in a glass jar.
 " 7. Portion of heart in a glass bottle.
 " 8. Portion of blood in a glass bottle.
 " 9. 225 grains of dried contents of intestines in a glass bottle.

"The several vessels containing these articles were securely closed, and duly labelled. I brought them direct to Glasgow on the day referred to, and, in accordance with instructions from the Crown-Agent, Edinburgh, I have, at my own laboratory, carefully analysed and chemically examined each and all of the said articles, for the purpose of ascertaining whether they contained any poisonous substance.

Dried Contents of Intestines.—The investigation was commenced with the contents of the intestines. From the information which I received, my attention was particularly directed to the detection of antimony; but, deeming it desirable to search for the presence of other metallic poisons, I subjected a portion of the said contents to the usual course of qualitative analysis for the detection of various metals of a poisonous nature. The results of this exhaustive examination gave distinct indications of the presence of antimony and mercury. For the purpose of establishing unequivocally the presence of these metals, and at the same time of estimating their quantities respectively, the following experiments were then carried out:—A known quantity of the said contents was dissolved with the usual precautions in hydrochloric acid, with the addition of chlorate of potash, and the solution being properly diluted with water, was subjected to the action of sulphureted hydrogen gas. An abundant black precipitate was obtained, which, by proper treatment, was separated into sulphide of antimony and sulphide of mercury. The sulphide of antimony, which was obtained of a fine orange-red colour, was washed, dried, and weighed. Its weight corresponded to a quantity of metallic antimony equal to 2·1 grains in one thousand parts of the dried contents of the intestines. The same sulphide was found to be readily soluble in sulphide of ammonium, and also in hydrochloric acid, and the acid solution, when poured into water, gave a white precipitate, and when boiled with copper-ribbon, deposited a violet-coloured coating on the surface of the copper. The coated copper, on being heated in a glass tube, gave no distinct crystalline sublimate. All these results are eminently characteristic of sulphide of antimony when thus treated. The sulphide of mercury was black; it was dissolved in nitric and hydrochloric acids, and the solution, being appropriately prepared, was treated with chloride of tin. A precipitate of metallic mercury was obtained, which, after being suitably washed and dried, was found to correspond to three grains in one thousand grains of the dried contents. A portion of this precipitate, on being heated in a dry glass tube, gave a sublimate of mercury in brilliant and mirror-like globules. Another portion was dissolved in nitric and hydrochloric acids, and the solution, after the removal of the excess of acid, was tested with caustic, potash, ammonia, and iodide of potassium, and with other re-agents and methods for the detection of mercury. In every case the peculiar reaction of that metal was satisfactorily produced. In order to corroborate the results of the foregoing experiments, another portion of the said contents of the intestines was subjected to Reinsch's process, and this was supplemented by Marsh's process. By the former process copper-foil was coated with a deposit which presented the peculiar violet colour and the general appearance of metallic antimony; and, by continuing the process till the copper foil ceased to be coated and the liquid was exhausted of separable matter, pieces of the copper foil were obtained with a grey coating, which, on being rubbed, became silvery and lustrous, like metallic mercury when similarly deposited. The coated copper was then digested in an aqueous solution of pure potash, and after being well washed and dried, it was cautiously heated in a small tube. A sublimate of metallic mercury in minute lustrous globules was obtained; and this sublimate, when dissolved in the proper acids, yielded with the well-known tests—the chemical reactions of metallic mercury. The potash solution from the coated copper was then treated in the usual manner for the separation of antimony in the form of the orange-red sulphide, which, when collected and weighed, was found to correspond very closely with the proportion obtained by the process previously described. The sulphide of antimony was soluble in sulphide of ammonium and in hydrochloric acid. The solution in hydrochloric acid gave a white precipitate when poured into water, and on being subjected to Marsh's process, deposited on a porcelain slab the characteristic stains of metallic antimony. In another experiment, a portion of the said contents was distilled with concentrated hydrochloric acid, and antimony was detected in the distillate. With a view of ascertaining whether the antimony and mercury existed in a form soluble in water in the said contents of the intestines, a portion of these was macerated in distilled water, and the solution carefully tested for both metals. The presence of antimony was distinctly detected, but no mercury. The said contents were also examined by Stas's method for aconite, morphia, and other organic poisons, but not the slightest evidence of the presence of such poisons was obtained.

Stomach.—The stomach was analysed by the same methods as those applied to the dried contents of the intestines. It yielded antimony in appreciable proportions, but no mercury. The quantity of antimony obtained was equal to ·05 of a grain in one thousand parts. The stomach was also minutely examined for morphia and aconite, but not a trace of these substances was obtained.

Liver.—The liver was found to contain antimony, but no mercury. The proportion of antimony amounted to one-tenth of a grain in one thousand grains.

Spleen.—The spleen yielded antimony in about the same proportion as that found in the liver, and it also contained mercury in well-marked quantity.

Kidney.—The kidney yielded about the same proportion of antimony as the liver, and it was also found to contain an extremely minute trace of mercury.

Heart.—The heart yielded antimony in a proportion rather larger than that found in the liver. It also contained mercury in smaller quantity than the spleen.

Brain.—The brain contained antimony in less quantity than the liver, but it yielded no mercury.

Blood.—The blood contained a small quantity of antimony, and also a faint trace of mercury.

Rectum.—The rectum yielded antimony, but in less quantity than the liver. It afforded no indications of mercury.

Having deliberately considered the results of my experiments upon the articles subjected to analysis, I have arrived at the following conclusions:—

1st, That all the parts of the body examined by me contained antimony. 2d, That in the dried contents of the intestines the antimony was partly in a form soluble in water, and most likely in the state of tartar emetic or tartarised antimony. In the liver, kidney, and the other viscera, the antimony was deposited in a state insoluble in water. 3d, That the contents of the intestines contained the largest proportion of antimony, next the heart, then the liver, kidney, and spleen; less in the stomach; and the smallest quantity in the rectum, brain, and blood. Not knowing the total weight either of the contents of the intestines, or of the several organs here enumerated, I was unable to calculate the total quantity of antimony in these matters, either separately or conjoined. 4th, That the contents of the intestines, the spleen, the heart, the blood, and the kidney, contained mercury; but that none of this metal was present in the liver, stomach, rectum, and brain. That, in all these matters, the mercury was in a state insoluble in water; and this result is quite consistent with the known property of mercury to form insoluble combinations with animal substances, even though it had been taken or administered in a soluble form during life. 5th, That the largest quantity of mercury was contained in the contents of the intestines, next in the spleen and heart, and extremely minute traces in the blood and kidney. 6th, That the presence of antimony and mercury in the contents of the intestines, indicates that these metals were being passed from the deceased up to the time of death. 7th, That no other metallic poison was contained in the matter examined. 8th, That no aconite, morphia, or other vegetable poison, discoverable by chemical processes, was contained either in the contents of the intestines, or in the stomach. 9th, Not having detected any organic poison, either in the said contents of the intestines or in the stomach, it was not necessary to examine the other articles for such poisons, and more especially as the quantities of these matters received for analysis were too small to hold out any prospect of a successful result.

All this I certify on soul and conscience.

Glasgow, 9*th May* 1865. FREDERICK PENNY.

Solicitor-General—Is that a true report? It is. You also at the same time received from Dr Maclagan portions of the body of Mrs Taylor? Yes. And you made a similar analysis of these? Yes.

Dr Penny then read the following report:—

Report of Analysis in the Case of the Death of Mrs Taylor.

ANDERSONIAN UNIVERSITY, GLASGOW, *9th May* 1865.

On the same day and occasion that I received the articles in the case of the death of Mrs Pritchard, Dr Douglas Maclagan delivered to me the following articles, certified to have been taken from the body of Mrs Taylor:—1. Portion of liver in stoneware jar; 2. Portion of stomach in glass bottle; 3. Portion of heart in glass bottle; 4. One kidney in glass bottle; 5. Portion of rectum in glass bottle; 6. Portion of blood in glass bottle; 7. 100 grains of dried contents of intestines.

The vessels containing these articles were securely closed and duly labelled, and were, on the day referred to, brought by me direct to Glasgow.

I have subjected all the articles above enumerated to a course of analysis and chemical examination similar to that applied to the articles in the case of Mrs Pritchard. The following were the results obtained:—

Liver.—In the liver the presence of antimony was unequivocally detected, and a quantitative estimation gave ·047 of a grain in 1000 grains of this organ. A careful analysis was also made for the presence of mercury, but not the slightest trace was detected.

Stomach.—The stomach yielded about the same proportion of antimony as that found in the liver. No mercury was detected. The stomach was also minutely examined by Stas's process for aconite and morphia, but not a trace of these poisonous alkaloids was obtained.

Heart.—The heart was found to contain antimony in less proportion than the liver. It yielded no mercury.

Kidney.—The kidney yielded about the same quantity of antimony as the heart. It gave a marked quantity of mercury.

Rectum.—The rectum gave antimony, but no mercury.

Blood.—In the blood, antimony was detected in rather larger proportion than in the heart. No mercury was detected.

Dried Contents of Intestines.—In the dried contents of the intestines, antimony was found to the extent of ·583 parts in 1000 parts by weight. It was partly present in a form soluble in water. No mercury was detected. The said contents were also carefully analysed for aconite and morphia, but no evidence of the presence of these poisons was obtained.

From a careful consideration of the results of the analysis and examination of the above-named articles, I am clearly of opinion that they are conclusive in showing:—1st, That all the articles subjected to analysis contained antimony. 2d, That the dried contents of the intestines contained the largest proportion of antimony; next, the liver and stomach; then the blood, and in less quantity in the heart, kidney, and rectum. 3d, That part of the antimony in the contents of the intestines is in a form soluble in water. 4th, That the kidney was the only article in which mercury was detected. 5th, That neither the stomach nor the contents of the intestines contained aconite or morphia in quantity sufficient to be detected by known chemical processes. 6th, That the articles subjected to analysis contained no other metallic poison than antimony and mercury as reported above.

To the truth of this report I hereby certify on soul and conscience.

GLASGOW, *9th May* 1865. FREDERICK PENNY.

Solicitor-General—Now, that is a true report? It is. You also made a report on certain articles which were delivered to you by Mr M'Call, Superintendent of Police? Yes.

Dr Penny then read the following report:—

Report of Analysis of certain Articles referred to in the case of Dr Pritchard.

ANDERSONIAN UNIVERSITY, GLASGOW, *17th May* 1865.

On Thursday, the 13th of April last, Alexander M'Call, Superintendent of Police, delivered to me, at my laboratory, the following productions, having sealed labels attached, referring to the case of Dr Pritchard:—A glass bottle, labelled "Batley's Sedative Solution," [B.] A bundle of seven small paper packages [C.] A quart wine bottle, containing ginger wine, [D.] A small glass vial, containing a white powder, [E.] Three small vials, two corks, and one stopper, securely tied together, [F.] Six small vials and six corks, attached with string, [I.] On the same day and occasion, John Murray delivered to me a paper package, having labels attached, marked A, and containing tapioca. On Friday the 21st April last, Alexander M'Call delivered to me a small glass phial, with label attached, marked G, and also a piece of cheese, marked H. On Thursday the 11th inst., John Murray delivered to me a paper package, with label attached, marked K, and containing tapioca. In accordance with instructions received from John Gemmel, Esq., Procurator-Fiscal, I have made a careful analysis and chemical examination of the contents of the several productions above enumerated. My experiments and investigations gave the following results, which, for the facility of reference, are reported in alphabetical order :—This paper package [A] contained 2850 grains of tapioca. The presence of antimony, in the form of tartarised antimony, was unequivocally detected. Its amount was found to be equal to 4·62 grains in the pound of tapioca. Not a trace of mercury was detected. This bottle [B] contained one ounce and five drachms of a dark brown liquid, having the odour and general appearance of Batley's Solution of opium. It was found to contain an appreciable quantity of antimony in a soluble form. The amount was equal to 1·5 grain per fluid ounce of the liquid. It contained no mercury. (I am at present engaged in examining it for other substances.) The seven paper packages [C] comprised in this production were marked No. 1 to No. 7 inclusive. No. 1 contained a small lump of crystallised nitrate of silver, weighing 16·5 grains. It contained no antimony. No. 2 contained 132 grains of cummin seed in powder. Neither antimony nor mercury was found in it. No. 3 contained 143 grains of sugar of lead. Nothing extraneous was detected. No. 4. The contents of this package consisted of a mixture of mercury and chalk, weighing together 6·5 grains, and it was evidently the medicinal preparation called "Hydrargyrum c. Creta." No antimony was found in it. No. 5 contained a lump of opium, weighing 110 grains. No. 6 contained 13·5 grains of morphia, contaminated with a small quantity of nitrate of silver, which, from the appearance of the paper package, had manifestly enfiltered accidentally from without. No. 7 contained 1350 grains of a white, gritty, crystalline powder, which was found to have all the physical and chemical properties of sugar of milk. It was carefully tested for mercury, antimony, and other substances, but the results were entirely negative. This bottle [D] contained 18 fluid ounces of ginger wine. No antimony or mercury was detected. This phial [E] contained 3·5 grains of a white powder, which was found by analysis to be tartarised antimony. The three phials [F] included in this production were labelled respectively 1, 2, and 3. No. 1 contained one ounce and three drachms of tincture of conium. No 2 contained five drops of the same tincture. No. 3 contained two and one-half drachms of the same preparation. This phial [G] contained nine drachms and a-half of a light yellow-coloured liquid, having the taste and odour of cinnamon, and consisting of a mixture of medicinal substances. It contained no antimony and no mercury. This cheese [H] was tested for antimony and mercury, but no evidence of the presence of these metals was obtained. This production [I] included six small phials, which were found to contain as follows :—No. 1. Four drops of tincture of aconite; No. 2. Twelve drops of the same tincture. No. 3. Thirty drops of the tincture of conium. No. 4. Fourteen drops of the tincture of conium. No. 5. Empty. No. 6. Nine drops of the tincture of digitalis. This paper package [K] contained 1695 grains of tapioca. Not the least trace of either antimony or mercury was detected in this tapioca. —All this I certify on soul and conscience. FREDERICK PENNY.

17th May 1865.

Solicitor-General—On the 15th May you received some other articles from Mr M'Call? I did. And you prepared a report regarding them? I did. The following was the report:—

Report of Analysis of certain Articles referring to the Case of Dr Pritchard.

ANDERSONIAN, GLASGOW, *May* 19, 1865.

This is to certify that I have subjected to careful analysis and chemical examination the following articles, which were delivered to me on the 15th inst. by Alexander M'Call :—No. 1. A brownish-coloured and turbid liquid, measuring three fluid ounces, contained in a glass bottle, labelled chloroform. It was tested for antimony and mercury, but not a trace of either metal was detected. It contained no aconite. No. 2. A white crystalline powder, contained in a small cylindrical wooden box, with screw cover. It weighed 15·5 grains, and was found to consist of a mixture of tartarised antimony and arsenious acid (that is, the common poison of arsenic) in nearly equal proportions by weight. No. 3. About ten drops of colourless liquid, contained in a quart wine bottle. It was found to be an aqueous solution of corrosive sublimate. No. 4. (A.) A white powder, contained in a circular red pasteboard box. It weighed 5 grains, and was found to be calomel. No. 4. (B.) A white powder, weighing 35 grains, contained in a green pasteboard box. It was found to be tartarised antimony. All the productions containing the articles subjected to analysis were securely closed, and had sealed labels attached.

FREDERICK PENNY.

Solicitor-General—That is a true report? It is. In your report about the bottle containing a dark brown liquid having the odour and general appearance of Batley's Solution of opium, you found an appreciable quantity of antimony in a soluble form? I did. And you say in that report that you were at that time engaged in examining it for other substances? Yes. Did you, in fact, complete your examination for other substances to the best of your judgment and ability? I did. What did you look for in particular? I looked for mercury and other metals. I searched for aconite, and also for conium. Did you find any of these? I found aconite. How do you proceed in order to search for aconite in another substance; is it by chemical or other processes? Chiefly by the taste of the extract obtained by evaporation, and by its physiological action upon small animals. Just explain to us as distinctly as you can how you proceeded with this fluid in order to determine whether aconite was present in it or not? A portion of it was evaporated to dryness, and the extract thus obtained was very carefully tasted, or its effects upon the tongue and upon the lips ascertained by applying it to them. And what were the effects? Tingling and a benumbing sensation. Characteristic of aconite? Yes. Another process was also carried out with the extract which remained after the evaporation. To another portion of the extract dissolved in water ammonia was added, and a precipitate was separated and examined in the same way, after being dissolved in diluted hydrochloric acid. The benumbing and tingling sensation produced by that precipitate was very slight. But the ammoniacal liquid, after the separation of the precipitate, was treated with hydrochloric acid and evaporated, and the sensation produced by this residue was very strong and distinct. With a view to ascertain the character of aconite when mixed with Batley, I purposely mixed known quantities of tincture of aconite with Batley's Solution, treating the mixtures in the same way. I took mixtures from 5 per cent. to 40 per cent. What tincture did you mix? Fleming's tincture. That is a strong tincture? Yes; a strong tincture. The results were precisely similar, but when the proportion was equal to 10 per cent., the sensation was by no means so strong. The addition of Fleming's tincture of aconite to genuine Batley to the extent of 10 per cent. of the mixture gave a sensation very much stronger than the liquid in this bottle. But the sensations were the same, although that one produced by Batley, with 10 per cent. of Fleming's tincture in it, was the stronger of the two? Precisely so. I draw the conclusion that in this solution there was more than 5 per cent., but less than 10 per cent. The sensation of benumbing and tingling is peculiarly characteristic of aconite? Yes. And well known to be so? Yes. You are acquainted with Batley's Solution? I am. I believe you procured some pure specimens of it, and treated it without mixture of any kind in the same way as the contents of that bottle? I purchased Batley's Solution at several establishments in Glasgow, and also in London. I examined all these samples, and I found that in no case were such sensations produced by the extract obtained as described. Did you buy some of it —I mean of the genuine Batley of Murdoch Brothers of Union Street, Glasgow? Sauchiehall Street. Did you find any trace of the presence of antimony in the genuine Batley? None. Your examination, I suppose, satisfied you that it contained neither antimony nor aconite? It did. [Bottle produced.] And your examination of the contents of that bottle satisfied you that it contained both antimony and aconite? Yes. You made some farther experiments with the contents of the bottle upon rabbits, I believe? I made in all about twenty-five experiments upon rabbits.

Lord Justice-Clerk—With the extract obtained from the bottle? And from genuine Batley and various mixtures.

Solicitor-General—Just take genuine Batley first. Did it kill any rabbits or not? Genuine Batley did not kill the rabbits with a dose even equal to fifty grains. The contents of the bottle—what effect did they produce? According to the dose. What dose killed? 40 grain drops. How did you administer it? By injection under the skin of the back, between the skin and muscles. You experimented with the contents of that bottle on the rabbits in the precise way that you did with genuine Batley? Precisely. Did genuine Batley, when injected to any extent into the rabbit, deprive it of life? I have already said that genuine Batley did not kill in any case.

Lord Justice-Clerk—To what extent did you try it? To the extent of fifty grains.

Solicitor-General—You did not try it any higher than that? No. Did you experiment in the same way with genuine Batley to which you had added Fleming's Tincture of Aconite? I did. Tell us the result of that? I made in all about ten experiments with the genuine Batley mixed with Fleming's Tincture. In different proportions? Yes. And what extent of Fleming's Tincture produced the same effect as the contents of the bottle? I will tell you the result of two sets of experiments. In one set I injected a mixture of Batley into three young rabbits, and in a third into full-grown rabbits. In the first set of experiments with young rabbits, I injected ten grains of genuine Batley's Solution; in the second experiment with a young rabbit, I injected ten grains of this Batley; and in the third experiment, I injected a mixture composed of nine grains of genuine Batley, and one grain of Fleming's Tincture of aconite. With the old rabbits, I proceeded in a similar manner, using forty grains instead of ten grains as with the young rabbits—first, with genuine Batley; and second, with the mixture; and third, with genuine Batley mixed with aconite. The general result was, that genuine Batley did not kill? It did not kill. Well, and the contents of the bottle? The following were the results:—The symptoms manifested by the rabbits, both old and young, subjected to the action of genuine Batley, were simple in character and few in number, and were not materially altered by variation of dose. The animal soon assumed a prone position, resting on belly and chest, and the head invariably resting on the ground. The fore legs were either sprawling or gathered under the body, the hind legs always extended sideways; the eyes remained open, and the pupils were natural and not contracted; the breathing was invariably gentle; no cries were uttered, and no convulsions or spasms of the body were apparent. There was a complete condition of inanity, and with the exception of the open state of the eyes, the animal seemed to be in a state of profound sleep. There was no indication of spasmodic movement; but when aroused or urged to motion, the movements were performed in a crawling tortoise-like manner. In this state the animal remained for several hours, and then gradually recovered. The effects produced by the mixture of genuine Batley with aconite were as follow, and presented a striking contrast to the symptoms resulting from pure Batley:—Very soon after the injection, the animal became restless and uneasy, and then began to crouch, resting on its flank, with the hind legs extended laterally, and keeping its head erect. It next assumed a sitting posture in an attitude of watchful expectancy, and commenced to twitch its lips and move its jaws as if chewing. Suddenly it staggers, rolls over, and quickly regains its feet. Saliva begins to flow from the mouth, and soon after piteous and peculiar choking cries are emitted. The head is retracted, and the breathing is painfully laborious. Convulsions now set in, followed by intervals during which the limbs are quite relaxed, and the animal lies helpless on its side. Frantic leaps are now frequently taken, accompanied by movements of a paralytic character. A state of utter prostration also occurs, variable in duration; and then a strong convulsion comes on, during which, or immediately after, the animal expires, the limbs becoming instantly relaxed. Then as to the results produced by this Batley, the symptoms exhibited by the rabbits subjected to this liquid corresponded in every important respect with the effects produced by the above mixture, and were so clearly similar that it was impossible to detect any essential difference in them. In the case of the small rabbits, the experiments were made at the same time, but, without knowing beforehand, it would not have been possible to distinguish the animal under the influence of this Batley from the one under the influence of the mixture of Batley and aconite. These results leave no doubt on my mind—joined with the taste and sensation—that that Batley contained aconite. All the other experiments, which were numerous and varied, confirmed these results.

The Solicitor-General—That bottle was about half-full, I think, when you got it? It contained 1 oz. 5 drachms. What, according to your judgment, as the result of your examination, was the whole quantity of aconite in that amount of liquid? Between five and ten per cent.

Cross-examined by Mr Clark—You said the bottle was half-full when you got it? It contained 1 oz. 5 drachms. Let me see how high that would come upon the label? I could not tell that. Would it go up half-way to the label? No; it would not come to it.

Lord Justice-Clerk—Aconite is a vegetable poison, I understand? Yes. What is the popular name of it? Monkshood. Were the experiments with the rabbits you spoke of made with the Batley's Solution purchased by yourself from Murdoch Brothers? They were made with the Battley purchased by myself from the Apothecaries' Hall, or from other places. That is not from Murdoch Brothers? No. Batley's Sedative Solution is a preparation of opium, I believe? It is. If you pursue Reinsch's test for the detection of antimony, and obtain, in the course of that process, a deposit upon copper foil, is that deposit conclusive of the presence of antimony? It would not be to my mind. Whatever the deposit might be? Whatever the deposit might be. Why is that so? Because other matters are liable to give a deposit similar in appearance to the eye. The only test that you have for antimony, when you pursue Reinsch's process to the extent of getting a deposit on the wire, is the colour that is seen on the foil? Yes; the violet colour on the copper. But that is not conclusive of antimony, because the same colour may be produced by other substances? It may. What are these substances—give us an example of them? Oily matters. Animal oils? Or vegetable oils; animal oils particularly. Anything else? No; nothing occurs to me at this moment.

Solicitor-General—[Shown No. 142.] That is a small phial containing a dark-coloured liquid? It is. When was that delivered to you? On the 16th May 1865. By whom? By John M'Millan, assistant to Murdoch Brothers. And did you make an analysis of that? I did. And was it similar to the Batley's which you purchased yourself? In every respect.

Lord Justice-Clerk—You analysed it, did you? I did.

Solicitor-General—That contained no antimony and no aconite? None. [Shown No. 143.] That is a bottle containing Batley's Solution which you yourself purchased at Murdoch Brothers? Yes; it was purchased by myself. And have you analysed that? I did. And it was in no respect different from that which was in No. 142, brought to you by Mr Macmillan? It corresponded in every respect.

Lord Justice-Clerk—And with the genuine Batley which you purchased elsewhere? Yes. And with which you had made experiments on the rabbits? Yes.

Solicitor-General—From whom did you get that bottle No. 85, of which we have heard so much? On Thursday, 13th April, Alexander M'Call, Superintendent of Police, delivered it to me at my laboratory. Can you tell me in a general way how much liquid there was in it at the time? It was much below the lower edge of the label. Of course you mean the original label? Yes. Can you tell me how much the bottle will contain when full? The entire capacity of the bottle was 5¼ oz. The top red line on the left side marked at the time by myself, as shown me by one woman, indicates 2¾ oz.; and the lower red line on the right side marked at the time by myself, as shown by the other woman, is 2¼ oz. Do you know who these women were? No; I have seen them in Court. When I received it, it contained between 1½ and 1¾ oz. Did you send some of the contents of that bottle to Dr Maclagan? I did. Or give them? I did not give them; I sent them.

Lord Justice-Clerk—Did you put it into his own hands, or send them? I gave up possession of the bottle to the officer Murray.

Solicitor-General—That was after you were done with it? After I had completed all my experiments—last week. I have marked on this label the date when I gave it up, which was on the 20th of June.

Lord Justice-Clerk—Was there anything in the bottle then? Yes. How much? There mnst have been about a drachm.

Solicitor-General—Was it sealed up? Yes; and bore my seal. Did Dr Maclagan get it with the seal unbroken? Yes. There was nothing in the contents which you sent to him that was not in it when it was handed to him originally? No; it was precisely in the same condition. Did you happen to be present when Dr Maclagan broke the seal? No; I was present at the experiments made in the University here upon rabbits by Dr Maclagan, in presence of Dr Christison, Dr Littlejohn, and Dr Gamgee. These experiments were precisely similar to mine, and were made with the same result, except that death was more speedy from the larger dose given. These experiments were made with the mixture in the bottle, the genuine Batley, and the Batley to which the tincture of aconite had been added? Yes. And these experiments which you witnessed, being exactly the same as your own, confirmed the opinion which you expressed, that aconite was present in the bottle? Entirely so. With the exception of the antimony and the aconite which you detected, the contents of the bottle were, I presume, similar to the genuine Batley? I examined it for the leading constituents of opium, and I found them there. In fact, it would be correct to say that it differed from genuine Batley, so far as you could see, only in the presence of the antimony and the aconite? It did.

The medical witnesses were here asked to leave the court, as the examination of Dr Penny was now to be directed to matter of opinion.

Dr Penny was then asked to read the latter part of his report upon the cause of Mrs Pritchard's death, which embodied the conclusions at which he had arrived. Having done so, his examination was resumed by the Solicitor-General. You heard read by Dr Maclagan the report of the *post-mortem* examination of this lady's body? I did. And I believe you have had previously an opportunity of studying it? It had been put into my hands by the agent for the defence. But you had read it before? Yes. The result of that report is, that the *post-mortem* appearances exhibited nothing to account for death? That is the result of the report. You heard the evidence as to the symptoms exhibited by Mrs Pritchard from the time that she was taken ill after the New Year down to the time of her death? I did. Are these symptoms suggestive to you of the action of any poison with which you are acquainted? Witness—From study only? I mean from study. I understand you are a chemist, not a medical man? Witness—Purely a chemist. And you have studied the action of poison? I have. Do these symptoms indicate the action of any poison to you? They correspond with those of tartar emetic. That is the other name for tartarised antimony? Yes. Tartarised antimony is one of the forms, and the common form of antimony soluble in water? The best known form. You detected the presence of mercury by your chemical examination? I did. Did you hear anything in the evidence which accounted for that? Yes, I did. What was that? Those powders prescribed by Dr Paterson. Containing calomel? Yes, and *hydargium cum creta.* Assuming that such powders had been administered shortly before death, that would correspond with the traces of mercury which you found afterwards? It would—to the extent given. Supposing that antimony had been applied to Mrs Pritchard's neck in the month of October—externally, I mean—when she was complaining of the swelling of a gland in her neck, would that account for any of the results of your chemical analysis? I have no experience in that direction; I am not qualified to answer that question. You confined yourself to the fact that these substances were detected by chemical analysis, and to the opinion, as the result of your study on the subject of the symptoms attending the administration of such a poison? Yes. And I understand you to say that the symptoms throughout Mrs Pritchard's illness—I speak only of the time after Christmas down to her death—corresponded with the symptoms produced by the administration of antimony? So far as the scope of my experience goes from study, they did. You also heard the account of Mrs Taylor's illness. Do the symptoms spoken of by the witnesses who gave that account suggest the operation and action of any poison to your mind? Merely the vomiting—from antimony. There were other symptoms in the case of the old lady—the comatose state in which she was? I am not prepared to speak to that. In regard to Mrs Taylor's case, what were your conclusions as stated in your report? From a careful consideration of the results of the analysis of examination of the above-named articles, I am clearly of opinion that they are conclusive in showing—1st, That all the articles subjected to analysis contained antimony. 2d, That the dried contents of the intestines contained the largest proportion of antimony, next the liver and stomach; then the blood; and in less quantity in the heart, kidney, and rectum. 3d, That part of the antimony in the contents of the intestines is in a form soluble in water. 4th, That the kidney was the only article in which mercury was detected. 5th, That neither the stomach nor the contents of the intestines contained aconite or morphia in quantity sufficient to be detected by known chemical processes. 6th, That the articles subjected to analysis contained no other metallic poison than antimony and mercury, as reported above. Is that the opinion truly entertained by you as the result of your examination? It is. You say the same in the concluding portion of your report regarding Mrs Pritchard? These are my conclusions. Is there any other matter on which, as a chemist, you can give any other information from the evidence you have heard? You have stated all you are able to state in respect to either Mrs Pritchard or Mrs Taylor? To the best of my belief I have stated all I know. Nothing occurs to my mind beyond what I have stated.

Cross-examined by Mr Clark—Has aconite a bitter taste? No. Has antimony a burning taste? It has, after a time, a metallic taste. When it enters the mouth, has it a burning taste? Not so far as I have tasted it. What it may be when it goes down the throat in sufficient quantity to poison I don't know. (Laughter.)

Dr Douglas Maclagan recalled.—Examined by the Solicitor-General—Dr Maclagan read the portion of his chemical report embracing his conclusions as to the death of Mrs Pritchard. That is a true report? Yes. You are now better acquainted with the history of the case? Yes. You heard the account given in this place of the illness of Mrs Pritchard, the first time she was taken ill after returning from her father's at Christmas? Yes. I am referring to the part of the evidence which relates to the account of the illness after her return to Glasgow up to the time of her death. Does that account of the history of her illness suggest to you as a medical man the cause of her death? It suggests a confirmation of the opinion I had formed from my chemical and *post-mortem* examination. Do the symptoms which she exhibited indicate the administration of antimony at an early period of the illness? I think so. If I remember right, there was vomiting at a very early period of the illness—that was a characteristic symptom—and muscular depression. Sickness and vomiting, and muscular depression, are symptoms of the action of antimony. Were there any other symptoms exhibiting the action of antimony which struck you? There was irritation of the bowels and cramp of the extremities, which are symptoms of poisoning by antimony. These are all characteristic of that poison? Yes. Then is it according to your opinion, judging from these symptoms, that the administration of antimony commenced with the commencement of the illness after Christmas, and continued down to the time of her death? I think it is most probable.

The Lord Justice-Clerk—You mean the administration of antimony was going on? Yes; from time to time. Then you think the symptoms she exhibited were such in all respects as you would have expected on the supposition that antimony was administered to her all along? I think so. Does the history of the case, as you have heard it in the evidence, and particularly of the symptoms which were manifested, suggest to your mind, as a medical man, any other cause of death? I don't know any natural disease that I could very well say I think it was due to. There is no natural disease to which you can ascribe the death? No, my lord, there is not.

Solicitor-General—The *post-mortem* examination did not indicate any natural disease whatever? No; no natural disease that could account for her death. There was an arrested pulmonary disease that had existed years before; but that had nothing to do with her death obviously. The result of the chemical examination accounted for her death in a manner entirely in accordance with the symptoms? I think so. Suppose that antimony had been externally applied to her neck in October last, when she was plagued with the swelling of a gland in the neck, would that in any way account for her illness? If it was rubbed in to the extent of producing postules on the skin—assume that? Oh, no! I never saw antimony rubbed into the skin produce any of the constitutional effects of antimony. And that would not account for the result of your chemical examination, finding it in the stomach and other organs? Oh, no!

Lord Justice-Clerk—It would not account for the results of the chemical examination, nor, I suppose, for the symptoms exhibited between Christmas and the death? No.

Solicitor-General—Suppose that years ago—I cannot give you any time more nearly, but just take the statement as I have given it to you now—Mrs Pritchard applied antimony internally on one occasion, when she had a tendency to inflammation of the eyelids—suppose that this was years ago, and that she had not used it internally except on that one occasion—would that be in any way connected with the symptoms of her illness, or with her illness at all? No. It would have nothing to do with it? Oh, no! You heard Dr Paterson mention the powders which he had prescribed for her? Yes. That was in the beginning of March? Yes. And the powder contained mercury? Calomel and gray powder. Suppose these powders to have been administered, would they account for the mercury which was found by your chemical analysis? Certainly. Had that mercury, in your opinion, anything to do with causing death? I do not think that there was any evidence of its having caused death. Or having had any concern with the death? Not that I can think of. But the traces of mercury which you found were such as you would expect in a patient who died while such powders were in the course of being administered? Yes. Were these proper powders to administer? Well, it is quite a usual prescription—calomel and gray powder. I presume you mean were they a safe prescription, generally speaking. I am not asking your opinion on the particular case at which you were not present; but they are a safe and common prescription? Yes. Then nothing in the history of the case as you have heard it in the evidence occurs to throw any doubt upon the conclusion at which you arrived by your chemical analysis? I cannot say that anything has occurred. But everything therein tends to confirm it? Rather so. Not entirely so? Oh, yes; I should say decidedly so—that is the proper answer. The symptoms during the whole of her illness, and the result of the chemical analysis, are in harmony with each other, and both concur in pointing to antimony as the cause of death? I think so. Was there anything in the case to indicate to a medical man that she was labouring under gastric fever? No. Do you mean that a medical man of ordinary intelligence attending her during the illness which you have heard described would not have concluded that she was labouring under fever? I should think not. Is there anything in the account of her illness to suggest gastric fever or any other fever to your mind at all? No. Now, will you read the concluding part of your report respecting the case of Mrs Taylor? Dr Maclagan then read the conclusions stated in his report, as given above.

From the above experiments I am led to the following conclusions:—1. That Mrs Taylor had taken a considerable quantity of antimony in the form of tartar emetic. 2. That, having regard to the absence of any morbid appearances sufficient to account for death, and to the presence in the body of a considerable quantity of a substance known to be capable of destroying life, her death must be ascribed to the action of antimony. 3. That it is most likely that this was not taken in a single large dose. Had this been the case, I should have expected to have found some morbid appearances indicative of the irritant nature of the drug. It appears to me more probable, from the amount found in the body, that it must have been taken in a succession of doses, not great enough individually to produce local irritant effects, but amounting in the aggregate to a large quantity. It is right, however, to add that a single copious dose, not large enough to produce marked local effects, might give rise to fatal depression of the system in a woman aged seventy-one, whose heart was enlarged and somewhat dilated. 4. That, from the fact that antimony was found copiously in the liver, was readily detected in the blood, and existed to the amount of a quarter of a grain in the stomach, some at least of the tartar emetic had been taken, probably within a few hours before death. 5. That, from mere chemical investigations, I am unable to say over what length of time the administration of the antimony had extended, supposing it, as I believe, to have been taken in a succession of doses. This can be learned only from a consideration of the history of the case, with which I am unacquainted. Douglas Maclagan.

That is your conscientious opinion? Yes. You heard and attended to the evidence respecting Mrs Taylor also? Yes. What cause of death does that indicate to your mind ? I am inclined to think, from the account we have heard of the case, that there was something more than antimony at the last. Antimony there must have been, for you found it ? Yes. You were inclined to think that there must have been something more than antimony. By "inclined to think" do you mean to say that you have doubt or hesitation, or do you actually think it ? I do think it. What else ? I think some powerful depressing poison besides antimony. Such as ? The symptoms might be produced by aconite. Aconite is a narcotic ? It is a sedative rather; but it is commonly described as a narcotic in books. It does not always affect the brain by any means, which is the proper meaning of the word narcotic.

Lord Justice-Clerk—What are its effects ? Its effects are to lower the circulation especially, and produce a paralysed condition of the muscles. The fatal result, I think, is generally due to its effect upon the heart as a muscular organ.

Solicitor-General—Just mention the symptoms in Mrs Taylor's case which you think were such as aconite would have produced. I think her being found with her head fallen on her neck, and hardly observed to breathe, and her pulse almost if not absolutely imperceptible, and in the dozing torpid state in which she was——

Lord Justice-Clerk—Coma, I suppose ? I am not sure if it was coma; I rather think it was the torpid condition of the brain from the lowered circulation. All these you say are what ? Are such as would have resulted from aconite.

Solicitor-General—Are they such as you would expect to result from aconite ? Yes. In short, they are the symptoms produced by the action of aconite ? Yes; but aconite, like most poisons, varies a little in the symptoms it produces in different individuals. You heard the result of the analysis of the liquid in the Batley bottle by Dr Penny, and you yourself experimented with it upon rabbits ? Yes; we made one series of experiments. Do you corroborate what Dr Penny said about the result of his experiments ? Yes. Would the aconite and the antimony existing in the liquid account for the symptoms under which Mrs Taylor appeared to be labouring on the evening of the 24th and the morning of the 25th February ? That must depend upon the quantity which she took of the liquid. But taking what quantity, would you say ? What would represent over five or ten grains of the tincture of aconite contained in it would do it. I say over five, because that has been indicated as a safe quantity of Fleming's tincture to be given, though I do not think it safe. Assuming aconite to have been taken, you would expect to have found it upon the chemical analysis which you made ? I might not; these organic poisons are very often not found, though they are known to have been taken. You mean in cases where they are certainly known to have been taken ? Yes. You are referring to aconite ? Yes; but the major includes the minor. I refer to the whole class of alkaloids. Antimony passes pretty rapidly out of the system ? Yes, a good part of it passes pretty rapidly out of the system. In vomiting and purging ? In vomiting and purging, and by the urine. And in that way the patient is weakened, and ultimately destroyed ? Yes. Would the administration of opium in any way interfere with the symptoms exhibited by the person who had taken antimony ? So far that I think it is possible it might make the tendency to vomit less. And also interfere with its effects upon the bowels, I suppose ? Yes. But would it, even in conjunction with opium, exercise a pernicious influence on the patient ? Yes; the depressing effect upon the muscular tissue would remain. Have you ever known a patient under the influence of opium, aconite, and antimony at the same time ? No. But if these poisons—opium, aconite, and antimony—were administered so as to be operating at the same time, are the symptoms which Mrs Taylor exhibited such as your science would lead you to anticipate ? I think so, because the aconite, being the more powerful, would probably predominate. I infer from your *post-mortem* report—but I wish to know whether I am certainly right—that the *post-mortem* appearances were not such as to indicate apoplexy ? No. When a patient dies of apoplexy will a *post-mortem* examination indicate that disease ? In most cases, but not invariably. And all you can say, therefore, is, that they were not indicated by the appearances you saw. That is all. But that is not conclusive ? Not absolutely conclusive. By most cases you mean the large majority of cases ? Yes. Are the exceptions very rare ? I have not met in my own practice, where I had an opportunity of making a *post-mortem* examination, any case where I did not find indications of apoplexy. But there are accounts of such cases ? There are. Was there anything in the symptoms which she manifested during life shortly before her death, or at any time before her death, which indicated apoplexy ? Certainly not. Then taking these appearances before death and the *post-mortem* examination together, is the idea of apoplexy satisfactorily excluded in your judgment ? Yes.

Lord Justice-Clerk.—That is to say, you are satisfied she did not die of apoplexy ? Yes. Was there anything in her symptoms which, in your judgment, would have led any medical man to think of apoplexy ? Not if he heard the account given by Dr Paterson. I am not asking your opinion upon the accuracy of the evidence; but, assuming it to be correct, would any man, seeing what Dr Paterson described, think of apoplexy as the cause? If I had seen what Dr Paterson saw, I would not have concluded that it was apoplexy, and I do not think any other man would. That is what I mean. The purport of the question is, whether it is a thing about which there could have been any reasonable difference of opinion? Doctors do differ; and I wanted to know whether this was a matter about which there could be a difference of opinion among intelligent men? I don't think it. Did you taste the aconite in the bottle? I did. Did it produce the sensation which aconite produces? It did. You are acquainted with the tingling and benumbing sensation? Yes. You are not likely to mistake it? I think not. Did that, irrespective of the experiments on the rabbits, satisfy you that there was aconite there? I should certainly have inferred that without any experiment upon the rabbits. Without any doubt? Yes. And the experiments upon the rabbits only went to confirm that? Yes. Did you get that bottle brought to you by the officer with the seal unbroken? Yes, by J. Murray. It is broken now? I endeavoured to keep the seal as entire as possible. Has aconite any effect in paralysing a patient? It does produe paralysis of the muscles, and sometimes convulsions. You are acquainted with Batley's Solution? Yes. It is a very well-known medicine? Very well known. I presume it is taken for all the purposes for which opium is used? It is a form of opium. What is a common dose of it? Well, I believe it is stated by those who prepare it as being a third stronger than laudanum, but in practice I have not found it to be so. What would be a good dose for an old lady of seventy? I would not give so much, perhaps, to an old lady as to a strong man. The medium dose of laudanum is commonly stated to be twenty-five drops.

The Lord Justice-Clerk—That depends upon habit entirely, and upon the circumstances of the case? Yes. You would give the patient a little less of Batley than of laudanum—about twenty drops or so.

Solicitor-General—Generally speaking, it has the same effects as laudanum? Yes.

Cross-examined by Mr A. R. Clark—You saw no indications of poisoning by opium in Mrs Taylor's case? No precise indications. It did not appear as if she had taken any opium? I cannot say that she had not taken any, but I did not observe any symptoms which specially pointed to opium. Were the symptoms which you saw exclusively the symptoms of aconite, as you thought? Well, it is very difficult to say; but I think aconite was the leading feature in the final part of the case. Did the symptoms in the course of the illness, as described by Dr Paterson, not indicate poison by opium or laudanum at all? I think not.

Lord Justice-Clerk—You mean that you now think that they don't indicate poisoning by opium? Yes.

Mr Clark—Are they inconsistent with poisoning by opium? I do not know that they are inconsistent with her having had opium; but they are not consistent certainly with poisoning by opium, and with the ordinary symptoms. Then you could not say that she had not taken opium? Oh, certainly not. Only that the symptoms of aconite predominated? That is what I think. If she had taken opium alone, what would you have expected to find different from what you heard? I would have expected to have found the pulse slow and full, and probably the breathing laborious and stertorous. But though these were absent, you cannot say that opium was not taken? No; particularly if the person was accustomed to the use of opium. I think Dr Paterson said her breathing was laborious? I think not; my impression was that he stated her breathing was barely perceptible.

The Lord Justice-Clerk here read from the notes that he had taken of Dr Paterson's evidence, from which it appeared that that gentleman had used the expression that her breathing was laborious.

Mr Clark—It seems, then, that her breathing was laborious. What did that indicate? It indicated some narcotic poison. Keeping that symptom in view, what modification does that make upon your opinion? Not much, because of the condition of the pulse, which shows the action of aconite upon the heart. You say it does not make much modification; does it make any? I do not think it does. You indicated first that you understood it was easy, light breathing? I indicated that the breathing was very feeble, but there I was wrong. Therefore not laborious? Not in the common case. Is laborious breathing an indication of opium? It is an indication of many things besides opium. Did Dr Paterson not also say that the breathing became stertorous? I do not think so.

The Lord Justice-Clerk here read from his notes again, from which it appeared that Dr Paterson had used the word coma.

Mr Clark—You observed that Dr Paterson makes use of the word coma? Yes. Does that indicate opium? Yes. Not aconite? Not generally; but here it was more oppression than true coma. Then you think that Dr Paterson was not right when he described it as coma? Coma is used by many persons to describe insensibility. Did Dr Paterson use it scientifically? Probably. But you pointed to the absence of coma as indicative of poisoning by aconite? I spoke of her being in a torpid condition, which I think was connected with the weakened state of the circulation, not from fulness of the brain. Now, in regard to the detection of organic poisons, you say that aconite is one? Yes. And is is not easily detected by chemical analysis? It can be detected. By chemical analysis? Not by chemical tests. Opium is another vegetable poison? Yes. When it is given, it is absorbed into the system? Yes. And so a person may be poisoned by opium without any traces of it remaining in the system? In the stomach. But in the system? I have not been able to find any in the system, though I have made experiments for that purpose. A person may be poisoned by opium without any trace remaining in the stomach or system capable of being detected by chemical analysis? Certainly. Antimony of course is a mineral poison? Yes. And it is more easily detected? Yes. And known to be so? All mineral poisons are known to be so. A person cannot be poisoned with antimony without the antimony being capable of being detected in the system? I am not quite sure that I would be prepared to say that. I can only reason analogically, and I am not prepared to give in to that statement broadly; because I know that a person may be poisoned with arsenic without its being detected. Do you know any case in which there was poisoning by antimony without the antimony being found? I cannot recollect of any such case. There was a very large quantity of antimony found here in both cases? The quantity was considerable. But the expectation is that, if a person is poisoned by antimony, chemical analysis will detect the antimony? Yes. It is possible there may be an exception, but you have not yet known it? It is possible. The pupils of Mrs Taylor's eyes are mentioned as being contracted? Yes. Is that an indication of poison by opium? Yes; but it occurs in aconite too. Is it a characteristic of poisoning by aconite? It seems to have been observed in a considerable number of cases, but they vary a good deal in that respect. In short, I understand there is a question as to whether aconite does contract the pupils of the eyes? There is a question; but that seems to arise from people having observed the symptoms at different stages, and the probability is that contraction had been produced first, and then relaxation at the time all the muscular parts become relaxed—viz., at the time of death.

Lord Justice-Clerk—You said that anything over five grains of Fleming's tincture of aconite would satisfactorily account for all the symptoms exhibited by Mrs Taylor? I mean the fatal symptoms at the end of the case. Now, referring to bottle 85, how much of that liquid must she have taken in order to take equal to five grains of Fleming's tincture? If Dr Penny's estimate be correct—and as I only made one experiment myself, I am not entitled to speak from my own knowledge—if his estimate be correct, that it contained from 5 to 10—say 7 per cent., she would require to take 7, which is over 5 a little, and that would give her 100 drops. I used the word "grains," though we don't measure such fluids by grains, because Dr Penny used it in his estimate. It would be more correctly minims, which are measured drops. Must it be all taken at once to produce these effects? Aconite might be given in divided doses, and it might not prove fatal, though the same quantity was taken, because the depressing effect of one dose might have gone off before the second dose was given. Then you are speaking of a single dose? I am speaking of single doses.

Mr Clark—Aconite is applied externally in some cases, such as neuralgia? Yes. There is a liniment in the Pharmacopœia which is of about the same strength as Fleming's tincture.

Lord Justice-Clerk—Are 100 drops of Batley's Solution an unusual quantity for a person to take who has been in the habit of using it for a long time? No, my Lord; there are many opium-eaters who would not thank you for 100 drops. (A laugh.) I am speaking of a person who has been in the habit of taking it in moderation. Would 100 drops be too much for such a person? Oh! he could take 100 drops quite well, a person who was in the habit of using it. Would 100 drops be a large quantity? 100 drops would rather more than fill an average-sized tea-spoon.

Dr Henry Duncan Littlejohn—Solicitor-General—You are Surgeon of the Edinburgh Police? I am. And, in addition to your general practice, you have had considerable practice there? I have. You acted along with Professor Maclagan in making the *post-mortem* examination of these two ladies, Mrs Pritchard and Mrs Taylor? I did. And you signed the reports along with him? I did. And you concur in these reports as being true? I do. Now, take the case of Mrs Pritchard first. Does that report indicate in any way that the lady had been ill of gastric fever at the time of her death? It does not. Nothing to suggest that? Nothing to suggest it. You took no part in making the chemical analysis? I did not. But you have seen the report of that analysis? I have. And heard it read? I have. You have also heard the whole evidence in this trial? I have. Now, attending to the evidence respecting Mrs Pritchard's symptoms during her illness, from her return to Glasgow after Christmas, down to the time of her death, what in your opinion was the cause of her death? Antimony administered in small quantities, and continuously. Do you mean from the commencement of the illness down to the time of the death? Yes; down to the time of the death.

Lord Justice-Clerk—That is from about Christmas-time till her death? Yes.

Solicitor-General—Supposing that to have been so, and that the poison was administered occasionally during all that time, the symptoms are exactly such as you should have expected? They are exactly such. Does any other way of accounting for these symptoms during that period occur to your mind as a medical man? None other. You cannot account for them in any other way? I cannot. And that way entirely accounts for them? Entirely. And the chemical analysis is, of course, such as, upon the same supposition, you should have expected? Quite. You also heard the evidence regarding Mrs Taylor's death—her illness before death, and such an account of her death as we have had here? I did. What opinion did you, as a medical man, form from the symptoms in her case as to the cause of her death? I had greater difficulty. It seemed to me that she might possibly have died from a dose of antimony administered shortly before death, or else from some of the sedative narcotic poisons. Have you any difficulty in her case in arriving at the opinion that she died from poison? None whatever. I so understood you that the difficulty you alluded to is as to the particular poison which killed her? Clearly so. Do you think the symptoms were mixed in her case to some extent like the symptoms of narcotic poison, and to some extent like the symptoms of antimony? Well, I am inclined to believe they were. Was there anything in her case to make you think that she died of apoplexy? There was not. Nothing to suggest that idea? Nothing. Was there any of the distinctive characteristics of apoplexy present at all? Not to my knowledge. And the *post-mortem* examination did not indicate any such disease? The *post-mortem* appearances did not. Do you recognise in the symptoms which Mrs Taylor exhibited prior to her death—do you recognise the action of antimony? In the failure of circulation I certainly do, and great depression and spasms. And in the state of insensibility in which she was? Yes; in the later stages of antimonial poisoning we have generally a state of insensibility. You heard one of the servants describe the sensations she felt on taking a bit of cheese on one occasion—a hot taste in her mouth, I think she said, like pepper—and a burning sensation in the throat. What does that indicate? Do you form any opinion as to what might be in the cheese? Not very decidedly. What does it suggest? It suggests a large quantity of antimony; and it also suggests a strong dose of narcotic poison.

Lord Justice-Clerk—It suggests many things? Yes, my Lord. Many things besides cheese? Yes.

Solicitor-General—And in one of the servants it produced violent sickness, lasting a considerable time—some hours, I think. That also is consistent with antimony? Yes; quite consistent with antimonial poisoning. Would antimony produce a burning sensation in the throat? It would in large quantities. I suppose you do not say that from actual experiment? I do. I have tried it in pretty large quantity. But in the throat? The secondary effect is always felt in the throat. And it did produce a burning sensation? It did. You also heard the account another servant gave of the effects following from some egg-flip she had swallowed. What do these symptoms convey to your mind? They point to some substance resembling antimony, if not antimony itself. Antimony would account for them. Does anything else occur to you at this moment that would do it? Various other emetics. Can tartar emetic be readily beaten up with egg-flip? With great facility. Rather a convenient medium for administering it? Yes. It dissolves readily? It does. Is it possible to convey antimony into the egg-flip in loaf-sugar? Antimony itself can be obtained in lump. But could you put tartar emetic into the sugar in sufficient quantity to produce sickness? It is quite possible by dusting it on. The sugar, being porous, would take up a quantity. It is a white powder? It is; resembling powdered sugar. If it was proposed not to kill by a dose, but to keep up the illness, a sufficient dose could be given in a lump of sugar? Quite easily.

Cross-examined by Mr Clark—Do I understand you to say that if the sugar—the two pieces of sugar—were put into a cup of egg-flip, enough of antimony can be conveyed by dusting over the sugar with tartar emetic—so that a teaspoonful of the egg-flip could produce the effects mentioned? It is quite possible. Egg-flip being a thick mucous substance, it would sustain mechanically a considerable quantity. You observe I am not speaking of the egg alone, but of the beat-up egg with hot water upon it. Suppose egg-flip is made in the ordinary manner, can you convey into the cup as much antimony upon two pieces of sugar as, taking a spoonful of the liquid, would produce the effect you have said? I think it is quite possible. Have you made any experiments to try it? I have made no direct experiments to try it. Have you made any indirect experiments? I have not. You have made no experiments at all? We doctors are continually making experiments. But I mean experiments for this purpose? I have made no experiments with direct reference to this question. You have made no experiments at all? Not with reference to this case. Then this is mere theory? Grounded on my experience of this drug. Without knowing the quantity of hot water that was poured upon the egg-flip, or the extent to which the egg and water were mixed together, you say that it is possible that as much tartar emetic could be put upon two lumps of sugar as would produce the effects referred to? I think it is quite possible. I may say that I am intimately acquainted with tartar emetic, and I hold I am entitled to answer the question the way I have done. You say that Mrs Taylor indicated poisoning by antimony and some other narcotic poison? I said "or" some other. Is opium included in sedative narcotic poisons? It is not. Do you mean to say that opium is not a sedative narcotic poison? I do not regard it as such. Is it not a narcotic? It is. And sedative? It is not. I regard aconite as a sedative narcotic. There was nothing impossible in the symptoms with her having taken opium? Nothing. You are inclined to the opinion that, besides opium, there was some other poison? Yes.

The Lord Justice-Clerk—I understood you to say that it was not impossible for Mrs Taylor to take opium, and the opium to contribute to produce those symptoms? It was not impossible.

Dr Paterson recalled—Solicitor-General—Dr Paterson, you heard the evidence in this case, and I hope you paid particular attention to that regarding the illness of the two ladies, and the symptoms? I have. Are you able to say, from the evidence, whether the impression you formed regarding Mrs Pritchard was confirmed or contradicted? In my opinion it has been very well confirmed so far as regards poisoning from antimony. Are you well acquainted, from your professional experience, with the action of antimony? I have seen a good deal of it from the thirty years' experience I have had, both in external and internal use. Have you seen it kill? I have. More than once? I have seen two cases of children that were poisoned by having it accidentally administered to them by their parents. These were the only cases of death? Yes; from antimony. Are all the symptoms which you heard described in the case of Mrs Pritchard such as would be produced by antimony? Yes; in what is called chronic poisoning by small and repeated doses. You include all the symptoms from the beginning of the illness, soon after Christmas, down to the time of her death? As far as I can judge from the general description, I certainly consider that there was antimony administered during the greater part of that time. Her appearance when you saw her in February entirely accorded with that? Yes. Her appearance was just such as you would have expected in a person who had been the victim of chronic poisoning by antimony? Yes. And the symptoms down to her death were also such as would be so produced? I certainly think so. That is my decided conviction. As a medical man, from the evidence as to the illness, the *post-mortem* examination and the chemical analysis, do you think that she was killed by poisoning by antimony? That is my decided impression. What is your impression as to Mrs Taylor's death? My impression was that her death was caused by opium; but there might have been some other narcotic combined with that unknown to me. Would aconite in combination with opium well account for the symptoms you saw? It would certainly contribute to the effect, and hurry the termination. Would these two in combination well account for the symptoms you saw? It never entered into my brain to suppose such a combination. Well, but let it enter your brain now. I suggest it to you now. Well, I believe it would. You have not in your practice seen any person poisoned by a combination of aconite and opium? Not to my knowledge. I have seen them poisoned by opium. Do you know experimentally or only from study the action of aconite? I tasted aconite just last week to determine its qualities. You mean the effect of it? Yes; of course I was very cautious in regard to the dose; I applied it to my tongue. And what sensation did it produce? In less than a minute there was an increased flow of saliva. This was immediately followed by a strong tingling sensation, very soon accompanied by numbness, and I felt the effects of it for at least four hours afterwards. You made such an acquaintance with the taste of it as you would know it again? Certainly; I will never forget it while I live. Attending now to the history of Mrs Taylor's case, along with what you saw of it yourself, do you think that any of the effects of antimony were exhibited by her? I had not the slightest suspicion of antimony in any shape or form when I saw her. Was what you saw inconsistent with antimony? The narcotic effect was such by the time I saw her that I do not believe I could recognise the effect of antimony. The narcotic effect would overpower the other? Yes. Would such a poison as laudanum interfere with the emetic effect of antimony? I believe it would. And also with its effect upon the bowels? I think it would.

Cross-examined by Mr Clark—Was there stertorous breathing in Mrs Taylor? Literally, there was what is called stertorous breathing, but I would call it oppressed breathing. You call it oppressed, but it is also called stertorous breathing or snoring? Yes. And snoring and stertorous breathing mean the same thing? The same thing.

Solicitor-General—In describing Mrs Taylor's condition when were you examined before, I believe you used the word *coma?* Yes; I did. What did you mean by the word? It signifies insensibility—insensibility especially under opium. And you were under the impression that it was opium alone? My impression was that it was opium alone, or some of its preparations; it might be morphia.

Lord Justice-Clerk—I would like to know before you go what your opinion is now, after hearing the whole evidence as to the cause of Mrs Taylor's death? It strikes me that she died from the effects of the narcotic. You mean the opium? Yes. That is your opinion? That is my opinion. You think, then, that she had taken so much opium as to kill her? I think so. Without the presence of any other poison? That is my own impression.

Solicitor-General—Do you mean that she had no antimony or aconite? I understand that now, but I did not understand that at the time.

Lord Justice-Clerk—I hope you understand me. You have heard all the evidence which discloses the presence of antimony in Mrs Taylor's body, and after having heard all the evidence, I want you to tell me what you now think was the cause of Mrs Taylor's death? I believe her death was occasioned by a combination of those two medicines—the antimony and the opium. A less dose of opium would have a greater effect, seeing that the body was previously under the influence of antimony. A smaller dose of opium would have a fatal effect in consequence of the condition of the body, produced by antimony? I certainly think so. Suppose that the opium which Mrs Taylor took had upwards of five per cent. of Fleming's tincture of aconite combined with it, what do you say then? The effect would be much more rapid, certainly. And more likely to be fatal? Certainly.

Hugh Orr—Mr Crichton—I am agent for the City of Glasgow Bank—the Charing Cross Branch, Glasgow. Dr Pritchard kept an account at our branch. It was overdrawn L.62, 11s. 11d. on 20th March last. [Shown No. 101.] It was overdrawn on 9th January to the extent of L.114. That was being gradually reduced till 20th March. It had been brought down to L.62.

Michael Balmain—Mr Crichton—I am assistant manager of the Clydesdale Banking Company, Glasgow. Dr Pritchard had an account at our bank. [Shown pass-book, No. 100.] On 20th March his account was overdrawn L.131, 12s. 4d. He was 2s. 4d. overdrawn in the beginning of November, and between that and December he overdrew the balance in three different sums.

William Finlay.—Mr Crichton—I am Secretary to the Scottish Equitable Life Assurance Society, Edinburgh. Dr Pritchard's life was insured in our office in two policies for £1500. He had got several advances on these policies, amounting to £255 in all. The last was on 13th May 1864, £35. The one policy was dated in July 1851, and the other in December 1851.

D. J. Macbrair, W.S.—Mr Gifford—I am an assumed trustee of the late David Cowan of Portsmouth. He was a brother of Mrs Taylor. We had charge of the trust funds under Cowan's will. They amounted to £3000. They were held for Mrs Taylor's behoof, exclusive of her husband's *jus mariti*. The whole sum was at Mrs Taylor's disposal. It was invested in railway debentures, and she got the interest. She was entitled to the capital when she pleased. She applied for a portion of the capital about two months before June 1864. She said she was desirous to give £500 of the money to Dr Pritchard, her son-in-law, as he had either purchased or was going to purchase a house. She got up that £500 in June 1864. The money was paid to herself. I attended a meeting held after Mrs Taylor's funeral. [Shown No. 149.] That is the minute of that meeting. It is in my handwriting, except the preamble. The docquet at the end is in my handwriting. That is a correct representation of what took place at the meeting. It is subscribed by Dr Pritchard, who was there. The last part of the minute is this—"Dr Pritchard further stated that the £500 above mentioned had been given to him by the deceased in July last, subject to no condition; but he expressed his willingness to have it secured over the property, which it was applied in part purchase of, for the benefit of Mrs Pritchard and family." That took place after the trustees had rather urged it on Dr Pritchard. [Shown No. 81.] That is an extract of the will of Mrs Taylor. It is dated 5th September 1855. It provides that the trustees "shall pay one-third part thereof to my son Michael Waistel Taylor, presently in Penrith; and they shall invest in such way and manner, and in such securities or security of such kind as to them shall seem best, the other two-third parts, and pay the interest or annual produce thereof to my daughter, Mary Jane Taylor or Pritchard, spouse of Edward William Pritchard, surgeon in Hunmanby, and that upon her own receipt as alimentary to her, and exclusive of the *jus mariti* and right of administration of her husband; and, in the event of her predeceasing her husband, the said interest or annual produce to be paid to him for the benefit of such of the children of my said daughter who may be under twenty-one years of age, and, upon their attaining that age, for his own use as he may consider proper." I have no means of knowing if Dr Pritchard knew the contents of that will. It was produced at the meeting at which he was present after Mrs Taylor's funeral.

Mr Watson—Mrs Taylor showed great anxiety to accommodate the prisoner with the £500. At the meeting after her death, Dr Cowan said he understood Dr Pritchard was to give a bond over the house. Dr Pritchard said he had not so understood; but he showed no unwillingness to do so. I thought he behaved extremely well.

D. T. Alexander—Mr Gifford—I am a writer in Glasgow. I acted as agent of the prisoner in purchasing a dwelling-house at Whitsunday 1864. The agreed-on price was £2000. I carried through the purchase. £1600 was borrowed on security of the house, and £400 was handed to me by Dr Pritchard. I understood he had got it from his mother-in-law. The transaction was settled on 9th July 1864. The cash was paid then.

Dr James Moffat Cowan—Mr Crichton—I am acquainted with the handwriting of Mrs Taylor. [Shown 22, 23, 27, 28, 25, and 26.] These are all in Mrs Taylor's handwriting. I am quite familiar with her handwriting. [Shown 19, 20, and 82.] These are all in Dr Pritchard's handwriting. In No. 19, under date 7th February 1865, there is an entry, "Dr J. M. C. here," and on Wednesday, 8th February, "Dr J. M. C. left. Dr Gairdner." "J. M. C." are my initials. On 9th February there is an entry, "Dr Gairdner."

Archibald Campbell Wells—Mr Gifford—I am salesman to Burton & Henderson, Sauchiehall Street, Glasgow. [Shown No. 113.] This is the scroll day-book kept by them. Under date Monday, February 13, there is an entry, "Dr Pritchard—3 lb. sugar, 4d.; ½ lb. tapioca, 8d." The entry is in my handwriting. I have no recollection of selling these things; but I have no doubt I furnished them for him. The prisoner was a customer of Burton & Henderson. Sometimes one of the servants came to the shop, and sometimes another.

John Henderson—Mr Gifford—I am a grocer in Glasgow, of the firm of Burton & Henderson. [Shown No. 95.] I sold to John Murray, sheriff-officer, a quantity of tapioca. This is the tapioca. I attached a label to it in his presence, and signed it. I had got a stock of tapioca in the end of 1864, from which I had been selling early in 1865. This which I gave to Murray was of the same stock.

John M'Millan—Mr Gifford—I am an assistant to Murdoch Brothers, chemists, Glasgow. I knew Mary M'Leod, a servant of Dr Pritchard's, by sight. In February last she brought a bottle of the capacity of 5 oz. to be filled with Batley's Solution. This was between 15th and 28th February last. [Shown No. 85.] This is like it in every respect. It had a label on it when she brought it, but I am not sure whether it was our label or Duncan & Flockhart's. I filled it with Batley's Solution for her, and she paid 8s. 4d. for it. We got our Batley's Solution from Barron, Harvey, Beckett, & Simpson, Giltspur Street, London. Our last invoice of Batley's Solution received from them before that was dated 13th December 1864. I supplied Mary M'Leod from the shop bottle. I cannot be certain if the shop bottle was filled out of the Batley we had got on 13th December; but if it was not part of that supply, it was part of a previous supply which we got on 7th May. [Shown No. 142.] I remember filling a half-ounce phial of Batley's Solution for Dr Penny. I took it from the Union Street stock, which I have reason to believe was the stock of May 1864.

Mr Clark—I remember filling the larger of these two bottles for an old lady some months before that. She told me to cork it well, as she had lost some of it the time before, in the train, by the cork coming out. She did not say she was going by the train when she asked me to fill this bottle.

Richard Bankes Barron—Mr Gifford—I am a partner of Barron, Harvey, Beckett, and Simpson, druggists, London. Murdoch Brothers, Glasgow, are customers. We have supplied them with Batley's Solution. We sent them a supply 13th December 1864, and 7th May 1864. We get that Batley from the proprietors of the receipt, Batley & Watts. The two quantities we sent to Murdoch Brothers were got from Batley & Watts the days the orders came. It is a private receipt which has been used for many years. We get it in sealed bottles. Murdoch Brothers ordered 5 lb. bottles, and that was the reason we got it direct from Batley & Watts. The bottles were securely sealed and corked. It was not opened on our premises; we were merely agents for it; and we sent it to Murdoch Brothers as we got it from Batley & Watts.

William Manning Watts—Mr Gifford—I am sole partner of the firm of Batley & Watts, wholesale druggists, London. I am proprietor of the receipt for manufacturing Batley's Solution, and I make it from that receipt, and sell it. It is a watery solution of opium. It contains no antimony or aconite—nothing but opium. It is sold in glass bottles, which hold from 1 ounce to 50 lb. Each bottle when sold is sealed and labelled. Can you tell me the ingredients of it? I think I must decline to do that.

Lord Justice-Clerk—But there is neither antimony nor aconite, nor any poisonous ingredient in it, except opium? Quite so.

By Mr Gifford—We have sold some of it to Messrs Barron, Harvey, Beckett, & Simpson.

ALEXANDER M'CALL, recalled—Mr Crichton—[Shown Nos. 139, 140, 141, and 144.] I found 139, a black porter bottle, in the consulting-room. It was empty. No. 140 two pasteboard boxes; No. 141, a small wooden box; and No. 144, were all found in the consulting-room.

Mr Clark—These were all found in the unlocked press, with the exception of the black bottle, which was found in the locked press.

Mr Crichton—These were delivered to Dr Penny in the same state in which I found them.

DR PENNY, recalled—Mr Clark—Dr Penny, I show you No. 13—that is the receipt or prescription which Dr Paterson read yesterday? Yes. Just tell me what it contains. Chlorodyne, 10 minims; solution of morphia, 19 minims; ipecacuanha wine, 30 minims; cinnamon water, 1 oz. Could that prescription have been made up from articles which you analysed, and which you obtained from Mr M'Call? Certainly not. There was nothing of that kind amongst them? No. You analysed all that you got? Yes. There was neither chlorodyne nor any of the other articles mentioned in the prescription given to you by Mr M'Call? No.

DECLARATIONS OF THE PRISONER.—The clerk then read the following declarations which had been emitted by the prisoner :—

No. I.

At Glasgow, the twenty-second day of March, Eighteen hundred and sixty-five years, in presence of Sir Archibald Alison, Baronet, advocate, Sheriff of Lanarkshire.

Compeared a prisoner, who, being judicially admonished and examined, declares and says:—My name is Edward William Pritchard. I am a native of Southsea, Hampshire, forty years of age, a doctor of medicine, member of the Royal College of Surgeons in London, and I reside at No. 131 Sauchiehall Street, Glasgow; and the charge of having caused the death of his wife, Mary Jane Taylor or Pritchard, by feloniously administering poison to her, having been read over to him, *Declares*,—I have always attended my wife in all her ailments of every kind during the whole period of our married lives, now fifteen years, and some of these illnesses were very severe, but I never saw her so ill as she was on this occasion which terminated fatally. As far as my judgment goes, her last illness was gastric fever, which commenced about the beginning of the present year. I gave my wife no medicines during her illness, excepting wine, champagne, and brandy to support her strength; and I gave her no medicine myself at all. I trusted to nature to right itself, with the assistance of those restoratives. During the last six weeks her power of sleeping entirely went away. In order to procure sleep I gave her, at the commencement of her sleeplessness, a small quantity of chloroform, but it entirely disagreed with her, and I discontinued it. I then called in Dr Gairdner, professor of medicine in the University, and he visited and saw her several times, and he continued to attend her till her old medical friend, who had attended her before our marriage, Dr James Moffat Cowan, returned, and he came from Edinburgh to see her. I then wrote to her mother to come to nurse her, and she arrived about the 11th of February last, and her arrival had a beneficial effect upon Mrs Pritchard for some time, but still the sleeplessness continued; and shortly after her mother's death, which happened on the 25th February, she relapsed and became much worse, and very apprehensive about herself, and she suggested to me the adoption of a medicine with which her mother was very familiar, Batley's Solution of opium, but I declined to give her any without first consulting with Dr James Paterson, who lived close by. I saw him and consulted him, but he did not see Mrs Pritchard on that occasion, and he did not approve of using the solution of opium. He prescribed granulated citrate of magnesia, calomel, mercury, and chalk, and I acted upon his advice and administered the medicine, and it seemed to have a beneficial effect. Some time after, finding her sleeplessness still continued, I, at her own suggestion, applied a solution of atropine to the external parts around the eye, and it had a little effect for some time; but the effects soon ceased. After her mother's death, she became rapidly worse; indeed, I ascribed her decease to the agitation consequent on her mother's decease. At the time of the last event, she was strongly impressed with the idea that she herself would die at the same time as her mother, and in fact she did die on a subsequent day at exactly the same hour. On the night preceding her death, she was apprehensive that unless she got sleep, she should not get through the night. I went for Dr Paterson, who came immediately, and sat for a considerable time by the bedside, and afterwards dictated a prescription, which was made up at the Glasgow Apothecary Company's shop at Elmbank Street. The prescription will be found in my desk at home. It was for two draughts, one to be given four hours after the first if it did not succeed. She got the first draught as prescribed by Dr Paterson about ten o'clock, but she said after drinking that it was not half strong enough, and asked if she might have some of her mother's medicine. I refused to give it her, and said I dare not do it. I gave her a glass of port wine, and sat carefully watching for a short time. I then went down stairs, and had supper; and after being absent for some time, returned to see whether she had got sleep. I found her awake, and she wished me to give her something to make her sleep. I refused; and she then asked me to come to bed, as I must be tired with the weary nights of watching. It was then about twelve o'clock. I tried to persuade her that I should remain up to watch her till past the time that her mother had died; but to please her I got into bed, and almost immediately I fell asleep from the state of exhaustion I was in. was awoke by her pulling at my beard, and found my wife struggling to get into bed. She appeared to have got out of bed. She said, "Edward, I am faint." I assisted her into bed, and asked her how long I had been asleep; but she answered, "Don't speak—look! do you see my mother?" I said "No; it is only a vision, only imagination," and asked if she had any pain. She said she felt cold, and that I need try no more skill, that I had failed this time, and that she was going to her mother. I got alarmed, and rang the bell violently, and the youngest servant came. I desired her to make a mustard plaster as quickly as she could; and on that my wife turned round and said, "Edward, I'm in my senses, mustard plasters will do no good;" and almost immediately she fell back in my arms and died. The servant came with a mustard plaster, and found her in that position. I did not give her any other medicine at that time except a little brandy applied to her lips. During the whole course of her illness I never gave her any antimony nor any medicine in which there was any preparation of antimony. Antimony is a poison; but it is used occasionally to subdue inflammation, and I applied it to her neck in October last, when she was plagued with a swelling of a gland in the neck. I rubbed it in externally on that occasion, and I have never given her any antimony since. On that occasion I recommended change of air, and I gave her a little bottle of antimony with her for the same purpose of rubbing in behind the ear. She went to Edinburgh at that time, and she returned to Glasgow very much better, and I have never seen the bottle of antimony since she got it away with her. There was a considerable quantity of antimony in my repositories at the time of my wife's last illness, as I used it extensively in my practice, and the antimony was kept in a cupboard, of which I have the key, but which was not always locked. I did not see any of it brought out, or lying about, during her illness. The cupboard where the antimony was is in the consulting-room on the ground flat, and she was so weak on the day of her death—Saturday—and on the Friday preceding, that I do not think she had strength to have gone to that cupboard herself. My wife took the antimony internally on one occasion when she had a tendency to inflammation of the eyelids. This was years ago, and I never knew her to use it internally except on this occasion. I never administered antimony internally to her on any occasion, nor any other substance calculated to injure or destroy life. All which I declare to be truth.

(Signed) EDWARD WILLIAM PRITCHARD.
A. ALISON.
JNO. GEMMELL.
P. MORTON.
BERNARD M'LAUCHLIN.

No. II.

At Glasgow, and within the North Prison there, on the twenty-first day of April eighteen hundred and sixty-five years,.

In presence of Sir Archibald Alison, Baronet, advocate, Sheriff of Lanarkshire,

Compeared Edward William Pritchard, presently a prisoner in the prison of Glasgow, and the previous declaration, emitted by him upon the twenty-second day of March last in presence of the said Sheriff, which is now docqueted and subscribed as relative hereto, having been read over to him and, he being again judicially admonished and examined, declares and says—I am entirely innocent of the charge referred to in said previous declaration, and I wish to add that to what is contained therein. As far as my memory goes, the declaration now read conveys correctly what I then said, and I adhere to the whole statements therein contained; and the charge of having, on several or one or more occasions between the tenth and twenty-fifth days of February 1865, within his dwelling-house in Sauchiehall Street, Glasgow, wickedly and feloniously administered, or caused to be administered, to Jane Cowan or Taylor, now deceased, several or one or more doses of tartarised antimony, or other poison unknown, in some article or articles of drink or food, or in some other manner unknown, in consequence whereof the said Jane Cowan or Taylor died, and was thus murdered by him, having been read over to him, and he being judicially admonished and examined by the Sheriff examinator, declares I elect to make a voluntary statement in reference to the said last-mentioned charge, and I now declare I was no way accessory to Mrs Taylor's death. I never administered poison to her. I did and do believe that she died from paralysis and apoplexy. I have no further statement to make, and by the advice of my agent, will make none, with the exception that I am entirely innocent of the charge preferred against me. Being asked by the Procurator-Fiscal whether he ever administered, or caused to be administered, tartarised antimony to the said Jane Cowan or Taylor, declares my agent recommended me to say nothing farther, and I decline to answer the question put, and as I act under my agent's advice, it is unnecessary to put any further questions. All which I declare to be truth.

(Signed) Edward William Pritchard.
A. Alison.
Jno. Gemmell.
Rob. Wilson.
Bernard M'Lauchlin

The Solicitor-General stated that this closed the case for the prosecution.

It being now nearly six o'clock,

Mr Clark suggested that the Court should adjourn till to-morrow, when the evidence for the defence would be led.

The Lord Justice-Clerk said he would like first to have an idea of how long the case was likely to last.

Mr Clark said that so far as the defence was concerned, he expected that the speeches of counsel might be concluded to-morrow (Thursday), as he did not anticipate that the evidence for the panel would extend beyond one o'clock.

The Lord Justice-Clerk remarked that in that case the Court would adjourn till Thursday morning at ten o'clock, and addressing the jury, he said:—Gentlemen of the jury,—You understand that you have not yet heard any part of the case for the defence; therefore I need hardly tell you, that it is in vain in the meantime to form any opinion on the case for the Crown.

The Court adjourned at a quarter to six o'clock till ten o'clock next morning.

FOURTH DAY—Thursday, July 6.

The Court met again this morning at ten o'clock—the Lord Justice-Clerk, Lord Ardmillan, and Lord Jerviswoode on the bench. The prisoner entered the dock a few minutes after ten, and his brother again took his seat beside him.

The prisoner seemed quite composed when he came into Court, although considerably jaded from the fatigue which he had undergone since the commencement of the trial. He was perhaps if possible more anxious than ever, and watched the proceedings with an attention amounting at times to nervousness. When his children were under examination, the composure which had hitherto characterised him deserted him, and shedding tears he covered his face with his handkerchief. After the first adjournment of the Court in the forenoon, the brother of the prisoner left the dock with him and did not return again. The anxiety of the prisoner became very great when the Solicitor-General began his address. During the whole of the learned counsel's remarks, he sat earnestly facing the jury with his hands clasped together as in a supplicating attitude.

The interest manifested by the public in the trial was much greater than on any of the preceding days, and large numbers of people in vain attempted to gain admittance.

EVIDENCE FOR THE DEFENCE.

The first witness called for the defence was

Dr Michael Taylor, Penrith—By Mr Watson—I am a brother of the late Mrs Pritchard, and son of Mrs Taylor. I was in Glasgow two days after my mother's death. I had not been there for a year or two before, and had not seen my sister during that period. I had some conversation with her on that occasion. She told me that Dr Gairdner had visited her some time before. She said that she did not think she would like him to see her again. I urged her to do so, as Dr Gairdner was a personal friend of my own, and I was sure would pay her every attention; she however had some prejudice against him. She said she would rather not see him again, but somebody else. She gave me to understand that such an intimation had been given to Dr Gairdner. She gave me to understand that that intimation was made to him at her request. I strongly urged upon my sister to have the benefit of a nurse, as there seemed to be no competent person about the house to fulfil that duty—no one but a young girl and a servant who had come recently. My sister made objection to it on the ground that it would create some confusion in the house, and that she did not like strangers about her. I was in Glasgow on 27th February for about an hour on the day my mother's remains were conveyed to Edinburgh. I saw my sister on that occasion, but had no particular conversation with her. I saw her again the following day, and was in Glasgow for three or four hours. It was on the second occasion that I had this conversation with her. [Shown No. 32 of Crown productions]:—

From letter, Mrs Pritchard to Dr Pritchard, commencing "1 Lauder Road, Edinburgh, My Dear Edward," and subscribed "Ever your Minnie." "Kenny and I arrived safely yesterday Grand P. and G. M. along with Fanny and Aili were waiting for us. To-day has been fine, but I have not been out. I feel better but no appetite. I suppose it will come."

That is the late Mrs Pritchard's handwriting. [Shown No. 34]:—

From letter, Mrs Pritchard to Dr Pritchard, commencing "1 Lauder Road, Edinburgh. My Dear Ted," and ending "Ever Dear Ted, your Minnie." (Found in an envelope bearing Edinburgh and Glasgow post-marks of November 28th, 1864.) "I am very vexed to hear that Dear Horace is ill. Had he taken anything to disagree with him when he was out? Your message by telegraph relieved me much . . . . Miss Moffat was mistaken when she said that I had been out to a party. Grandmamma and grandpapa were at Mrs John Moffat's, but I was sitting quietly at home. They wished me to go but I did not feel well enough. I have been out two or three times, once to get under woollen clothing, which has kept me much warmer and more comfortable. Yesterday I went with grandma to hear Spurgeon preach—an immense number of people. I have made no calls yet except to Miss Bain, as I had promised to go the first time I was out . . . . . Grandmamma is better. She sends her love to you, and thinks I have improved very much since I came here. My eyes are much better."

This is also her handwriting.

Cross-examined by Solicitor-General—Mrs Pritchard was my only sister. She and I were the only two children of our parents.

JOHN SIMPSON—By Mr Watson—I am one of the partners of Duncan, Flockhart, and Co. I personally attend to the business at our premises on North Bridge. We carry on a very extensive dispensing trade. I have been eleven and a half years engaged in that shop. I recollect seeing the prisoner in Glasgow about four years ago. Shortly after that, some purchases were made in our shop in Edinburgh in his name of Batley's Sedative Solution. Some person came to the shop with a bottle and paper, instructing us to fill the bottle for Dr Pritchard. [Shown 85.] That is very like the bottle which was brought. That bottle was very often brought back to our premises to be filled. I had no personal communication with Dr Pritchard on that occasion. [Shown No. 52 of the Crown list of witnesses, Mr James Thomson, commission agent, Edinburgh.] That is the person who came to our shop with the bottle for the Batley's Solution. About 7s. 6d. was charged for it. It would have been charged higher for any other person than a doctor. The bottle was frequently sent back to be filled. It came about four years ago first, and frequently after that down to the beginning of the present year. I think it came very regularly; I could not say if it came more frequently at the end of the period. I could not say how often it came—there are so many people in the shop. I know Fleming's tincture of aconite. We dispense it in our retail trade. In the course of a year we dispense not less than half-a-gallon, or eighty ounces. I have very frequently made up prescriptions of half an ounce in a mixture. I would not consider it at all unusual if a medical man were to get an ounce at a time from us.

By the Solicitor-General—We get our Batley's Solution direct from the manufactory in London. There is no antimony or aconite in the Batley we sell. It is quite impossible they could get into it accidentally in our premises. We keep it in a separate place. I know the Glasgow Apothecaries' Company. That is a large establishment, and very well known in Glasgow. It has two branches—the one at Sauchiehall Street, and the other in Union Street. They are both large establishments.

By the Lord Justice-Clerk—The half-ounce of aconite which I frequently made up was for a medicine, and it would be a fourth of the entire mixture. Such a mixture is chiefly used in heart disease. Eight drops is the usual dose of such a mixture; that is equal to two drops of Fleming's tincture of aconite.

Thomas Fairgrieve—By Mr Watson—I am a chemist and druggist at 46 Clerk Street, Edinburgh. I knew the late Mrs Taylor. She was in the habit of making purchases at my shop. She purchased Batley's Solution from me for some years before her death, She very frequently came herself and occasionally sent for it. [Shown No. 85.] Only once that I know of I sold her a bottle of this size, holding five ounces. Afterwards she got it in 2-oz. bottles, and sometimes in 1-oz. bottles. This is a bottle made for Batley's mixture. So far as my recollection goes, when Mrs Taylor herself called for the medicine she paid for it. When it was sent for, it was generally put down to her account. Her purchases were sometimes at considerable intervals, and at other times frequent. [Shown No. 30 of productions for the defence.] That account was rendered by me to the late Mrs Taylor. On 18th January 1865 there is an entry of two ounces of Batley's Solution. On 29th January there is another entry of two ounces; on the 4th February also an entry of two ounces. Batley to that amount was furnished to Mrs Taylor on these occasions. I know Fleming's tincture of aconite. My business is entirely a dispensing retail business. In the course of a year I sell about fifty ounces of Fleming's tincture; that is within the mark. It is generally prescribed in the form of liniment. I have made up prescriptions containing two ounces of Fleming's tincture of aconite for a liniment; and I am not sure but I have made up more. I would not be at all surprised at the purchase by a medical man of one ounce of it at a time.

By the Solicitor-General—Medical men are in the habit of sending prescriptions for the tincture of aconite—not of coming for it themselves. Medical men have bought unmixed aconite in my shop; but it is not very common. I should say it is rather uncommon for them to do so. I am not prepared to say for what they got it, but I should say it was for outward application: I don't think it was for experiments in a laboratory. I have sold half-an-ounce and an ounce to medical men. I have sold it to Dr Fleming himself—the inventor—in three, or four, or six ounces. I don't sell much antimony or tartar emetic now. It is not so common as it used to be. There has been a change since croton-oil has come into use. In the last year or two there has been less antimony sold. I have sold it in large quantities to veterinary-surgeons, and persons come to me and get it mixed up with lard as an ointment. There is scarcely a day but antimony is ordered, either as a solution or as antimonial wine. Frequently, in prescriptions, the two or three grains are dissolved in a given quantity of water. I could not say how much I sell of tartar emetic in a year. It might be two or three ounces in a year. That would include what I have sold in lard, but not what I have sold to veterinary-surgeons. The quantity of tartar emetic in a prescription to be taken internally is very small. It is measured in grains. There are 480 minims or measured drops in an ounce of Batley. I should think 20 minims would be equal to 30 drops dropped from a bottle, without being measured.

By the Lord Justice-Clerk—There is an imitation of Batley, which I keep. I never sold it to Mrs Taylor. I am able to say that her purchases in January and February last were of the genuine Batley. The imitation of the real Batley is a perfectly safe thing; it is supposed to be the same, but it is made by a different maker. It is made from the extract of opium. Fleming's tincture of aconite is very largely used in an unmixed state for severe tic doloureux. It is never used internally unmixed. I have found it act as a specific for toothache at times.

By Mr Watson—It is generally used in neuralgic or rheumatic pains. I don't remember its having been used for affections of the ear; but I see no reason why it should not be.

James Thomson—Mr Watson—I am a clothier's traveller and commission-agent, and was for some time in the employment of Mr Michael Taylor. It will be three years in August first since I left his employment. I was clerk and assistant in the business. I sometimes executed small commissions for Mrs Taylor. I went occasionally to Messrs Duncan & Flockhart's for her. I understood it was for opium; but when I went for it I did not know what it was for. During the first twelvemonth or so I got a line and the bottle. The bottle was generally wrapped up in the line. [Shown bottle.] It was a bottle the same as that. I could almost say that was it. I have gone to Messrs Duncan & Flockhart's with the bottle oftener since I left Mr Taylor's service than I did before, as I still continued to do small things of that kind for Mrs Taylor. I once read the line on Messrs Duncan & Flockhart's counter—that was the only time ever I saw it open. After some time she just gave me the bottle, and told me to go and get it filled; and I went and presented the bottle, and it was filled at once. I went last for it the night before Mrs Taylor went to Glasgow immediately preceding her death. The bottle was filled on that occasion, and I took it back next morning, and gave it to her. For about a year or so before her death, I would say, I got the bottle filled for her once in every two or three weeks.

By the Solicitor-General—When I first entered Mr Taylor's service I only got the bottle filled once in every two or three months, but gradually it came to be that I went for it every two or three weeks. When I saw the line on Messrs Duncan & Flockhart's counter, I could see "5 oz. opium" marked on it. There was something else which I could not read, as the line was lying at some distance from me. It was in Mrs Taylor's handwriting. I sometimes used Dr Pritchard's name there. When I went with the bottle and without a line, she told me, if they asked who it was for, to say that it was for Dr Pritchard. She told me she got it half-a-crown cheaper by saying it was for a doctor. Although I had left Mr Taylor's service I generally went such messages for Mrs Taylor. She asked me to come and see them occasionally, and I generally called about twice or thrice a week.

By the Lord Justice-Clerk—The medicine was always corked and sealed, and put up in paper, when I got it from Messrs Duncan & Flockhart. Sometimes I delivered it to Mrs Taylor herself, sometimes to the servant, but always in the state in which I got it. The bottle I got filled on the night before Mrs Taylor went to Glasgow. I gave it next morning to Miss Pritchard, her grand-daughter, who delivered it to her.

James Foulner—Mr Watson—I am a corkcutter, Carrick Street, Glasgow. I consulted Dr Pritchard about an affection of the ear in November last, and up to the evening of his wife's death. I did not know him before I consulted him. It was by his solicitation, through one Miss Clyne, that I went to see him. On these visits, the doctor generally painted my ears inside and outside, and frequently syringed them, and sometimes he dropped a liquid into them. It was in a room on the street floor of his house in Sauchiehall Street that he did so. I could not say what he painted my ear with, but it coloured the ear. I think he took it out of a press in the room. The application was not painful till afterwards. It had a smartish sensation afterwards. Shortly before I stopped going to him, he told me to buy some iodine, and paint my ear myself. He gave me several small phials; the first two or three contained a white thickish matter. He also gave me a bottle larger than the rest; it was labelled "poison."

By the Solicitor-General—I have the larger bottle with me which I got from him. [Witness produced it.] I never gave it up to any one. It has been in my possession till this moment. The label is, "Two drops in each ear every night—poison." It still contains part of the liquid; it was scarcely half full when I got it from the doctor.

The Solicitor-General—I don't know whether the Court would think it necessary to order an examination of the bottle.

By the Solicitor-General—I showed that bottle to the Fiscal yesterday. I was at Mr Hart, the Fiscal in Glasgow, about it on Tuesday, and he advised me to bring it here. Nobody else, except my wife, has seen it; and nobody interfered with it. What he told me to get to paint my ear myself was tincture of iodine; and I got some.

By the Lord Justice-Clerk—That iodine produced the same yellow colour that his painting had done.

By Mr Watson—I was examined by a gentleman on behalf of the agents for the prisoner. I told him I thought I had none of the bottles I had got from Dr Pritchard.

The Lord-Justice-Clerk, after consultation with the other judges, said—Mr Clark, have you any desire that the contents of this phial should be examined.

Mr Clark—No, my Lord, I have no desire to do so.

The Lord-Justice-Clerk—You don't wish it.

Mr Clark—No.

The Lord Justice-Clerk—(To witness)—Then you may go.

Mr Clark—Give him this bottle.

The Solicitor-General—I am told it might be examined in a few minutes.

The Lord-Justice-Clerk—If the prisoner's counsel doesn't think it desirable, we don't order it.

Mr Clark — The prisoner's case is just about to close; we shall be done in a few minutes.

Mr Clark was handing the bottle to the witness, when

The Lord Justice-Clerk said—There is no reason why the bottle should be given up. Let it remain.

George Kerr—By Mr Watson—I know the prisoner. He attended me for an affection of the ear; about the end of February or beginning of March 1865. He gave me a little medicine. He gave me a prescription to get medicine, which was obtained at the Glasgow Apothecaries' Company, Sauchiehall Street. He did not give me a bottle to drop into my ear. It was just a tonic. I remember something about his giving me a bottle labelled glycerine and strychnine. It was to be used externally to the ear; but I only used it twice, as the ear was so much inflamed, and I did not think it would do the ear any good in that state. The doctor gave me the bottle in his consulting-room. I have the bottle still. I think I could find it for you, as it is still in my possession. I got the bottle about the end of February, as near as I can remember.

alternative, it is your duty—and you will gladly avail yourselves of it—to acquit rather than convict any one bearing the form of a man of anything so atrocious. The observation is a sound one—I accept it, and commend it to you as in my opinion sound and just; and, indeed, I make these observations to you, not to excite prejudice, but for the fairer purpose of assuring you, that I should appreciate the gravity of the charge which I make, and now press, and duly estimate the burden which is upon me of establishing it by satisfactory evidence. Gentlemen, I am charged, in my official capacity, with the interests of public justice and of society at large. The interests of society are indeed great. It is unnecessary to express them. There is no protection against murder by secret poison except the reasonable certainty of after detection and punishment. Against open violence we may defend ourselves; we may avoid an enemy; we may protect ourselves against him. But against the secret poisoner there is absolutely no protection, except in the fear of detection and punishment. It is, therefore, for the best interests of society that the prisoner, if he be guilty, and be proved to be so by convincing evidence, should not escape. But it is not for the interest of society that any man should be convicted upon insufficient evidence, and it is not according to my duty to press the case, or any part of it, or any view of it, against the prisoner beyond what justice and truth, according to the evidence, and legitimate and convincing argument, exactly warrant. The interest and the right of the prisoner to be acquitted if he is not satisfactorily proved to be guilty is as important and sacred in the estimation of the law, and will be in yours, as the interest of society is that, if proved to be guilty, he shall not escape. I rejoice, therefore, to think that his interests have been committed to hands so able and experienced as those of my learned friends who now appear for him. Gentlemen, I have told you that the prisoner is charged with two acts of wilful murder—the one committed upon his wife, the other upon her mother. And what you have to say—it is a solemn and important duty—men cannot in this country be engaged in any duty more solemn and more important—is whether both or either of these charges is proved to your satisfaction. Upon me the burden of proof lies. The prisoner is entitled to every presumption in his favour to begin with. It is for me to prove it, or if I do not he is entitled to be acquitted. Let me then, with all the impartiality and candour which I can command, proceed to consider with you the evidence upon which each of these charges rests. The first matter for consideration in this and every similar case consists of what lawyers are accustomed to call the *corpus delicti*—that is, the question whether or no the crimes charged were both or either of them committed by anybody. Were these ladies murdered by poison, or were either of them murdered by poison, by any one? It is for me to establish by convincing evidence the affirmative of the proposition that each of them was so murdered. If I fail, of course there is no further question of any moment in the case: the murders charged in that view were not committed, or are not proved to have been committed. But if I satisfy you—if I should say I have satisfied you by the evidence upon which I rely, and to which I shall immediately advert, that not one only, but both of the women were murdered by poison, the only question which remains—I say only, not because it is not vitally important, indeed the vitally important question in the case, but it is the only question—is, was that murder perpetrated, or were these murders perpetrated, by the prisoner at the bar? Let me begin, as naturally I ought to do, with the first question—Were the murders charged, either of them, committed by any one? That, of course is the question stated in another form. The question then comes to be, did the ladies die by poison not taken wilfully with a view to suicide, or accidentally either through negligence on their own part or somebody else's, or, if they did, the conclusion is inevitable that they were foully murdered? Did, then, both or either of the ladies die from the effects of poison? And let me here take the cases separately, in so far as it is possible to make a separation between them. I begin with the case of Mrs Pritchard, because, although she died last—about three weeks after her mother—she was, if there be any truth in the case for the prosecution, the first victim of the foul acts with which the prisoner is charged. That poisoning of her commenced before her mother came to nurse her on the 10th February, which, I believe, was the true date, although the poison did not terminate fatally until the 18th March, the mother herself having died upon the 25th February. But naturally, I think in whatever view you regard the case, the death of Mrs Pritchard is one which first presents itself for consideration; the murder of the mother being something like an episode occurring in the course of the murder of the child. Mrs Pritchard died upon Saturday, the 18th March, at a very early hour of the morning. The first question as to which you must make up your minds is, what was the cause of her death—of what did she die? The prisoner said to those who asked him, and to the registrar after her death, that he was her ordinary medical attendant, and that she died of gastric fever. The public prosecutor now says she died of poison. It is for you to determine which of these two assertions is the true one. It is painful to be obliged to say that the question admits of only one answer; for could I see any reasonable view upon which a different answer from one confirming the assertion of the prosecutor could be given, I should not fail to advert to it, and to state to you what I think. But I can see no materials. You will judge whether you can, in the whole of the evidence which has been laid before you, see materials to justify even doubt or hesitation in asserting that Mrs Pritchard died on the 18th March from the effects of poison. The evidence upon this subject is singularly clear and conclusive—I say singularly so, because cases of this description are of rare occurrence in my experience. This is the first in which a doubt was not raised, and raised upon medical testimony, upon the question whether death was to be ascribed to poison. Here there is none. The testimony is all one way, and you see distinctly how no doubt could have been thrown upon it. The poor woman's body was opened after her death. It presented, on the examination of the doctors, nothing to account for death—no appearance of natural disease. The conclusion of the report of that examination by Dr Maclagan and Dr Littlejohn is this—"We have to report that this body presented no appearances of recent morbid action, beyond a certain amount of irritation of the alimentary canal, and nothing at all capable of accounting for death. We have therefore secured the alimentary canal and its contents, the heart and some of the blood, the liver, the spleen, the left kidney, and the urine, in order that these may be submitted to chemical analysis." Nothing indicating gastric fever comes under their notice. Therefore these gentlemen thought the cause of death was to be ascertained by a chemical analysis of the portions of the body and the contents of the intestines here specified. That chemical analysis accordingly took place, with the result which you know. Poison was found diffused through the whole organs and parts of the body. It was found in the stomach, in the liver, in the spleen, in the kidney, in the heart, in the brain, in the blood, and in the rectum. The body was all impregnated with it, and notwithstanding the copious discharges which it produced upon the patient so long as she had strength to make them, the large quantities mentioned by the doctors in their evidence before you, were found in these various parts of the body, showing that the poison had diffused itself through the whole system, and satisfying them that the case was one of aggravated poisoning—that is, that poison had been administered in small doses, each of them insufficient to kill, but administered in small doses, and during a long course of time. That was the conclusion at which they arrived before knowing anything of the history of the case. Dr Maclagan stated in his report that the period over which the administration had extended cannot be determined by mere chemical investigation, but must be deduced from the history of the case. And Professor Penny, giving the same result—I don't trouble you with reading that part of the report in which he refers to it—Dr Penny, on examining portions of the same parts of the body and the contents of the intestines which had been examined by Dr Maclagan, arrives at the same conclusion. You understand this, gentlemen: Dr Maclagan did not experiment or operate upon the whole of the various portions of the body and substances which he had extracted. He operated only upon a portion of them, leaving another portion, in order that the additional security might be obtained of submitting that other portion to another chemist, in order to see whether the result which he arrived at was the same or different. You know from his report the result of his investigation. He found the article antimony diffused through the whole body, as I have stated to you—so diffused as to satisfy him—he being a person well able to judge upon such a matter—that the administration had been chronic, extending over a period of time. The other portion is submitted to the examination of Professor Penny. He conducts his own experiments really in the same way, because the mode of proceeding in order to ascertain the presence or absence of this poison is well understood. He finds the same poison in the same parts of the body, diffused in the same way through the system, and he arrives at the same conclusion. If there had been any possible doubt, we should have had some other testimony on the subject; but in the face of these reports of gentlemen of the greatest eminence, and upon whom, and such as whom, we must place reliance, unless we are to abandon altogether the idea of detecting the crime of poisoning, the matter was too clear to admit of any hesitation. But Professor Maclagan says:—"The period over which the administration extended must be ascertained by a reference to the history of the case; the medical examination and the chemical analysis could only lead to the conclusion that it had extended over a considerable period." Then you had the history of the case. I am not to go into that now. But you remember that the poor wife was taken ill, the symptoms being sickness and vomiting, these being the most marked symptoms—at all events, no others were stated—before she went on a visit to her parents in the end of November. She went there when she had got a little better, and with the view of her permanent recovery. She did recover. She was not visited by the sickness in Edinburgh—you have her own testimony to that effect. She went an invalid; she returned, not in perfect health, but still comparatively well. She had been free from the only symptoms which her illness indicated while she was at home, which she could not account for in any way; and it was painful to hear detailed in her own way the remarks which the poor creature made in the absence of her husband that it was strange that she was always well from home, and ill at home. She could not account for these sicknesses; nobody in the house could except the author of them. Well, she returns from her father's house two or three days before Christmas. Her mother is with her and her eldest child, and she is comparatively well; but only for a few days. The sickness and vomiting return within a few days, and after her return to her husband's house, as unaccountably as ever. They continue with more or less frequency. Generally every day, although sometimes she escapes a day, she is sick and vomiting, cramped. She at last went to bed—and kept it more or less for a week. The sickness, along with this vomiting and purging, leading to that general debility which it is the nature of this particular poison to cause, was upon her. Well, it goes on. The poor mother says that she became one day a little better, and two days worse—sick sometimes before breakfast, sometimes after breakfast—sometimes after dinner, after tea; sick during the night, ill with cramp; nothing in the world to account for it. These are the symptoms down to the period of her death—one day better, two days worse, until she sinks, completely exhausted, and dies upon the 18th March. What were these symptoms of—symptoms occurring under the eye of her husband, a medical man, the only medical attendant, living in the house with her day and night? Of gastric fever? No. They were the symptoms which would be produced by that poison which was found in her body after death, and so diffused through it as to lead inevitably to the conviction that it had been administered in small doses over a considerable period of time. The history of the case, therefore, confirms what the medical gentlemen and the chemists were led by the chemical analysis to anticipate; the poisoning of that poor woman was going on. I take no account of the period before she went to her father's house, but from very shortly after the time of her return, and it continued almost day after day down to the time of her death. Gentlemen, take the symptoms how you like—the symptoms indicating the action of antimony—exactly the symptoms which antimony would produce—and finding antimony in the body, diffused through the system, on the examination after death, I say the conclusion is so irresistible that it is not wonderful that it should not be disputed that this poor woman, however she came by it, had antimony administered to her, and died in consequence. If you cannot resist that conclusion, then, in respect to Mrs Pritchard, that part of the case is established—she died, not of gastric fever, but of poison. Now, attend for a moment to the case of Mrs Taylor — this murder occurring as an episode in the course of the perpetration of another. Mrs Taylor came to Glasgow on the 10th February, I believe—that is, according to the evidence, I mean about that date. But I think we have the correct date in the only two references which I mean to make to the journals of the prisoner. In them it is stated that Dr Gairdner visited Mrs Pritchard on the 8th February. That was the same day that Dr Cowan left, for on page 13 of this diary we have, under the head of 7th February, "Dr J. M. C. here;" while on the next day, 8th February, "Dr J. M. C. left." The statement was that he came the one day and left the next; and under the same date there is the entry, "Dr Gairdner"—that is to say, Dr Gairdner was there on the night of 8th February. In the same journal, on page 14, we have, first, on the 9th February, "Dr Gairdner"—that is, that he visited again that day; and Friday 10th, "Grandmamma"—that is, the old lady. And then, looking further into the dates in the journal, we are reminded that Catherine left on the 16th February, at 10 P.M., and that Mary Patterson, cook, joined his service. Mrs Taylor then came upon the 10th February. She does not appear to have been sick after she came until after taking some tapioca, and I think that was on the 13th February, three days after she came. But she was sick then, and vomited. So far as we know from the evidence, she was not sick after that till Friday the 24th—that was the last day of her life. An old lady of seventy-one—you will find the appearance which she presented to the experienced eye of Dr Paterson was that of a hale, healthy-looking person, fine form, good complexion, nothing in her appearance to indicate anything the matter with her. On Friday the 24th, she is going about the house all day quite well, as she used to be. It is true, one of the servants—I think Mary Patterson—said that she was a little peevish that afternoon, as she thought, over the affliction of her daughter; for she was with her day and night—in the same room with her—after she came. But between six and seven o'clock, according to the evidence, I think, of Mary M'Leod or Mary Patterson, the old lady showed a tendency to sicken. She wanted to be sick, and thought that she was about to be in the same condition as that in which she had seen her daughter. At this time she was apparently quite well, and there was nothing in her appearance to attract any attention to her. But I think it was about nine o'clock that she goes up from the consulting-room, in which she had been writing, to her own bed-room. I am speaking from recollection in saying that it was about nine o'clock that she went upstairs; but if I am wrong, his Lordship will put me right. But the precise time is a matter of comparatively little moment. The important matter is that she walks upstairs, nothing, so far as any one can see, the matter with her. In about half-an-hour the bell of her room was rung, and the servant upon going upstairs finds her sick, but not actually vomiting. She was wanting to vomit, and went to the basin and tried to vomit, but did not. She asked for hot water to make her vomit. This was about half-past nine. The servant goes down to get the water, and then afterwards she got some more. The old lady becomes very ill, and goes into a state of almost insensibility, sitting upon the chair, her head hanging down. The servant girl is sent for the doctor—that is, Dr Pritchard—who so far as she knew up to that time had not seen the old lady at all. He was in the consulting-room engaged with a patient. The patient went out shortly after, and the servant told him that Mrs Taylor was ill, and he went up to the bed-room. Then it was she was found with her head hanging down upon her breast, and he sent for Dr Paterson. You have the description which Dr Paterson gave you of her appearance—a very distinct description. He had no doubt that she was labouring under narcotic poison—opium, or some preparation of opium. Dr Paterson did not doubt that that was the case. We shall see the account given to Dr Paterson by the prisoner of her disease afterwards; but in the meantime, I merely want to direct your attention to his description of the symptoms of her disease. He said she had all the symptoms of poisoning from a strong narcotic. Opium would produce such symptoms, but the effects of the opium would be increased and quickened by the addition of a still stronger narcotic and stupifying poison—aconite. The state of depression and general weakness under which she appeared to be labouring were like effects such as antimony would produce. After the *post-mortem* examination, antimony was found in her body. Antimony is found there, and must have been administered to her. It must have found its way there, whether she took it herself, or it was accidentally administered, or it was administered to her. There is no doubt that she did not die of apoplexy any more than the wife died of gastric fever. She died of poison, and the symptoms were those of narcotic poison—the effect of narcotics administered along with antimony, in order to obscure, by overpowering, the symptoms of the antimony. But none of these narcotics were found upon the chemical analysis after death. It was explained to you that analysts usually fail in finding these poisons These narcotics are vegetable poisons, and are not detected in the same way as metallic poisons, such as antimony. In the case of narcotics we are indebted for the means of ascertaining the poison from the symptoms exhibited during life, rather than by the chemical examination afterwards. If metallic poisons are administered, these will be found on examination after death—the vegetable poisons most likely will not. The symptoms shown by the deceased lady were not the symptoms of any known disease—they were not the symptoms of any known kind of apoplexy; but during her life we have the symptoms of narcotic poisons, and we have the metallic poisons found in her body after death. Did she die, as her daughter died afterwards, of poison, although not entirely the same poison? or did she—as the prisoner, her medical attendant, had stated during her daughter's life, and to the registrar—die of apoplexy? I am afraid, gentlemen, there is no room for any other answer than that which I now make. She died of poison—narcotic poison, opium, aconite, antimony. The antimony they found in her. I am not speaking of the felonious administration of it at this moment. It is merely of the fact that she was poisoned, and that she died of poison. It doesn't follow necessarily—though I think it does in this case—but as a general proposition, it doesn't follow necessarily—that, because a death is occasioned by poison, that poison was murderously administered. The victim may have committed suicide, or got the poison accidentally somehow or other. It would be almost an insult to your understanding to suggest suicide in the case of either of these ladies, except to throw aside the suggestion at once. Neither of them had indicated any desire to get rid of life. With respect to the wife, suicide is not committed, as the tonic poison, which might be given in some cases, was so administered as to keep on the illness for months. Murder is committed that way sometimes, as from criminal annals we know. The suicide does not choose a long, lingering, and painful death. The murderer, however, sometimes chooses that course for safety to himself, to make the death appear the result of natural disease. Suicide in the case of the wife is therefore extravagantly out of the question; and in the case of the mother equally so. However they came by that poison, neither the one nor the other took it wilfully. Then, gentlemen, what is the next suggestion? I don't mean to say that the suggestion has been made by anybody; but it is made by the evidence in the case, and I shall bring you rapidly to the real occasion on which it occurred. Accidental is the next question which we have to consider, but only for a moment. Let us take the case of the wife. A person may get poison by accident. One bottle of medicine may be mistaken for another, and poison mixed with it by accident. But antimony administered by accident over a course of months—from the season of Christmas down to the 18th March—is widely out of the question. I mean poison taken by accident by some person, or by some other person giving it accidentally, and not wilfully—that is out of the question in this case. In the case of the mother, the question we have to consider is, whether or not the prisoner was the murderer. It is difficult to conceive that aconite and antimony got into the poor old lady's Batley's mixture by accident. It is not accident. I therefore put aside accident as entirely out of the case, as much so as suicide. There is no such suggestion as this in it. It is excluded in the prisoner's own declaration that any antimony was administered medicinally to the poor wife and to the mother, as he denies that it was so. She had no illness for which any one for a moment would think of administering antimony. The only illness which she had was the one which suggested the action of antimony. The action of antimony was vomiting, sickness, and cramp, burning sensations, and the rest of it. Antimony was therefore not administered medicinally. If the idea of suicide is out of the question—if the idea of accident is one not to be entertained—see what you are shut up to. You are shut up by a process short, but clear and convincing, that the poison which killed the woman was administered wilfully by the hand of some person in the prisoner's house; for out of it she does not appear to have been, from the time when she was first taken ill at the end of December or the beginning of January, until she was carried away to her grave. This is a sad conclusion which cannot be resisted. Then, who was the murderer? For there was a murder committed in that house—a deliberate, cold-blooded, cruel murder. Who was it? We know the inmates. There were two students of medicine. I suppose you may lay them aside as having nothing to do with it. Suspicion does not attach to them, neither had they the opportunity. The servants changed in the course of the enacting of this dreadful tragedy—all but one. Catherine Lattimer was there until the 13th of February. The poisoning went on after she left—the deaths both occurred after she left. She was not the poisoner, nor was there a breath of suspicion about her. Mary Patterson comes upon the 16th of February. The poisoning, indeed, goes on after she comes; but it had commenced long before—weeks before. We therefore leave her aside. There was Mary M'Leod—a girl under seventeen, the only remaining grown person in the house during the whole course of the administration to which I refer. I need not take any notice of the children, who were the only other inmates of the house. See, then, to what we have come. There was a murderer in the house—a murderer in that house practising the dreadful art of slow poisoning from the end of December till past the middle of March. The only two grown persons, except the boarders, who were in the house during that time—the only two who had access to the patients—were the prisoner at the bar and Mary M'Leod. This is narrowing the case to a very short question. I have excluded every other idea from the case by fair, legitimate, convincing argument, upon evidence which is not open to dispute. I have excluded the notion of natural death. I have established the fact of death by poison. I have excluded the idea of suicide, the idea of accident, the idea of administration medicinally. You are shut up, therefore, to murderous administration. I lay aside the children; I lay aside the two boarders; I lay aside the two servants, one of whom was in the house only during the first half of the period, and the other only during the last half, and I find that the only two who had access to these miserable victims, and had any opportunity to perpetrate the murders with which they are charged, were the prisoner and this one girl. Now, pray, consider with respect to the wife, upon the question whether or no the prisoner is not the man clearly proved by irresistible evidence to be so, what was the nature of the murder? It was a murder in which you almost detect a doctor's finger. It is gradual poisoning—poisoning so as not to kill but to weaken: leaving off for a day and then resuming again—one day better, two days worse. During the whole time the patients exhibited the symptoms of vomiting and purging, the result of the action of antimony. You have that going on during that long period; ay, and under the very eye of a medical man—the husband of the victim, who was in close attendance upon her. Do you think anybody else—do you think a girl of seventeen could have done that deed? She knew nothing about antimony. If she did not, the prisoner at the bar must have done it. And what is his case? His case respecting his own wife, who was thus demonstrably poisoned by inches under his very eye during this long period—what is his case? I thought it was gastric fever, he says. Gastric fever! Nobody could have thought it was gastric fever. Nothing like gastric fever in it. Nothing like anything except what it was—slow, cruel poisoning, which brought, in the course of two or three months, this poor woman to the grave with such an amount of the poison in her body. And, gentlemen, how does he speak even of the prescription of Dr Paterson? He writes to her father, I think, or mother—I forget which—that among other things Dr Paterson ordered was Dublin stout. Dublin stout! The last thing you would think of ordering for a person in that condition at least. Now, Dr Paterson says he did not order it; he swears he did not order it, and you are bound to believe him. Something was said in the course of the cross-examination by Dr Paterson which I must advert to, though not in the language of complaint. He was very much struck, when called in to visit Mrs Taylor, with the appearance of Mrs Pritchard. He was not called upon to visit her professionally. He was called to visit her mother, whom he thought dying, although the prisoner would not admit it. He was so struck with her appearance that the idea pressed upon him with the force of conviction that she was under antimony. My friend Mr Clark very properly put it to him, "Did you not think of stating your suspicion either then or when you went back on the 2d March?" Well, one was not in the least surprised certainly, that, being called in on the night of the 24th February to visit the old lady, he should not have volunteered a statement to his professional brother, living a few doors from herself, "Your wife there is under antimony: I have a grave suspicion of you that you are practising upon Mrs Taylor and that woman by antimony." He would have been a very bold man—bold to rashness—that would have ventured upon that. He might have scared the murderer from his victim for a moment—for a while: but he never would have gone to the house again—he would not have rescued her; and what position would he have been in himself? A consulting physician, called in to see the mother, volunteering to state the suspicion—although it was a strong one, and with the force of a conviction upon his mind from what he saw—that the daughter was being poisoned; and there could be nobody who could poison her except one. You see where his suspicions pointed, I daresay confirmed to such an extent by what has occurred—by what he has heard since—that the language which he uses upon that impression upon the 24th February is more emphatic than it would otherwise have been—that she was under antimony. She was under antimony beyond all question; but it would have been a rash thing, I think, for him to have made any accusation against anybody, or made any statement to anybody on the subject under the circumstances, upon the 24th February. Perhaps he had a fairer opportunity upon the 2d March. On the 1st March he says he was asked to call on the next day. He was not the medical attendant in Dr Pritchard's house at all. He had never been over his threshold before the 24th February, and he was not asked back again; but on the 1st March Dr Pritchard met him accidentally—that is to say, there was no designed meeting. They were both in the same street, and, speaking as persons who had met once before, he explained that naturally there was a conversation about the death of the mother—an allusion to it, and about the wife being a little better; and he says that on the forenoon of the 1st, about eleven o'clock, Dr Pritchard said to him, "I am going to Edinburgh to-morrow; and I should be glad if you will call and see Mrs Pritchard about eleven o'clock." Dr Paterson said his impression was—and there was no reason to doubt it—that it was an entirely accidental meeting, and it had occurred to Dr Pritchard upon the spot, while they were in conversation, to ask Dr Paterson to call next day; and he regarded it more as a mark of sympathy with the daughter upon the death of the mother, which he had almost witnessed, being the last person who had seen her except Dr Pritchard upon the night of his professional visit. But he saw her, and did prescribe for her. She was better, and he did prescribe for her. His suspicions were not removed—that is to say, he did not see from her appearance that day that he was entirely wrong in anything which he had suspected before. But do you think that he could have even then denounced the husband? I do not know whether he might not, by securing something in the room—something that had passed from her, and, having that chemically analysed, have ascertained whether antimony was there, or any poison. I do not know whether it was possible. Probably it depended on any recent administration of the antimony. But, without any proof—with nothing except his own suspicion—to appeal to the husband as to the state of the wife, it would certainly have been a strong measure for him to have given utterance to any warning on the subject. Without expressing any opinion as to what was Dr Paterson's duty in the circumstances, I shall only say that probably most men would have found it exceedingly embarrassing; and I shall not take upon me to express or to imply a censure upon the course which he took, of being discreetly silent by expressing any opinion whatever. It has no effect upon my mind; you can judge whether it ought to have any effect upon yours. It may be that you will be appealed to in this way, that if any of you were placed in similar circumstances, what would you have done? Would you have allowed a feeling of professional etiquette and professional dignity to interfere with your taking steps to save the life of a fellow-creature? Now, I would say again, that if he had said to the husband, "I suspect you of administering improper drugs to your wife," and if he had put the wife upon her guard against the husband, he might have scared the murderer from his prey from a time; but he would have done so at an immense risk, possibly at an immense sacrifice to himself. Nobody can tell what the world would have thought of him. There was not the opportunity which we have had since of ascertaining the facts conclusively by an examination of the body of the victim. But, gentlemen, I shall be asked what motive had Dr Pritchard for committing this crime? This question of motives is a very delicate one, and the importance of it is apt to be too much exaggerated—indeed, I think, is commonly exaggerated—and the very nature of it as evidence to a great extent misunderstood. There are many men whose worldly interests would be vastly promoted by the death of others. There are hundreds of persons who are in that position; but God forbid that it should weigh a feather's weight in the scale against any one of them if charged with murder, that it could be said—"You succeeded to money," or "You succeeded to estates by this death!" I say I believe there are hundreds, there are thousands—ay, possibly, there may be millions—in this world who are in that position, who would be benefited in their worldly means by the death of another, but who would shrink with absolute horror from the idea of hastening that death by a moment. Motives, therefore, of that description are of no weight whatever unless you have convincing evidence that the act was committed by the man; and if you have that, the supposed motive is an altogether secondary—almost unimportant—consideration. No doubt, in cases of murder proceeding from revenge, feelings of revenge, and passions stirred, you have a motive generally strongly indicated as one which is operative. The man who is in a passion—who is moved by the feeling of revenge, and who manifests it and sometimes expresses it, supplies proof of a motive in actual operation; but in cases of murder such as this, pray consider how the matter of motive stands as a question of evidence. There was here a cold-blooded, protracted murder committed—that is a fact with which you have to deal. The person who committed that must have been dead to all the ordinary feelings of humanity. It is difficult to enter into the feelings of such a one, to consider what the feelings may be of any person, man or woman, capable of committing such a murder as was, in point of fact, committed here—for I am assuming that I have convinced and brought you to the conclusion, upon grounds which are satisfactory to your minds, that the murder was committed by somebody. You are dealing with this case, therefore, that the poisoner here was some one who was dead to all the ordinary feelings which actuate a man—no compassion, no kindness, no sympathy for the person; bent upon the destruction of a victim, bent upon it for months; able to repress his or her feelings, and to conceal a design, to proceed in a cool, calculating way, producing and keeping up sickness, attending upon the sickness of his or her patient, down to the last fatal moment. The person capable of doing that is not demonstrative, but able to repress his or her feelings, able to conceal them, and to act without expression. Now, I impute to Dr Pritchard the murder of his wife under circumstances which, I think, exclude every reasonable ground for supposing that it could have been committed by anybody else. I do not know his feelings towards his wife. I know, indeed, that he was not a virtuous, affectionate, loving husband, for we know the footing upon which he was living in the house with the poor girl whom he had seduced almost at the age of fifteen. I do not know his feelings towards his wife, for the person who could commit that crime is, I repeat, not demonstrative. He is apt to be an excellent actor, able to repress—I shall not say repress his feelings—for I do not think any strong feeling could exist in the case, except the cool, calculating, deliberate determination to carry out a purpose. I say so much for motive. I know nothing about him or about the terms on which he lived with his wife. I know the terms upon which he lived with his servant-girl. You know it from the evidence. Whoever committed the murder attended apparently affectionately at the bedside, must have been in attendance upon the patient, and must have been in attendance with such apparent kindness that the patient received him and took food from his hands. But, gentlemen, I have more than anything I have stated yet against the prisoner. He had every opportunity. No poisoner could have a better opportunity than he had of poisoning in the very way in which the poisoning was committed here. He had an opportunity of putting it in almost everything. He had the material, and in abundance. He bought antimony—he bought it in abundance, in unusual quantity, represented, so far as the evidence of the Glasgow manager of the Apothecaries' Company goes, as very nearly unexampled in the case of antimony—a quantity unexampled even in the experience of the apothecary who was put in the witness-box for the prisoner to-day. He bought some ounces—two ounces at one place, and one at another. During the period between the 16th November and the 18th February he purchased two ounces—a very unusual quantity. Two ounces would equal the whole quantity used in practice by the customers of this apothecary for a year. About the same quantity would serve the whole dispensing practice of the apothecary who was examined here to-day. The prisoner had abundance of antimony. He is a medical man who used it; and he had abundance of opportunities of doing so; and he used it wholesale, so as to produce the gradual effect he desired. His servant-girl knew nothing about that antimony. She knew nothing about these doses. She was incapable of doing such a crime as this under the eyes of an innocent husband—a medical man attending upon his wife; but you will judge of that. But cannot we trace from his hands to the victim some particular articles of the poison? We have a bit of cheese which he cut and sent by his servant to his wife. The wife would not take it. One servant-girl ate a bit of it and Mary M'Leod swallowed a piece. It produced burning sensations in her throat, and what she called a bitter taste in her mouth. She never tasted anything like it before. It was a bit from the cheese in the house. She took the cheese downstairs and put it in the pantry. The mistress would not eat it. It was the first thing she had been asked to taste. The servant-girl took it down to the pantry, and next morning the other servant girl picked up a bit of the cheese there, put the bit into her mouth, and it produced in her such sensations as she never had before, and she was sick for hours after—from seven in the morning until ten. Then she has to go to bed. Can you doubt there was poison in that cheese? It was during the period that the wife was in the course of being poisoned, and within a few days of the fatal termination. This was a piece of food which was sent to her by her husband, and produced upon the servant-girl the effects of antimony. You must take that in connexion with what I have mentioned—that it was in course of his wife being poisoned, as we know, by somebody—by a murderer's hand—it was during that time that the husband sends to her a bit of food which, being tasted by two of the servants, produced upon them all the effects of antimony. You will remember that at the time there was some camomile tea made by him. His wife immediately after taking it became ill. I do not dwell upon the fact that the prisoner frequently prepared her tea, spread the butter upon her bread; but I cannot pass over the egg-flip; for that, again, is a substance which I trace from the hands of the man whom we charge with murder to the lips of his victim. The egg-flip was prepared by Mary Patterson. The prisoner gave her the egg; he told her to beat it up well in a porter-glass, very smooth, otherwise Mrs Pritchard would not take it; and he said he would add the sugar. The sugar was kept in the dining-room, not the consulting-room—it is medicine that is kept there. He goes to the dining-room for the sugar for this girl, who was in the pantry beating up the egg-flip. He does not go into the pantry with it, but into the consulting-room where antimony was kept, and then he goes from the consulting-room into the pantry, and puts the sugar into the mixture of beat-up egg. Hot water is then poured upon it. The cook tasted it, and what is the effect? Painful and violent illness is the effect produced by antimonial poison; not a doubt about it. Now this again occurs in the course of the period when the woman was being poisoned by inches in the house. She was very ill after taking food, and thought that she would die during the night, and was so ill that nobody could see her. I say again, can you doubt? Why, you see it almost as much as if you had seen the prisoner take the sugar from the dining-room into the consulting-room, and sprinkling the antimony upon it, and from thence to some place, and drop it into the egg-flip. The cook, upon tasting it, was ill, as she described, precisely as she would have been under the action of antimony. Gentlemen, these are very strong circumstances. I submit them to you for conclusion. You cannot fix the murder upon anybody else. You have no ground for suspecting anybody else. You must fix it upon the man who had the means and opportunity; but you will judge of that. You will judge whether it is probable a girl of seventeen, under the eyes of a medical man attending, as the prisoner was, upon his wife, was poisoning her with these subtle drugs, and he thought all the while it was gastric fever. Now, let me come to the case of Mrs Taylor, and that case throws some light upon the other. It is impossible it should not. It is even part of the same tragedy. I say again that I cannot enter into the mind of the man who is capable of committing such a murder as was certainly committed here by some one, or even conjecture what motives may be sufficient to set him upon the practice of the terrible art—for it is a terrible art that of slow poisoning. But it appears that he was in very poor circumstances. Indeed, he doesn't seem to have been possessed of a farthing. He was to some extent, not a great extent, I believe, in debt. His bank-book was overdrawn, and had been so for some time. His house, which he had bought recently, was not paid for except to the extent of £400, which he had taken out of the £500 given him by the old lady. It was a £2000 house, and of this £1600 was borrowed upon it. He had two policies of insurance, on both of which money was borrowed. That was his condition pecuniarily—living in a house of the value of £2000, but not paid for, with a practice, the extent of which I have no means of judging; but with his accounts overdrawn, even after applying £100 of the £500 which he got from the old lady, to some other purpose than the house. The old lady he knew was possessed of money. He had got £500 from her. She was very fond of him—particularly proud of him. She gave him the £500; but she gave him more money. She was possessed of £2500 more. According to her will—if he knew of it—that sum would come to his wife, and, failing his wife, he was to have the liferent of two-thirds of it. That would come to him immediately upon her decease. That was her will, and these were the terms upon which this moneyless man would succeed to two-thirds of the liferent upon her death. Am I to be told that it is inhuman to suppose that a man would kill the mother of his wife, who had been kind to him, for such a paltry motive as this? Kill her by poison! Gentlemen, she was killed by poison for some motive or other. There can be no motive known conceivable which will satisfactorily account to a well-constituted mind for the perpetration of an act so foul; but the foul act was perpetrated, and was perpetrated by some one for a miserable motive—a dreadfully miserable motive—by somebody void of heart, and void of ordinary feeling. That is the necessary condition of whoever perpetrated that murder. If there is no murder, it is an end of the question; but if there were a murder, the condition of the perpetrator was that of a man—a heartless unfeeling wretch, into whose motives it is impossible to enter—what would appear to one to be sufficient for his conduct! Well, then, as to the death of the old lady. Let us consider his conduct with respect to her. She has watched over his destined victim, if there be truth in the case which I have presented to you with respect to the wife. Let us see how he behaves with respect to his mother-in-law. The mother was sent for, Dr Cowan being the messenger upon his recommendation that she should be sent for. I do not insinuate that Dr Pritchard was averse to it, but Dr Cowan did suggest it, and he was the messenger to the mother to get her to watch over the sick and dying daughter. Well, she is there at the time, and I think it is proved almost to demonstration, as clearly as such a matter can be established—that she died from the effects of such poisons as were in the drug she was accustomed to use, when mixed with that drug itself. In the bottle of Batley's Solution which was found in her pocket—I suppose you will have no misgivings in your own mind about the identity of that which was taken possession of—it was the only one in the house with Batley in it, it was taken possession of after the prisoner's apprehension, and it was subjected to analysis, and in it was found antimony by chemical analysis—in it was found aconite—the presence of that being ascertained otherwise. Aconite is known to produce a peculiar tingling and benumbing sensation when applied to the lips and the tongue—so the chemists and medical men of experience recognise it at once by these effects. When the contents of the bottle which had been taken from the old lady's pocket were so applied to the lips, they produced the tingling benumbing sensation to a greater degree than the addition of five per cent. of Fleming's Tincture of aconite to Batley's Solution, although to a less extent than the addition of ten per cent. Aconite, therefore, had been added to that tincture to the extent of from five to ten per cent., Dr Penny thinks about seven per cent. The presence of aconite in that mixture is otherwise conclusively ascertained. It is conclusively ascertained by the fact, that the contents of the bottle killed small animals in precisely the same way as Batley's with from five to ten per cent. of Fleming's Tincture of aconite in it. So that the test of the sensation produced, and the test of the destruction of animal life, both together lead you to the conclusion that the contents of that bottle taken from the old lady's pocket consisted of Batley's Solution, with from five to ten per cent. of tincture of aconite added. And there was antimony in it; that was ascertained, too, by the chemical analysis. Who put antimony—who put aconite into that bottle? Here, again, you probably trace the finger of a medical man. It was not like a servant-girl between sixteen and seventeen, to find her way to the doctor's repositories and put in a little antimony and a little tincture of aconite. It seems to have been skilfully done; but it is done, and it must have been done before the old lady's death; for it entirely accounts for that death, and there is no other way of accounting for it. Her symptoms were precisely such as would be produced by taking a considerable dose of the mixture to which these poisons had been added. Now, gentlemen, let us see how the prisoner behaves with reference to her illness. You will remember from the short narrative which I gave you of the facts attending her death, that, although the old lady had complained of an inclination to be sick between six and seven, she had after that gone into the consulting-room and had written letters, and had left the consulting-room to appearance well enough and alone, and walked upstairs. She passed the servant-girl—I think, Mary M'Leod—on the stair about nine o'clock, and she was half-an-hour in the bed-room with her daughter before she left the room. And then she wants hot water to make her vomit. She complains only of the inclination to be sick even then, and has hot water brought to her twice for that purpose. And it is not till the bell has been rung a third time that the servant goes to the consulting-room to bring up the doctor, and, finding him there with a patient, he is delayed some minutes, and goes up, and for the first time sees the old lady after the attack. That is the evidence. Dr Paterson is sent for, and the account he gives is very striking and very important—so much so, that I must take the liberty of reading a part of it to you. [The learned gentleman here read that portion of the evidence which referred to the prisoner's account of Mrs Taylor's attack and illness upon Friday night, the 21st February; and also extracts from the evidence of Mary Patterson and Mrs Nabb, describing the finding of the Batley's mixture bottle in the pocket of Mrs Taylor after her death.] He continued:—I think you will be satisfied that there is not proof for the statement which he made to Dr Paterson, that she was in the habit of taking a drop occasionally—meaning that she was in the habit of taking spirits; that there was nothing to justify the expression that she was in the habit of taking a drop. There is no proof, and there is no reason to suppose there was any truth, in the statement he made that she (the old lady) had been indulging in liquor for a few days, and had also been taking an overdose of opium. It is certainly unfortunate for this—in other respects the most unfortunate of men—if he should prove to be innocent of the crimes with which he is charged—to have stumbled into the terrible error of making these false statements. One of these was when the old lady was still living; he stated to the doctor whom he had sent for to come and see her that she was in the habit of taking a drop occasionally: the other, that he stated to the washerwoman when she was in the room that she had been indulging in liquor for some days, and had been confined to her bed by an overdose of opium. In addition to that, the first statement of all, which he makes to Dr Paterson, is a very strange one. He had told the young man Connell that it was apoplexy, when he came down from the bed-room, and was going into the consulting-room, after the short time, so far as we know, he had seen the patient. He sticks to that main point, or rather to an account that looks something like it, for Dr Paterson had been told that for half-an-hour or an hour before, when writing several letters in the consulting-room, after having partaken of some bitter beer, the bitterness of which was remarked upon, she had tumbled off a chair in a fit on to the floor, and had been taken up to the bed-room. That, however, is not according to the truth, for she had walked from the consulting-room, where she had been writing her letters, in all probability up to the bed-room herself at nine o'clock. She had had no tumble or fit at all. Now, the doctor knew nothing of her having the attack till the bell had rung three times—that hot water had been taken to her by the servant to make her vomit. And even after the third attack he was prevented from going up for a short time from having a patient waiting upon him in the consulting-room. The accounts, therefore, do not agree. It was a strange explanation he made in presence of the servants, as if he had only accidentally discovered from Mary M'Leod—who, by the way, swore that she knew nothing about it—that she had got her a supply upon the Monday. Then it is a singular admission in connexion with it that before her death—before anything was found in her pocket at all—he told Dr Paterson that a few days before she had purchased something like half a pound of the solution, that she was in the habit of taking it regularly, and that, probably, her illness was to be accounted for by her having taken a good swig of it. That she was in the habit of taking this mixture—this solution of opium—is clear enough, and also that she had done so for years, so that an ordinary dose would have little effect upon her. That he knew that is also very true. Nay, that he knew it is certain, according to the case which is presented to you by the witnesses, if he had availed himself of the knowledge—he had got the bottle which the old lady had to allay her neuralgic headaches, or to ease herself from the excessive perspiration from which she suffered. He had availed himself of the knowledge, and had got hold of the bottle, and into it had introduced what he alone had the opportunity or means of introducing—that is, these two deadly poisons. Gentlemen, these falsehoods are very striking—very striking indeed; and they were followed by others. Dr Paterson showed his feeling upon the subject by refusing to grant any certificate of Mrs Taylor's death, and by informing the registrar that the death was sudden, unexpected, and to him mysterious, and that he would grant no certificate. Then Dr Pritchard grants a certificate himself. He says that twelve hours before her death she had been suffering from paralysis, and that apoplexy had supervened an hour before her death. He says—"Primary disease, paralysis; duration of that, twelve hours; secondary disease, apoplexy; duration of that, one hour." Dr Paterson had refused to certify. He then certifies himself, and certifies falsely. She was not suffering from paralysis twelve hours before her death. And he says she was suffering, and again falsely, from apoplexy one hour before her death. There was no paralysis, except the paralytic affection which was caused by the aconite, and that was not before she went upstairs at nine o'clock in the evening, which was only four hours before her death; for she died about one o'clock, or rather at half-past twelve. There never was any apoplexy at all—she died of poison. Now, gentlemen, here is a murder—a crime occurring as an episode in the course of another carrying on in this doctor's house—and you have a false certificate from him, a false statement of the cause of death. Who could have poisoned her if he did not? Allow me to supply an omission—that there is a mysterious matter in this case—indeed two of them—the one relating to the poisons—the same tapioca which had been got from a grocer's, I think, on the 13th February—and the other regarding the sickness of the assistants lodging in the house. I suppose it is clearly shown that poison—that poison antimony—that was the poison used in the tapioca that had been got and given to Mrs Pritchard, and that that antimony had been put into the parcel. It was purchased entirely for her use. A sufficient quantity of antimony was put into it, not to cause the death of anybody, but the sickness of anybody who took it. Keep in view that the method of poisoning alleged against the prisoner here is not the giving of a dose that would kill, but the introducing the poison into the food in such quantities that the taking of it would not kill, but produce sickness merely; the intention being, in dealing with the victims who used the food, to produce and continue the sickness for months, the fatal termination then supervening. A poisoner in this way practises the dreadful art successfully, and could not be very apprehensive of even himself or any one else taking the food accidentally, as it would only make them sick. He knows that to produce death it will be necessary to continue it for a long time. Into this tapioca antimony is introduced—sufficient to produce sickness in anybody taking it, but not to produce death. It was intended as part of this scheme to extend the poisoning over a long period of time. But Mrs Pritchard does not get this tapioca. She does not want it after it is made. It is taken by Mrs Taylor, and she is immediately seized by symptoms of poisoning by antimony. She is sick in the same way—I think she expressed it—as her daughter was; because the effects were the same. That tapioca was not put out of the way, as it might be required again; and if Mrs Pritchard had wanted tapioca again, she would have got that, and the poisoning would have been carried on by means of it. If anybody else got it, it would be a misfortune, but not much more. It would produce sickness, but not destroy life; and who could have introduced antimony into the tapioca except the master of the house, who was an adept—as I think I have proved against him—in such a mode of poisoning? The bag containing what was left of the tapioca which had prodnced sickness in Mrs Taylor is found afterwards in the kitchen, is analysed, and found to contain antimony. I don't know how many, if even more than one in November partook of poisoned food; but some food had been poisoned. I take that for granted, and that it had been taken by one of the boarders, named Connell, I think. But that is not presented as part of the case. He is one day more or less sick. If the lad is sick after he had taken something into which poison had been dropped—sugar, tea, or anything else—and that produced illness lasting for some time, I say nothing was more likely to happen in that house. The prisoner does not seem to have been alarmed about it—he does not seem to have been alarmed even when he himself was sick upon some occasion in February. He knew very well there was no occasion for alarm, for sickness was the end of it; that it would require a long sickness in order to produce anything like a fatal result. Gentlemen, I have now stated to you, I think, all the views of this case which occur to my mind as material. I have stated to you, to the best of my udgment, the questions and the considerations upon which your verdict must depend. These questions, to resume very briefly, are these :—Did both ladies, or did either of them, die from the effects of poison? If so, was that poison taken wilfully to commit suicide by both or either? Was it taken accidentally, by the mistake of the persons themselves, or of some others? If you answer the first of these questions in the affirmative, and the second and third in the negative, you are then shut up to this other question—Who committed the murder? for murder, upon the assumption of these answers to the questions I have stated, was committed. It is quite competent for you to find the prisoner guilty of the one charge, and to acquit him upon the other; but I submit to you, as the truth of the case, that he is guilty of both. I have stated to you the various considerations which appear to me to be of weight to determine conclusively your answers to the various questions which I have put to you in the manner which I have stated. By presenting the case to you, as I have done, maintaining the charge now at the close of the evidence as it was stated at the beginning, I have discharged my public duty to the best of my judgment, and, you will believe, I am sure, conscientiously. It is for you now, after you shall have heard the powerful, and I am sure altogether becoming and proper defence which will be stated for the prisoner by my friend Mr Clark, to consider how you are to discharge yours. If my friend shall be able to convince you, by arguments which you shall think the evidence warrants, that the evidence is insufficient—that you cannot, without serious doubt and misgivings, pronounce the prisoner guilty of both or either of these murders, then undoubtedly it will be your duty to acquit him; for in that case he shall be entitled to be acquitted. But if, on the other hand, you are satisfied upon the evidence that he is guilty of both or either of these charges—if the effect of the evidence, considered calmly and dispassionately, is to produce that conviction upon your mind, then your duty—you duty to the public, to yourselves, to the oath which you have taken—is to pronounce a verdict according, in that view, to what is your opinion of the truth of the case, finding that he is guilty.

[The Solicitor-General resumed his seat, having spoken about two hours and a quarter.]

MR CLARK'S ADDRESS FOR THE PRISONER.

Mr A. R. Clark commenced his address for the prisoner at twenty minutes to three. He said—Gentlemen of the jury, under this indictment the prisoner is charged with the commission of two murders—the one the murder of his mother-in-law, Mrs Taylor; the other, the murder of his wife. The annals of human crime are indeed black enough; but if he be guilty of the charges that are made thus against him, I do not hesitate to say that he is the foulest criminal that ever lived. He is a member of an honourable profession, whose duty and whose pleasure it is to assuage suffering, to ward off the attacks of disease, and to do their best to prolong human life; and we all know how nobly, how generously, how unselfishly that duty is discharged. But here it is said that the physician became the destroyer, and used his art of healing to sap the foundation of life. Black indeed would be a crime such as that, but it in no degree indicates the measure of the prisoner's guilt if he indeed be guilty. He is charged with having murdered two defenceless, trusting, devoted women—of one of whom (to use the expressive language of Dr Cowan) he was the idol, and to the other of whom he was united by the most tender of human ties—who was the mother of his children, and who loved him with a deep and lasting love. He cannot plead that any angry passion drove reason for a time from her seat, and led him to the commission of this foul act. Provocation cannot even be pleaded as a weak palliation for the crime. No; I accept the words of the Solicitor-General, and say that, if he did commit the crime of which he is charged, it was a cold-blooded, deliberate poisoning of these two trusting and loving women. Yet, even yet, the measure of his guilt, if he be guilty, is not full. His cruelty knew no compassion; for if it be true that he poisoned these women, he did not resort to the use of drugs that in a few minutes or hours might have put them beyond the reach of pain, but chose rather to practise his devilish arts by slow degrees, so that the poison which he was administering should stop his wife's life by slow degrees. It was a poison which, if the case against him be true, was administered day after day, and week after week: and yet, during the two months or three months which elapsed from the commencement of the administration of this subtle agent, he is represented as watching over the being whom he was destroying, and holding loving intercourse with—nay, sleeping by the side of—that woman, whom his infernal practices had doomed to death. Gentlemen, that is the crime with which he is charged. It is not less, but it is indeed, I believe, much greater; for I have only attempted feebly to portray those feelings of horror which must necessarily arise in every well-regulated breast, in conceiving a guilt so great as that of which the prisoner is charged. But if, indeed, it is true that that is the charge, then, I think, gentlemen, I am well entitled to say that, before you can hold him guilty of offences like these, you must have presented before you overwhelming evidence; for I think it is hardly in the mind of man to believe that there ever was made a wretch so foul—a person so utterly devoid of human sentiments, of human feeling, as to practise deeds so frightful as those that are stated against the prisoner. I make these remarks simply for the purpose of pointing out to you the character of the charge, because unless you have before you the character of this charge which is made, you cannot well appreciate the evidence which the Crown says establishes it. You must have had before you evidence in which there can be no doubt—evidence strong, clear, overwhelming, that brings home to your minds and consciences, without the slightest suspicion on the accuracy of the testimony, that the prisoner is guilty. But if there be any doubt—and I hope to be able to show you that there is much doubt—if there be any reasonable doubt on your minds of the truth of this charge, I need not say what has already been said by the public prosecutor, that the prisoner is entitled to the benefit of that doubt. But, gentlemen, I have not yet seen any reasonable ground on which it can be said that so fearful a crime has been proved against the prisoner; for I beg again to say, that you must consider that the public prosecutor has not been able to assign or suggest any motive for the commission of such a crime. True it is that the Solicitor-General endeavoured to show that he need not assign or suggest a motive, and I am not here to plead that murder may not be committed though there is no motive for the murder. But still, gentlemen, in considering whether there is evidence sufficient, it is hard to throw out of view whether or not there were considerations which might in any degree have been impelling him to the commission of the crime or these crimes; and all that the Crown have been able to suggest are, I think, these trifles arising from the connexion which it is said he had with Mary M'Leod, and from the expectation of some succession to be derived from the death of his mother-in-law, Mrs Taylor. Gentlemen, if it be true—if Mary M'Leod upon this matter is to be believed—if, without any corroboration whatever, Mary M'Leod's statement is to be taken for proof—if, in the absence of the proof of any familiarity whatever observed in that household between the prisoner and her, the statement which she gave you on the first day of the trial is to be taken for proof, I cannot help it; but you cannot conceive that the motive which the Crown suggests should have influenced the prisoner to the commission of this crime. The motive seems to me, if I can understand it, that he desired to marry that girl—to marry the girl of whose person he had already had possession, and that he had chosen, in order to carry out that intention, to tread over the dead bodies of those two defenceless women. Marriage may, as she said, have been spoken of, but in jest, and it may have been the motive to some one to commit the crime; but it is impossible to conceive it to be a motive to him. And in the case of Mrs Taylor, surely the motive was less. It appears —for the Crown have been at the pains to show it—that this unhappy man had his bank account overdrawn by some £300, and had borrowed upon two policies of insurance to the extent of £200—insurances which he had effected in 1851; and they tell you that, though he was the idol of Mrs Taylor, and was able, I daresay, to obtain anything which that woman could give him, nevertheless, to obtain some chance of succession—for he did not even know of the existence of the will which settled the life-interest of her estate upon his children, and, in the event of her daughter's death, gave him the annual interest until his children reached a certain age—he murdered this old lady who had trusted him, and who had loved him so long. Gentlemen, it is not in human nature to believe that these motives which were assigned or suggested by the Crown could ever have, in the least degree, actuated any human being to the commission of offences so hideous as these. And therefore, gentlemen, you must approach to the consideration of the evidence in this case, keeping fully before you the fearful crimes which are charged against the prisoner, and keeping this further before you, that there is no assignable motive or motives that can be suggested that could in the least impel him to the commission of these crimes. But my learned friend says the crimes are so like—the fever of the daughter is so very like that of the mother —that probably you would trace in all this the finger of the medical man, to use my learned friend's expression; and he dealt with the probabilities as proof upon which you are to proceed in this case. But put the likelihood before you, and consider then—Is this such a crime as a doctor would in such a position be likely to commit? You had it proved in evidence yesterday that in poisoning by metallic poison—of which antimony is one—the poison is necessarily found in the body of the victim, and proves always to be the best detection of the crime. No doubt Professor Maclagan said that it was possible that there might be a case in which all traces of metallic poisons might disappear; but his long experience—and no one has had longer experience than he—did not enable him to cite any case which had actually occurred. And consider further that, this was not only a crime which a medical man was unlikely to commit, but it was a crime which was not committed in the best way; for he used, not an occult poison, of which, as a doctor, he had the knowledge, but he used antimony which, as a medical man, he must have known left clear unmistakable traces When you assume the likelihood of his committing these offences, yet from the character of the crime, from its mode of commission, it is impossible to say there is anything to lead you to suppose that as a medical man he would commit it in the manner in which the Crown accuses him. Now, to sum up these considerations which the Crown have pressed upon you as indicating that he must have been the person who committed the crime, they are—that, in the first place, he had an opportunity of committing it; and, in the second place, he was in possession of the means. It is far from me to deny or dispute that he was. If the charge of poisoning be a charge of poisoning by a husband against a wife living in the same house, to say that there was opportunity is simply to allege that the one was the husband and the other was the wife. That particular goes a very short way—indeed, goes no way at all—in even suggesting or indicating guilt. True, in many cases it is so, and forms a great topic in this Criminal Court, but never in such a case as this. If you find a case where the crime is committed, and where the person who has been charged with committing the crime has made an opportunity for himself—has been zealous in obtaining opportunities—then opportunity is of the greatest possible importance and the strongest possible evidence; but to say that he has opportunity in this case is nothing more than to say it was likely, as, indeed, it was true, that the husband who was attending the sick-bed of his wife should carry to her some of her meals, and send up others with her meals. But that he should do so is, I am sure, nothing unnatural—nothing to suggest guilt. It would have been frightfully suggestive of guilt, if instead of sending up these meals, and taking them up himself, he had always chosen some other agent to carry up these meals and administer the food she was taking. If that had been the case, I would have been inclined to say that the Crown would have had the case much more strong to indicate guilt, than they have when, as is stated here, that he was administering to the comfort of his wife while upon her death-bed. Was it remarkable that he was possessed of the means of killing this woman, by the legal possession of poison? He was by profession a doctor, and had, no doubt, as I daresay most doctors have, considerable quantities of drugs in his possession. No doubt it came out yesterday from the evidence of Mr Campbell, that the quantity which he had of aconite was greater than that gentleman had ever sold to a medical man—as much, indeed, as he used in his dispensing business in the course of a whole twelvemonth. But see how little you can trust evidence like that, for we put into the box to-day two gentlemen who told you they were in the habit of making up prescriptions of aconite containing in each no less than half-an-ounce, and that they were in the habit of selling large quantities of that tincture in a year. No doubt the prisoner was in the habit of using large quantities of tartarised antimony, and much of this he is charged with having administered to his wife. But does that prove anything in the case? It merely proves that he was in possession of the substances which he is charged with having administered to those women. To that extent the Crown have proved their case; but how far is it possible to say that he obtained those poisons for the purpose of committing murder? The possession of those poisons is founded upon by the Crown as showing that he intended them for a felonious purpose. But is it possible to conceive that he bought those quantities of antimony and other drugs at the apothecaries' room for the purpose of committing murder? It is perfectly out of the question to suppose so. If those poisons had been so used, they must have been most destructive, as the strength is most enormous. The amount of aconite necessary to kill is a very minute dose indeed. But it is not unimportant, in considering this question, and it is very important especially in considering the argument of the Solicitor-General—that these poisons were not kept in any locked press, but, upon the contrary, were within the reach of the household. If one thing is established in this case, it is the fact to which I now allude—and I am not commending the prudence of leaving drugs exposed to those in the house. It is not a question of prudence, it is a question of crime we are considering, and it is established by all the evidence we have heard that those poisons were kept in an unlocked press in the consulting-room, within the reach of the other persons living in the prisoner's house; and taken in connexion with this matter, which I think the Solicitor-General could hardly explain, that it appeared Connell, one of the boarders in the house, took ill in November, when Mrs Pritchard was absent, and that his illness was referred to February, when no doubt Mrs Pritchard was in the house, and that the doctor himself took ill precisely in the same way, and indicating all these symptoms of poisoning which are relied upon as to the food of the persons whose death we are inquiring into. The Solicitor-General says, "Oh, the doctor will take no harm; I can hardly conceive of the prisoner being poisoned." It is perfectly incredible to say that while in the course of poisoning his wife he so suffered and took no notice of it. I think I shall be able to show you that this is not the case. It is a remark I have made, and I think it is right we should have it in view that, when we come to consider the articles of poisoned food which are in question, which the Crown say are poisoned, that there was not one of these articles of food which ever reached the lips of Mrs Taylor or Mrs Pritchard without passing through other hands than those of the prisoner; and it is odd enough that in regard to each of these three articles of poisoned food, the person who administered it, and who carries away the food left, is this girl Mary M'Leod. Now, gentlemen, these are the preliminary observations which I think it right to make in considering the question upon which you are now called upon to decide. And it will not do, I again repeat, to proceed upon suspicion or probability. You can only proceed upon proof, as distinct from conjecture, suspicion, or probability. It will not do for the Solicitor-General, in conducting this case, to say, "I have established that one of two persons must have committed these crimes," and that you can trace the particular finger of the medical man in connexion with those crimes. Probability will never support a conviction. It will not do for my learned friend to say, as he said at the close of his speech, as regards the death of Mrs Pritchard, it was the act of either the prisoner or of Mary M'Leod, but that it was not likely that a girl of fifteen would have the skill to do it. Do you not think that he shrinks from the onus of proof when he accepts this convenient mode of getting rid of the difficulty, as he must prove that it is one of those two persons who did it. He must prove by evidence that it was not Mary M'Leod, or some one else in the house, and it was only by showing that it was not Mary M'Leod, that he can bring this charge home to the prisoner. And, gentlemen, while on the topic, let me examine further and more minutely the evidence of the case. I was struck, in the course of this trial on the part of the Crown, by a very singular omission intentional on their part, as it must have been. They were speaking of the persons who cooked the food; and they came to Catherine Lattimer, and spoke to the tapioca in which they said antimony had been placed. They asked Catherine Lattimer if it was true that she put nothing into that tapioca, and she told you that there was nothing in it except tapioca; and that Mrs Pritchard chose to put the sugar into it to suit her own taste. But it is remarkable that when the Solicitor-General puts that dilemma to you upon which his whole case is founded, he said that it was either Mary M'Leod or the prisoner; but in the course of his examination of Mary M'Leod he did not venture to put the question —"Did you put nothing into these poisoned articles which by your hands you have carried to the lips of these two victims, Mrs Taylor and Mrs Pritchard." It is a singular omission in the case of the Crown, which necessarily depends upon being able to select between those two persons whom the Solicitor-General stated were the only two persons who could have committed the murder, that they did not venture to put the question to exclude upon her evidence the fact that she might have been guilty. And this is all the more strong, please to keep in view —all the more strong that I shall trace immediately through her hands, and through her hands alone, every article of poisoned food which we have heard of; and I think I will be able to show you that the prisoner had nothing to do with any one of them. Now, gentlemen, let us take the two cases separately; and as Mrs Taylor was the person who first died, I shall state shortly the case which I have to submit to you upon the evidence applicable to this unfortunate lady Mrs Taylor was taken ill on the 24th February. Some uncertainty there appears to be about the hour. She had come on the 10th; she was taken ill on the 24th February; and ultimately died on the Saturday morning. Her illness was not long. There were certain symptoms observed upon by the Solicitor-General of her vomiting and purging in the course of that forenoon; but it is quite certain that she did not die of the administration of antimony. It is proved by the medical evidence—and it is the case of the Crown—that in her case antimony was not the agent which caused her death; but it is said that it was a more subtle poison still; and they attributed it to the aconite which existed in that solution of morphia which she was possessed of, and which she used to a considerable extent. Now, let us see what the evidence is as to the cause of this lady's death. Antimony was found on her person, on the medical examination after her death; but, as I said before, we may discard that, for it is not said now to be the cause of her death. There is a question whether it was opium which she herself possessed, or whether it was aconite which had been murderously introduced into the opium. The case for the Crown—that aconite was the cause of death—necessarily depends upon their being able to show, from the symptoms which were observed by Dr Paterson—the only person who saw her alive when she was suffering under the influence of the poison—whether these symptoms are to be attributed to aconite to the exclusion of opium, or at all events to be attributed to aconite given along with opium. And what is the evidence which we have upon this matter? I take what I think is not unnaturally the evidence which is best to be relied upon—the evidence given by the gentleman who observed the case; because all the others—the only two others who were examined upon the matter—Dr Maclagan and Dr Littlejohn—were merely giving scientific opinions; and Dr Paterson stated on his examination that he believed, when he saw Mrs Taylor on the 24th February, that she was narcotised—suffering under opium, dying from its influence—and he described the symptoms, which I need not go over. Amongst others, he described the symptoms of laborious oppressed breathing, which he at a subsequent examination described as what some people would call stertorous breathing; described further coma as existing—a coma which, at the time of observation, he looked upon as the coma which is produced by the attack of a narcotic poison, such as opium. Now, no other person has anything further to go upon, so far as symptoms are concerned, except what Dr Paterson himself observed—the only observer; and Dr Paterson, having heard the whole history of the case, and having been examined, retained the opinion of the case which he had expressed before—which he had expressed at the time, and attributed the death to Mrs Taylor taking too much opium. He did not suppose that there was any indication whatever of the presence of any other poison. No doubt he said, in answer to a question put from the Bench, that it was not impossible that aconite might have been present; but surely the statement that it is not impossible that aconite is present is not a statement which can in any degree support the case of the Crown. And what does the other gentleman say? I asked Dr Maclagan, who studied the question, if they were the symptoms of poisoning by opium, and he said they were not. I asked him why he said there was no coma, and that the breathing was imperceptible and not laborious. Dr Maclagan had not observed very minutely what Dr Paterson said; for Dr Paterson said there was coma; that there was laborious oppressed breathing. I referred Dr Maclagan to the testimony which Dr Paterson gave, and he said, "Oh, you may throw that out of count altogether. It is in consequence of the imperceptible breathing; it does not indicate aconite as distinct from opium." Upon this he founded his opinion that aconite was present, and that she was not suffering from opium. He threw out that, but omitted to notice that Dr Paterson was particular in establishing that there was oppressed breathing as contradistinguished from imperceptible breathing, which indicates the presence of aconite. But Dr Maclagan went further, and said, "Oh, it is oppressed breathing only, not stertorous breathing." But Dr Paterson was recalled, and we have him afterwards stating that he preferred to call it oppressed breathing, and that most people called it snoring or stertorous breathing. Therefore, I think it is out of the question to say that the Crown have anything like established the proposition upon which the whole case of the Solicitor-General rests, that the aconite was the agent which led to this lady's death. I am assuming—I don't care to enter into the question -- that that lady had not died a natural death. But I only ask you to consider whether there is evidence on this point on which the whole case for the Crown turns, of the administration of aconite. For I think the best evidence—that of the observer at the time—an observer not, as I shall afterwards be able to show, in favour of the prisoner, but against him—the only one is the observer who tells you both at the time and now, that he is of opinion opium was the agent which caused death. Let us see now whether it was not possible for this death to occur without in any degree being connected with the prisoner. Assuming for a moment that opium may be the cause of death—I am not bound to put it in the least degree higher—assuming that opium may have been the cause of death, let us see whether it was not possible that this act might have occurred without the agency of the prisoner Assume, if you like, that antimony had been administered—I shall consider the proof of the antimony—but assuming it—what was there more likely than that this old lady might have taken a great dose of opium, as was suggested at the time by Dr Paterson, and was spoken of by the prisoner himself, who said he believed she had been indulging in that stuff? It is the case for the Crown that she was suffering from vomiting and purging; and what, I ask, more likely than that, to relieve the pain from which she was suffering, she might have overdosed herself with the drug, which she was so plentifully in possession of? And if this is a fair and reasonable theory to take, why should you go upon the probability of the Crown, and say we shall prefer the probability of the Crown to the probability of the other side, and find that Mrs Taylor died from the administration of aconite, though it might have been that opium was the cause of her death, of which she herself was abundantly possessed? I do not say that the old lady committed or intended to commit suicide; far from that. But a person having these dangerous drugs, and so much given to the use of them, may have killed herself by her own hand, more especially if it be true, as the case for the Crown indicates, that her system had been reduced by antimony previously administered. Nothing more likely to have happened than this—that being so reduced, and taking a dose of that by mistake for the purpose of relieving herself from the pains and vomiting which she suffered from—nothing, I say, is more possible than that she may have taken too much for her reduced system of body, and died from taking that opium in the possession of which she was to such an extent. But, gentlemen, all these considerations are of very little consequence until you come to the question of considering whether there is proof of the administration. It is of very little consequence in what way this unhappy lady died; but it is of consequence whether it was from the prisoner's hands, or through his instrumentality, that the poison was received. Now, I think I can show you that, as regards this unhappy woman, there is no proof whatever that he administered any poison. The only poisoned article which the Crown can even by any evidence suggest that she received, was the tapioca which she obtained, I think, upon the 13th for Mrs Pritchard's use. Let us see what about this tapioca. The case of the Crown is that antimony was put into this tapioca by the prisoner; for the tapioca no doubt contained antimony. Let us look at the history of this tapioca; it is a very important item in the case. It would have been well if the Solicitor-General had explained at a little greater length how he connected the prisoner with this tapioca. Let us have the history of it. It appears that after Mrs Taylor came to visit her daughter on the 9th February—on the Monday following, I think, on the 13th—it was suggested, apparently through Mrs Taylor, and in the course of the forenoon of that day, that Mrs Pritchard would like some tapioca. There was no talk previously of their having been any tapioca required for the use of Mrs Pritchard. She was ill, and in bed, and her mother thought that tapioca would be food which she might relish; or it may be, Mrs Pritchard herself may have suggested that she should like some of it. Accordingly some tapioca is got by a little boy who is sent to buy it, and it is brought in and received oddly enough by Mary M'Leod. She says it was placed for some short time—she does not tell how long, about half-an-hour, perhaps—she says it was placed on the lobby table for that time. According to Catherine Lattimer's statement, Mary M'Leod takes down the tapioca to Catherine; but according to Mary's statement, it was taken down by Mrs Taylor herself. Now, the suggestion of the Crown here is that the prisoner put in this antimony into the tapioca, and that it was nicely adjusted to the tapioca which had been bought, so as to produce sickness leading to death, but not to produce death itself. From what the Solicitor-General said it would have been certainly of some importance to have shown that the prisoner had any opportunity whatever of administering or putting any poison into the tapioca, but it is not even proved—there is not a shadow of evidence—that he had any opportunity. The tapioca was received by Mary M'Leod, taken down to the kitchen after having lain a short time on the lobby table; and there is not a vestige of evidence to show that the prisoner was in the house at the time. Catherine Lattimer and Mary M'Leod could have told you that, but there is not a suggestion on the part of the Crown that Dr Pritchard was present in the house at the time. He was a man accustomed to exercise an active profession, and, of course, naturally, would be out at that period of the day; but, at all events, it is not even shown that he was aware in the least degree that his wife desired tapioca, or that his mother-in-law had ordered it. It is not even shown that there was the least possibility of his introducing antimony into that bag. The antimony must have been in the bag before it was taken down to Catherine Lattimer, because Lattimer prepared the tapioca from it, and that tapioca is said to have been poisoned. It is prepared and carried up by Mary M'Leod to her mistress, who declines to take it, and it is taken by Mrs Taylor, who, according to Mr Connell, one of the students living in the house, was taken ill after partaking of it. Now, when you have poison found in a house, passing through certain hands undoubtedly, and among those, through the hands of the only person whom the Solicitor-General says he must exclude before he can convict the prisoner, how is it to be supposed that he could have anything to do with putting poison into this tapioca, of the existence of which he did not know, and seeing, moreover, that he was not in the house at the time, and there is no suggestion of that kind? The antimony was put into the bag in the house; but then the prisoner is not proved to be there. Are you to hold, therefore, that his was the foul hand that put in that antimony for the purpose of taking away his wife's life, or that he adjusted it with such nice admeasurement, to see that too much poison was not taken in any portion? To have done this would have been to have taken much more time than he could have had, even though he had had the opportunity of putting it in. On the contrary, gentlemen, I suggest to you that it is almost inconceivable that he could have done it, and that there is upon the proof, as the Crown have chosen to lead it, and upon which you must find your verdict, a greater probability that it might have been another hand than his that put in the poison. Yet with all the probability in favour of another person, the Solicitor-General's whole case was this—the murder was committed by one of two, and it was not likely that a girl like Mary M'Leod was the person. Is there any further proof of administration in this case? Not the slightest—there is no other proof whatever of administration. No other poison could be traced to the prisoner, or even to show that he was connected with this case. As regards Mrs Taylor—that is the whole evidence of administration. But there is another bottle—a bottle of Batley's Solution—which she had in her pocket, and which, apparently, she carried with her; and it is suggested that the prisoner may have put the aconite and the antimony which was found in it into the bottle in the pocket. He knew, no doubt, that she was taking it; but it is not in the least degree proved that he knew where it was, in what bottle it was, or where Mrs Taylor kept the bottle. Mary M'Leod did know, for she bought it for Mrs Taylor. But what is the ground of the suggestion that aconite had been put into that bottle before Mrs Taylor had it? What is there to prove it? All that you have is that Drs Maclagan and Littlejohn say there was, that they were contradicted by the person who actually observed its effects. And what became of this bottle? It was found after her death on her person. Is it possible to suppose that he had means of getting at the bottle before her death to administer the poison? How could he? It was carried about upon her person, and there is not the slightest suggestion that he ever had access to it; and yet you are asked to act upon that suggestion, because, to use the words of the Solicitor-General, "You may probably trace the administration to a medical hand." You are to act upon probabilities so general that I wonder the Solicitor-General put it to you. No; probabilities are not in this case—probabilities are not here. It is proof, and proof alone, that we can go upon. Now, what was the history of that bottle? It was found in her clothes, no doubt, when the body was being dressed by these two women, Mary Patterson and Mrs Nabb, and even they did not know the very great quantity, perhaps, that this old lady had taken. But still more; supposing that she should take no aconite, she had taken sufficient of the mixture to account for her death. Assuming that the highest mark on the bottle, as taken by Dr Paterson, is a correct one, it would come to be not more than 2¾ ounces that had been taken. It was shown that the bottle was put by for the time, but if it was taken away after the murder, that is of very little consequence. If he had put the antimony into it, would it not have been very easy for him to have thrown the bottle aside? But instead of that, we have him expressing his surprise to these two women that she had taken such a great quantity of the medicine which she was accustomed to take. He takes away the bottle, and brings it back again, and there it remains until examined by Dr Penny, who then finds that there exists in it some aconite and antimony. But where is the shadow of proof that he put it there? The bottle was lying open—the bottle was not locked up in any way—it remained in the house from the death of Mrs Taylor, from the 25th February till after the prisoner was apprehended, more than a month afterwards. Any person in the house might have access to it, and yet all that can be suggested to prove that the prisoner put in this antimony and this aconite before her death was contained in that observation of my learned friend, that you could trace, or that you could probably trace, here the finger of the medical man. It is a singular request to you to proceed in such a case on such a suggestion. Then another consideration on which the Solicitor-General founded a good deal was, that the accused gave an account to the registrar that Mrs Taylor had died of paralysis and apoplexy, which is not, as he says, true, and which he could not have believed, and that he considers to be another proof of his guilt. Now, in the utter absence of any proof of the administration of poison to Mrs Taylor, it is stated that he said this woman had died of some disease of which she did not die—that she had died from natural disease, while really she had been poisoned. But what did he say to these two women? He said, when they found the bottle, "Good heavens, I am surprised to find what a quantity she has taken." But it seems that she was able to take about 150 drops a day, and was it, therefore, unnatural for him in the circumstances to use the expression that she had died from natural causes? Then Dr Paterson had previously told him that, in his opinion, she had died of poisoning by opium; and what was therefore more natural than for the prisoner, on being visited next day by his father-in-law, to say, "Oh, the death was sudden and apoplectic?" Was it very unnatural for the son-in-law meeting his father-in-law to ascribe the death to natural disease, though he knew it was to be ascribed really to taking opium? It may have been wrong—it was quite wrong in him to send an improper account to the registrar, who was bound to register the cause of death. I am not justifying the act—I am not justifying the act at all—I am considering only the question of whether you can infer guilt from the circumstance that he tells his father-in-law that death resulted from natural causes. Well, knowing that the unfortunate woman died from taking too much opium, I do not think that is a very unnatural circumstance; he does not wish the true cause of his mother-in-law's death to appear—he wished rather to conceal it. He tells his father-in-law what he thinks of it, or rather tells him to go to Dr Paterson; but Dr Paterson declines to give the information, for he refers the father-in-law to the son-in-law again for the cause of death. But if he was intending to conceal the cause of death, so as to prevent inquiry, and that, too, with a guilty knowledge, would he have sent the father-in-law to Dr Paterson? Would he not at once have certified the death himself, as he afterwards did? Dr Paterson would not do it. His dignity or etiquette would not allow him to do it; he was the consulting, and not the attending physician, and he takes no notice or little notice of the old gentleman, but refers him back to his son-in-law, who says, and, I think, says humanely enough, the cause of death was apoplexy, and does not choose to ascribe it to its real cause, which would indeed be painful enough for a husband to hear. I do not say that he was justified in doing as he did; I am not justifying the morality of the act; but, looking at the circumstances that are presented to us, is there any degree of guilty knowledge when he asked Dr Paterson to inform his father in-law of the cause of death, and he was only forced to take that step by Dr Paterson refusing to act upon the suggestion? But, gentlemen, there are some other aspects that he gives of it—some false aspects which the Solicitor-General founds so much upon, and which all depend upon the evidence of Dr Paterson; and Dr Paterson, I think, in a case of this kind, is not justly entitled to all the consideration with which he was treated by the Solicitor-General; for I venture to say that no witness in a case of murder ever exhibited so great an animus as that gentleman did exhibit when he was examined in the box, and I would call attention to one or two curious facts connected with his examination. Why, he had got the exact distance between his house and the prisoner's house; for when he was asked, "How far is it?" he replied at once, "195 yards." A criminal detective could not have answered with greater precision, or given it off with a better air; but there was still something worse suggested by him, which he had no reason to suggest. What he told you here in the witness-box was, that he met Dr Pritchard accidentally on the 1st of March, and that Dr Pritchard asked him to come and see his suffering wife next day; but Dr Paterson added, with something which I confess seemed like a sneer, "he would not have asked me if it had not been for the accidental meeting." How does Dr Paterson know that? I should think Dr Paterson regrets extremely having made the observation from the witness-box when he was sworn to speak upon oath, for it was merely conjecture, which could proceed from nothing but animus in his mind against the prisoner. He had no right to draw his own conclusions in that way. It might have been an accidental meeting, or it might not. Granting that it was an accidental meeting, as Dr Paterson describes it, he has no right, because he is asked at this accidental meeting to visit the prisoner's wife on the following day, to say that that request would not have been made had it not been for that accidental meeting with Dr Pritchard on the street. And I do think that, considering the bias which that gentleman has shown, and the conduct which he has displayed with regard to this melancholy case, I am not too strong in saying that very little credence is to be placed on his observations or remarks upon this case as against the prisoner. From the position Dr Paterson occupied in the box—a position which the Solicitor-General declined to characterise, and an example which I shall follow—I will leave you to consider whether the gentleman is speaking exactly the truth, or has been speaking, I do not say distinctly untruths, but speaking from impressions which he has unreasonably taken up, when he reflected upon this case from the time it commenced; and when you consider what he said in speaking of Mrs Pritchard, that when he was called in to see Mrs Taylor on the night on which she died, on the 24th February, he did not speak to Mrs Pritchard, but saw her, and seeing her, he formed the conclusion that she was being poisoned—slowly poisoned by some person to him unknown. That was the conviction which he affirmed. Well, gentlemen, he says he was frightened to tell Dr Pritchard about it—"It was an unsafe thing," said the doctor. Was it unsafe to tell the poor father the next day when he came to call upon him to ascertain the cause of his wife's death—was there any danger in telling the poor father, or suggesting that he should take some steps to save his daughter from being murdered, which he, Dr Paterson, as a medical man, knew, or which he was convinced was being done? There was no danger—nothing but a suggestion to be made, and the woman might have been saved. Yet Dr Paterson, in the face of the conviction that murder was being done, would do nothing whatever to arrest its course. Nay, more; even a more fearful thing was said by him in the witness-box. He was asked by the husband, in the manner which I have stated, on the 1st March to visit the wife on the 2d March, and he did so. On doing so he found that that woman was being murdered by some one to him unknown, and, retaining that conviction when he saw her upon the second occasion, that conviction was, he said, confirmed. And, gentlemen, Dr Paterson told you that either through fear or etiquette or dignity, being but a consulting physician, and not attending the patient, he did call in then merely as a friend to express condolence—he gave no hint to this unhappy lady as he and she sat alone, about the murder which he was convinced was being practised upon her—was being slowly carried through. I will not characterise the position which Dr Paterson holds; but if what Dr Paterson says is to be believed, I beg you, gentlemen, to judge of the conduct of that medical man, who was afraid, from motives of his own—fearful of his purse—fearful of his person—fearful of his dignity and of his etiquette—to arrest the progress, or take any steps to arrest the progress, of a murder which he was convinced was being perpetrated. Gentlemen, for Dr Paterson's sake, I refuse to believe that statement. It is a statement which I think cannot be believed; it is a statement which has grown upon this man, as that expression clearly indicated—which he has attained by brooding over this case. I do not believe that he saw any symptoms of poisoning, or he would have acted as every medical man would have acted—unselfishly, nobly, and generously in the matter. And when you see that this is inconsistent with the whole conduct of the profession to which he belongs, I ask you to disbelieve many of the statements which he makes. You cannot rely upon these statements, given with a bias, for he tells you what is incredible or only credible at the loss of his own honour, which I am sure he will strive studiously to guard. He has become a partisan in this matter altogether, and forgot what is due to his position and his profession. All that can be said of Dr Paterson is this—that he speaks about the prisoner, of his mother-in-law, and speaks further about what the prisoner said about her falling; yet even after all, this is merely an account of a circumstance given by Dr Paterson some months, or, if you like, a month after the case occurred. And because the prisoner made some statements which are not consistent exactly with the truth as now disclosed upon the evidence, are you to believe upon Dr Paterson's statement, and upon his statement only, that these statements were made so as to show guilty knowledge. I can quite understand how it should be that, after there is proof of administration, you may support that proof by evidence of falsehoods which the prisoner may tell, if you have reliable evidence to prove the truth that falsehoods were stated. But when you have no evidence of the administration of poison—when the evidence is all the other way—when you have no evidence that he had administered that poison; then I think you cannot eke out the probabilities of the case by appealing to these probabilities, or appealing to falsehoods depending upon evidence like that here, showing conclusively, beyond reasonable doubt, that this prisoner was the person who committed that foul crime upon the person of his mother-in-law. Gentlemen, that is the examination, which I make of the evidence in the case of Mrs Taylor; and you will please to observe that, though I think I have brought out the whole proof which attaches upon this matter, there is no proof whatever to convict the prisoner with any administration of poison except suspicion—this suspicion arising from the fact of his being a medical man. Let us see if it stands differently in the case of Mrs Pritchard. No doubt, he attended her bedside, as he was bound to do as her husband—as he was bound to do as a physician; and no doubt he ascribes her death to gastric fever, to which gastric fever that death undoubtedly was not due. But is it so very clear that a disease, which indicated itself in the manner which was described, might not have been mistaken even by a skilful medical man for gastric fever? On that matter, if I am not mistaken, we have no evidence. We have, no doubt, evidence now given in the course of the trial, that the symptoms were symptoms of poisoning by antimony; but are the symptoms of poisoning by antimony so easily distinguished by a person assumed to be innocent of the administration of it? It is all very well at this present time, when the case has come out, and the chemical analysis has been made, for medical men to say that the symptoms are consistent with poisoning by antimony, and suggest that poisoning by antimony—to make that statement not only when their suspicions are aroused, but when they know by the chemical investigation that antimony was present in the body. But, gentlemen, it is a perfectly different case when the administration is going on; and I do not think there is any evidence whatever to show that the symptoms of poisoning by antimony are capable of easy detection. No such question that I know of was put to the medical witnesses. Therefore, the whole case of the Crown necessarily fails upon this matter, upon which they have founded so much; because they say that Dr Pritchard is to be presumed guilty of those offences because he should easily and at once have known that something was wrong, and that he was absurd in putting it down to gastric fever. All very well, when one is wise after the fact, to ascribe it to this poison, because it has been previously ascertained; but consider, if you please, whether there is any evidence to show that, though he might have been wrong in the existence of fever and the existence of gastric fever, he could have known or suspected that there was poisoning by antimony. The only evidence which we have upon this matter, I think, is simply an expression which we have from Dr Gairdner, who saw Mrs Pritchard upon two days, on the 8th and 9th February, and, I think, in answer to questions from my friends on the other side, he said, "The case puzzled me very much." So much for the easy inference which was here made as inferring Dr Pritchard's guilt, that Dr Pritchard ought to have discovered the poisoning by antimony which was going on in his own house, himself a medical man, as the Solicitor-General so often repeated. But if the prisoner was guilty of this crime, why was he so perfectly willing—nay, desirous—that the wife should have the assistance of attendance? It was he who brought Mrs Taylor, according to the assumption of the Solicitor-General; and after Mrs Taylor, poor thing, was taken away, what is the history we have upon this matter? It was suggested by him that she should have a nurse to attend her; and the suggestion would have been carried out but for whom? For his wife. For you will remember that the witness Catherine Lattimer, when examined upon the first day of the trial, stated that she conversed with Mrs Pritchard upon that subject, and Mrs Pritchard said that the doctor wanted her to have a nurse, but that she objected to strangers. And, again, the same statement was made by her brother, Dr Taylor, who was examined to-day, and who tells us that Dr Pritchard offered to get a nurse, but that Mrs Pritchard refused. Is it suggested, therefore, by some persons here who had some knowledge of the disease of his wife, that the prisoner wanted to prevent his wife from getting daily and nightly attendance? Now, the evidence shows that it was owing to her own act and wish that the attendance was not got. That is proved by the evidence of Catherine Lattimer, and still more clearly by that of Dr Taylor. Was the prisoner desirous that medical men should be excluded from her bed-room? It was said that Dr Gairdner was called in; and some evidence has been shown that she was desirous of a medical attendant; and that she called her husband a hypocrite. To this the Solicitor-General made no reference, and very properly so, I think, as there was no doubt it was spoken under the influence of delirium. Dr Gairdner was there on the 8th and 9th February, he says; and he told you that a message had been sent to him telling him not to come again, and that it was from Dr Pritchard; but when we examined Dr Taylor to see whether Dr Gairdner was stopped from going again to see Mrs Pritchard, we found that it was Mrs Pritchard herself that took exception to his attendance, and prevented it. No doubt this was so, according to Dr Paterson's statement with reference to this matter, for which there is no foundation; and it would have been better if he had kept it to himself, as the statement appears to have been made to bias the case—so that there is no reason to suppose that, in order to poison her, the prisoner kept persons away from the bedside of his wife. It was her own act that prevented her having Dr Gairdner, and it was also her own act that prevented proper attendants. I think that there is no probability in the circumstances on which the Solicitor-General founds, that the prisoner was desirous of secluding his wife from supervision, that he might the more secretly practise the art which he was accused of practising against her. It is very idle for the Solicitor-General to say, "I reduce the case to a question between Mary M'Leod and the prisoner." It is not enough to say that a girl of seventeen might have been guilty of it, but I should have liked the Solicitor-General to have shown anything like proof of the administration of poison by the prisoner. He should have shown that the poison ever reached his wife by another than his own instrumentality. With reference to the question of poisoned food, the first thing I shall notice is the poisoned cheese; and it is said that the cheese was poisoned by the white powder which the prisoner is said to have had in his possession. We will see if there is any evidence to show that that was done by him. It is spoken to by the girl Mary M'Leod. She tells you that she had taken up the tray for the supper, and that on the tray was the cheese and other things which were placed on the table at which Dr Taylor and the other inmates of the house are sitting; that she came out, and that, on returning again, Dr Pritchard handed to her a piece of cheese to take to her mistress. She did not see it cut off the cheese; but Dr Pritchard handed it to her sitting at the table; and it is perfectly obvious that it must have been cut off the cheese eaten by the family at supper. If he had placed antimony upon it, it must have been placed upon it in the presence of the persons at supper. You have heard the cheese described—a piece of yellow cheese—which must have indicated the powder of tartarised antimony, if placed upon it. It was antimony that was placed upon it if you believe the medical witnesses, because Drs Maclagan and Littlejohn stated that it indicated antimony in the symptoms. Dr Littlejohn suggested the possibility of his putting the tartarised antimony into the egg-flip; but it was not asked if it were possible to put this tartarised antimony upon the cheese while sitting at supper; and I leave you to judge if it were possible. The piece of cheese was taken up oddly enough—I cannot help noticing the coincidence—by Mary M'Leod. She says she ate a part of it, and that it did her no harm; but the residue was taken down to the kitchen and eaten by Mary Paterson, and she suffered from vomiting. Now, will you take it into your minds if it was possible that the prisoner could have poisoned the cheese by putting on antimony when it was in the dining-room—sitting in the presence of others who were in the room. If he had wanted to do that, would he not have done it in a cooler way than in the presence of all those people who were sitting there, and could not help seeing it done? Look again at the egg-flip, on which I will say a single word or two. The egg-flip was prepared in this way. The doctor comes and tells his servant to prepare some egg-flip, a thing not unnatural to be taken by a person with a delicate stomach, as she undoubtedly was suffering from, and not an unnatural thing for a medical man or a friend to order. But the Solicitor-General says that this was a plot for Dr Pritchard to get in his drugs in this way; and he says, with a sort of sneer, that he told her to take it very soon, as if for the purpose of administering poison. He supposes that he went through the dining-room and got the sugar, and then into the consulting-room, and then that he went into the pantry and dropped the pieces of sugar on which he had put antimony into the egg. Does he give any proof of this? Does he suggest anything more than suspicion? What is the proof of his being there? The Crown seem to have doubted whether he could with sugar have put in so much antimony as to have produced the effects which the servant girl says that she suffered. And he asks Dr Littlejohn if it was possible. Dr Littlejohn says, "I think it is possible." I asked Dr Littlejohn if he ever made an experiment. He answered, "Not a direct experiment." Then I asked, "Did you ever make an indirect experiment?" To which he replied, "No." "Then you made none at all?" "No, I did not, but from my medical knowledge I think it was quite possible." Dear me! is that the kind of evidence you are to be asked to rely upon? A possibility at the best, according to the statement of Dr Littlejohn — a large possibility — that he could have put in the drug. If he could have put it in the sugar, it was only by possibility; and it was hardly possible to suppose it could have been out of the sight of the girl Mary Patterson. The easiest thing, in his mind, would have been to have prepared some pounded sugar in the adjoining room, into which he had introduced antimony, and gone for it, and never to have come near the consulting-room at all. That was the natural course for a poisoner to pursue. The next question is, whether egg-flip was capable of producing the effects which are said to have been caused by it. It was barely possible, according to Dr Littlejohn's opinion. Let us see the history of the egg-flip. Does it pass through his hands? No. It does pass through Mary M'Leod's and Mary Patterson's hands. It was left by Mary Patterson in the pantry, and Mary M'Leod came down for it to the kitchen. She was told that it was in the pantry, and she goes up to bring it down. There, again, you have Mary M'Leod intervening in the matter, notwithstanding the dilemma on which the Solicitor-General placed his case; and she it is who carries it up to the bedroom; and she it is who administers it to the patient who is suffering there. There is another remarkable thing in this case. The amount of antimony introduced must have been a very powerful dose indeed; because taking only a teaspoonful of it, as Mary Patterson did, she lay vomiting and suffering all night. It was stated that Mrs Pritchard took a wine-glassful of the egg-flip, and she vomited for about half-an-hour or thereby afterwards. But surely if the strong woman took only a teaspoonful and the weak woman took a glassful, she would have been destroyed by the action of a poison which had so powerful an effect upon the servant girl. How is that to be explained? That is a matter which the Crown have not in any way cleared up at all, and I say there is no proof whatever that in any case the prisoner has put any poison in any food taken by his wife. The whole case stands upon mere probabilities—mere suggestions, that opportunities and means were in his possession, and that either he or some other person must have been the guilty party. But I wish you also to notice that, instead of being worse after taking that egg-flip, as Mary M'Leod has said, Mrs Pritchard was rather better, and therefore it is very inconceivable that there was anything in this egg-flip which caused Mary Patterson to suffer. It must have been from something else she took. She did not notice at first that there was anything peculiar in the egg-flip, but that it had a very bad taste. Then it is a curious thing that Drs Maclagan and Littlejohn have stated that tartarised antimony is a comparatively tasteless substance. Mary Patterson, speaking of what she experienced when she took the egg-flip, says that the moment she put it to her mouth she felt a burning sensation, and said—"Oh, what a taste it has?"—not the burning sensation in her throat, which was afterwards spoken to—but when she put this substance to her lips. This must have been caused by some other substance, not antimony at all. The fact that she experienced a bad taste is inconsistent with the theory that there was any antimony there; but be there antimony there or not, how you are able to reconcile those discrepancies I do not understand. Sufficient for me to say that there is no proof whatever that the prisoner's hand did put in the antimony. There is as much proof that it was put in by another, through whose hands every one of these articles had passed. Gentlemen, I have now considered pretty nearly all the evidence which I think the Solicitor-General relied on, and with which it is necessary to detain you in this case. These are the only instances of poisoning on which the Solicitor-General proceeded, so far as I know. And it will be unnecessary to attempt to detain you upon the evidence upon which the Crown do not rely in this case. Now, you will keep in view that this is a case where the Crown undertook to prove the administration of poison. It is not a case on which they can obtain a verdict, as I would again repeat, by probabilities, or inferences, or presumptions. They have stated the case against the prisoner, and are bound to show by conclusive evidence, without any reasonable doubt, that the prisoner is guilty of the crime with which he is charged. It would have been desirable in a case of this kind that the Crown would have satisfied the burden of proof which is upon them by proving that on some one occasion the prisoner was detected in administering poisons. If the case was proved that the poison had been administered in the course of months in a house of which he was the head, but in which also there were other persons, how is it possible, if you are to accept the case for the Crown as conclusive of the prisoner's guilt, that throughout the investigation they have made in that house during these months they have not been able to trace one case of poisoning to the prisoner's hands? In every one of these cases Mary M'Leod is concerned. In the case of the tapioca it is impossible to conceive the prisoner concerned. In the case of the cheese it is almost equally impossible to suppose that the prisoner could have been concerned in it. And yet while I think the evidence frees him from suspicion as regards these cases—though freed from suspicion as regards cases in which, according to the Crown, poison was put in Mrs Pritchard's food—yet they concluded without a shadow of evidence that he was the foul poisoner who, during these three months, protracted his wife's sufferings until she died in his arms on the 28th March. The case is utterly beyond belief. The Crown admitted their obligation to prove this case by the clearest possible evidence. And yet the elaborate speech of the Solicitor-General is reduced to this, that there were but two persons who could commit the crime—the prisoner and Mary M'Leod. Mary

M'Leod's hand is found in connexion with every one of these acts of administering poisoned food; and yet, without asking her whether she put anything into the food, the Crown asks you to believe that she was not guilty, and therefore that the prisoner was guilty. If one of two persons committed the crime, then most assuredly the burden rested upon the Crown to exclude one of these two from the possibility of having committed the offence, and they never can discharge that burden by the mere suggestion that it is unlikely that a girl of seventeen would commit that offence, because though that it may be unlikely an improbability does not meet the case. Therefore, I ask you to consider the whole of the case upon the evidence as I have stated it to you, whether it is proved beyond reasonable doubt that the prisoner committed this crime ; or whether rather, to take the case that has been presented to you, if it is not a series of suspicions and probabilities upon which they entirely depend, and not legal proof which would satisfy your mind in consiguing this prisoner to a guilty cell. Consider that he was the idol of his wife—that he lived on the most affectionate terms with her, though it is admitted that he was unfaithful to his marriage vows. His children, who were very capable of noticing all that was going on, proved this. The little boy stated they lived happily together. There is not a suggestion of anything between them, and yet, upon the evidence of mere conjecture, such as the Crown founds upon, the prisoner is to be held guilty of an unparalleled and hideous murder. The Solicitor-General spoke of his nerve. Well might he speak of his nerve. I cannot conceive of anything so hideously unfeeling; for during all her suffering he slept with his wife, and held her in his arms when she was suffering those tortures. You will remember that, when her body was brought home to her mother's house, at his own request the coffin was opened, and this foul murderer, if the story of the Crown be true, showed the body of his murdered wife to his relatives, and, kneeling down in the face of God, kissed for the last time those lips which his hand is said to have closed. A more cold-blooded, a more frightful, a more dreadful atrocity could not be supposed. It is impossible to suppose it upon the evidence. Suppose such a case—one would almost believe the thunderbolt of the Almighty would have stricken down the man who could have done it. The whole evidence of the Crown hangs upon probability, and can never justify you in believing that he, in the first place, was capable of committing the crime; and, in the second, it is hardly conceivable that anything so unnatural should be committed by such a man. Gentlemen, I have asked a verdict of acquittal from you. In your hands alone are the issues of life and of death. In your hands, to you and you alone, is the responsibility of the verdict. I ask you to restore the prisoner by your verdict to his orphaned family and sorrowing relatives.

The Lord Justice-Clerk, addressing the jury, said—I put it to you, gentlemen, whether it would be your desire that I should proceed with my charge, or whether you prefer an adjournment till to-morrow morning. In order to enable you to form an opinion, it is right to state to you that I cannot promise to finish to-night. My examination of the evidence will extend over several hours, but whichever course is most agreeable to you, I shall be most happy to follow.

The jury intimated that they would prefer an adjournment.

The Court adjourned about half-past four, to meet again next morning at ten.

FIFTH DAY—Friday, July 7.

The Court met again this morning at ten o'clock, and resumed the trial. The Lord Justice-Clerk, Lord Ardmillan, and Lord Jerviswoode occupied the bench.

The prisoner took his seat in the dock at ten o'clock precisely. He was not, as on former occasions, accompanied by his brother.

The Lord Justice-Clerk proceeded to charge the jury. He said—Gentlemen of the jury—In considering the social and professional position occupied by the prisoner at the bar, the great atrocity of the crimes laid to his charge, and the singular means by which it is alleged he perpetrated these crimes, this is indeed an extraordinary and appalling crime. It would be a public calamity and a great scandal upon the administration of justice if, in such a case, the guilty should escape punishment. But let me remind you also, that it is not the less a crime that the verdict, which is to be followed by the sentence of death, should rest upon untrustworthy or imperfect and unsatisfactory evidence, or that any unsatisfactory foundation should be laid for such a verdict as you are called upon by the prosecutor to return. I am sure it must have been a great satisfaction to you, as it certainly was to me, to see this trial conducted throughout on both sides of the bar with such eminent ability, and at the same time in such good judgment, and moderation, and good temper. Everything the legal professor could furnish for arriving at the ends of justice has certainly been performed by the learned gentlemen who have conducted this case. The responsibility henceforth rests with me and with you, and with you eminently; for it is your verdict that must determine whether the prisoner is guilty or innocent. My duty is to advise you in matters of law, and, at the same time, so far as I can, to aid your deliberations upon the evidence by digesting it for you for your use, and placing it in such a form as will enable you best to appreciate the several questions which you must consider and solve. Gentlemen, in order to enable you to return a verdict of guilty, in regard to either of the two charges contained in this indictment, there are three things of which you must be satisfied upon the evidence. In the first place, that the deceased died by poison; in the second place, that the poison was wilfully administered, for the purpose of destroying life; and, in the third place, that it was the prisoner at the bar who so administered or caused it to be so administered. If the evidence is defective in any one of these particulars, the prisoner is entitled to an acquittal; but if, on the other hand, you are satisfied of these three things, then there remains nothing for you but the stern and painful duty of conviction. We must consider the three different questions which are raised, therefore, separate from one another; and I proceed to call your attention, in the first place, to the evidence as to the cause of death in regard to both of the deceased ladies, for it is not my purpose in dealing with the evidence here to separate the two charges entirely from each other, simply because I think it is impossible. I must consider them in combination, because in truth they form both necessary parts of one history. And as regards the death of Mrs Pritchard, which, although it occurred after the other, was first made the subject of investigation and inquiry by the authorities, we have very clear and satisfactory evidence in the medical and chemical reports which you heard read in the course of the trial, and to the results of these reports, and the opinions of the gentlemen who had framed them, I shall now shortly call your attention. Mrs

Pritchard's body was subjected to a *post-mortem* examination very soon after her death by Dr Maclagan and Dr Littlejohn — two gentlemen, from their professional pursuits, eminently qualified for the conducting of such an inquiry. Both have devoted their time and attention to the study of medical jurisprudence. They made a very careful examination of the body, and particularly of the condition of all the vital organs, and in the details of their report there is not the slightest trace, as they themselves say, of any morbid action—no appearance of any disease, anything at all to indicate how the patient came to die. They, therefore, report that these bodies presented no appearance of recent morbid action beyond a slight amount of irritation of the alimentary canal, and nothing at all capable of accounting for death. They, therefore, proceed to say, "We have secured the alimentary canal and its contents, the heart and some of the blood, the liver, the spleen, the left kidney, and the urine, in order that they may be submitted to chemical analysis." And in taking that course, I need hardly tell you that these gentlemen did only what was their clear and obvious duty, and accordingly the portions of the different parts of the body which had been thus secured for examination were submitted to chemical examination and analysis by Dr Maclagan, and another portion by Professor Penny, of Glasgow. These gentlemen again came substantially—one may almost say exactly—to the same conclusions; and, without entering into any of the details of the processes by means of which they attained these conclusions, I may merely say in passing that nothing has been shown to throw the slightest doubt upon the sufficiency or the chemical tests which they applied, or the perfect ease and accuracy with which they were applied. Dr Maclagan, in examining the urine of the deceased before entering upon any very careful and complete experiments, found that it yielded what appeared to be antimony, and that in considerable quantity; and he, therefore, applied himself chiefly in examining the other articles which he secured for consideration to the detection of the well-known poison in these articles. In the liver of Mrs Pritchard he determined at last that the amount of antimony, in the shape apparently of what is called tartar emetic, was almost exactly four grains, and gave us further information regarding the total amount of the antimony contained in the contents of the intestines, which appears to me, in connexion with what I can now say, of the greatest possible importance. He took a portion of the contents of the intestines, and submitted that to a quantitative analysis, having already submitted other portions to a quantitative analysis, for the purpose of determining the nature of the poison; and that quantitative analysis enabled him to say what amount of antimony there was in the portion of the contents of the intestines which he so examined. Thus, having the proportion which that part of the contents of the intestines bore to the total contents of the intestines, he was able to arrive at the conclusion with perfect accuracy as to what amount of antimony there was in the total contents of the intestines; and that he determined to be very nearly 6 grains—that is to say, 6 grains of tartar emetic. In these two places alone, therefore—in the liver and in the contents of the intestines—you have found in this lady's body after death not less than ten grains of tartar emetic. In other parts, in the kidneys, the stomach (that is to say, the contents of the stomach), and the blood, there were other and more minute portions of the same mineral poison found. But it is unnecessary to go into any details about this, because I am sure you must be satisfied from what I have already said, that the presence of ten grains of tartarised antimony, or tartar emetic as it is popularly called, in the intestines and liver of the deceased, was very sufficient to justify the conclusion which Dr Maclagan came to, and which he thus expresses at the end of his report. [His Lordship read the concluding part of Dr Maclagan's report]. That portion of his opinion is, you will see, altered by a subsequent experiment, the results which he gave you, and which I have just read, regarding the large quantity that there must have been in the contents of the intestines. Then, gentlemen, you have Professor Penny's report, and he confined himself entirely to his duties as an analytical chemist, and expresses his opinion thus. [His Lordship also read the last portion of Dr Penny's report, the fifth conclusion of which is as follows, "That the largest quantity of mercury was contained in the contents of the intestines next to the spleen and heart, and extremely minute traces in the blood and kidney."] You will recollect that that was perfectly accounted for without any suspicion of poisoning by mercury, in consequence of the administration of the powder that Dr Paterson gave Mrs Pritchard upon 2d March. That is the result of the *post-mortem* investigation, and it is for you to say whether or not you are satisfied upon the evidence that Mrs Pritchard died of antimony—that she was poisoned by antimony, in the sense that by taking antimony she was deprived of life. I am not now speaking of an act of poison, but of the sufferings of the deceased, that she, by taking or having antimony administered to her, died of the poison. I do not think that it was attempted by the prisoner's counsel to resist this conclusion, and upon the evidence I fairly confess to you it is impossible to entertain any doubt. Now, let us consider what is the similar evidence in the case of Mrs Taylor. She died, you will recollect, on the 25th February. She was buried in the Grange Cemetery here; but, in consequence of the suspicions attaching to the death of Mrs Pritchard, Mrs Taylor's body also was disinterred, and subjected to a *post-mortem* examination, and the result of that is very similar to the result of the *post-mortem* examination of the other body. Dr Maclagan and Dr Littlejohn made their report on this subject on the 30th of March, and they very naturally, in consequence of the recorded causes of death—paralysis and apoplexy—devoted a great deal of their attention to the condition of the head and brain of the deceased, the result of which was, that there was not the slightest trace of anything like disease, or any of those local affections of the brain likely to produce apoplexy, and so cause death. They examine also the other vital organs of this old lady, and they find them all in healthy condition, with this exception, that as regards her heart, it was somewhat enlarged. I shall read to you what they say of the organs of respiration and circulation. [His Lordship here read the parts of the report referred to.] Now, it was explained in the evidence of these gentlemen that, although that old lady's heart was large, and slightly dilated, there was nothing either to account for death, or to be the cause of death. But there was undoubtedly this remark, that in consequence of the condition of the heart, she was a perilous subject. She was a person upon whom effects might be produced from slighter causes than upon a perfectly right subject; and you will be kind enough to bear that along with you in considering the other parts of the evidence to which we are to come by and by. In the other respects this Mrs Taylor was obviously a strong and healthy woman for her time of life, which was about seventy, and altogether the appearances presented upon the *post-mortem* examination again led these gentlemen to the same conclusions, that there was nothing to account for death, and therefore they took the course which they had done before in the case of Mrs Pritchard. They secured for chemical examination and analysis the alimentary canal and its contents, the heart, and some of the blood, the liver, the spleen, the kidneys, the bladder, the uterus, and a portion of the brain; and these articles having been thereafter subjected to examination again partly by Dr Maclagan, and partly by Professor Penny, of Glasgow, we have the results of their examination before us. Dr Maclagan concludes his report thus. [His Lordship here read the conclusions arrived at by Dr Maclagan.] Now, you will observe there are some differences between this report and that which was made on the examination of the contents of Mrs Pritchard's body, because it would rather appear, from what was found upon chemical analysis in the case of Mrs Taylor, that she had taken a dose of antimony very recently before her death, whereas, in the case of Mrs Pritchard, a day or two might have intervened, according to the views of Dr Maclagan, since any antimony had been received by Mrs Pritchard. Professor Penny again, states, as the result of his examination and analysis on portions of the liver, stomach, heart, kidney, rectum, blood, and contents of the intestines of Mrs Taylor, "that all the articles subjected to analysis contained antimony. That the dried contents of the intestines contained the largest proportion of antimony; next, the liver and stomach; then the blood, and in less quantity in the heart, kidney, and rectum. That part of the antimony in the contents of the intestines is in a form soluble in water. That the kidney was the only article in which mercury was detected. That neither the stomach nor the contents of the intestines contained aconite or morphia in quantity sufficient to be detected by known chemical processes. That the articles subjected to analysis contained no other metallic poison than antimony and mercury." Now, gentlemen, with regard to the case of Mrs Taylor, it is not necessary to add that, according to what was observed of her symptoms by Dr Paterson at the time of her death, and according to the evidence which you have had of the contents of a bottle that was found in her pocket, there may be a question whether she died, like her daughter, from the simple action of antimony, or whether she died from the embodied influence of antimony and other poisons, the other poisons being opium and aconite. It is not necessary for the present purpose to go minutely into that part of the evidence to which I am now referring, but which I shall be obliged to call your attention to more particularly by and by for another purpose. It is sufficient for the present as regards that part of the case, to say that Mrs Taylor died from the combined operation of opium, antimony, and aconite. Of that there can be no doubt, and we are now considering wholly that present question—whether the two deaths which are laid at the prisoner's door were in point of fact caused by poison. Gentlemen, that exhausts all I think it necessary to say upon what I have represented as the first question for your consideration—namely, whether the two deceased ladies, one or both of them, died by poison; and you will consider whether in the circumstances it is possible to resist these conclusions—First, that Mrs Pritchard died from the action of antimony alone, administered in large quantities, as present in her body—I should say in large quantities; and, second, that Mrs Taylor died from the action of antimony, either alone or in combination with the vegetable poisons of aconite and opium. The next question is, whether these poisons were administered to them by some person for the purpose of destroying life; and here there are various possibilities that naturally suggest themselves to inquiring minds, and which must all be passed in review before we can be quite certain whether we are reasoning safely and correctly or not. There may be accidents of various kinds; there may be suicidal acts; and in either of these cases, of course, there can be no guilt against any living person. It is indispensable, therefore, that in considering whether anybody is to be held responsible for the administration of these poisons, we should entirely negative the idea of either accident or suicide. Now, as regards the case of Mrs Pritchard, it will, of course, occur to you that accident is utterly impossible, if the reports of Dr Maclagan and Professor Penny are to be relied on, because there is not a single tittle of evidence to show that death was caused by one dose. It is not proved that there was any single dose administered to Mrs Pritchard and taken by her, capable of itself of destroying life. On the contrary, the evidence goes to show that it was a long-continued administration of poison given in small doses, frequently repeated, that brought about the death of the lady. That cannot be questioned, so far as I can see. Ingenuity might suggest, that if a person were persuaded that some large quantity of this poison was really something else than it was, and had continued for a month or two to use it as if it was something proper to be put in ordinary articles of food—had mistaken the white powder of tartar emetic for pounded sugar, or for salt, and had consequently used it in her food, that that was an accident that might have accounted for death. It is possible; but then we search the evidence for the slightest trace of any such mistake. It is not reasonable, and I suggest it only for your consideration, because I desire you to be most scrupulous at every step of this inquiry to satisfy your minds as you go along whether there is anywhere—and if there be anywhere, where it is—a defect in the evidence which I am now reviewing. If you can receive such a supposition as that—that there is any portion of the case unsupported by evidence—good and well. Then, gentlemen, as to suicide—suicide by slow poison, is, I rather suppose, unheard of. A person who desires to destroy his own life generally selects the speediest and least painful mode of doing so; and even although, in that respect, there may be great varieties in different cases, I certainly never heard it suggested that suicide was committed by a person taking poison with his own hand continuously over a period of weeks or months. Add to all this that there is nothing in the history of this lady, Mrs Pritchard, to indicate any such state of mind, any such morbid condition either of mind or body, which would suggest the idea of suicide, and I think we arrive pretty safely at the conclusion that neither by accident of any ordinary kind, nor by suicide, could the death of Mrs Pritchard from poison be traced. The position of the prisoner suggested one species of accident, which is possible in some cases—namely, unskilful treatment. Unskilful treatment in the administration of a strong and dangerous drug administered to a person may sometimes produce death, and that would be accidental poisoning; and if the case of the prisoner had been that he was treating his wife with antimony, and had unconsciously or accidentally given her too much, and so produced death, that would have been a case very well worthy of your consideration. But it is entirely excluded by the position which the prisoner himself has taken up in his declaration. [The Lord Justice-Clerk then read the portion of the declaration of the prisoner in which he stated that during the whole course of her illness he had never given Mrs Pritchard antimony, nor any preparation of it; that he had it in stock, but only used it externally for her neck; that he had some years ago treated her with it for inflammation of the eyelids; that he kept considerable quantities of it in a press, which was not always locked.] I need hardly state that the accidental application of antimony to the deceased's neck in October, and the use of it in moderate quantities years ago, had nothing to do with the appearances presented by the chemical examination of the intestines and other organs of Mrs Pritchard. Then, gentlemen, if it be clear that Mrs Pritchard died by poisoning by antimony, and if the evidence excludes the possibility of either accident or suicide, it seems impossible to resist this conclusion, which answers the second question I submitted for your consideration, that the poison must have been administered by some one for the purpose of destroying her life. Now, with regard to Mrs Taylor again, in reference to this second question, the case stands in a somewhat different position. There is a very considerable portion of antimony found in her also—not to the same extent as in Mrs Pritchard, still quite a sufficient quantity of antimony to account for her death. Dr Maclagan and Professor Penny were quite clear upon that, when they made their first examination of the intestines and other organs subjected to their examination. But then there again comes that other part of the evidence to which I have already slightly adverted, I mean the symptoms exhibited by Mrs Taylor at the time of her death, and the circumstances connected with the finding of the bottle in her pocket. The contents of the bottle have been analysed. It is clear, from the evidence, that the bottle which was subjected to the examination of Professor Penny was the same bottle as that found in the pocket of Mrs Taylor. The steps of the evidence I will state to you very shortly, without reading the depositions of the witnesses. The two women who dressed the body, who took off the clothes of the deceased after death, Mary Patterson and Jessie Nabb, found the bottle in her pocket about half full of a brown liquid. They put it aside for the time. The prisoner soon afterwards came into the room, and said he had been informed about that bottle, and desired to have it. He got the bottle, and took it away with him. I am not now speaking of the manner in which he conducted himself on that occasion. We shall consider that by and by in the third branch of this inquiry. He took the bottle away with him. It was then found upon the same chest of drawers upon which it had stood in Mrs Taylor's room. That chest of drawers had in the meantime been removed out into the lobby. It was afterwards put in a drawer, and from that place it was taken and delivered to the police-officers, who gave it to Professor Penny. Beyond all question it would in such cases as this be more satisfactory, if it were possible to prove the utter impossibility of any change of the state of the contents of such a bottle, to exclude the possibility of any doubt as to the identity of the bottle. You must, however, take the evidence just as the circumstances of the case produce it. It cannot be made any better than the circumstances of the case allow it; and it is for you to say whether you are reasonably satisfied. And it is for you to say whether you are reasonably satisfied that the contents of the bottle which was found in Mrs Taylor's pocket after her death reached the hands of Professor Penny in the same condition. If so, then observe what is the result. The bottle contains Batley's Solution of opium, which is a strong narcotic, which a person unaccustomed to take could not take much of without very serious consequences. But I need hardly tell you, that the quantity of opium or laudanum which any person is able to take depends entirely upon habit; and we have it in evidence that Mrs Taylor was in the habit of taking this medicine for a number of years; and the quantity she was in the way of taking had gradually very largely increased. One of the witnesses, who acted as a messenger, frequently told you he was in the way of getting her bottle filled, and it used to be about once in two or three months when he was first employed by her, but that increased till it came to once in two or three weeks, so that it is quite obvious that the habit of taking opium was growing upon Mrs Taylor, as it almost invariably does in all such cases; and at the time of her death she was in a condition to take a quantity of opium that would have poisoned any person not accustomed to it. Now, she had taken some of the contents of this bottle, and it was suggested that she had taken a very large quantity of the contents from the time it had been got in on Monday down to her death. I think it was said by the prisoner's counsel, from calculations he had made, that she must have taken 150 drops a-day. I have not followed out the calculation, but it is improbable that a person who had been in the habit of taking opium for years, would take 150 drops without the slightest effect, further than the carrying on of a very bad habit. Now, that is the state of matters. Let us consider, in the next place, what else there was in this bottle. There is a considerable portion of antimony found in the bottle of Mrs Taylor afterwards. There is also in the bottle another poison of a more subtle kind, and one less easily detected—aconite—a vegetable poison, which cannot be discovered by the same tests as the mineral poison of antimony. But the skill of Dr Penny discovered the presence of aconite in the bottle, and enabled him to say, that not only was there some aconite there, but also determine with quite sufficient precision for the purposes of this case, what proportion the tincture of aconite bore to the other contents of the bottle. By a series of experiments, which were conducted with great skill and care, he arrives at the conclusion that the proportion of aconite in the whole of the contents of the bottle must have been under ten per cent., but above five. Now, if anybody took a single drop of that mixture, that person must inevitably have swallowed more than five drops of tincture of aconite. The conclusion, therefore, that one is almost forced to arrive at in regard to Mrs Taylor is, that her death was brought about by the combined action of three poisons—aconite, antimony, and opium ; but the opium, probably, not in such quantities as to cause death, although it might have been a powerful agent in combination with other poisons—even to a person accustomed to take opium. The question, then, for your consideration upon the second point is this : whether, taking all the facts in view, you can arrive at the conclusion that the poison from which Mrs Taylor died was given to her by the hand of some other person, and was administered to her for the purpose of destroying life. Here, again, as in the case of Mrs Pritchard, you must endeavour to consider whether you can exclude the question of accident or suicide. I need not dwell upon that, as I have done before. It is sufficient to observe, in the case of Mrs Taylor, that, whether she died through the influence of antimony administered in several doses, as the chemical reports clearly bear out ; or whether her death was brought about immediately through swallowing some of the contents of bottle 85, it is very difficult to understand. Now, was her death brought about by accident ? I have said enough about continuous administration of antimony as being inconsistent with the notion of accident, and I need not repeat that ; but do you think it was by accident that tartar emetic and tincture of aconite found their way into her Batley's Solution ? It was proved to have been bought from the apothecary, from a part of a stock which the apothecary had in his possession for a very considerable period, and which was shown to have come from a wholesale London dealer. The maker himself was brought to prove that antimony and aconite are substances altogether foreign to the medicine. Was it, then, by accident that these two subtle poisons found their way into this lady's medicine-bottle, or, if it was not by accident, did she put it there herself, or had she any knowledge of such things to enable her, if she were willing, so to poison herself apparently by using her own medicine ? There is no appearance of that, and the character and conduct of the old woman, her natural condition both of body and mind as you heard it described by the witnesses, is such as not to suggest the idea of suicide in her case as a possibility at all. Consider, then, gentlemen, with reference to both o the deaths—that of Mrs Pritchard in the first place, and that of Mrs Taylor in the second—whether you can arrive at the conclusion, or whether you can resist the conclusion, that the poison by means of which they were deprived of life was wilfully given to them for the very purpose of destroying life. And that brings me to a consideration of the third and only remaining question, but a question of vital interest in this case—Was that poison administered, or procured to be administered, to either or both of these deceased ladies by the prisoner at the bar? This must be decided by entering into a careful and minute investigation of the evidence in the case; and you have paid so close attention to the evidence in all its details as it was laid before you, that in any ordinary case I confess I should have been inclined to shorten this part of your labour and mine; but I rather think that you will sympathise with me in the feeling, that I cannot, for the sake of mere brevity, or for the purpose of saving your time or trouble, omit any one particular that appears to me to be important for your consideration. The time over which this history runs is but short. It commences in the month of November, or perhaps rather more probably about the commencement of this year, and it terminates with the death of Mrs Pritchard upon the 18th March. The scene of the double tragedy is equally compact. It is all confined within the four walls of the dwelling-house in Sauchiehall Street; for from that house, so far as I can see, his wife never removed from the time that she returned from Edinburgh a little before Christmas until her death; and from the time that Mrs Taylor came on the 10th February until her death on the 25th of the same month, she was in constant attendance on her daughter. The other persons in the house were, during the earlier part of the period, and prior to the 16th February, Catherine Lattimer, Mary M'Leod, the children, and two more, besides the prisoner and his wife. After the 16th there is this alteration, that Catherine Lattimer goes away, and is succeeded by Mary Patterson. And then on the 10th February, six days before Catherine Lattimer went away, Mrs Taylor came. Now, keeping these things in view, let us attend to some of the prominent occurrences during this period; and I think here, as in other cases, it conduces to clearness to take events precisely in the order of time. You will recollect that Mrs Pritchard went to visit her friends in Edinburgh in the month of November—the precise day is not fixed. She had been ailing before that time, and according to the account of Catherine Lattimer, her ailment was just a little less severe. Afterwards it increased in intensity, and accompanied her down to her last moments. It was sickness and depression. She got better while she was in Edinburgh; but she returned a few days before Christmas, towards the end of December. She returned home, and after that she got gradually worse. There was a return of the sickness and depression, and the vomiting seemed to be more violent. On the 1st of February there was a severe and alarming attack—so much so, that Catherine Lattimer, who was to have left the service next day, Candlemas-day, was obliged to return, in order to make herself useful to Mrs Pritchard. Now, I wish to call your attention to Catherine Lattimer's account of this attack on the 1st February. I think that is the first event of particular importance in the history of these last two months—February and March. [His Lordship read at length the evidence of Catherine Lattimer, as to the attack which Mrs Pritchard had suffered on the 1st February, and in the course of which, after she had got to her bed-room, cramp had seized her, and she was afflicted with sickness and vomiting.] It now appeared from this evidence that Mrs Pritchard had said to the witness that she was generally sick after slops and after tea. Having read this evidence, his Lordship proceeded—Now, gentlemen, that was the first very serious and violent attack which Mrs Pritchard had, and we may be sure that it was such as Lattimer described it, for she has apparently been very accurate and judicious in her observations. She appears to have observed everything minutely, and gave her evidence in such a way as to command respect. We then come to inquire at the medical gentlemen whose opinions we have before us, whether these symptoms are or are not reconcilable with the opinion which, they formed upon the most careful and minute chemical examination, and they say they correspond exactly—that they are just the symptoms they would expect from a person to whom antimony was being administered. Now, in the course of the week, Dr Cowan makes his appearance upon the scene. He comes on the 7th, and visits Mrs Pritchard, converses with her, sees that she is very unwell, and makes some little suggestions as to the way in which she should be treated, which are now very material to the question into which we have at this stage to inquire. He remains there till next day, leaving upon the 8th, and during the time that he was there Mrs Pritchard had no serious attack of any kind; but, strangely enough, a second attack, and a serious one, does come on on the evening after he left—the 8th. You have the description of that attack by Catherine Lattimer again; and you have also, as applicable to that, the evidence of Dr Gairdner—the first appearance of any medical man upon the scene other than the prisoner himself. Now, attend if you please, to what these two witnesses say about this attack on the evening of the 8th. Catherine Lattimer had made a little mistake about the dates of these two attacks, which she set right when she came to describe the second attack, and which was set right by Dr Gairdner, who, as a medical man, preserved a note of the case, and kept it in perfect precision; and, as that is the case, there can be no doubt about the time that Catherine Lattimer is speaking of as the second attack. [The Lord Justice-Clerk then read over a portion of Catherine Lattimer's evidence, in which she described the second attack which she saw her suffer, when she went to her bedroom, and found her in great pain, and was asked to send out Mary M'Leod for Dr Gairdner, and when she called her husband a hypocrite.] Now, as regards that little episode, I confess I do not attach much importance to it, because it was perfectly plain that Mrs Pritchard was not in her right senses at the time. This was made quite plain, I think, by the testimony of Dr Gairdner; but I mention it because at the time when the evidence was given it did appear of some importance, though afterwards it was deprived of that character by the evidence of Dr Gairdner, and therefore no importance is to be attached to anything Mrs Pritchard said at the time. [The Lord Justice-Clerk read further from Catherine Lattimer's evidence as to the weak and exhausted condition of Mrs Pritchard after the attack.] Then we have Dr Gairdner's evidence upon the same occurrence, who was sent for by Mary M'Leod, acting under direct instructions from Mrs Pritchard. [The Lord Justice-Clerk read from Dr Gairdner's evidence as to the state of Mrs Pritchard when he visited her—who found her in an excited and hysterical condition, which led him to suppose that she was drunk; and when he ordered the use of stimulants to be stopped.] Dr Gairdner, however, said that there was no fever in the case. Yet it is a very remarkable circumstance that throughout, whenever the prisoner had occasion to explain to anybody what he thought was the matter with his wife, he called it gastric fever. The prisoner's counsel says, "That any man might be mistaken about that—the most skilful might be mistaken in such a case as hers, and Dr Gairdner himself was quite puzzled." And well he might be, if it be the fact, as I suppose you have assumed it to be, that the lady was at that moment under the influence of the metallic poison of antimony. No doctor could guess at that, and, therefore, there was good reason for his being puzzled. But he was not so puzzled as to believe that she was under fever when he found all the symptoms indicating the very reverse, nor could any man be so puzzled as to call it gastric fever. But it is remarkable that there was no appearance of fever even upon the occasion of Dr Paterson's visit; because if at any time, then was the time to expect indications of fever, when apparently she had received stimulants to a considerable amount—whether it was champagne, chloroform, or iodine. And by whose directions had these been administered? The prisoner told Dr Gairdner it was by the direction of Dr Cowan. Now, it is important to see what Dr Cowan says in regard to Mrs Pritchard. He does say something, and from it you will judge for yourselves whether what was suggested by Dr Cowan was likely to justify the opinion of Dr Gairdner that she was in a state of intoxication. [His Lordship then read a portion of Dr Cowan's evidence as to the state of prostration in which he found Mrs Pritchard, and his recommending that she take small quantities of champagne and ice.] That was the second point for their consideration. The next important event is the arrival of Mrs Taylor on the 10th. We will not pause upon that, because, at the time of Mrs Taylor's arrival, we have already had a very good account of the condition of Mrs Pritchard, from the evidence of Catherine Lattimer. She is described as suffering from severe attacks of spasms from eight o'clock in the morning of the 9th; but after Mrs Taylor arrived there is an episode in the case, which has been dwelt on as of very great importance on both sides of the bar, and which I think does deserve your most serious consideration. On the 13th February it was suggested by Mrs Pritchard, or somebody else, that she should have some tapioca. Now the tapioca is said to have been poisoned by an admixture of antimony, and thus some of it was being taken by Mrs Taylor, who immediately after, in consequence, was taken ill. Now, as to the evidence of Catherine Lattimer on this point. [She stated that she prepared the tapioca for Mrs Pritchard a few days after Mrs Taylor came, and that Mary M'Leod brought the order to the cook. The tapioca was in a paper bag, and witness did not notice whether it had been opened. She made half a breakfast-cupful, and Mary M'Leod took it into the dining-room. Witness did not put any sugar or anything else into it. On returning to Glasgow, she found the remains of the tapioca in the press, and gave it to the Procurator-Fiscal. The tapioca was brought to her by Mary M'Leod. There was just one making of the tapioca while she was there.] Then, in the next place, let us see what Mary M'Leod says about it. She says that "the tapioca was bought from Burton & Henderson by the prisoner's son Kenneth. He gave it to me. It was either a pound or half-a-pound. I laid it on the lobby table, but it did not lie there long, not an hour, before it was taken down to Catherine Lattimer. Mrs Taylor took it down," and I think that is all she says about it. Mary M'Leod took it up, and then it was proved that Mrs Taylor had some portion of it. Whether Mrs Pritchard had or had not does not appear, but Mrs Taylor afterwards was sick and vomited, and said she thought she was getting the same complaint as her daughter. Now, gentlemen, the tapioca, you may observe, was bought from a grocer, and was proved to be part of a store of tapioca which these grocers had, and it was proved to be perfectly free from antimony. It was brought to the house by the little boy, given to Mary M'Leod, prepared by Catherine Lattimer, and taken upstairs by Mary M'Leod, and the consequences were such as I have related to you. Now, the remainder of the tapioca—that which was not cooked by Catherine Lattimer—was put by her into the kitchen press, and Mary M'Leod mentions in her evidence having found it in the kitchen press. Catherine Lattimer was brought back for the purpose of saying whether it was there she put it, and she said it was. That tapioca was handed over to Professor Penny for examination. Now see what he says about it in his report. He says this paper package contains 2850 grains of tapioca. The presence of antimony in the form of tartarised antimony was unequivocally detected. Its amount was found to be equal to four grains and sixty-two parts in the pound of tapioca. Now here unquestionably was a parcel of tapioca out of which the preparation had been made for Mrs Pritchard's consumption, which had interfused into it antimony in the proportion of about four and a-half grains per pound; and, consequently, it is not surprising that Mrs Taylor, after having taken some of it, was taken unwell with sickness and vomiting; and having seen the symptoms of her daughter's illness, said, "I am afraid I am going to have the same complaint as my daughter." Still, gentlemen, it is not very easy to see what opportunities the prisoner had of mixing this antimony which is found in the tapioca. It is not proved, as a matter of absolute fact, that he was in the house at the time when this tapioca was brought in, still less is it proved that the tapioca was in his hands. It was left on the table for some time, Mary M'Leod could not say for what time—"not so much as an hour;" but more precise than that she could not be. And, therefore, there is certainly no direct contact between the prisoner and this parcel of tapioca, which undoubtedly was poisoned, and which produced the symptoms upon Mrs Taylor that might have been expected from the action of the antimony which was in it. This was upon the 13th, and upon the 16th there was a change of servants. Catherine Lattimer went away, and Mary Patterson came in her place, and from that time onwards you have a description by Mary Patterson of what she saw of the illness of Mrs Pritchard, the details of which, I think, I may dispense with reading, because they correspond with what has been already brought under your notice in the evidence of Catherine Lattimer; and so far as I have read it, of Mary M'Leod. But I may in the meantime abstain from referring much to the evidence of Mary M'Leod. From the 13th to the 25th February—that is a period of twelve days—there is no occurrence of any very remarkable kind to which I think it necessary to call special attention. I therefore now go on to the period which is marked by the death of Mrs Taylor. She was taken ill, as you are aware, upon the evening of the 24th; and here we have the evidence of Mary Patterson, a very reliable and good witness, according to my estimate of her, but you will judge for yourself how far that opinion is justified by what you saw. [His Lordship here read from the evidence.] Now, in like manner, Mary M'Leod gave her account of the matter. [His Lordship read Mary M'Leod's evidence on this point.] Then Mrs Taylor's body was removed. You will recollect that Jessie Nabb, the woman that was sent for, as Mary Patterson tells us, for the purpose of dressing and stretching the body of Mrs Taylor, gave almost the same account as she does of what took place between them and the prisoner when he came into the room after Mrs Taylor's death, and after the finding of the bottle. And that scene, I beg now to recall to your attention, as it is given by Mary Patterson. She says—"When the bottle was found he expressed great surprise that she should have taken so much of its contents within so short a time." Now he was quite aware, as you will see from the evidence, that the old lady was in the habit of taking a great quantity; and you will consider whether the surprise was real or feigned. That is but a very small point, however, in reference to this matter. His expression in regard to it seemed to me to be much more strong. He expressed surprise at her having sent "a girl like that for it"—that is to say, sent Mary M'Leod—to the apothecary for a bottle of Batley's Solution. I cannot see that there is anything so very startling in that. Did he mean to suggest that in consequence of such a messenger being sent for it, there might be some mistake as to the contents of the bottle? Why, what was it? "To send a girl like that for it"—what was the harm of sending the girl—an intelligent servant girl? What was wanted was Batley's Solution, because it was what Mrs Taylor wanted—what she was accustomed to take. But still he thought that was a very serious matter. And he thought, further, that it was one of those things that it would not do to have spoken of as having occurred in his house—a man of his profession. You will consider what is the true bearing and import of all these statements of the prisoner. He then says further to these girls that Dr Paterson, when he had been there before Mrs Taylor's death, had pronounced that she was paralysed upon the left side. That is not so. Dr Paterson had never said that. But is it not strange that he should have made that false statement to these two servant girls, when you come to consider what is the cause of death which he assigned in the case of Mrs Taylor in his report to the registrar? He was the medical attendant of Mrs Taylor. He must have known perfectly well that he was the person who must make the report to the registrar. He sent the old man, Mr Michael Taylor, to Dr Paterson, to ask him for a certificate, which he could hardly expect Dr Paterson to give. I do not suppose any medical man who would have been called in in the way Dr Paterson was would have ever dreamt of giving in a report in the way Dr Paterson was asked to do, with a medical man resident in the house, and constantly in attendance upon the patient. And consequently the prisoner must necessarily have known that he would have to make the return; and what return did he make? He made a return to this effect—"That the primary disease of which she died was paralysis, and that that paralysis had been in operation for twelve hours before her death." But, as you know from the evidence, that was absolutely false. She was down taking her tea at seven o'clock—nothing the matter with her—down in the kitchen visiting Mary Patterson, who saw nothing peculiar in her, except, as she said, that she was "a little peevish," which she ascribed to the fatigue which the old lady had to undergo in watching her daughter. At nine o'clock she is seen walking upstairs, nothing the matter with her, and in the course of the evening she calls to one of the servant-girls, "Go out, and bring in sausages for supper;" and that woman is represented in the report to the registrar as having been paralysed during the whole of that day. Further, the secondary disease, the disease which immediately preceded death, according to the prisoner's report, was apoplexy, and that had lasted for an hour; but now we have it demonstrated upon the medical evidence, that there was not a trace of apoplexy in the case. Ah, but it is said the prisoner might have been mistaken as to the symptoms. It is very odd that he should be always mistaken about such things. And further, with regard to the paralysis, as to that he could not be mistaken. It is said that he ascribed this as the cause, out of a feeling of kindness towards Mr Michael Taylor; he didn't like to let it be known to poor old Mr Michael Taylor that his wife had died of an overdose of a poisonous nature; and, therefore, he falsified a public record by inserting therein as a fact circumstantially stated, twelve hours turn of paralysis, which he knew was an absolute falsehood. These are strange facts. But Mrs Taylor's body is removed, carried to Edinburgh, and there interred. I need not say more at present about the circumstances attending the death of Mrs Taylor; but I will have to refer again to them, and yet for another purpose. I pass on in the meantime to consider the evidence applicable to the period between the death of Mrs Taylor and the death of Mrs Pritchard—between the 25th February and the 18th March, a period of little more than three weeks. I ought to have read to you, but omitted it at the proper time, a statement of Dr Paterson's about what he saw of Mrs Taylor; but I shall advert to the circumstances at another time, and, therefore, I need not go back to it at present. But Dr Paterson had not only seen Mrs Taylor upon the evening of the 24th February; he had also seen Mrs Pritchard, and for the first time. He had formed an impression of a very peculiar kind regarding Mrs Pritchard, which he stated to you in the box, and when he visited her again on the 2d of March, that impression was confirmed. Now, there have been a good many observations of an unfavourable kind made with regard to the conduct of Dr Paterson; and I do not think I should be doing justice to the case or to you if I did not advert to them. It is said that Dr Paterson formed a very strong impression at the time he saw Mrs Pritchard, on the 24th of February and the 2d of March, that she was being foully treated, or, in other words, that she was in the course of being poisoned; and that having formed that impression, he came into the witness-box with a strong feeling against the prisoner, and that he exhibited that feeling in a very marked way. Now, gentlemen, if he formed the opinion that Mrs Pritchard was being poisoned on the 24th of February and the 2d of March, in the hands of her husband as her medical attendant, you cannot be surprised that he will come here as a witness in a strong feeling against the prisoner. No feeling human being could feel otherwise if he had formed such an impression. To be sure it is said that he exhibited the feeling in a very marked unpleasant way. That is a matter of manner, and if the feeling existed I do not know that he could have made his evidence really more valuable if he had concealed the existence of it. It may be an unpleasant thing to see what is called an animus in a witness exhibited in the witness-box, but a man who has a feeling very strongly upon him, and that on good ground, may come into the witness-box and entirely suppress all appearance of it, and give his story as calmly and deliberately as if he had no feeling at all. It is only because he has more command of his feeling, or a better manner of concealing it. The fact remains, that if he takes up the position which I have described, he cannot, as a man of ordinary feeling, feel otherwise than unfavourably prepossessed against the prisoner. So far, I confess, the observations made upon Dr Paterson's appearance did not seem of great weight. But there is another matter which stands in a somewhat different position—the conduct of Dr Paterson when he formed this opinion on the 24th of February. He said, in answer to the questions put to him, that his meaning was—what he intended to state in the box was—that he was under the decided impression, when he saw Mrs Pritchard on these occasions, that somebody was practising upon her with poison. Now, he thought it consistent with his professional duty, and I must also add, in his duty as a citizen of this country, to keep that opinion to himself. In that I cannot say that he did right. I should be very sorry to lead you to think so. I care not for professional etiquette, or professional rule. There is a rule of life and a consideration that is far higher than these—and that is the duty that every citizen of this country—that every right-minded man owes to his neighbour, to prevent the destruction of human life in this world, and in that duty I cannot say but Dr Paterson failed. Now, gentlemen, you will consider what effect that is to have, or whether it is to have any effect, upon your minds. It is a very painful subject—a subject which I would fain avoid—but the exigencies of this case drive me to its consideration—and I am bound to say that, because a man is so mistaken in regard to his duty to fellow-citizens, and his fellow-creatures, as to act in the way in which he then did, it does not by any means follow that he is a man undeserving of credit as a witness. It does not follow. You may consider his evidence always in the light of the failing, and if you see reason to modify anything that he says because of the existence of the failing, it is your bounden duty to do it. But it does not by any means follow, I repeat, that because a man who has acted in what we must consider to be an improper manner, and has disregarded what was undoubtedly a public duty, that he is therefore going to speak what is not the truth when he comes to give his evidence in court. Now, with these observations, I proceed to call your attention to the evidence of Dr Paterson. It is extremely important evidence to this case. If it had not been so, I would not have felt it to be so imperatively my duty to make the observations I have done. The evidence stated that he was sent for to see Mrs Pritchard on the evening of the 24th, between ten and eleven o'clock at night; that Dr Pritchard met him in the lobby, and took him into the consulting-room, and told him that his mother-in-law, while writing a letter, had taken suddenly ill, and fallen off her chair, and that she had been carried upstairs. Now, the moment this medical man comes into the house, his mind is prepared by the prisoner for seeing a case of sudden death from apoplexy or some other cause. But the whole of this story, as you know, of the falling off her chair and being carried upstairs, is an absolute fabrication, because we have it clear upon the evidence of others that she was perfectly well until she went upstairs, and that she walked upstairs at nine o'clock, and that it was in her daughter's bed-room she was taken ill. [His Lordship read Dr Paterson's evidence with respect to his asking Dr Pritchard whether he could assign any reason for the illness. Dr Pritchard said his mother-in-law and Mrs Pritchard had been drinking bitter beer for supper, and were immediately taken sick and vomited. Dr Paterson said there must be some other cause than that, and asked him as to the old lady's present health and social habits, when Dr Pritchard, by insinuation, gave him to understand that she was in the habit of drinking spirits occasionally. He told him also that his wife had been ill a long time of gastric fever, and that some days previously he had telegraphed for her mother to come and attend her.] I will not describe to you the evidence which he gives as to the appearance of Mrs Taylor, for we have already concluded that part of the case which relates to her death; but with regard to Mrs Pritchard's appearance on that occasion, I am particularly anxious that you should attend to this. Dr Paterson stated that, in the bedroom, he was very much struck with the appearance of Mrs Pritchard. She seemed exceedingly weak and excited. Her features were sharp and thin, and a hectic flush was on her cheek. Voice very weak, particularly like the voice of a person approaching the collapsed stage of cholera. The expression of her face was semi-imbecile. He supposed at first this was produced by recent gastric fever, of which he had been told by the prisoner, but he (Dr Paterson) could not banish the conviction that she was under the depressing influence of antimony. Now, that is all that he says as to the impression he received with regard to Mrs Pritchard, on the first occasion of his visit on 24th February. But then he visits her again on the 2d March by the prisoner's desire, and I shall read you his description of that visit. [His Lordship read extracts, showing that Dr Paterson's conviction that Mrs Pritchard was suffering from the action of antimony had been confirmed by his subsequent visits to her, and continued]—These were the first marked events in the interval between the death of Mrs Taylor and Mrs Pritchard. There are other two very important circumstances which also naturally take their place in the interval—the one is the matter of the cheese, and the other is the matter of the egg-flip. [His Lordship read the evidence of Mary Patterson and Mary M'Leod, giving the story of the bit of cheese, and after concluding the evidence of Mary M'Leod, he said]—That is not a satisfactory piece of evidence, you will see, gentlemen, from the variations that occur in the course of it; but it is obviously the time that is spoken to by the other witness, Mary Patterson, because that is the night that they both speak of as the night that Mrs Pritchard had the cheese for herself. Now, with regard again to the egg-flip, Mary Patterson gives this account, and this episode of the egg-flip occurs just the next day, the 15th. [His Lordship here read Mary Patterson's evidence relating to the egg-flip, and proceeded]—Now Mary M'Leod's evidence confirms this to this extent, that when Mary Patterson tasted the egg-flip she did say "it had a bad taste," or something to that effect. Also when Mary M'Leod came down at four o'clock she told her how ill she had been. The egg-flip was carried upstairs by Mary M'Leod, and Mrs Pritchard had taken some of it, and after she had taken it, had become very ill in consequence of it, or after it,—I shall not say in consequence of it,—as sufficiently demonstrated by the fact that Mary M'Leod was obliged to remain with her till four o'clock in the morning. Now, gentlemen, with regard to these two matters of the cheese and the egg-flip, there has been a good deal of comment offered to you upon the part of the prisoner. It is said to be very difficult that cheese could be poisoned with antimony—that it would be very difficult to make a powder like tartar emetic adhere to a piece of cheese in sufficient quantity to have any effect, and that if it did, it must have been visible to the naked eye, because the cheese was yellow, and the tartar emetic was white. But, gentlemen, we know from the evidence before us that tartar emetic was very easily dissolved, and the poisoned cheese could have been poisoned by dipping it into a solution, quite as easily as dipping it into a powder. With regard to the flip, again, it is said that if the sickness with which Mary Patterson was visited in the course of the night was so dreadful as she had represented it to be by merely taking a teaspoonful of the egg-flip, the half wine-glass which Mrs Pritchard took ought to have absolutely killed her. It is difficult, gentlemen, to offer any answer to that. It is impossible to say what is the precise point to which a poison of this kind will kill—what is the precise amount which will at once destroy life as compared with that which will only inflict suffering and torture. But that Mary Patterson did suffer these severe vomitings and pains immediately after having tasted this egg-flip, I suppose you will not be disposed to disbelieve, looking to the general character of the evidence which she gave here as a witness. Now, gentlemen, these are important incidents in this story, occurring particularly as they do in the course of the week in which Mrs Pritchard died—one of them on the evening of the 13th of March, and the other on the evening of the 15th. The first must have been on the 13th, if it is the case that it was on the morning of the 14th that Mary Patterson found the cheese in the pantry. And now we come to the last scene of this tragedy, the death of Mrs Pritchard herself, which occurred, as you will recollect, early on the morning of the 18th March. I give you the account of the scene from the evidence of Mary Patterson, because I think you will agree with me that she is the safest witness to trust to in the circumstances. [His Lordship then read from the evidence of Mary Patterson, in which she stated that about twelve o'clock on the 17th Mrs Pritchard's bell rung three times, and she (Mary Patterson) went up at the third ringing. She went first to the prisoner's consulting-room, and asked for the prisoner, who came to the door. The door was partly open, but it would not open further, although she pushed it up. She then went away to go upstairs, and it was then that he came to the door and asked her how was Mrs Pritchard now? She said she did not know—she had not been upstairs, as he had told her on going out in the morning not to go upstairs, as Mrs Pritchard seemed disposed to go to sleep. Patterson then went upstairs and saw that he was following her; and after him came Mary M'Leod.] After reading the passage, his Lordship said—This is rather a remarkable incident, because Mary Patterson, being alone in the kitchen, and, hearing the bell rung, had to go up; and at the consulting-room, finding that it would not open, although it was a little let open, she turned to go up. Then the prisoner came to the door and asked her, "How is Mrs Pritchard now?" having himself previously told her not to go upstairs that morning; and then immediately behind comes Mary M'Leod. I do not say, gentlemen, that that proves that the prisoner and her were in that consulting-room then together, and that the door was kept purposely from opening when Mary Patterson came; but you will consider whether there is not some reason to believe that that looks like a secret intercommunication between the prisoner and Mary M'Leod upon that particular evening. [His Lordship then read the evidence given by Mary Patterson as to the death of Mrs Pritchard, and the conduct of the prisoner on that occasion. He also read Dr Paterson's evidence in regard to the condition in which he found Mrs Pritchard on the night of the 17th March, immediately before her death; and pointed out that Dr Paterson had denied that he had ever ordered wine for Mrs Pritchard, which was asserted by the prisoner, and also that he had ordered Dublin stout—another gratuitous assertion which the prisoner made.] His Lordship then continued—Now, gentlemen, such is the scene of Mrs Pritchard's death, and that brings to a close the main facts of this history, during the period which I referred to at the outset—I mean from about the beginning of February down to the 18th of March—and such is mainly the evidence upon which the prosecutor relies for a conviction against the prisoner. But in connexion with the death of Mrs Pritchard it is also necessary that I should call your attention to the return which Dr Pritchard made to the district registrar of what caused her death. You see what he had been calling her complaint to other people, and even to medical men—gastric fever. These medical men saw plainly enough that that was not true, whatever her complaint might be, and yet he persisted in that to the end, and returns the cause of his wife's death to the registrar as gastric fever. It is not possible to say here, as in the case of Mrs Taylor, that that is an assertion of a physical fact—like the case of Mrs Taylor—where paralysis was stated to have taken place twelve hours before her death, but you will consider whether in the case of a professional man like the prisoner, he could ever under the circumstances—if his wife died under the effects of antimonial poison—be so far deceived as to believe she died of gastric fever. But now let us consider what is the general effect and import of all this evidence. As I said before, Mrs Pritchard appears never to have been out of the house from the time when she became seriously ill. There is no appearance of her ever going out. Mrs Taylor, from the time she came on the 10th February down to the date of her death on the 25th—a period of fifteen days—was engaged in attending upon her daughter and in managing the house, and whether she was ever out of doors or not does not appear, but it cannot have been much or long. Therefore, the two deceased ladies during the whole of the important period in this case were in the house, and we may say generally were never out of it. The prisoner was living in the house through the whole of the time uninterruptedly. It does not appear that he ever went from home during the time,—of course he was out in the course of the day. We saw instances of that, but then we had in evidence that he was resident in the house constantly. There were two boarders in the house, Mr King and Mr Connell, who were examined before you, and very properly examined before you although they could say nothing very material in the case. The other inmates besides the children, previous to the 16th February, were Catherine Lattimer and Mary M'Leod, and subsequently to the 16th February, Mary M'Leod and Mary Patterson. And if you are satisfied upon the first question which I presented for your consideration, that Mrs Pritchard certainly died of antimony; and if you are satisfied that Mrs Taylor also died of poison—although it might be from the combined action of three or four; if you are further satisfied that those deaths were not produced accidentally nor suicidally; and further that the poison which produced their deaths must have been administered by some one of the parties in the house, then the inquiry comes into a narrow compass. There is very little to choose upon. If the poisoning was continued so as to become chronic, as it was very aptly called by some of the medical witnesses, and particularly in the case of Mrs Pritchard it was chronic poisoning, extending over a period of several months, then the inquiry comes to this, Who amongst the inhabitants of that house did the deed? It is common in a question of that kind, and very natural, to consider in reference to any individual charged with such a crime, first, what motive he had; secondly, what opportunity he had, and whether he was in possession of the agent or instrument by which death is caused, and it is right that I should direct your attention for a few minutes to this point. In regard to the matter of motive, I would suggest to you that the motive that his pecuniary difficulties would be relieved by the death of Mrs Taylor, does not seem to have been made out satisfactorily. You will consider the evidence which was laid before you on the subject, but I confess I do not think it worth while to set it before you again. Then, the question comes to be, Was there a motive? What is there in the shape of a motive that may be conceived or supposed to account for the perpetration of two such horrid crimes? That is the way it was stated, and ably stated by the prisoner's counsel. But, gentlemen, there are some considerations applicable to that part of the case, which I am bound to suggest to you. The absence of motive, in the ordinary sense of the word, is not a very uncommon thing in the experience of a criminal court. In truth, the existence of any adequate motive for the perpetration of a great crime is a thing impossible. There is no adequate or sufficient motive for the commission of a great crime. Still there may be what is called an intelligent motive—the existence of some foul passion, or some immediate and strong excitement, which, in a moment of half frenzy, drives a man to the commission of murder. These are all very evident and intelligible incentives to crime. But when we find that, in the opinion of the prisoner's counsel, there is no motive for the perpetration of this crime, it means no more than the motive has not been discovered if the crime has been committed—and that it was committed by somebody I fear admits of little doubt. There must have been a motive or incentive, and yet we may never discover what it was. You are never in a condition to say that there was no motive, but only that the motive has not been discovered; and the motives of human action, we know from history and experience, are often inscrutable. Another motive or incentive for the perpetration of the murder of his wife has been suggested against the prisoner, and that is the existence of illicit relation between himself and the girl Mary M'Leod. This is a very important part of the case undoubtedly, and one to which you are bound to give due attention. The prosecution suggests that the existence of that intercourse between him and the servant was the reason or the desire that led him to get rid of his wife. If that was the incentive for the commission of the crime, I do not think there will be much difficulty in explaining the incentive to the commission of the other crime of murder—that of his wife's mother; because we presume in the course of the chronic poisoning of his wife, she would have been a great obstruction and interference with his plans. But it is for you to say, gentlemen, whether you think that the existence of an illicit connexion with the servant girl is sufficient to account for his taking up this nefarious purpose of murdering his wife. It is a fair question for consideration, and one that I should desire you to turn your minds to very seriously, keeping only this in view, that, even supposing you find it impossible to assign an intelligible motive for the commission of one or both of these murders, the entire absence of evidence of motive is not a sufficient reason for acquitting the prisoner, if you are satisfied from the other evidence in the case that he was guilty. Motive, after all, can but create a presumption one way or another. It is not evidence of the fact of murder, that a man has an obvious motive to commit it; and just as little can the absence of proof of the existence of a motive be a reason for finding the prisoner not guilty, if the evidence of the fact of the murder be satisfactory against him. But then, gentlemen, in the second place, as regards the opportunities, it is scarcely necessary to say a single word. His opportunities, of course, were such as a man could not possibly have who was not at once the husband and medical adviser of the one, and the son-in-law and the medical adviser of the other. Mr Clark very properly said, "It is not his fault that he had abundant opportunities. The relation existing between him and these ladies is not his fault, and it was the existence of that relation that gave him these opportunities." Quite true, gentlemen, a very just observation; but remember, on the other hand, that as the opportunities did in point of fact exist, he cannot argue the case as if they did not. Then, lastly, with regard to the accused person's possession of the agent or instrument by which death was accomplished, that circumstance is also a strong case in evidence. His possession of poisonous drugs to such an extent is not a suspicious circumstance in the case of a medical man. They are in some degree necessary; but the peculiar position of the matter in this case—the nature of the drugs found in his consulting-room—is certainly not to be lightly passed over, and still more the nature of the purchases that he had been making from two different apothecaries during the period to which our inquiries particularly refer. In his consulting-room there were found some parcels of tartaric acid—not a very large quantity; some phials containing the remains of tincture of aconite and of white powder to the extent of some three or four grains, containing a strange and somewhat unexplained mixture of tartarised antimony, or tartar emetic and arsenic. These things were found in his consulting-room; but what had he been purchasing during the period to which our inquiry refers? We have the evidence first of apothecaries upon this subject, and we find that on the 16th of November he purchased an ounce of tartar emetic, and upon the 7th of February he purchased another ounce of the same poison—very unusual quantities, as the apothecaries state.

He had purchased no less than 5½ ounces of tincture of aconite, some of it being Fleming's tincture, and the others being the common tincture. That, the apothecaries have stated, was a very unusual quantity for a medical man to purchase; but I think it was a mistake in some respects to push this statement to the extent to which the prosecutor pressed it, because some of the other witnesses of the same description who were examined said that for external application tincture of aconite is sometimes used in considerable quantities, and if it were used for that purpose, we might account for such a large quantity being used by the prisoner. But I do not think that anybody said, that two ounces of tartar emetic within a month or two was a usual quantity for one medical man to use, who was not in the practice of mixing it at home, which the prisoner, in his conversation with Dr Paterson, says he was not. Besides, there were other very strange purchases, which have no immediate connexion certainly with the prisoner in this case, but which it is fair to bring under your notice—strychnine conine, and laudanum, and digitalis, and morphia, and antimony—all strong poisons. The prisoner, therefore, was undoubtedly possessed of a very large quantity of different kinds of poisonous substances; but what is most important is, that he was in the possession of that very poison to which the death of Mrs Pritchard is undoubtedly to be traced, and to which, in combination with others, the death of Mrs Taylor is also to be traced—that is, antimony. So that whether we adopt to the full extent the conclusions of the inquiry now suggested by the Crown, it appears beyond a doubt that some one had been practising a system of poisoning; and that in the possession of the prisoner were the agents which were necessary to carry it on. Then, gentlemen, as I said before, who else could have done so? Catherine Lattimer, before the 16th February, Mary Patterson, after the 16th February, Mary M'Leod during the whole period, and the prisoner were in the house. Are you disposed to connect any suspicion with Catherine Lattimer? or any suspicion with Mary Patterson? You saw them both examined in the box, and heard their evidence. You are as good judges as any men can be whether there is ground for supposing the accession of either the one girl or the other to the accomplishing of the death of the two women in the manner you have heard. I suppose you will not have any doubt on these points. And the prisoner's counsel has said there was another girl there who stands in a very different position, and that it appears, singularly enough, throughout the whole evidence that whenever an article of food was to be carried to Mrs Pritchard, Mary M'Leod is the hand that bears it. In short, if I understand aright the theory of the prisoner's counsel, it is that Mary M'Leod is the person who caused these two murders; and he invites you to choose between her and the prisoner at the bar, and to pronounce upon a balance of probabilities which of the two it was. Gentlemen, that is a very painful position for you to be placed in. If it be necessary that you decide absolutely between these two, it must be done. At the same time, the prisoner's counsel did not seem sufficiently alive, in considering the point, to the possibility that both might be implicated, and if that was so, I suppose we should have little doubt which was the master and which was the servant; and although the one might be the active hand that administered the poison, if two were concerned, you could have very little doubt who was the master and who served the other. And, in fact, if you should arrive at that conclusion, every article that the prisoner's counsel alluded to for the purpose of showing the guilt of Mary M'Leod, would be an article of evidence to implicate the prisoner at the bar. But, gentlemen, I do not desire you to take this theory. On the contrary, I think it is quite right that you should consider upon the balance of probabilities, as has been very well said, which of the two is the perpetrator of the crime; and in considering the question, it is necessary for you to advert to this—poisoning, if proved at all, extended over a considerable period of time—that the poisoning was administered in doses—in doses, any one of which was quite insufficient to produce death, but which was quite sufficient in the agony which it produced, and by the gradual reduction of the strength of the patient, at length to lead to a fatal termination. Is it conceivable that a girl of seventeen or sixteen years of age, in the position of a servant maid, could have herself conceived and executed such a design, and if she had conceived it, could she have executed a design like that, within this house, under the eye and subject to the vigilance of the husband of her victim, himself a medical man? Gentlemen, that is very hard to believe indeed. On the other hand, if you can suppose that the prisoner at the bar was the person who conceived and executed this wicked design, it is not so difficult to believe that Mary M'Leod may have been the perfectly unconscious instrument of carrying out his purpose—suspecting nothing, knowing nothing, of what was being done, and seeing nothing but great kindness on the part of the prisoner towards her mistress, and seeing them both dying, not rapidly, as in the case of Mrs Pritchard, and, though rapidly in the case of Mrs Taylor, still in a way the prisoner accounted for as a medical man. You may understand easily enough that a girl in the position of Mary M'Leod might be made to be the unconscious means of carrying out these designs, and perfectly innocent on her part. But there is no difficulty in this question. Somebody did it. If, then, you are satisfied the murder was committed, somebody did it. The parties who had access to her only could have done it. Some of them are plainly innocent, and in the case of others the probability of guilt is reduced to two. Of these two, one or both of them are guilty of this deed. Gentlemen, there is only one part of the case which I have not touched upon, and that is because there did not occur any fitting opportunity for it before—I mean the way which has been suggested as the true cause of Mrs Taylor's death. It is contended, on the part of the prisoner, that Mrs Taylor died of opium, and that that opium was administered by her own hand; and he says that if that were so—if she really died from the effects of opium, and that opium administered by her own hand—it is impossible to say there was any murder in her case at all. Now, observe exactly how the case stands with regard to her. There is no doubt that when Dr Paterson saw Mrs Taylor, he was under the impression that she was dying from the effects of a narcotic poison. He was not then aware of what were the contents of the bottles, by reason of the taking of which she died; but we are now in possession of the contents of that bottle. We know that it consists partly of opium, and partly of two other poisons—antimony and aconite. We have the testimony of a medical man that with a quantity of the opium taken on the occasion, more or less, it must have been accompanied by a certain proportion of aconite and antimony; and if she took any more than her accustomed quantity of opium—of Batley's mixture—say a hundred drops, or something of that kind—she must have imbibed along with it a sufficient quantity of the other poison to cause her death, from the proportion in which they were present. If that be so, and if you are of opinion that, upon the evidence, the poisons of antimony and aconite were put into the bottle by the hands and through the instrumentality of the prisoner, who, as he contributed these poisons in the mixture, thus caused her death, there can be no doubt in the world that in law, and, I think I may submit, to any grave common sense, that she died by his hand from poison. But, gentlemen, on the other hand, if you should think from what has been suggested on the part of the prisoner, regarding Mrs Taylor's death—if you think there is the slightest room for conjecture that she was done to death by poison administered by her own hand—if you think there is any doubt about it—of course you will give the prisoner the benefit of the doubt, however little it may relieve him of the grave fact—if you are satisfied with the fact—that these poisons were introduced into the bottle by him. But even supposing you acquit him of the murder of Mrs Taylor, you will bear in mind in dealing with the charge of his wife's, Mrs Pritchard's, murder, you will not throw out the circumstances which you conceive to be pointed out by the evidence connected with the death of Mrs Taylor. These are the most material parts of the case which you have to consider, bearing upon the murders of Mrs Taylor and Mrs Pritchard. And now, gentlemen, I have done. I am extremely sorry that it has been necessary for me to occupy you with these details so very long, but I feel and know the inducement I have in doing so. I could not do less than present to you everything that appeared to me to be material in the case. You will be now kind enough to consider your verdict, and I hope it will be a satisfactory one.

The Jury then retired to consider their verdict, and after an absence of fifty-five minutes, the jury returned with the following verdict:—

THE JURY UNANIMOUSLY FIND THE PRISONER

GUILTY

ON BOTH CHARGES.

The Jury retired at twenty minutes past one o'clock, and came into Court about a quarter past two. Several of the jurymen were weeping when they came into Court, which at once made known to the audience the nature of their verdict. The names having been read over, Mr Syme, who had been appointed chancellor, announced that the Jury had agreed upon the following verdict:—

"The Jury unanimously find the prisoner

GUILTY

of both Charges as libelled."

The sentence was then read over in due form and signed by the three judges.

The Lord Justice-Clerk, addressing the prisoner, said—Edward William Pritchard, you have been found guilty by the unanimous verdict of the jury of the two murders charged against you, and the verdict proceeds upon evidence which, I believe, leaves in the mind of no reasonable man the slightest room to doubt. You are aware that upon such a verdict one sentence only can be pronounced. (The prisoner bowed.) You must be condemned to suffer the last penalty of the law. (The prisoner again bowed.) It is neither my duty nor my inclination to say one word which shall have the effect of aggravating your position. I leave it to the ministers of religion to address to you exhortations to repentance, which, by God's blessing, will be found suitable to your position. Let me only remind you that you have but a very short time to live, and I beseech you to take advantage of it.

ANOTHER CONFESSION BY DR PRITCHARD.

DR PRITCHARD has since his committal to the condemned cell been in the most taciturn state of mind—at one time expressing a desire for religious instruction, and in a short time thereafter concocting what have proved to be a parcel of lies. In the intervals between the visits of several reverend gentlemen, the unhappy man seems to have employed his thoughts in writing and re-writing confessions, no less than four having been handed to the governor of the jail by him, but all differing very materially, and the two succeeding the first so palpably false that they were not deemed worthy to see the light of day.

On Thursday, however, it was made known to the Rev. Dr Norman Macleod, the Rev. Mr Reid, of Christ Church Episcopal Church, Mile End, and the Rev. Andrew Bonar, Glasgow, that the convict had made another confession, and it was accordingly submitted to these rev. gentlemen, and a consultation was held with Governor Stirling regarding it. It was compared with the first confession, and with the others which have not been thought worthy of publication from their evident falsity, and the reverend gentlemen were of opinion that it exhibited a truthfulness which the others did not possess. The document, which is at least as singular as the first drawn up by the unhappy man, is as follows:—

Confession by Edward William Pritchard, M.D., made in the presence of an all-seeing God, and of the Rev. J. Watson Reid, my present spiritual adviser, on this 19th day of July 1865, at Glasgow Prison, for communication to the proper authorities.

"I, Edward William Pritchard, in the full…

r on "English Ultramontanism" we take the
wing sensible concluding passage:—

o one doubts that there was once great power in
apal organisation; no one denies that even now

reakwater. Rennie died October 16, 1821,
buried in St Paul's Cathedral. Rennie's great
an engineer consisted in his almost intuitive
n of what was proper to be done to effect the
purpose. Another striking characteristic of
is the remarkable combination in them of
d durability. In this respect Rennie had no
d though his works are frequently objected to
ound of their expensiveness, yet their lasting
will in the end more than compensate for this.
Rennie was of extraordinary stature and
strength—characteristics which have for a
d period distinguished his family, and with
to which numerous tales are still current
many of his relatives."

n Fireside, in describing itself in its sub-
"a magazine of home literature for the
mily," indicates very fairly the
ts contents. It is a cheap but well-
tolerably well illustrated monthly,
lergyman, and containing a good deal
atter amongst its very varied contri-
this present number for July that
speaker and writer the Rev. Dr
communicates a slight sketch of
Braemar, and Deeside," filled out
extract from *Black's Guide*. It
following description of the Queen at

ngular and cheering sight in these modern
Queen Victoria treading the heather, and
ong the mountains and streams, where
nce rose *en masse* to resist that dynasty
e is so illustrious an ornament. With

The Lord Justice-Clerk, in commenting on
that I had acted in this dreadful tragedy,
care not for professional etiquette, for profess
There is a rule of life, and a consideration
higher than rule, and that is the duty w
citizen of this country—which every right-m
—owes to his neighbour to prevent the des
human life, and in that duty I cannot say bu
Paterson failed."

His Lordship may pardon me for return
the compliment, when I tell him that, as
guished officer of justice under the British
an impartial Judge upon the Bench, he mo
failed in doing his bounden duty to me, i
back part of my evidence on this point, a
the fault, the gross carelessness of the re
my shoulders, and holding me out as to a gr
responsible for not trying to prevent the des
human life, when the blame in this case l
upon the District Registrar! Permit me
before you part of my evidence on this poi
cross-examined by Mr Andrew Rutherfurd
was asked if I had done nothing to try and
Pritchard's life when I suspected that sh

Lightning Source UK Ltd.
Milton Keynes UK
UKHW03f2004160418
321153UK00002B/171/P

9 781375 550123

wordery
your online bookshop

Your Details

Adrian Smith
ADDLESHAW GODDARD
EXCHANGE TOWER 19 CANNING STREET
EDINBURGH
Midlothian
EH3 8EG

Order date: 15/04/2018
Order reference: AUK-34751478
Dispatch note: 20180418936101

Your Order

ISBN	Title	Quantity
9781375550123	A Complete Report of the Trial of Dr....	1

For returns information visit wordery.com/returns. Please keep this receipt for your records.

Thank you for your Wordery order. We hope you enjoy your book #HappyReading

wordery
your online bookshop

20180418936101